I0779071

HIT MAKERS

HEATHER O'BRIEN

Hit Makers

Copyright © 2025 Heather O'Brien

All rights reserved.

No part of this book may be used or reproduced by any means—graphic, electronic, or mechanical—including photocopying, recording, taping, or by any information storage retrieval system without the prior written permission of the publisher, except for the use of brief quotations in a book review and certain other noncommercial uses permitted by copyright law.

This is a work of fiction. All characters, names, incidents, organizations, and dialogue contained in this novel are either the product of the author's imagination or are used fictitiously. Similarities to real persons and events, living and dead, are unintended.

Bendemeer's Stream: Irish Melody
Lyrics by Thomas Moore; Traditional Irish melody (1893)
Public Domain

The Souling Song (Soul-Cake)
Lyrics & Music compiled by Rev. M.P. Holme (1893)
Public Domain

Second edition 2025
[First edition 2023]

Published in Fernley, Nevada – USA by *Word Rites Media*

eBook ISBN: 978-1-962501-15-6
Paperback ISBN: 978-1-962501-14-9
Hardback ISBN: 978-1-962501-13-2

Library of Congress Control Number: 2025904168

Cover by Warren Design

The Music is Murder saga

Lockhardt Sound

A Fate Worse Than Fame

Ballad of Someday

Hit Makers

Feels Like the End

Betrayer's Lullaby

High Water or Hell

To learn more, visit: www.booksbyheather.com.

ACKNOWLEDGMENTS

We can all blame my husband for the existence of this book. He conceived its foundation, sparked my creative juices, and unwittingly set in motion the fictional trajectory of *Hit Makers*, which simultaneously changed the course of the overall story arc of the Music is Murder saga.

I must thank author R.E. Pringle, whose brilliant research and deductive imagination regarding certain events that transpired in the music business in the late '60s and early '70s (what many dismiss as "conspiracy theory") altered what I'd originally believed I'd envisioned on my own, transforming it into the most provocative and controversial novel I've written. This, coupled with an anonymous source privy to these same events, framed the premise of *Hit Makers*. If nothing else, music history buffs may find it interesting to debate the real-life circumstances at the heart of this fictitious tale.

Thank you to my daughter, Scarlette, who found Mr. Pringle's writings and, as a result, breathed life (and a certain measure of danger) into this book.

Thank you to those who assisted in my continued research on the Kray twins. Their names are intentionally withheld per their requests.

My deepest and continued gratitude to my Beta readers:
Erin Adams, Emily Conner, Christina Naughton, and Kim Timperio.

Thank you to Sgt. Ethan Ragsdale of the Santa Barbara Police Department, who gave generously of his time and expertise as I pieced together certain procedures and the historical lay of the land that was 1973 Santa Barbara.

(And Henry? Everything done in the darkness eventually comes to light.)

SPECIAL THANK YOU:

Christina Naughton, who not only beta read *Hit Makers* (going back to the beginning of the saga and reading straight through) but emerged as an invaluable source in the British leg of my exhaustive research. She was integral to the integrity of this book.

"I would not be concerned with the secrets, the lies, the mysteries, the facts. I would be concerned with what makes them necessary."

~ Anais Nin

For Randy

This book is dedicated to those lost in the
South Hallsville School bombing of 1940.

PROLOGUE

Canning Town, East London, England
Sunday, September 8, 1940

By all accounts, Mary Nock should have dropped the toddler clutched against her hip. The twenty-four-pound bundle's terrified, spasmodic shrieking should have had her in a panic. Normally, mother's instinct would have kicked in. She would have painstakingly checked Francis for signs of injury. Doubtless, she would have found at least minor cuts or bumps beneath the oily soot blanketing his skin and clothes. Instead, she patted his back, held him close, and instructed the two-year-old, "Now then, Francis. Settle down."

Of course, what was normal about herding one's seven children into the basement of a primary school on a Sunday evening after receiving stern warnings from police and Air Raid Precautionary Wardens that one's house— and indeed the houses of most one's neighbors—might soon be obliterated by parachute bombs?

No more "nuisance raids" for Britain. Yesterday afternoon, at 4 PM, the phony war had become all too real.

From behind her, Mary's husband stretched his thin arm around her shoulder. He pointed a bony finger at a small section in the far corner of the basement. "I should think we'll fit quite nicely over there, love."

She conducted a visual inventory of her kids, then hastened for what may have been the last remaining unoccupied area of their makeshift dwelling. Nodding at their neighbors as they passed, they behaved as the rest of their community behaved: brave, prepared, and calm. They knew what was coming. No cries or screaming from Canning Town residents. No shouting. No din or frenzied panic. Not even from Mary, whose every nerve had been numbed by fearful uncertainty the moment she had heard the first of Hitler's calling cards the night before.

Ten-year-old Daisy appeared at her side as the twins sprinted ahead to lay out the shabby afghan they had grabbed on their way out of the Anderson shelter after the all-clear had sounded at 6:10 PM that evening. With steady hands, Daisy reached up. "Here, Mummy. I'll take Francis. You sit down."

Mary handed the toddler to her oldest daughter with a grateful nod. She thanked her sons for the provisional covering, sat down on the hard floor, then patted the space beside her and gestured for her husband's cane.

James shook his head. "I saw Daniel talking with some of the other men. Think I'll ask 'em what he knows."

She craned her neck to scan the room. "Have you seen Elizabeth? Is she with him? And the kids?"

"I didn't see 'em." James surveyed their surroundings, mentally cataloguing the familiar faces. At last, his brows arched in relief. He pointed his cane. "There. I see her. Kids're with her. All accounted for."

Mary clutched her chest and began to stand. "I'll go see her."

"No, Molly. Stay here until I return. Everyone's just settling in, and more are comin' by the dozen. We need to stay together."

Mary relented. She watched James hobble off to consult with their neighbor, George, and a hoard of others trying to get checked in or ascertain their current circumstances. Hopefully, they would all know more, soon.

She held, then released a strained breath. With a reassuring smile, she glanced down at Francis, then Daisy. "Thank you for your help, darling. Daddy'll return straightaway with news."

"I heard someone say the coaches are on their way," thirteen-year-old Oscar called over his shoulder. He and twin, Owen, stood just off the afghan, facing the throng like scrawny sentries guarding their small stake of territory, watchful and steady in the midst of the orderly chaos of the cramped shelter.

Eight-year-old Polly sat fidgeting to Mary's left. Of all her children, Mary knew Polly would take their confinement the hardest. She had barely lasted the two hours in their Anderson shelter—and that with sirens and bombs all about. Who knew how long the promised transport would take to collect them? The only possible consolation for Polly would be the assurance that, once outside the greater London area, their northern country relocation would provide not only more safety but a more open area in which she and her siblings could play.

Mary patted Polly's knee, which Polly then covered with her threadbare, damaged dress. "It won't be too long, then, will it Mummy?"

"No, my darling," she comforted. "Not long at all."

"Might we see cows up north?"

"We may, yes."

"I should like to find someone to stay with who has a farm. I would very much like to milk a cow."

"And all the fresh milk we can drink," Daisy added with a chirp as she bounced a now-quieted Francis on her lap.

Mary's heart swelled with pride at the calm, idle chatter and soft giggling of her children, given the general state of trauma. But that was the way of things in Britain. Even in such an overwhelming crisis, the countenance of their fellow refugees, of their community, was one of pragmatic coping. Packed together in the school like a tin of sardines, strangers and familiars alike suffered together, but did not discuss it. They hunched down or sat perched upon their luggage in their tattered, torn, and singed garments. Some had escaped their homes in such haste in response to the urgent beckoning of authorities, they still wore their night clothes. Ruined, all. Their faces were blackened with soot, grime, and smoke. Like the Nocks, these families had either lost, or feared they would lose, their homes and every possession.

Tragically, some had already lost precious more.

An unexploded bomb, dropped that very morning by Goering's Luftwaffe atop a terraced house over on Martindale Road, had prompted 10 Downing to make the hard decision. Canning Town needed to evacuate immediately. The South Hallsville School had been identified as a rest centre and temporary shelter for those locals who had not already begun migrating—mostly on foot— for the relative safety of the fruit-picking fields up around Epping Forest or under the Thames toward southeast England via the Woolwich foot tunnel. Now, the huddling masses of those who would not, or could not, leave assembled therein, anxiously awaiting coaches to rescue them from the hell reigning down upon London's docks.

Lord willing, James and the others would return quickly with news of a brilliant strategy relayed to them from the small group of authorities hovering around the ARP Warden who had checked them in upon her family's arrival. Surely, their Prime Minister would not forget them.

With a start, Mary sat straighter on the afghan, realizing she had seen neither Paul nor Ronnie since their arrival. Her eyes darted about the area, a sense of dread enveloping her beneath the layer of black gunk stuck to her person. "Have you seen your brothers?" she asked no child in particular. "They've not gone outside, have they?"

Oscar pointed to the far end of the basement. "Paul's over there with the Gunns," he assured. "But I don't see Ronnie."

"He told me he wanted to go outside and watch the sky," Owen added.

"He what?" Mary's heart throbbed inside her chest. She frantically scanned the dense crowd for any sign of her second born.

"I want to see the sky," Polly complained, hopping onto her knees. "It was all orange and lovely because of the fires. Can we, Mummy? Can we go outside? Just for a moment? It smells horrid in here."

Mary found her feet. Before setting out to search for Ronnie, she tried again to spot him amongst the Canning Town community crammed by the hundreds into their basement shelter. She noted the Quirkes, the Chandlers, and the Maskells. A growing number of locals, including her husband, had surrounded the authorities, demanding with increasing intensity information about their promised departure. Bustling about the area, volunteer rest centre staff handed out cups of tea and what blankets they had to offer. But nowhere amid the throng of people could Mary locate her son.

She caught her husband's eye and motioned him back. He limped over as quickly as he could, careful to avoid accidentally stabbing his cane down on a random toe or finger belonging to some unsuspecting fellow refugee in his path.

"They say it'll be tomorrow afternoon before the coaches arrive," he announced upon his return. "We'll need to stay here tonight. It's not safe to go

out. It's a wall of fire out there. But no worries, love. Ol' Winnie's on top of it, you mark my words. He knows these docks're a prime target. He won't let us dow—"

"Ronnie's gone." Mary's voice broke. "Owen said he'd wanted to go out and look at the sky."

"And I want to go, too, Daddy!" Polly pouted, crossing her arms.

James's face grew solemn, then angry. When anger gave way to fear, he turned and searched the room. "We told him to stay close."

"If you'll stay here with the kids, I'll go on up and collect him if he's outside. And don't let Polly out of your sight!"

James grabbed her arm as she rushed past him. "No, Molly. If anyone should go, it's me. You stay with the children. They need their mother."

"They need us both," Mary said. "And we need them. James, darling, you shouldn't be navigating the stairs again with that leg. I won't be a moment. He wouldn't have gone far."

She blew kisses to the girls, sent the twins to fetch Paul and bring him back to the family, and made them promise to keep watch for their rebel brother. But before she reached the stairway, the terrifying shrill of the air raid sirens began again, throwing Canning Town residents inside the South Hallsville School into grim silence.

The Luftwaffe was back. And Ronnie was gone.

CHAPTER 1

THE IDEA OF LEAVING LONDON next month left Ross Alexander strangely conflicted. On one hand, he and his bride would relish settling back into the quiet normalcy of their Greenwood Lake home in New York. On the other, Ross believed he had become a new man since returning to England—his first visit since 1940, when he and his mother had stopped accompanying his father on business trips due to the war.

In London, Ross had excelled in his new position. He had come to terms with his father's inevitable death last year. Combined, these two major life events found him free of chains he had scarcely before dreamed himself a captive.

"Don't hurry back to the hotel," he instructed the cabbie he had employed both personally and professionally over the course of the Alexanders' stay. "I'd like to take in the city lights."

"Saturday night," the cabbie mused with approval, talking over his shoulder while keeping close watch on the road. "Fancy a turn 'round the Circus?"

"Excellent. And maybe a detour around the Palace after that. Not too far out of the way. Jo's already annoyed I worked on a Saturday."

"A bank holiday at that."

"Indeed."

The commute from Olympic Studios back to the Park Lane Hotel was pleasant, if congested. By the time they turned onto the Putney Bridge, Ross had fully relaxed despite a long day finalizing Crimp's contract renewal. More challenging than he had anticipated, considering the young band had yet to produce a hit. Still, the negotiations had handed a big win to his employer. Good for them. Good for him.

"Looks like we'll be leaving in a couple of weeks." Ross shuffled through some papers on his lap, then stowed them in the briefcase beside him. He folded his suit jacket atop the briefcase.

The cabbie eyed him through the rearview mirror. "Job done, then?"

"Yes. The contracts are all finalized. And none too soon. My bride has thrice threatened to leave me if we have to stay much longer."

"I'm always happy to show her about, you know."

"I know. You've been a godsend to us both. Turns out, she can only shop Carnaby Street and King's Road so many times. I'm not sure how many A-line skirts and shift dresses a woman of thirty-two needs. As it is, we'll require double the luggage to return as we had on our arrival. Leave it to me to be assigned to the new fashion capital of the world."

"You're a lucky man. She's a beauty."

"She is. And I am." Ross squared his shoulders at the compliment, then gazed out the window as the Austin FX4 motored through Fulham toward Westminster. "Speaking of. Any word on your wife and son?"

The man shook his head but did not immediately respond. A thoughtful moment later, he said, "I keep trying. There isn't much hope as long as I'm driving a taxi for a living, is there? They deserve better, and she knows it."

Ross propped his elbow atop the window ledge. He tapped his index finger against his bottom lip. "Ever consider a new line of work?"

"Only all the time."

"I'd told you I recently changed my area of practice."

"You did."

"So I'm no stranger to switching focus. It may seem impossible, but finding your place in the world—your true calling—is liberating. Even if I was forty years old when I did it."

"I'll be forty-two in November."

"And I'll be forty-one next month."

"So you'll be back in the States for your birthday."

"With any luck, I'll just miss it." Ross repositioned himself in his seat. "In any case, maybe it's time for a change in your vocation—like you said."

Through the rearview mirror, Ross glimpsed the knowing, sideways smile stretch across the cabbie's face. "I'm looking forward to it."

It was an unlikely friendship they had developed over the months. One that bucked social mores and class distinction. But where that mattered greatly in British society, Ross did not care a whit. His London circle was as small as his circle back home. Rock'n'roll was not only relatively new, it was chock full of younger, hungrier, cut-throat types. His driver's ability to converse over a diverse number of topics ranging from business to world affairs was refreshing. Ross considered the man more peer than hired driver.

They wove in and out of West London's scenic spots, enjoyed the lights of Piccadilly Circus, and wound around past Shaftesbury Memorial Fountain. The driver pulled in a side street and parked so they could have a walk and grab a to-go coffee from a local coffee bar, which they enjoyed as they sat and chatted on the steps of one of Trafalgar Square's fountains. They discussed the cabbie's eleven-year-old son, whom he had not seen much of in the seven years since his wife had taken him to America. She had wanted more for herself, and the child, than her husband had to offer.

"How about you? Any plans for a family?"

The question deflated Ross. With a somber shake of his head, he said, "Children aren't in the cards for us."

Details were neither requested nor given.

Taking in the evening bustle of pedestrians moving about Trafalgar Square, Ross decided he had to hand it to Josephine. She had tried. Yet no matter how she pretended otherwise, she did not care for city life. Not in New York, and not here. Far from a hippy or part of the mod scene, hers was a classic beauty with classic contentment. Quiet. Refined.

Still, despite their less-bohemian leanings, the couple had savored the city's theaters, museums, and an arm's length observation of the heady spirit of youth permeating the post-austerity culture. And, of course, Josephine adored her shopping.

For his part, Ross had enjoyed Swinging London's diversions. London had emerged from the devastation of World War II stronger, brighter, and flourishing. It had remade Britain's image into what *Family Weekly* journalist, Geoffrey Bocca, had described back in January as, "morally shaky, economically disintegrating, but fun."

Hedonism was intoxicating—even if his participation in it was predominantly voyeuristic.

At least entertainment law held a modicum of excitement. Certainly, more so than the trap of the corporate law career his father had pressured him into. Better yet, his employer had told him just last week that if their label realized their projected success, they might soon rival Brian Epstein's NEMS. A lofty goal, and one that thrilled Ross.

He missed his father, though deep down, he knew the man would have never forgiven him for switching areas of practice. Irving Alexander could have never comprehended that, here in London, a lifetime of reliability—dependability—had given way to a previously unacknowledged carnal aspect of his only son's nature. Perhaps something Ross had inherited from his carefree mother. At least she understood. She always understood. Though why that mattered to him at his age, he did not know.

Ross wondered if the change would prove permanent or if he would eventually revert back to his more stoic temperament after leaving the United Kingdom. Josephine would certainly hope so. But Ross? He was less eager to shed his newfound sense of whimsy.

They finished their coffee, then returned to the taxi and headed toward the Park Lane. Ross admired the sights as they drove, lost in pride over the day's win and an eagerness to share his victory with Josephine over dinner, for which he realized with a guilty wince, he was late.

The Austin Princess slowed to a stop at an initially unfamiliar corner. Ross noted they had veered off course. He glanced around, confused. Then, he recognized the neighborhood's rows of large, white-quoin and brown-brick townhouses with their iron gates and balconies.

He had visited this place once before. Two months before, to be exact.

His troubled eyes darted about as he rubbed his naked jaw. The lamplit streets appeared empty and still. Not so much as a resident walking their dog or a couple strolling the sidewalk. Surprising for a late-August Saturday evening in Belgravia.

He cleared his throat, checked his watch as best he could in the dim glow of streetlights, then addressed his driver. "What are we doing here?"

The cabbie shifted the car into park and killed the engine, then reached across to his left and grabbed a small paper bag from the passenger's seat. He did not answer the question. Rather, he gripped the door handle with his free hand.

"It may be seen as a conflict, my being here," Ross pressed. "You know this."

"You'll be fine," the driver dismissed with a grunt as he opened his door. "A former fare left something in the car earlier. I need to return it. I won't be long."

Ross voiced no further objections. He watched the man trot up the four cement stairs and knock on the door. No one answered, so he knocked again. When the second knock met the same end, the cabbie descended the steps backward, visually scanning the top three stories as if looking for a sign of life via a light shining through one of the sheers sheathing the multi-paneled windows.

The man stood silent for a moment, then performed a quick survey of the front of the building before turning his head to peer left, then right, up Chapel Street to assess his surroundings. Ross also glanced up and down the street. He checked his watch again. Nine o'clock. Where had the time gone?

Josephine would be worried. And angry.

When his driver friend disappeared around the corner of the house, down Groom Place alleyway, the hair on the back of Ross's neck stood on end. Odd behavior for someone merely returning an abandoned item from a black cab. Odder still that the owner of this particular residence should have ever been in the cab to begin with.

Ross sat alone in the back seat for many long minutes. He wondered how mad his bride would be when he finally returned. His throat tightened as he fought the paranoia of being recognized. Perhaps some unsavory character was watching. Perhaps they would report back to another interested party. Perhaps this seemingly impromptu visit would result in his being dangled by his ankles off some balcony ledge, à la last year's infamous altercation between the Small Faces' music manager Don Arden and impresario Robert Stigwood, after Arden learned that Stigwood had tried to poach the band from him.

Might someone accuse Ross of conducting an off-hour meeting with pop music's most notable entrepreneur? Of trying to edge himself in and somehow oust show-business lawyer David Jacobs, the flamboyant senior partner of M.A. Jacobs Ltd.? Or worse—claim Ross had come by for something more...*personal*?

Insiders knew, if only via hushed discussions, of Chapel Street's most famous resident's proclivities. Then again, the proposed Sexual Offenses Bill had just received royal assent a month ago. Any day now, the bill would become law, and Brian Epstein and others of his persuasion would be free to conduct their private lives without fear of prosecution.

Once again, Ross eyeballed his surroundings. He hoped his time in London would not end his still-new transition from corporate to entertainment law.

For a moment, he considered walking what he guessed was a little more than a half-mile back to the hotel. But as he gathered his coat and briefcase, the driver reemerged from around the corner.

With no hint of distress or caution, the man climbed back into the cab, started the engine, and navigated in ominous silence to the Park Lane Hotel. He periodically checked his rearview and side mirrors.

Ross had questions. Instinct cautioned him not to bother. He was probably overthinking, as he sometimes did. The important thing was, they had left 24 Chapel Street. He would soon get back to face his bride.

He paid the driver, then grabbed his belongings and exited the vehicle. Before closing the door, he said, "I'll see you Tuesday morning. Same time?"

The driver glanced over his shoulder at him, a feigned and fearsome grin tugging at his cheeks. "Actually, you inspired me tonight. I think I *will* start a new career. You're my last fare."

Ross reached in to accept the cabbie's outstretched hand, unsure how to respond. Perhaps out of habit, he reached inside his suit jacket pocket, pulled out a business card, and handed it over.

With lifted brows, the man gave the card a little shake. "Who knows?" he said as Ross shut the door, "I may see you again someday. Have a safe trip back to New York."

***

Too old to play about and too young to make the rules, Chris dangled mercilessly on the middle branch of the Grant family tree. But how come Jordan got to play out front and Ben managed to maneuver himself into his bedroom "to work," while *he* got all the girl jobs?

"Straight and tidy," his mum had trilled with delight as Ben had informed Chris he had to help her clean up that Sunday after church. "Daddy'll be home for dinner. Mustn't welcome him with a mess."

Somehow, "straight and tidy" had resulted in Jordan's assigned task being to pick up the few toys they had left outside yesterday. Ben was on standby to cut the grass whenever Jordan finished playing with those same toys and actually put them away. Meanwhile, Chris was left to unclutter the sitting room and scrub the toilet. How was that a fair distribution of labor?

His Mum bustled about the kitchen, prepping vegetables and baking bread for dinner. The typical kick in her heels whenever their father returned from the road. She bobbed her head and danced to the radio, humming or singing along with the hits every bit as enthusiastically as her sons did. A byproduct of her former career.

Lynda Grant had been a famous dancer—at least until Chris had come along. Or so he had heard time and again whenever Ben guilted him into taking on more responsibility around their house. Given her sacrifice for them, surely they could sacrifice for her, too. They could help out more and should do it without grumbling. In the last five years, Ben had turned into a gigantic mum's boy.

Chris used a thin, worn section of fabric from an old T-shirt to dust the furniture as his mother sang along to Anita Harris's "Just Loving You" on the radio. Next, he emptied the ashtrays, then ran their Gemini Sweeper across the rugs.

Glancing out the picture window, he spied Jordan. Still playing. A right focused one, he was. At this rate, Ben might not be able to manage the grass before their father's return. It would not in the least bother Chris to see some blame fall on his older or younger sibling, except he suspected it would result in him getting more chores.

He knocked on the window to get Jordan's attention, then raised his arms, palms up, fingers splayed. Jordan nodded, then began picking up in earnest.

After stowing the carpet sweeper, he assessed the room to ensure everything looked ship-shape. The sooner he finished, the sooner he could disappear into his guitar—his father's gift to him for his eleventh birthday last December. From the moment Chris had picked up the instrument and run his thumb down its strings, he was hooked. Now, some eight months later, his parents had started complimenting him on his progress, complete with a hint of astonishment in their praise. It was probably not intended to hurt him, even though it did.

The sitting room looked suitable. The only thing out of order was his mum's stack of magazines strewn about the coffee table. Chris gathered and patted them into place, then ran his dust rag over the table before fanning them out the way his mum preferred.

August's covers of both *Vogue* and *Good Housekeeping* caught his eye. The doe-eyed, tawny-haired beauty staring back at him sent an immediate surge of electricity straight to his trousers. The tilt of her head on one magazine and the parting of her lips on the other unraveled him right where he stood.

Jean Shrimpton was the most beautiful woman in the world.

He eyed the kitchen, then the hall, then looked back down at the magazines. The one task remaining on his list of duties spurred him on. He rolled up and then slipped both magazines into his front trousers for a future, more intimate, review. To disguise their bulk against his lanky frame, he untucked his T-shirt.

"I'm finished here, Mum," he called into the kitchen. "I'm off to clean the loo."

Lynda padded into the sitting room for a quick inspection, humming as Anita Harris faded away. "It's lovely, son. Thank you. You always do such a good job."

Hands crossed before him, holding tight the nicked magazines, Chris gave a sharp, single nod but surreptitiously rolled his eyes. As he headed for the hallway, the music on the radio abruptly cut out. The DJ's urgent voice announced breaking news out of London.

The ensuing report froze him in place. His mother's eyes widened, then arched in sadness. With a slow shake of her head, she returned to the kitchen. "How tragic," she said under her breath. "That poor man."

Chris collected himself and bolted to Ben's room. On the radio, the DJ concluded his mini-eulogy by spinning a fitting "All You Need Is Love" by the Beatles.

A handmade Do Not Disturb sign hung from his oldest brother's door. Inside, Chris heard faint singing and humming, but no radio. Composing again, as usual. Ben spent more and more time writing songs lately. Their father had encouraged him to send them around to see if anyone would record them. Some had already been sent on to London.

He raised his hand to knock on the door. The rolled-up magazines dislodged themselves from the waist of his trousers, so he slid them out and clutched them in his fist. He again poised himself to knock, then reconsidered. Why should Ben have his own room when Chris had to share one with a seven-year-old? Just further inequity in the Grant household.

Chris burst inside. A hint of satisfaction flashed across his face at his brother's startled reaction.

Sitting bedside, Ben jumped and blinked several times as the guitar slid from his grasp in a discordant thud onto the floor. He narrowed his eyes at his brother's visible satisfaction. "Don't you know how to knock?"

Chris ignored him. "Didn't you send some of your songs to Gerry and the Pacemakers?"

Ben eyed him suspiciously. "I've sent them all over. You went with me to the GPO just last week, remember? You ran into that girl from school."

The memory momentarily stole Chris's focus. "That's right. A pretty one, Clara."

Ben glanced with disgust at the contents of his fist. He scoffed. "I see you found Mum's new magazines with your girlfriend on the cover."

Chris crossed his arms. "Who do you fancy, then? Or do you save it all for your lyrics?"

Ben lifted his head. "Did Jordan finish picking up?"

"I'm not his keeper."

"Are you finished, then?"

"You're not Dad. I don't answer to you."

"You don't answer to anyone much, do you?" Ben gathered the papers strewn about his bed, patted them into place, and slid them into a worn folder pregnant with partial and completed compositions. "So go on, then. Why'd you ask about Gerry Marsden?"

Chris flopped down onto his brother's bed. He released his grip on the magazines, letting them unscroll atop the comforter. "You'll never guess who just died."

***

Kelley O'Conner was living proof that romance could be both thrilling and practical. Some might argue his timing missed the mark. On the upside, they had their favorite restaurant almost completely to themselves. The wait staff fawned over them, as usual. Besides, opting for an earlier seating accomplished two things. First, they would make it home from their date early. Second, they would avoid suffering any ill-effects as the world began another work week.

This rationale suited Kelley. Truth told, he could not wait to share his news.

Beth O'Conner sipped her champagne. She emitted an indulgent sigh as she set down her glass. "Drinking on a Sunday afternoon."

Smiling, he reached for her hand. "Should I have let you squirm until next weekend?"

She raised her brows and shoulders. "I don't know. You still haven't told me."

"I haven't told you how beautiful you look tonight, Mrs. O'Conner?"

"Not that," she scolded. "What's the news?"

"Which news? The good news or the bad news?"

"Bad news?" she echoed, deflating in the upholstered chair.

Kelley nodded, his cheek muscles pulling his closed lips to one side. "Afraid so. It's not often we get the good without some bad, right?"

"I—I guess so."

He motioned for their waiter and told him they were ready for dessert. The server cleared the nearly finished beef bourguignon and disappeared to procure their last course.

"So." Kelley cleared his throat, reaching beneath the table. He produced two small, brightly wrapped packages, which he placed on the table. "What'll it be? The good news or the bad news?"

Beth beheld the gifts, flat-faced. "Why would anyone wrap *bad* news?"

He chin-pointed to the purple paisley paper and red ribbon package. "See for yourself."

With halting movements, she reached for the first gift. She eyed her husband, weighed it in her palm, then gave it a shake.

"You don't want to break it, do you?" Kelley asked.

"Oh no—is it breakable?"

He grinned. "Nope."

She leveled a softened gaze upon him, shooting him that patient, scolding glare she gave him whenever he teased. More curious now than defeated at the prospect of bad news, she removed the outer wrapping to reveal a plain brown cardboard box. Inside lay a roll of packing tape covered in tissue paper. She blinked, unsure what to say.

He propped his elbows on the table, touching his clasped hands to his lips. "Like it?"

"Is the bad news that my husband's suddenly forgotten how to give thoughtful presents?"

"Oh, I remember, and I've thought about it since the day we met."

"Ten years? I'm impressed." She placed the opened box on the table.

He pinkie-pointed at the second gift. "You forgot the good news."

Less enthusiastically, Beth unwrapped the orange package with the yellow bow. It was light, as if empty. Inside was a folded piece of paper. "This one isn't fragile, either."

"You didn't open it."

Out of the corner of her eye, she spotted three waiters headed their way. One carried a silver ice bucket with a bottle of champagne and two crystal flutes. Another balanced a dessert tray above his left shoulder. The third cradled a bouquet of long-stem red roses encircled in cellophane.

Confused but flattered, she tilted her head. "What have you done?"

"Open your good news, Beth."

She lifted the paper from the box and unfolded it to discover what looked like a paper insert for a picture frame. The image of a sunset met her, complete with tilted white letters on the bottom right corner that read "5 x 7."

Kelley leaned back as the waiters dressed their table with the champagne and pineapple upside-down cake. One of them handed Beth the roses.

"Tell me," she urged, smiling her gratitude to the staff. "What is all this?"

He rose long enough to grab a chair from a nearby unoccupied table, nodding a friendly acknowledgment to the three other tables of patrons whose attention they had aroused. Scooting the chair between them, he then took the roses and laid them on the seat.

"Let's toast." He held aloft one of the fizzing flutes. "To Seattle."

She scrunched her nose but touched the lip of her glass to his. "What's there to toast Seattle about?"

"Its abandonment," he said without pause. He winked and took a sip.

A sigh of frustration escaped her.

He slid his dessert plate aside and leaned toward her. "The bad news," he said softly, "is that you're going to have to pack up the house."

Her jaw slacked, all expression fleeing her beautiful features as she began to understand.

"The good news is, I spoke to Joseph Williams yesterday."

Breathless, she whispered, "California."

He smiled and nodded.

Her hand covered her open mouth.

Kelley lifted his chin to their server. "I think we'll take the cake to go. My wife needs to get home. She has a lot of work ahead of her."

The typical cloud cover filling the northwest Washington sky had cleared, augmenting their short drive home as the sun waned in the late afternoon sky. They spoke little, but Beth's excitement over their impending move was evident. Kelley felt the tremble of her fingers as she held his hand.

Much still needed sorting out. Not tonight, though. Tonight, they would have a private celebration after they tucked Farin into bed. Tomorrow after he returned from work, they could start discussing the details.

He had promised her sun and beach when they married nearly six years ago. For a while, he had wondered if he would ever deliver.

"I love you," she whispered, facing him. It was a serious "I love you." Factual. Deeper than emotion.

He brought her hand to his lips and kissed her near her wedding ring. She gave his fingers a gentle squeeze.

When they pulled into their driveway, Beth gathered her flowers and the two packages. "I'll get Farin in the bath while you drive Rosie home."

Kelley agreed. He grabbed the doggie bag from the back seat, which contained two extra servings of cake—one for his daughter and one for their sitter. All in all, it had been a pleasant, if early, dinner. Perhaps a bit too ambiguous with the gifts, but it had turned out well.

He sauntered across the threshold, whistling "Silence is Golden" by the Tremeloes. But inside, his happiness dissolved into concern when he found Rosemary sitting on their sofa, wiping tears from her eyes. He dropped the doggie bag on the coffee table, then sat down beside her. "Are you okay? Where's Farin?"

Rosemary sniffed and tugged at her miniskirt. She pointed down the hall. "Mrs. O'Conner took her to run a bath."

"What's wrong, Rosie?" He placed a comforting hand on her shoulder.

With a grateful nod, she plucked a tissue from the box he grabbed from an end table. "It's just so sad. What do you think they'll do, Mr. O'Conner?"

"Who?" The missing pieces of her puzzling mood made him empathetic to Beth's earlier frustration over his admittedly confusing surprise.

"The Beatles." She scrunched up the tissue and dabbed beneath her lower lids, careful not to further damage her heavy mascara.

"Did something happen to them?" Kelley's brow creased. He and Rosie often discussed their common love of music, an interest Beth did not share.

"Not them." Her voice broke. "It's their manager."

His eyes narrowed. "Epstein?"

She nodded.

"What happened?"

"I don't know." Rosemary continued to softly weep. "All I know is they found him at his home today. He's dead."

CHAPTER 2

*F*OURTEEN YEARS RAISED IN THE *poor, working-class neighborhood of Canning Town. A slum back in Victorian times. Over the past decade, its mean and narrow streets had been cleared of the rough stuff. Yet now, Ronnie could scarcely navigate the short route between the South Hallsville School and the modest terrace house he had shared with his family. Through the choking oily haze, it appeared many of the streets had been reduced to rubble.*

"Think it's still standing?" Paul shouted above the whir of plane engines and the whistling and explosions of falling bombs in the near distance as they climbed and crawled over rubble that had once been—to the best of their discernment—Roscoe Street.

Ronnie lost his footing on a pile of ruined masonry, coming down hard and twisting his ankle. The sharp, sudden pain made him cry out. The last thing to do when with one's older brother—no matter the terror of their circumstance. "I hope so. Last time she snuck out, she'd mentioned wanting to go get something to take with us when the buses arrive."

Paul scoffed bitterly. He offered a hand to help steady his faltering sibling. "If they ever arrive."

Their best guess was that Polly had wandered outside sometime after dinner that night—the second night in their basement shelter—as they continued to await the promised transportation that would relocate them north of the city. She had told their mother she was going off to play with a friend whose parents had set up a small space at the opposite end of the basement. With many hundreds of evacuees occupying the space, coupled with the authorities' decision to move the men and boys to one corridor and the women and girls to a separate one as the shelter burst at the seams with increasing numbers of evacuees, it had proven impossible to keep an eye on her.

When their mother had gone to collect her later that night, the friend's parents said she had left them some two hours earlier. Panicked, Mary Nock had rallied several men to join Paul and Ronnie on a fruitless search of the school. When they came up with nothing, Paul and Ronnie had set out alone to find their spirited youngest sister. However apologetic, none of the men had volunteered to help. It was too late. Too dangerous. Despite the close-knit community, they needed to consider their own families.

The cacophony of anti-aircraft guns, bomb explosions, and the incessant rumbling of plane engines terrified Ronnie. His hands shook as he plowed through the crumbled ruins of their neighbors' homes on his desperate pilgrimage to their place not three blocks from the school.

An orange, misty glow arising from the raging infernos illuminated the night sky. When they had first left the shelter, they had looked southward toward the docks, where—judging by the foul smell of burning molasses saturating the air—it appeared the old sugar refinery had suffered a hit. It looked as if the entire bank of the Thames was afire. These same fires were a guide for the Luftwaffe in their now-nightly air offense against the East End.

"We've been gone a long time," Paul shouted as they reached what they surmised used to be Forty Acre Lane. "Mum'll be frantic."

"She'll be all the worse if we return without Polly," Ronnie shouted back. "If you want to go back, go back. I can keep looking for her."

"What if she's not at home? What if there's no home left?"

Ronnie clamped shut his jaw. He did not respond. Instead, he defied his fear, harnessed what courage he could, and forged ahead. When he picked up the pace, Paul followed suit.

As they reached Hemsworth Street at last, he heard a near-deafening whir and whistle. It was dangerously close. The noise and pitch rose at an alarming rate.

He searched their immediate surroundings and spied what looked like an Anderson shelter close by, in what used to be a neighbor's garden. Unfortunately, there was no time. "Get down!" he shouted.

Ronnie cast himself against a pile of broken stone, pulling his jacket up over his head moments before the bomb exploded. Without his bearings, he had no point of reference where it landed or how far away.

The blast wave nearly blew out his eardrums. His insides ached in protest of the concussive force; his lungs felt as if they would explode. Glass, rock, and metal projectiles shot through the heavy fabric of his jacket, some puncturing all the way through to the skin of his side and back.

It took time to regain his faculties. For several moments, breathing proved difficult. The thick smoke and grimy air nearly choked him. He found himself covered afresh by a heavy layer of dust and debris.

He coughed several times, sputtering out grimy spit from his mouth. When he eventually attempted to stand upright on his trembling legs, he called for his brother. "Where are you? I can't see anything."

The surrounding uproar sounded muted and filtered inside his ringing ears. He strained to hear his brother's voice. "Paul? Can you hear me?"

Ronnie pulled off his jacket and waved it around in vain, as if doing so would simply fan away the smoke and clear the air enough to recognize his surroundings. Unable to see or hear clearly, he used his hands for guidance.

At last, he came upon something warm and soft.

A body.

He jerked back his hand, emitting what sounded inside his head like a hollow squeal. His heart thumped with fear and shock. A part of him wanted to believe he had stumbled upon one of the many unfortunate souls who had lost their lives fleeing German bombs as they raced, too late, for shelter. It could not possibly be anyone he knew. Certainly not his brother.

"Paul?" he shouted again into the dense air. He discerned no response.

In the distance, he thought he heard something. Something like screaming. He could not tell from which direction it had come.

"Paul!" he called once more, coughing in the dusty haze.

"Ronnie!" came the muffled sound as if it had originated from inside his head instead of from several feet away. The voice was not Paul's. It came again, this time closer. "Is that you?"

He peered through the thinning murk and perceived a small figure stumbling and clambering his way. Before he could respond, he peered down to the form at his feet.

Paul's body lay bloody and misshapen against the rubble. His lifeless eyes remained open. Blood trickled from his eyes, ears, nose, and mouth, cutting swatches like rivers along his blackened skin. One of his arms was missing, along with both his shoes.

"Ronnie!" The voice grew less faint as the figure advanced, though it remained muted in his mind. "Help me!"

Aghast, he looked up to see the shadowy bundle hastening his way. Despair over his brother collided with instant relief as he recognized his missing sister headed his way.

As she stumbled and bounded nearer, Ronnie recognized the whirring of another bomb. Like the one before, it sounded close.

He stood and leapt over the rubble, defying his injured ankle and aching lungs, snatched a terrified Polly up into his arms, and dove into the neighbor's Anderson shelter mere seconds before the second explosion.

***

Bobby Lockhardt eyed his mother's sleeping form for some time before leaning over to smell her breath. Good news: she was breathing. Better news: no alcohol.

He nudged her shoulder and whispered, "You gonna get up, Mom? You promised."

Most eleven-year-old boys hated clothes shopping. Especially with their mother. Though clothes did not particularly excite him, Bobby looked forward to having lunch at one of La Cumbre Plaza's nearby restaurants and maybe running into some of his classmates. His summer had been long and lonely, what with his mom's odd behavior and all.

Only a few days left before he started sixth grade. Sixth grade! No more older kids around to tease or bully him. This year, he would work harder to cultivate a friend or two. Maybe even talk to a girl. Maybe, he would start today—despite his mother's presence.

He nudged her shoulder a second time. "C'mon, Mom. Please?"

Sarah Lockhardt's closed eyelids flickered. She squinted against the morning light of her bedroom's open curtains. "What time is it?"

Bobby indicated the clock on her nightstand. "Nearly ten."

"Ten?" She groaned in protest, running her slim, dainty fingers through her crumpled Marilyn Monroe mane. "What day is it?"

He stared at the floor.

"Don't do that." She peeled back her bedding, rose on unsteady feet, and searched for her pink silk robe. Once discovered, she twirled it about her shoulders. "I haven't had my tea, yet. Bear with Mummy, won't you? What day is it?"

The amiable inflection of her voice belied her flat expression. As he found himself doing more and more lately, he humored her. "It's Monday, Mom."

She gripped his shoulder for balance, sliding into her house shoes.

"You promised," he reminded her, defeated.

"I know."

"Want me to go make your tea?"

She nodded, then disappeared into the master bathroom.

Bobby marched through the living room as if avoiding paparazzi. Hands shielding his side view like blinders as he strode purposefully toward his destination, he chose not to confront the shambolic wreck he had just tidied up yesterday. He had heard her up and about last night after he had gone to bed. Lately, an early retreat to the seclusion of his room had become routine.

He filled and set the kettle on the stove, then switched on the burner. As the water heated, he readied her cup and filled the tea strainer. The grocery bags sitting atop the counter caught his attention. They had not gone to the store yesterday. He had not heard anyone stop by last night.

Peeking into one of the bags, he noted the bug spray and ant traps. Dozens of them. In fact, all three of the bags contained similar products of varying brands. It looked as if she had bought out the store. She likely had.

Her wallet sat open beside the paper bags. ID intact and checkbook closed, it could have simply been abandoned for a more pressing interest—except it appeared she had no cash tucked into its bill sleeve. Odd. His mother always kept a fair amount of money in her billfold. He hoped she had not been robbed while at the store picking up enough pesticides to treat the entire neighborhood.

By the time Sarah finally emerged, Bobby had prepared her tea just the way she liked it. He even made toast with jam. Perhaps she would perk up if she had a little something on her stomach. That was what she used to say to him when he was younger.

Something about her movements and appearance unnerved him as she entered the kitchen. Small movements, semi-dragging her feet as she shuffled along. It appeared she had tried to dress herself, yet her clothes hung disheveled about her. Usually, Sarah Lockhardt wore the finest and most recent fashions. Today, she wore wrinkled slacks and a bulky button-up shirt. The buttons were misaligned; the slacks had a grease stain on the left thigh.

Her eyes avoided his as she approached the breakfast table. They flitted cautiously around the kitchen, as if expecting something to jump out at her.

Bobby watched without comment. Part of him had grown accustomed to her peculiarities. Another part of him lived in terror and confusion.

"Toast's still warm," he said when she took her seat. "I made your favorite. Orange marmalade."

She nodded, expressionless, and reached for her tea. The cup's radiant heat prompted her to recoil. She leaned back in her chair, crossed her arms and legs, and waited for it to cool. Eyes narrowed in suspicion, she picked up a piece of toast, sniffed it, then set it back down. "Did you bring in the paper?"

Bobby slipped out of his seat, trotted past the cluttered living room, and opened the front door. Bending down to grab the morning's *Santa Barbara News-Press* off the front doorstep, he froze in place. "Mom?"

There came no reply.

He backed inside, then lunged forward to grab the paper before closing the door. "Mom?" he called a second time.

The phone rang as he hurried back to the kitchen. Before he could say another word, she had risen to answer the phone. The one side of the exchange he heard left no doubt as to the identity of the caller.

"What's changed?" she accused, her tone again masking her stone-like expression. "Are you still working for them?"

Bobby never could understand why his mother got so angry about his dad's job. Had she not told him hundreds of times what a respectable, honest, successful man his father was?

"How would that change anything?" she continued in a stern voice. "Of course, I know. I never said that." A moment later, she huffed and shoved the receiver his way. "Here. Talk to your father."

He stepped forward, reaching for the phone. His mother snatched it back momentarily and buried it in her chest. She focused her glacier-blue eyes on his. "It's none of his business what happens here, son."

"Can I tell him you're taking me clothes shopping today?"

She paused, then nodded in concession and handed him the receiver. Without another word, she sat back down at the table and again tested her tea. First with a sniff, then the tip of her tongue.

Bobby smiled as he greeted his father. "Hi, Dad! How are you?"

"I'm grand, Bobby. It's good to hear your voice. How are you and your mother doing?"

"Okay. I miss you. Well, we miss you. Are you coming for a visit soon?"

"I'm working on it."

"Really? When?"

The ensuing refusal to give a clear timeline deflated Bobby. In the years since his parents split up, he had seen his father twice. They spoke a couple of times a week, but never for long and never with any concrete plans to resolve the lack of consistent contact. Despite his mother's reassurances, Bobby sometimes suspected his father wanted to speak with his mother more than him.

"How's Mum, really?" his father asked. "She sounds tired."

Bobby stole a glance at his mother before answering. She had dumped her tea and toast in the sink. Now, she busied herself scrubbing out the kettle and tea strainer. "She's great, Dad. She's cleaning up the breakfast dishes. We're going to the mall soon. Mom's taking me clothes shopping."

"School starting soon, then?"

"A week from tomorrow."

"Excellent. I expect you'll keep up your marks as good as last year, yes?"

"Promise."

Their conversation waned once they had gone through all the usual pleasantries. Bobby's heart ached with rejection when his dad asked him to put his mother back on the phone.

She sneered, nostrils flared, as she snatched back the receiver. "Go get ready. We're leaving in five minutes."

Shoulders slumped, he left to brush his teeth.

"Is that a threat?" his mother shouted into the phone. "Are you threatening me?"

Bobby did not want to further agitate her while she fought with his father on the phone. She would find out soon enough that their car was not parked in the driveway.

He wondered if someone had stolen it or if she had abandoned it somewhere and called a cab to return home. It would not be the first time.

***

"I'm refilling my ice water, dear. Can I get you anything? Water? Soda?"

"You're avoiding the question."

"No, I'm thirsty."

She declined his offer as usual, but he always asked. The most dedicated student he had taught in his twenty-plus years, she spent every minute of their twice-weekly lessons learning or practicing, and—if her mother was to be believed—most of her time at home, as well. Twelve years old and already at an impossibly advanced Level 9.

Still, it was 1967. Given the era, it did not shock him to witness her interests shift from Rachmaninoff to something more rebellious, but it did disappoint him. Worse, it would horrify her parents.

The Petersons had high expectations for their daughter. His task was to ensure she met them.

He left the room as Faith fingered the first few notes of Bach's Sinfonia No. 4 in D minor, BWV 790. The upbeat piece soon had him humming and bobbing his head. He took his time, praising her aloud from the break room as he emptied then refilled ice trays. When the tune concluded, he slid the last tray into the freezer, pausing to applaud.

Then, it began.

Without warning, she erupted into a largely improvised "Lucille." The Little Richard melody invaded the pomp and elegance of the studio, swapping out serenity for a raucous that epitomized everything wrong with the day's most popular music genre.

Austin Jones detested rock'n'roll.

"No-no-no-no-no," he protested with a disapproving huff as he marched back into the studio, arms waving as if cautioning oncoming drivers that the road upon which they drove was washed out ahead.

Faith remained undeterred. She shot him a rebellious smile, stood, and continued to punish the keys with an unmerciful pounding that would have doubtless impressed the song's composers.

He wrinkled his nose as if the melody had emitted a foul stench, then stood beside his young pupil, arms akimbo. When he caught her eye, he lowered his head and raised a scolding brow.

The outburst continued. She steadily slowed the tempo, then riffed into "Come On Down to My Boat" by Every Mother's Son, transitioned into Stevie Wonder's "I Was Made to Love Her," and ended with an impressive nod to Ray Manzarek's popular intro for the Doors' "Light My Fire." Halfway through, she reached around with one hand to unpin the thick bank of red spirals she usually kept pulled back into a taut bun. She whipped her head around until they spilled down her back and shoulders, then continued without missing one tickled ivory.

Austin gritted his teeth and endured the outburst. What she lacked in taste, she more than made up for in talent. Hopefully, she would not lose focus. Glancing at the clock on the far wall, he envisioned her parents standing outside at this very minute, listening in horror.

A triplet of sharp claps restored order. No applause this time. Prodigy or no, she needed to practice discipline. Her parents did not pay him good money to let their only child squander her lessons on the Billboard charts.

"I trust that won't be part of your Juilliard audition." He drew his browline glasses halfway down the bridge of his nose and peered disapprovingly over the frame.

Faith rolled a shoulder. "Maybe I won't audition."

He gave a doubtful snort. "You can discuss that with your mother. For now..." He flipped the pages of the *Repertoire Music Book* propped open face against the music rack until he came to Debussy's "Cakewalk."

"Answer the question first," she challenged, a mischievous glint in her chartreuse orbs.

Austin exhaled. "My personal life is none of your business, Faith."

She jutted her chin. "I won't play another note. And I won't audition."

He studied her hard, lips pursed, weighing the sincerity of her threat. "His name's John. And we're just friends."

Faith twisted her lips into a victorious smirk. Then, like a toggle switch, her expression flattened. She transformed again into the dutiful student with which he preferred to deal.

With a curt nod, he indicated the sheet music before her. She straightened her posture, positioned her delicate fingers above the keys, and responded accordingly.

The last fifteen minutes of their hour dragged by for Faith. But as endless as it seemed, she knew the instant Austin told her parents about her little improvisation, it would be an even longer evening.

And she was right.

Once the initial shock of her musical mutiny had subsided, the lectures ensued. Clipped but kind at first, they began in the studio with the three adults reminding her that she had a future to consider.

Wild-eyed, her mother wrung her white gloves. Staring first at Austin, then Faith's father, she insisted, "Well brought up girls don't play such music."

"And you just won the Leventritt in May," Austin scolded, arms folded, lips scrunched to the side. "That was quite an honor, you know."

On the way home, she sulked in the back seat of the family Fairlane as her father picked up the baton. "We're just worried about you," he reasoned, eyeballing her through the rearview mirror. "There're so few real opportunities for girls in your field."

"I'm twelve, Dad. There aren't any opportunities—"

"—yet," her mother corrected, smoothing her freshly applied lipstick with the tip of her pinkie finger. She looked over at her husband. "Stop by the house before going on to the restaurant. I need a pill."

Faith eye-rolled. She peered out the window, absent as they continued the lecture. Rows of brightly painted track homes with manicured lawns zipped past as the Fairlane carried them away from their tree-lined, upper-middle-class neighborhood to the restaurant to meet their dinner companions from her father's club.

She wished they would have let her stay home. She hated spending stuffy evenings in posh eateries, where her folks pretended their station in life was grander than it actually was. At least it was the Tuffins tonight. At least the husband would crack a smile sometimes, unlike most of her dad's fake friends. In fact, for an older man, Faith found him rather handsome.

Just six months to go. Although not officially a teenager yet, Faith understood the big secret they never shared with her. She had demonstrated unequaled talent at a very young age, and now had a mission in life that her parents would ensure she completed. Walt and Millie Peterson's only child would elevate them to the status they had long-coveted—and that meant more than money. The outwardly proper, cultured couple would legitimize their standing amongst the upper crust one way or another. After all, whatever Mrs. Peterson wanted, Mr. Peterson had best provide.

"You know, Mr. Tuffin's on staff at Juilliard," her mother chirped over her shoulder without looking back. "Remember that when he asks about your progress, darling, and for Pete's sake, don't mention today's... incident...at practice. It'll be our little secret. Agreed?"

Faith watched the Manhattan cityscape come into view.

"*Okay*?" her mother demanded, twisting around in her seat and glaring over her shoulder. "Are we on the same page here?"

Faith crossed her arms in a daring, if flimsy, attempt at...what did Austin call it? Rebellion? "*Okay*, Mother."

Millie Peterson stared open-mouth at her husband. "Did you hear the way your daughter just spoke to me, Walt?"

Her father eyed her from the rearview mirror. "You all right back there, kitten?"

"I'm fine," Faith spat. She nestled into her seat, agitated for reasons that went beyond the irritation her mother evoked within her. Lately, she felt this way a lot.

The woman continued her indignant rant the rest of the drive. "I can't understand what's gotten into her."

"Maybe her blood sugar's low. We'll be at the restaurant soon enough."

Millie shook her index finger at her husband. "Don't start that, Walter. Food isn't the answer to everything. Just because you can stuff yourself like a pig—which I'll remind you to refrain from doing tonight, thank you very much—doesn't mean everyone else can. Women need to watch their figure." Her eyes affixed themselves to the reflected image of her daughter in the rearview mirror, displeased at her folded arms and scowling face. "You hear that, Faith? Don't let yourself go. Especially now that you're nearly thirteen. Puberty is not your friend, young lady."

Everything inside Faith wanted to believe her mother had not shot that last comment as one of her many poisoned arrows. They always hit their mark. This one was no exception.

Sometimes, Millie Peterson feigned concern over her only child's lack of companions. Mostly, though, it appeared she reveled in it. Friends might distract her. That was the sentiment. And nothing—nothing— would come between their musical prodigy and the illustrious future her parents banked on. They would see to it.

Little did they know, they were too late. Faith had found an entire group of friends some months ago. And not a bunch of long-dead relic composers, either. Every one of them, from Otis Redding to the Monkeys to the Beach Boys, was alive—and they made her feel alive too.

CHAPTER 3

ROSS FISHED HIS HOTEL ROOM key out of his pocket, smiling despite his exhausting day at the lilting trill of Josephine's voice through the door. Happy laughter reserved for friends and family, neither of which she had here in London. Before inserting the key into the lock, he checked his watch and subtracted five hours. Just past 1 PM in New York. Thankfully, such time conversions—however natural they had become over the last several months—would no longer be necessary.

As far as Ross was concerned, a week from Friday could not come soon enough. He wanted to put as much distance between himself and England as possible.

Inside, Josephine beamed radiantly, her features blossoming as he entered and draped his suit jacket atop his briefcase, which he set near the door. "Oh wait—I think he just walked in."

Wide-eyed, Ross rapid-shook his head and waved her off. He needed a drink. More than that, he needed better answers than he had received from the papers and his insider contacts.

"My mistake, Evelyn. I'm sorry. Looks like we're both still waiting on him." She placed a hand on her hip and frowned. "Yes, he is a busy man. Of course I'll tell him you called. Yes...yes, that too. Okay, then." She giggled, moved closer to the receiver, and bent down to replace the handset as she signed off. "Will do. Take care. We'll see you in a couple of weeks. Okay. Bye for now."

Ross hooked a finger into the knot of his tie, tugging it side-to-side as he carried his three-finger pour to one of the two upholstered armchairs facing the sofa. He sat down and took a hearty swallow, then yanked his loosened tie free from his collar.

Josephine brought the decanter of scotch over and placed it on the table beside him. She gave his shoulder a gentle squeeze before crawling into his lap. As he draped his arms around her waist, she brushed her lips against his. "Your mother's upset we won't be back for your birthday."

He regarded her with wary eyes. "There must be a party involved."

She locked her arms around his neck. "A surprise party."

"She knew we wouldn't make it."

"Did I mention how upset she is?"

"Trust me. She'll get over it. The party's for her and her society friends anyway, so she won't have to cancel. And I won't be missed."

"She's trying, Ross."

He barked out a doubtful but good-natured breath, maneuvering his glass through the maze of their locked arms to take another drink. "She usually is."

Nonplussed, Josephine vacated her husband's lap to check her hair and makeup in the entryway mirror—a recent compulsion since letting local "it" stylist, Daniel Galvin, talk her into hacking off her beautiful dirty-blonde locks and brickworking it into the increasingly popular Twiggy do he had created. "Shall we go out tonight or order something from room service? You look like you've had quite the day."

Ross rubbed his temple with his free hand, the other clutching his rocks glass as if it was glued to his palm. "Thank you for understanding. I'm not very hungry, anyway. We ordered a late lunch and ate at the office."

The typical vibrancy of Josephine Alexander's countenance faded to pensive empathy. She stared at her husband through the mirror. "Have they heard anything yet?"

He scooted back into the armchair. "The autopsy didn't establish a clear-cut cause of death," he said, his tone laced with what sounded like a cross between fear and scorn. "The coroner's ordered a full-scale inquest."

"How long will that take?"

His eyes fused, his mind desperate to disremember the events of last Saturday night. "Doesn't matter, really. My understanding is the results won't be released to the public."

She pivoted to face him, her short skirt softly twirling around her thighs. "So...that's it, then? They're ruling it a suicide?"

He looked at, then past, her. "I don't know. Like I said..."

She went to the bar, grabbed another rocks tumbler, then returned and helped herself to a generous pour before gently collapsing on the sofa. "So what now? What about NEMS? What about the band? What about Cilla Black? What about the others?"

Ross set down his drink and stood with a grunt. He unbuttoned his dress shirt as he trudged toward the bedroom to change into something less suffocating. "I don't know, darling. I don't work for NEMS. I've heard a bunch of rumors. That's all I have."

"I didn't mean to upset you," Josephine called after him. "I've been getting calls from my friends in New York all week. Everyone's curious what happens now. And, well...I am too, I suppose."

The last thing Ross needed was for his bride to grow suspicious. Yet somehow, he could not shake the growing tension he felt every time the topic arose—as it did, constantly. "I'm sorry," he called back to the living room. "The whole world's waiting to see what'll happen. Most are concerned the Beatles will disband."

"Have they said anything yet?"

"There was a meeting at NEMS today. Rumor has it the boys' copyrights could be sold to an American consortium to pay the eighty percent owed on Epstein's estate. I imagine there'll be some internal reshuffling and rearranging. Maybe some additional mergers, or maybe Clive'll come in to try to run the business."

"Clive?"

"Eppy's brother. Anyway, it's really too early to guess. But I did hear that Lennon said they'll be managing themselves 'for a time,' whatever that means."

"I guess I figured Robert Stigwood would step in, what with that merger earlier in the year."

The proposition elicited a burst of laughter from Ross. "He wishes. But no. The boys made it crystal clear they won't consider Stiggy."

"Really? Why not?"

Ross peeked his head out of the bedroom to steal a glance at his bride's loveliness. "Who knows. Apparently, the lads are all heading back to India for a couple of months to study with that guru. Honestly, Jo, I don't know."

Josephine scrunched her lips into a contemplative frown. Then, her features softened. "It's so tragic. He was my age, you know. Handsome. Successful. It's so shocking."

Shocking, indeed. More shocking than she knew. Worse, he had yet to see his cabbie friend again since Saturday night. Had the man gone off to find a new career after all?

The good news was that no one had approached him on the matter, other than the normal gossip that ensued when the news hit the airwaves. No heavies had come to his office to hang him out a balcony window. No anonymous phone callers wanting hush money to forget they had seen him in the area. And no call from Eppy's attorney, David Jacobs, demanding an explanation.

Instead of giving into paranoia, Ross decided he needed to start packing and forget the bizarre cab ride back to the Park Lane. Technically, he had no idea what had transpired when his driver disappeared down that alley. Technically, he could be blowing it all out of proportion. And maybe he was. Maybe it was a suicide after all. Or maybe even an accident.

He changed into his nightclothes, donned his robe and slippers, and then returned to the living room. The scotch had already produced a slight buzz. He went with it, determined to salvage the evening with his bride.

She smiled up at him as he grabbed his drink and relocated to the sofa to sit beside her. "I think I'm a little overdressed."

"Always," he groaned seductively, leaning in for a kiss. "And stop fretting over your hair. It's beautiful—and it'll grow back before you know it."

***

Outwardly, Lynda Grant displayed little reaction as her seven-year-old joined her in song. One never knew how a young man might react to a fawning mother telling him what a lovely voice he had. She did not want to make him self-conscious. That was how she and George had handled the older boys when they first showed musical promise: 83% nonchalance, 17% encouragement.

But inwardly, she was thrilled. Though not one to believe in premonitions or other such rubbish, Lynda flashed forward a decade or so and envisioned her little man all grown up, singing on stage, with adoring crowds cheering him. A blond Fabian with a set of golden pipes. The vision was so clear, it could have stolen away her breath.

She wrestled back a grin as she continued singing, waltzing her way to procure flour and sugar and then back to the counter, as if her youngest's mastery of an old Irish folk song was the most natural thing in the world. "That's right, love," she instructed matter-of-factly with an approving nod and zero direct eye contact.

Seated on the counter near the mixing bowl, Jordan fidgeted with his fingers. He cast shy eyes upon the kitchen floor but sang louder from his mother's encouragement.

> *... That bow'r and its music I ne'er can forget ...*
> *... But of when alone in the bloom of the year ...*
> *... I think, "Is the nightingale singing there yet?" ...*
> *... "Are the roses still bright by the calm Bendemeer?" ...*

Her head gently swayed as they measured the ingredients together and finished the tune. "And what color frosting, Jorie? I've some food coloring, so we don't have to settle on boring old white."

"His favorite color's blue, Mummy. Can we do blue?"

"Of course we can. Splendid idea." She kissed the top of his head, then cracked the eggs and folded them into the batter. "You'll need to lick the spoon once it's all mixed up, though. We want to make sure it's perfect. And you're the best tester."

Would-be stage fright gave way to sugary anticipation. His green eyes grew as large as saucers. He began the second verse without prompting or reservation.

> *... No, the roses soon withered that hung o'er the wave ...*

... But the blossoms were gathered while freshly they shone ...
... And the dew was distilled on the flowers, that gave ...
... All the fragrance of summer when summer is gone ...

She had sung "Bendemeer's Stream" hundreds of times—most often while cleaning or cooking or performing similar mindless tasks. The idea that her boy had not only listened when she sang but also learned the lyrics—and accompanied her in perfect harmony—made her swell with pride. And today, she needed the lift. Especially today.

"Don't decorate, Mum," Ben had scolded earlier that morning after stumbling upon the box of streamers and such she had pulled out of the attic in anticipation of his birthday, but had failed to adequately hide. "Decorations are for kids, or girls. I'll be fifteen. I'm a man, now."

The adamant request had stung. Every one of the last fourteen previous birthdays, she had gone all out. The same with Chris and Jorie. She reveled in celebrating birthdays and holidays. And yet, as early as last year, she had seen the proverbial writing on the wall. Ben was growing up. He was right. No more balloons and streamers for him, no matter how it hurt to let go.

Not that she did not have plenty of practice letting go of the men in her life. George was always on the road, it seemed. His career had never given her a moment's pause until Chris came along. She had had her own career. Bothersome worries about schedules and a lack of time together had rarely crossed her mind.

Only now, with sons who seemed to remind her every day that they would not be with her for many more years, did it nag at her insides. And that nagging, she admitted, was something she freely spread around. George had started getting his fair share of it over the last few weeks.

She wondered how much of her growing discomfort was George's career and how much of it was her lack of one. She missed the stage. Then again, with all the cultural changes in entertainment anymore, she probably would have retired by now, anyway. And in fairness, she should probably support George as much as possible. Not only was he the sole support of the household, his profession's expiration date loomed ever near as well.

When they finished their duet, Jordan reached for the wooden spoon. "May I stir the batter?"

"Of course you may." She remained close by, humming while he gave the mixture a thorough turn. When the silence in the kitchen registered, she sidestepped to the radio and switched on the power. Engelbert Humperdinck filled the room with "The Last Waltz." The tune made her smile. She found herself recalling her first dance with George on their wedding day.

In that moment, all irritation evaporated. George was doing his best. Ben was growing up. And at least she still had Chris and Jordan—for now.

"That's a fine job, son," she cooed, reaching for the greased and floured pans she had pre-prepared. "Time to pour."

"Can I help?"

"I'm counting on it. You know, Jorie, you should be sure to learn to cook for yourself. You might not always have someone to do it for you. Or, you might fancy whipping up a meal or two on your own anyway."

He cupped his hand atop hers as she smoothed the creamy batter. "But I have you."

"I mean when you're older. And married. Sometimes, it's nice for daddies to cook, too."

He made a face. "I'm not getting married."

She set the spoon in the bowl and the bowl in the sink. "Not any time soon, but someday. And you'll want to be a proper husband."

"Does Daddy cook for you?"

She dipped her finger into the remnant batter in the bowl and dotted his nose. "Daddy's hardly ever here, now is he?"

Jordan hopped down from the counter. "Will he be home for Ben's party?"

"He wouldn't miss it," she promised, wiping her hands on her apron. "Now go grab the timer so we can get these pans in the oven."

Carefully setting the timer as he had been instructed on previous occasions, he adopted a look of stern contemplation. "But if the party's not until tomorrow night, why're we making the cake today?"

Lynda opened the preheated oven and gently slid the pans inside. "Because your brother wants Sunday roast for his Friday birthday, along with leek and potato soup for a starter. What with the roast beef, potatoes, boiled cabbage, and Angel Delight for dessert, it's a lot of work for one oven."

"Why does he get Angel Delight if he's getting a cake?"

She tousled his hair. "Not complaining, then, are you? When you're fifteen, you can decide to have two desserts as well. Besides, if he gets it, you and Chris do, too."

"When I'm fifteen, I want all dessert and no roast."

The idea of her youngest turning fifteen, leaving school, and beginning his own life was not something she wanted to consider. "Let's cross that bridge when we get there, my darling. You're mine for at least eight more years. Now come along. Let's wrap your brother's gifts before he gets home and says he's too old for presents."

***

Huddling at a worn corner table of what lore and locals dubbed the "Bun House" in Bromley-by-Bow, strategically positioned for an optimal view through its large pane windows so he could monitor the passersby outside, he waited—alone. For over an hour.

He wondered which one of the boys had chosen this particular establishment to meet. The Widow's Son. The irony was not lost on him.

Tourists and regulars alike sat at or leaned against the long, dark wood bar, laughing and chatting over pints of ale or stout while glasses clinked from toasts or were cleared away. A steady, upbeat stream of patrons for a Thursday afternoon, even for such a popular pub. But no one bothered him as he slouched in his seat, nursing his scotch and soda. He had ensured his privacy by opting for a table over the more exposed bar stools. The last thing he needed was the company of friendly, smiling strangers.

He glanced regularly at the passings of pedestrians and cars along the street outside, then up at an aging net of hot cross buns hanging from the famous pub's ceiling, and then at the front door. Forty-five minutes in, he almost wished he had taken up smoking. Anything to pass the time without dulling his necessarily sharp senses. Alas, the filthy habit had never taken hold of him. Not that it mattered in this place. A dense layer of smoke floated above the patrons, covering them like an awning, so thick it caused him to periodically cough into his fist.

The first time they changed the meeting location and time, he had understood. Too much heat, especially with Scotland Yard's endless—and heightening—obsession with the Firm's every move. Besides, it had only been a few days since the events in Belgravia. The second time the meet had been rescheduled, frustration had niggled him. The third, he had grown concerned.

Surely, Reggie and Ronnie wanted him as far away from London as they could get him. Surely, the twins were as anxious as he. After all, one villain gunning down another known villain at the Blind Beggar in broad daylight was one thing. Who would mourn a common East End thug like George Cornell, save his wife and son? But *this*? Last weekend's job was a game changer by anyone's estimation. Particularly after what they had done to music producer Joe Meek back in February.

If the brief contact he had had with their go-between the day after the news broke was to be believed, no one had expressed interest in how the job went, if there were complications, or even if anyone had seen him. At this point, maybe those things mattered less than him keeping his head down and dwelling in the shadows.

Fair enough. They had known he would leave nothing behind. That he was a professional. Besides, they were his associates, not his counselors.

Privately, the heaviness of that night haunted him. It would forever, even though he fought and despised his self-accused weakness. He had wrestled with the assignment more than anyone might have guessed, considering the many years he had yoked himself to this dark world. Not to mention the personal cost. In fact, had the boys known his sole reason for accepting the job that finally earned him his bones, they might have chosen someone else.

But what was done, was done. Now, he could only bank on them holding up their end of the Devil's bargain. Undoubtedly, things would get tricky. Everything had become tricky since Ronnie Kray had upped the ante by graduating from fists to guns to settle scores. Now, there was no going back to the more civilized way of doing business. For any of them.

Was he the only one who felt things shifting? The time had come to get out.

Three drinks and an hour and a half in, he decided to leave. The crowd grew as afternoon gave way to evening. With the fading sunlight, foot and vehicle traffic along Devons Road would soon render it a challenge to distinguish the innocent from the guilty. It would leave him vulnerable. Besides, someone might later recall seeing him sitting alone, perhaps looking dodgy. He could not risk that.

From across the pub, the bartender caught his eye. The man lifted his chin, indicating the empty glass of melting ice cubes before him. He shook his head to decline a refill, stood up, and straightened his shoulders. As he wove through the crowd, he leaned in and slipped the bartender a fiver. Then, as he approached the door, he caught sight of the rugged, familiar face of his liaison standing outside and across the street.

Henry. One of the toughest enforcers in the East End. And not one to be crossed.

A part of him was disappointed Ronnie Kray had not come himself. An absurd notion upon further consideration. The whole idea of banishing him from Vallance Road and all the usual places was to ensure distance between the twins and the events of last Saturday. An imposing, black Jaguar 420G motoring up to collect him from the pub would have garnered unwanted attention. Not to mention the possibility of Detective Nipper Read tailing them in his typically obvious manner.

Zigzagging against traffic, he jogged across Devons Road to join Henry. They shook hands, but neither spoke at first. Instead, they stalked north up Campbell Road toward the tracks, two suited, middle-aged, high-foreheaded, heavyset Eastenders out for a leisurely neighborhood stroll.

A couple of blocks up, Henry scrutinized their surroundings with dark, narrow eyes. "All right, then?"

He nodded down at the road. "No worries."

"Witnesses?"

"None," he lied. As soon as he had been assigned the job, he had known he would need an insurance policy. He could think of no one better than his new solicitor buddy. An alibi, should he need it. A plausible scapegoat should things take a bad turn. Mutually assured destruction would ensure his freedom far better than anything anyone closer to the situation could have. Brains over brawn rarely failed. And brains were something he had in spades.

"Right then."

Another two blocks up, the seasoned heavy stopped and faced him. Henry withdrew an envelope from inside his suit jacket and handed it over.

He tucked it into his own suit pocket. Fleetingly, he wondered if the stack of bills inside it had come from Epstein himself, having been previously extracted on pain of being exposed for his many dirty secrets. Secrets that could have ended his illustrious career faster than any amount of Carbrital could have. The twins had been blackmailing him for some time.

"You need to disappear for a while."

He nodded. "We'd talked about that."

"Things're coming apart. Last year, it was Cornell getting his at the Beggar—and then his wife, Olive, throwing that brick through the window at Fort Vallance. This year, the business with Frances dying."

The last thing he needed was a summary of past events. Everyone in Reggie Kray's sphere knew how cruelly the villain suffered over his young wife's recent suicide.

Selfishly, he was more concerned about his own wife. "Any news about America?" he dared to ask.

"America?" A sardonic burst of laughter escaped the man. "What're you on about?"

His lips flattened into a straight line. He cautioned himself to maintain his calm façade. "About branching out. I've done some research."

"*Research*?" Henry mocked, giving his back a hearty slap. "You mean that music business rubbish? They tried that. It never worked. And do you know why it never worked?"

He set his jaw and peered up, then down, Campbell Road. "No, Henry, you tell me why."

"Because they're villains, not managers."

"But they said—"

"What?" Henry stretched his arms wide, a provoking smile revealing a mouthful of gnarled and yellowed teeth. "What did they say?"

He stuffed his hands in his trouser pockets and clenched his fists. "If they're not looking to take advantage of the situation, what was all this for? They'd said they wanted to manage—"

"You think that's what this was about?" Henry tucked his chin.

"Wasn't it?" The tension overtook him as his worst fears began to materialize.

Henry gave him the once-over, his squinting eyes curious and distrusting. Then, with a lethal edge to his tone, he said, "There were other reasons. Many reasons. Personal reasons. But if you think what you did changes anything, you're nuttier than the Colonel."

His body chilled as the reality of the situation beset him. What he had done. Why he had done it. And who it had made him.

His knees weakened, but he willed his body to behave. Nothing would change the events of that night on Chapel Street. Not their reasons, and not his own. But if he could not make it to America, he would likely die on the street or in prison. All he could do now was wait.

Henry stood tall, yanked taut his jacket, and slapped him again on the back. "You did the job, right? Got a bit a dosh? As soon as we're sure nothing'll come back to the lads, you'll be back to work."

He looked away. "I'm done driving."

"That's right. No more cabs for you. But for now, disappear. You got somewhere to stay?"

"Yes."

"Right then. Check back in next month."

He cast his eyes down the street at the Bun House, debating whether he dared go back and start drinking in earnest.

"Hey." Henry reached out, cupped his neck with a strong grip, and fixed him with hard eyes. "You listen, now."

He met the man's stare with matched intensity.

"No one grasses."

He assured the man with a single shake of his head.

"No one left behind."

He gave a curt nod.

"And no more talk of America."

Forehead-to-forehead, they glared at one another. The man never minced words and always spent them economically. With a firm jerk of the hand around his neck, Henry demanded a response.

"Okay," he said at last, too frightened to argue.

With that, Henry released his grip. He dipped his head, then pivoted and lumbered up Campbell. "You know, I always thought you were smarter than this. It'd be a shame to prove me wrong."

On that point, he would not argue. He *was* smart. And because he was smart, he would find some way out of this life and over to America—with or without the Firm's assistance.

CHAPTER 4

*W**ITH THE ARRIVAL OF THE second bomb in the pre-dawn hours of that fateful Tuesday morning, Ronnie Nock learned some life-altering lessons.*

First of all, Anderson shelters were fine for protection...except against direct hits. Had this bomb, in particular, landed any closer than it had, he and Polly would have died. As it was, they had barely made it inside. In fact, Polly's already-tattered dress had been blown off her, leaving only her undergarments—and had all but shredded them as well. He had lost his jacket, and his breath, from the concussion caused by the blast. Dirt and dust filled the inside of the shelter, leaving them choking for air.

It took several minutes to dig, claw, and push their way out, only to find they would need to climb a mound of debris to find a patch of solid road. His shoes must have been blown off, not unlike his sister's clothes. His injured ankle throbbed as he assisted his younger sibling, whose normal, chatty disposition had dissolved, leaving her stunned silent.

"C'mon, then, Polly," he urged, stretching out one of his scratched and bruised hands to assist her as she stumbled behind him. "You'll be all right."

"I want Mummy." The proclamation started her weeping even as she accepted her older brother's assistance.

"We'll head back soon. I'm not sure about the way or how much damage there might be, though. The smoke needs to clear a bit before we start."

"What about the bombs?" She squeaked in terror. Teardrops spilled down her plump cheeks, streaking her soot-covered face.

Ronnie squinted and cupped his free hand above his brows in an automatic response to the light, as if shielding his eyes from a glowing sun instead of the raging inferno along London's docklands. "We'll be all right, Polly. No worries. Just stay close."

She clutched the prize for which she had left the school to search. A stuffed brown teddy bear she had dropped in the chaos as they had evacuated. A present received two Christmases ago from their parents. Like Polly's undergarments, the blast had nearly shredded its fur. Its left eye and leg were missing.

As little as three days ago, the sight of such a beloved, shabby possession would have sparked incessant teasing from all four of her older brothers. Today, Ronnie's heart ached for Polly. That bear was the only item she had from the life they had lost. His second lesson: war made men out of boys—

ready or not.

"We can't stay here," Polly complained, her voice trembling as much as her tiny frame. "Please, Ronnie. Let's get back to school. I want Mam."

He toed aside a nearby brick with his stockinged foot and collected his thoughts. "We need to make sure we don't go the wrong way. Morning should be here soon."

"But the buses!"

"The buses won't be here before the dawn. Once the bombers stop for the night, they'll come for us. Let's just sit down here and have a rest. I'm sure bombs are like lightning, Pol. And what does Mam say about lightning?"

Polly shuddered as she scooted close to her brother. She nuzzled her head against his arm, snuggling the bear close into her sheer, soot-saturated undershirt. "Lightning never strikes the same place twice."

"Right." He nodded, projecting unfelt courage, and patted the balled-up hand with which she clung to her tattered treasure. "We're in the safest spot in London, you and me. As soon as dawn breaks, we'll head back. It'll take no time once we can see properly."

Despite their dire circumstances, Ronnie found himself conflicted. A part of him agreed they should get back to the school. Their parents would be sick with worry. In truth, the buses could show up at any time. Yet another part of him ached at the idea of abandoning Paul on a heap of broken beams and rubble. Surely, morning would bring rescue workers. Someone would need to identify the body. He could not fathom a group of strangers loading up his brother in a morgue van, figuring he was just one of many anonymous unfortunates claimed by Hitler's air raid.

Lesson three: when in doubt, stay put.

Minutes passed slowly as they hunkered together on the dirty ground, the foul smell of dust, burning tobacco, and molasses thick about them. Polly wept into his chest as he watched the red glow that was the London sky. They listened in terror as the bomber planes continued their dark mission, simultaneously heartbroken for their close-knit neighbors and relieved when no additional bombs fell in their immediate vicinity.

Except one.

Without a watch, Ronnie could only guess the time. He recalled leaving the shelter before midnight and calculated the hours he had spent first with Paul, then Polly. The sun would chase away the enemy in the next couple of hours, he imagined.

The explosion must have come right around 4 AM, if his calculations were correct. Just southeast of them. For a moment, he worried. He could not be certain, but it looked as if it had hit near the school. He hoped not, but comforted himself with the idea that—unlike their poorer homes—the school's building could withstand one of Hitler's air assaults.

When Polly did not scream at the explosion in close proximity to their location, he looked down and saw that she had somehow managed to fall asleep against him. Probably sheer exhaustion from the trauma. He wished he could do the same. His ankle throbbed, as did his head.

He glanced down the road as the slightest hint of morning began to banish the night. Though too far away to see, he imagined Paul's lifeless body where it had fallen. He chastised himself for not moving closer to wait for rescuers to collect his brother. Then again, the dirty, blood-caked body was nothing Polly should see.

That Paul, the brother who had taught him to fish and recite his multiplication tables from memory, would die nameless and unaccounted for distressed Ronnie. Paul Nock would never be forgotten. Not by him.

With the sunrise, he noted burning pockets of smoldering remains all about them. He nudged his sister awake as soon as there was light enough to move on. "C'mon, Pol. Time to get back to Mam."

Groggy and spent, Polly struggled to walk the small trek back to the safety of South Hallsville School. He considered his injured ankle, then had her climb up onto his back. When he hefted her in place, she wrapped her arms around his neck. The broken teddy bear dangled from her clutched fist.

Rocks and pebbles in the road hurt his feet, but he defied the pain and labored on toward the school. Polly wept softly into his shoulder. Periodically, he would hush and encourage her.

They had survived the night. Well, two out of three of them had. Soon, he would deposit his rebel sister—who had doubtless learned some lessons of her own from the hell of their evening—into the waiting arms of their mother. He had brought her back, as he had promised before he and Paul took off to begin their search.

Another lesson learned: never give up.

But as he limped down Agate Street, less than a hundred meters from the school he had attended with his siblings, every thought left his mind. He stopped abruptly, his arms falling to his sides. Immediately, Polly slid down his back and landed bottom-first on the dusty road. She cried out in shock and pain.

Half the school had vanished. In its place was a deep crater. Police, rescue workers, and others shouted, coordinating as best they could as they took turns descending its depths to listen for the voices of any survivors.

"Mummy!" Polly screamed, scampering to her feet.

Ronnie recovered his thoughts in time to grab her waist. "No, Polly! Stop!"

She shrieked as she watched with growing intensity the reality of the situation settling upon them in waves.

Once he could walk again, he held his sister's hand and approached the ARP Warden who had checked them in two days ago. He was standing on the edge of the crater with a small group of men. One of the men looked up at the sky, tears streaming down his face, and cried, "My God, my God...this should have never happened."

How the ARP Warden had survived, Ronnie could not guess. But if he did, maybe the Nocks had, too.

The men spun around at the sound of Polly's mourning cries. Two of them rushed toward the children. One grabbed Polly to assess any wounds that might need urgent attention. The other asked Ronnie if he was okay, and if he had been in the building at the time of the blast.

Stunned as he surveyed the ruined schoolyard, he asked, "Where are the survivors?"

"Was your family staying here, lad? Were you with them?"

He nodded, slack-jawed as one of the men reemerged from the crater with what looked like a body part. Instantly, he thought of Paul.

"Ambulances are on the way," the stranger told him.

"Where are the buses?" he muttered, almost to himself.

The men spoke, but he could not understand them. His ears still rang from the two close blasts they had withstood. Every word they spoke sounded garbled and wet.

"Where are the survivors?" he demanded again, ignoring their inquiries.

The ARP Warden moved closer and clutched his shoulder. He shook his head. "Son, there aren't any. The buses have been canceled."

The last and most painful lesson Ronald Nock learned that fateful September day in 1940, the day his family had perished: never trust the government.

***

The fire brigade arrived at dusk, just as birthday party guests began to trickle in. From his vantage point in the living room, Ben glimpsed his mother standing near the kitchen, wringing her hands. She did that a lot in matters pertaining to her middle son.

Their father greeted the men at the front door with a measure of annoyance and resignation, a pinched expression on his face.

The family firebug had struck again.

Ben slipped upstairs without notice, impressive since the day's attention had focused on his transition from boyhood to manhood. He searched the bedrooms, the loo, and all the closets to no avail. Finding nothing, he decided the window was the best way out.

He slid open his window and hoisted one leg out onto the roof.

"Where are you off to?" came a small voice from his doorway.

Ben held his index finger to his lips. "Don't tell anyone."

Jordan nodded, eyes big. "I won't. But where are you off to?"

He shifted to straddle the windowsill. "Where do you think?"

"Gonna go get him?"

Ben winked. "Someone's gotta do it, right?"

"Gonna pound him?"

"I might."

Jordan fidgeted with the toy ball he held in his hands. "What about all your presents?"

"I won't be gone long."

"Promise? 'Cause I made you something you're gonna love!"

"I promise. And I'm sure it'll be the best present I ever received. Now go on back downstairs and help Mum for me, okay?"

All the boys had become experts at exiting the house through their bedroom windows. For the most part, it was novelty. With one exception, they only used their cat-like skills to show off. Only Chris employed it as a means with which to sneak out at night. Or, apparently, during his older brother's fifteenth birthday party...to light a nearby field on fire.

Ben stomped the entire way from the house to Chris's regular hiding place up near the ridge. Doubtless, he had heard the sirens. How long he might intend to hide away, Ben did not care to guess.

In the distance, he saw a dissipating pillar of billowing smoke rising from the meadow. A grove of fir trees and thick shrubs obscured his ability to see the ground itself, but Ben could imagine the charred earth in the middle of an otherwise golden, late-summer field. The brigade had already worked the flames before arriving at the Grants' to have a stern word with the parents of Bledlow's most notorious petty arsonist.

He followed the footpath that snaked around the thicket, pawing through branches to reach the hiding place he had lived to regret showing his younger brother. The one he used to go to for privacy. The place he had first started writing music. Now, it was nothing more than a place to skulk away to until the worst of whatever situation Chris concocted had passed.

At the center of the thicket, which he himself had cleared out and turned into a makeshift fort, Chris sat...with a girl. Always a girl, these days.

A supercilious grin stretched Chris's lips as he lay casually against the would-be wall, propped up on one elbow. "Ah, there he is. The man of the hour. Prince Charles, the mum's boy." He glanced at the girl sitting cross-legged beside him, then back at his brother. "Took you long enough."

Ben raised his hands to his waist, leveling stern eyes upon the unrepentant form before him. "Say goodbye to your friend here and let's go."

Chuckling, Chris winked at the girl. "C'mon, brother. This party's just getting started."

He hitched a thumb over his shoulder. "The party's back at the house. And instead of being there, I'm here with you. Now, tell your friend goodbye and let's go, or I'll head back alone and let the brigade know where to find you."

The threat brought him to his feet. He stared cleavers at his sibling. "You wouldn't!"

Ben stood, nonplussed. "Try me."

The lecture began after the girl left, replete with the same condemnation voiced with every previous incident. The authorities were furious over the damage Chris inflicted on a semi-regular basis. Perhaps the time had come to leave Bledlow. To leave England altogether. Maybe pack up and take their boys to Australia. And had Chris given any consideration to the humiliation he had caused their parents? Did he want them driven from their home?

A scowl fixed Chris's face. "At least Mum would see Aunt Grace more than once a year. Maybe Australia wouldn't be so bad. Beaches, better weather..."

"Not the point," Ben scolded, stomping more than walking.

They continued on in silence for a time. Ben hoped his absence had gone unnoticed by those who had come to celebrate. He figured his father would have talked down the brigade by now, assured them he would deal with the offender, and that Chris would be at their offices first thing Monday morning to account.

George Grant was well-known in Bledlow, and something of a celebrity due to his big band days. For this reason alone, Ben figured, they continued to endure Chris's escapades. Any other family would have been run out by now.

"You going to the cinema this weekend?" Chris asked, probably hoping to ease the tension before they returned.

Ben set his jaw. "And there it is. As if nothing happened. Yes. I'll likely take Jordan to the cinema tomorrow unless Dad and Mum have plans. You're welcome to come with us—if you can tear yourself away from the matches and all the girls in town."

Chris folded his lips in on themselves to suppress a grin. His purposeful gait became more of a saunter. "Her name's Claire."

Ben shook his head but stared straight ahead. "A pretty one, isn't she? You've made quite the rounds lately with all the pretty faces. I suppose that's impressive for a kid your age."

"And what's wrong with pretty faces? Pretty faces are a good thing. Maybe if you weren't waltzing about all the time, pretending you're Dad, you could get a bird of your own."

The barb hit its mark, though Ben wrestled it down. "I'm thinking of the future. You'll understand when you grow up."

"You won't grow up being Billy No-Mates...mate."

Ben spun and grabbed Chris's upper arm, jerking him around to face him. "As much as you know. See, you left too soon. You weren't there when Dad gave me my birthday present. A trip to London. Turns out, he's been showing my songs around. And people like them. We're going into the city next week."

A look of sheer envy, raw and uncut, sheathed Chris's stunned face. "Congratulations," he muttered through tight lips.

Ben released his grip, and they continued down the ridge. The casual superiority in Chris's step disappeared. The satisfaction of putting him in his place was the best present Ben could have asked for.

"Why don't you ever share your songs with me? I could play them. In fact, I'm thinking about starting a band."

"You'd have to be serious. And so far, the only things you seem serious about are girls and pyrotechnics."

"Just watch. Someday I'll be bigger than Mick Jagger."

Ben guffawed. "Guess I'll see you on *Top of the Pops*, then."

"Laugh all you want. I don't care."

As they neared their home, they noted the number of cars parked about their property. Ben had no idea his parents had invited so many friends and neighbors. Yesterday, he had heard their mother whisper to their dad, asking something about industry people dropping by as well. The thought made him nervous.

"So..." Chris opened the back gate, stepping aside so the birthday boy could pass him. "Got a date coming for your big celebration?"

Ben scrunched his mouth to the side. "No, Chris, I don't have a date coming. Let me guess. You do. Is it this Claire? Or someone else?"

"There're two," he said matter-of-factly. "And no, not Claire. Lucille Smith. You can have the other one if you like."

"Lucille," Ben echoed, unimpressed. "Thanks just the same. I don't fancy younger birds."

Chris glanced around to the front of the house to ensure the fire brigade had left. "You might not fancy Lucille, but I'd wager you'll fancy her older sister."

An image of Marge Smith stopped Ben in his tracks. Lovely girl.

However annoying, his younger brother's ability to attract females—

apparently even older ones—impressed him. Maybe he would take some time to get to know Marge better if she showed up. After all, what good was striving for a career and future if he had no one to share it with?

Chris stopped him before they entered the house. He looked up at him, suddenly sincere. "Happy birthday, Ben."

***

Thankfully, the ringing of the phone drew her away from the sandwich she had purchased from the store earlier that morning after dropping Bobby off at school. She had stopped by their local grocer to pick up a few items for dinner and decided to have the deli department make her a to-go lunch while she shopped.

Big mistake. The ham tasted funny. Like much of her food, lately. She had noticed it with the first bite. The small bag of potato chips was fine. But the sandwich? Also, the way the gentleman who prepared it had stared at her, she knew. He was in on it.

And she had finally figured out why. Only one person would want her poisoned. All his overtures about reconciliation did not fool her. Jameson would stop at nothing to get rid of her and take Bobby.

She pushed the plate away, rose from her seat, and picked up the kitchen wall phone, glancing right at the brief image that flickered at the corner of her eye. Shivering suspiciously, she brought the phone to her ear.

"Sarah?"

"Father!" she exclaimed, closing her eyes and exhaling with relief that whatever shadow she had just seen had disappeared. She stretched the phone cord as she walked, settling upon the kitchen chair opposite the one she had just vacated. "How are you? It's late there, isn't it?" She eyed the wall clock and automatically calculated the eight-hour time difference. "Is everything all right?"

"Yes, thank you. It's been some time since I checked in on you. I trust all's well?"

"Bobby and I are quite well."

"You sounded a bit odd when you answered."

Sarah's shoulders drooped. *Not again.* "Odd? In what way?"

Ever since the funeral two years ago, her father had accused her of...something, though he had never come out and said exactly what.

Pinning the receiver against her shoulder with a tilt of her head, she picked at, smelled, and again pushed away the plated sandwich. She briefly considered the possibility her father might be behind the attempted poisoning. Or maybe he and Jameson were in on it together.

"Tired, perhaps? Overwhelmed?"

Robert Wellingham III had always resented her. He resented that his only child was female, and that her birth had cost him his wife. He resented the effort his own mother had to exert stepping in to help raise the child—at least in those areas outside the expertise of his servants. Things like breeding, manners, and choosing a suitable husband. The latter was the one thing she had failed at...a fact about which Robert often reminded his daughter.

He also resented Sarah for his own mother dying two years ago, having convinced himself that the woman's death was not due to brain cancer, as the doctors had insisted, but rather as a result of the years wasted trying to ensure Sarah took her rightful place as the Wellingham heir.

The balls, the presentation to Court, the would-be suitors who had something to offer by way of a dignified future. Sarah had rejected all propriety by running off with someone far below her station. While Queen Elizabeth had been ascending the throne, Sarah Wellingham was falling in love with an ill-bred pretender with zero ability to keep her in the manner to which she was raised. Why Robert had deceived the family matriarch into believing he had withdrawn all financial support from his recalcitrant offspring, he could not explain.

But Sarah knew. She knew all along. Somehow, he and Jameson were conspiring to take her son. They were in on it together. Everyone wanted Bobby back in Britain. And as soon as they could get her to take the poison, their plan would work.

Well, too bad. She had them all figured out and would never fall for it.

For fifteen minutes, Sarah chatted with her father about Bobby's upcoming first day in sixth grade, how lax and inferior American schools were, and the continued success of Robert's financial dealings. Of course. It always circled back to money.

"Which reminds me," he said, slipping in as he always did. "Did you receive my most recent check?"

"I deposited it this morning, thank you." She stood and grabbed her plate from the table, then stretched the telephone cord as far as she could reach as she leaned toward the garbage can. Just short, she flicked her wrist, causing the offending sandwich to slide from the plate into the bin.

"And you still won't consider moving back? Bring your son up in a more civilized environment?"

"California isn't uncivilized, Father."

He harrumphed. "Come now, Sarah. Let's not do this again."

"Then stop bringing it up. Where's fear, father, and we're praying." She winced at the mistake. Sometimes, she jumbled her words. Always frustrating. She knew what she wanted to say, but sometimes— particularly when agitated—she miscommunicated. "We're staying," she corrected, speaking slowly.

For a moment, the line fell silent. It occurred to her that her father sounded "small" today. Perhaps weak, or ill. She asked after him, but he denied any ailment. In fact, he insisted, his physicians had recently given him an excellent bill of health.

"And what about you?" he asked, a hint of what almost sounded like worry in his tone. "You'd mentioned some concerns of your own, healthwise."

"I'm better, now." *I'm on to you. I know what you're trying to do.*

"Have you heard anything from your ex-husband?"

"Have you?" she blurted out before she could stop herself.

"*Indeed!*" he roared at the preposterous notion.

The rest of their conversation eluded her. Lately, she had found it increasingly difficult to concentrate. Between warding off their repeated attempts to poison her food and trying to get a handle on the growing ant problem at her house, she had more important things on her mind.

"I should like very much for you to bring Robert over for Christmas," he told her as their conversation devolved, reaching its maximum level of discomfort.

She lowered herself into a kitchen chair. "You want us...to visit?"

"Very much, yes."

"You said you'd never accept my son as a Wellingham."

"I said that years ago, my dear—"

"My dear?"

"—and made myself clear at that time. I disapproved of your marriage. That marriage is over now. I should think you'd want your only child, your son, to know from whence his future will come. I'll not have Wellingham descendants growing up as paupers. That is not the legacy I worked to maintain my entire life."

Despite herself, she defended the man she had once loved. The man she still loved, regardless of their inability to stay together. The man she had, in fact, still not technically divorced. "Bobby's future will come from his father, as it should be," she insisted.

His response escaped her. She felt something on her skin. Glancing down, she saw an ant crawling up her forearm. Immediately, she flung the phone away and began slapping her arm with loud *thwacks!*

The phone hit the floor, the curlicue of the cord contracting back up into place, dragging the receiver across the kitchen floor until it dangled from its base to just above the linoleum.

"Sarah?" came the muffled, faraway call of her father. "Are you there?"

CHAPTER 5

KELLEY O'CONNER ASSESSED THE PACIFIC Ocean view from the patio and generous backyard. Not the perfect vantage point to watch a sunset, what with two mature trees situated too far apart to install a hammock and the fact that Cabrillo Boulevard and a row of houses and businesses snaked along the coast, creating a barrier between the house and the beach, but they could hardly complain. A smaller home, to be sure. Especially given the O'Conners' more than comfortable means. But this was Beth's dream—and Kelley determined to make it a reality.

He asked the real estate agent for a moment alone to consult with his wife, then beckoned Beth outside. "What do you think?"

"It's a bit small!" Carol Williams singsonged from the kitchen.

Beth leaned into Kelley, her voice low and amused. "I just love her," she whispered, slicing the air with her open hand. "She's been a godsend, helping us look. I can't explain it. We just...*get* each other, you know?"

Smiling, Kelley rubbed the red stubble of his beard. "I knew you would. And you two'll have plenty of time to bond, co-parent, shop...whatever. But right now, we need to think about where we're going to live when we get you out of Seattle."

Eyes closed, Beth savored a deep breath of ocean air. Her features radiated a contentment he had never seen. Head high. A blissful, upward curve to her lips.

She blew out her breath and looked at him. "It's perfect."

"Not too small? You heard your new best friend. What about that place over in Hope Ranch? It's closer to them. You can still see the ocean from there."

"Not like this." She stepped into his arms and gazed out at the sea. The late afternoon sun shone down, beckoning her. If only they could stay for sunset. "Farin and I can walk to the beach from here. Besides, three bedrooms, two baths, and a den for that heavy old desk of yours? The rooms are on the small side. I'll grant you that. But did I mention Farin and I can walk to the beach?"

He pulled her closer, rubbing her upper arm. "Sounds romantic until you realize you have to wait for the streetlight to change in order to get there."

She gave him a playful slap, then buried her face into his chest. "Stop ruining the image. You and I both know this is going to be our new home.

And Farin will love it."

"She sure will." He squeezed her shoulder.

It had been a long but fruitful day. Kelley and Beth had met the Williamses at a coffee shop on State Street for a quick breakfast before searching out office space. They had spent the entire day weighing options. Collectively, the vibe was high. The foursome chatted as if having lived and worked together for decades, instead of two former law school students whose wives had never, until today, laid eyes on one another.

Despite having struck up a friendship in law school, Kelley O'Conner and Joseph Williams had only loosely kept in touch after graduation. They reconnected sporadically, mostly to discuss notable cases that made headlines, such as Memoirs vs. Massachusetts' obscenity laws, the Supreme Court's Miranda rights decision, and Louisiana's District Attorney Jim Garrison's announcement that he intended to solve the JFK assassination. They debated the Civil Rights movement and the Vietnam War, and traded jokes about the election of actor Ronald Reagan as California's new governor. Just enough contact to remind them of their similar approaches to the law and their potential compatibility should they ever decide to partner up.

They had not, however, been involved with the details of each other's lives. They had not attended each other's weddings. Their children had never met. It had been anyone's guess if the women would have any chemistry—something both men agreed bore consideration. But if this first meeting between them was any indication, it appeared as if their impending partnership was providential. Not unlike this house.

Joseph had begun the search for office space days before the O'Conners' arrival. He had narrowed down their choices to three: a small, two-office startup; a mid-sized, three-office space with a kitchenette; and a two-office lease within a larger firm. Ultimately, they had agreed on the mid-sized space, which lay closer to the O'Conners' future house off Mason, over the smaller, less private office near the Williamses' Hope Ranch home. This way, they could add another partner if they wanted to at some point. Not too big, but enough to build a successful business. Besides, more than three names in a partnership sounded pretentious.

Now, it seemed everything was settled. The minute they had stepped foot in this house—much to the surprise of their hosts—Kelley had watched Beth come alive. Whimsical. Beautiful. All the things he had fallen in love with her for, yet heightened with the anticipation of leaving the dreariness of Seattle and an abusive upbringing for the sun-drenched, healing beaches of California. The only thing missing from the perfection of this moment was his daughter. But Beth was right to leave Farin with friends for a couple of days while they took this working vacation.

Regardless of her assurances, he still believed the house too small. But they could always move if she grew claustrophobic. Maybe they would finally revisit the idea of giving Farin a sibling, once they settled in. Unlike Beth, who contented herself dedicating all her maternal affection to an only child, he wanted an entire menagerie of children. He hoped they could come to a compromise. Farin needed more than adults in her immediate orbit.

They called the real estate agent back. Kelley and Joseph talked business for a few more minutes while the women went inside for further inspection. They agreed to meet at her office in the morning to start the ball rolling. Yes, they would make an offer. And yes, they wanted to fast-track escrow. All they needed was the home inspection and to settle on a fair price.

Beth was one step closer to freedom.

The women joined them on the back patio. "Beautiful oak tree," Carol mused, surveying the backyard. "It doesn't even impede the view...much."

Kelley nodded, his eyes narrowed in thought. "Maybe I'll build a treehouse for Farin."

Carol moved into her husband's arms. "Ooo. Our Marci would love that."

"Think so?" Joseph asked. "All those frilly pink dresses you keep her in? Hardly the tomboy."

"You don't have to be a tomboy to enjoy a treehouse."

"We can decorate it so they're both comfortable," Beth added, giving Carol a sly wink. "Farin's no tomboy, either, but it'd be great to have a place the girls can play alone."

"And out of our hair." Carol smiled.

Beth returned the genial expression, nodding enthusiastically. "That too."

Joseph stretched his arms wide. "Productive day. We found our office space, your home, and a place for our girls to play. Now all we need to do is decide where to have dinner. Anyone else getting hungry?"

Carol turned to her husband, eyes sparkling. "We simply must take them to the Harbor Restaurant," she said, brushing his chest with her hand. "They'll die for the view."

"I love the idea of a view," Beth mused. "And I'm dying for seafood."

"I could go for a nice steak," Kelley added.

Carol fluttered her wrist. "They have both—as well as the view. And speaking of views, Beth, did you see your attic? I'll tell ya, what this place lacks in square footage, it sure makes up for in character." She linked Beth's arm, then marched her back inside.

Kelley watched them disappear to give the house a final look. He pushed out his chest, plunging his hands in his slacks pockets, satisfied with the day and the trajectory of his life. "We're actually doing this, eh, Joe?"

Joseph nodded, his gaze fixed out toward the sea. "Looks like it."

He inclined his head to the back door. "I'm glad they get along. I'd hoped they would."

"Me, too. The last thing we'd need is for them to take a dislike to each other. I'm not sure it'd work out if we had to worry about mediating our private lives."

"We'll have enough professional drama, I'm sure."

"We'll be fine," Joseph said, slapping his back.

"Maybe our girls'll get along, too."

"Can't see why they wouldn't."

"We'll cross that bridge when we get there. For now, let's grab the ladies and get out of here. Champagne's on me."

"Sounds good. I'm starving."

As they left for the restaurant, Kelley glanced left and noticed a porch swing. The graying wood was old and probably needed replacing. In his mind, he imagined himself rocking and cuddling with Beth, Farin squeezing herself between them.

This would be their home. A whole new life was on the horizon. Kelley could not wait.

***

Evelyn Alexander had a way about her. She possessed an inexplicable charisma that captivated her son and simultaneously drove him away. A genial hostess in her day. A society butterfly. Elegant. Gregarious. The life of every party. And seemingly oblivious to the everyday cares of the outside world. Whenever Ross found himself in her sphere, which, he confessed, he avoided as much as possible, reality melted away. Like a character out of an F. Scott Fitzgerald novel. Daisy Buchanan minus depth or internal conflict. No honest person had ever described the eighty-year-old widow as "authentic."

"I *adore* what you've done with the house," Evelyn gushed, accepting the second martini Josephine had handed her in the half-hour since her arrival. She air-kissed in Josephine's direction.

Lounging sideways atop the drawing room settee, she drew her legs up and locked her ankles as if she still owned the place. As if holding court. And, of course, she was. She always was. "I know I say it every time I visit, but you truly have a knack, my dear. Ever consider interior decorating? It's the age of women—we can do anything, now! Not like in my day..."

As if Evelyn had ever desired a career. She had barely agreed to raise a child.

In many ways, Ross took after his more self-effacing father, the late Irving Alexander. An investment banker at the House of Morgan, he had only managed to convince his non-maternal wife to bear his child after coming face-to-face with his own mortality the day of the Wall Street bombing of 1920. Though he had survived, he had lost a couple of friends.

Irving had suffered minor injuries that day, but had gained a son in the end. As he told Ross during a rare moment of father-son bonding not too long before his death, "The reality that a life could be so easily extinguished and immediately forgotten wounded me in a way that spraying debris and second-degree burns never could."

His father had earned more than his respect. Ross missed him. Especially now that he again questioned his life's path. The music business was shadier than late afternoon in the middle of a dark forest—and far more dangerous.

Evelyn imbibed a healthy sip of martini, set the glass atop the accent table beside her, and affixed a cigarette to the end of her jade cigarette holder. Ross dutifully swooped over to light it. "So enough chitchat. Tell me all about London. I simply adore London! And don't scrimp on the details. After all, it is the reason you missed your birthday party. And what a party it was, Ross! Nearly three weeks ago, and I confess, I'm still recovering!"

"Well." Josephine grew animated, something she only did when endeavoring to keep up with her spirited mother-in-law. She hopped out of her chair and left the room, talking over her shoulder as she strode with an elegant nonchalance. "I'll do better than details. I brought visual aids!"

Evelyn clapped the tips of her fingers. "Oh darling, I can always count on you!"

When Josephine cleared the room, Evelyn leveled a mischievous glint upon her son. Head cocked, she pointed her cigarette at him, her beringed fingers pinching the jade-tipped holder at an arch, bobbing a shoulder in that semi-flirtatious way of hers. "And don't think you're getting out of this conversation. I see you there, nursing your drink and judging me. Something's up. Something happened."

Ross adopted his most innocent, most unaffected expression. "Must be the jet lag. I should've taken some time off before returning to work so soon after the flight. I'm not as young as I used to be, Mother."

She narrowed her eyes as if setting a target. "You know, we never really discussed your decision to abandon mergers and acquisitions for entertainment law."

He downed the remnant of his rocks glass and went to the minibar for a refill. More than the liquor, he needed to move out of her crosshairs. "If it's any consolation, my former skillset might soon come in handy."

"Really? So soon? Welp, that's show business for you. Here today, gone tomorrow. I imagine you've set yourself on quite a course." Her haughty, high-class demeanor dissolved. An uncharacteristic hint of sadness laced her words. "Your father wouldn't have been pleased, you know. He had such high hopes."

Imagine how he'd feel if he knew I may or may not be an accessory to murder.

Ross relaxed into his wing chair and loosened his tie. "Don't worry. With the experience I've gained in the last few months, I won't be without gainful employment. There's something to be said for starting small. I may not be my father, but I'm not doing as badly as you may think."

Josephine returned with several oversize store bags stuffed full with choice selections from Lady Jane, Biba, Irvine Sellars—all the most fashionable boutiques. And all in Evelyn Alexander's size. "Since you can't get to London these days, I brought London to you."

The octogenarian squealed like a teenager. She stamped out her cigarette, then swung her legs around to sit upright on the edge of the settee. With aged, slender hands, she began lifting out the treasures, one by one. "Oh, you shouldn't have! *Oh!* I simply adore that skirt! And the pattern!"

Josephine backed away to sit on her husband's lap. Smiling, she patted and rubbed his back, ever mindful to dedicate her full attention to the Alexander matriarch. "I knew that one would be your favorite."

Evelyn removed a dress from one bag and held it up against her body. "It is, and—oh!" She stopped, momentarily deflating in her seat. "But we shouldn't be spending all this time on gifts for me when it's your birthday coming up. Where are my manners?"

As if on cue, the doorbell rang. Josephine rose from her husband's lap, insisting he stay while she answered it. "Trust me, Evelyn, seeing you happy is the best gift I could ever wish for."

"And I am, my dear. I am!" Evelyn resumed admiring her new frocks.

Josephine opened the door, thrilled to find Betty standing on the other side. She hugged her sister as if they had not seen each other in years, although they had just had lunch together some hours ago. She whispered in her ear. "Ross has been brooding for a month now, and Evelyn's here. You're just in time to save me!"

Betty recoiled, wild-eyed. She stepped back as if readying to sprint off the way she had come. "Oh Jo, I can't go in there!"

Josephine took her hand. "Why not?"

"Look at the way I'm dressed. I thought we were going to have some wine and unclutter your post-London shopping spree."

"We are," Josephine assured her in hushed tones, drawing her across the threshold. "Now get in here. I have the wine. And most of the clutter will be leaving after dinner. There's a party in the city tonight. Her car will be here in an hour and a half."

Betty beheld her more casual house dress with distaste. She smoothed it with her hands, then fussed with her hair. "I don't know."

Josephine gave her sister a knowing look. "Oh, stop. You can't leave. We both know you have to get Ross alone so you two can finish planning my surprise party."

Betty's eyes widened, then softened with disappointment. She crossed the entryway with a heavy sigh. "You weren't supposed to know about that."

"I always know." Josephine closed the door, then linked her sister's arm, marching her toward the drawing room. "And I promise to be the most surprised birthday girl you've ever seen. Besides, wait until you see what I brought you back from London!"

Another elated squeal echoed from the drawing room. "Oh Josephine, this pleated tent dress is to die for! I'm wearing this one tonight!"

***

A soft wrap on her bedroom door sent Faith into sullen silence.

"You decent, doll?"

Doll?

She ignored her mother's saccharine tone. It fooled no one. Ever.

"Faith? You in there, sweetheart?"

Sweetheart?

She wanted to be alone. More than that, she wanted to avoid the inevitable lectures about things like "sacrifice," "commitment," or "...after all we've done for you."

A second, less amiable, wrap at the door drew her off her bed with an angry jolt.

"Faith Annelisa Peterson!"

She jerked open the door to stare bitterly at her mother. "What?"

"I-I..." Millie stammered, pearl-clutching as if endeavoring to taper her aggression and adopt that false sweetness she used whenever she suspected a more diplomatic approach was needed, "that is, we...well, we weren't finished talking."

Faith scowled. "I was."

The indignant huff came next, as she knew it would. Millie did not take rejection well.

"Wh—don't you want dessert?"

"I'm full, Mother."

"But I made Jell-O parfait to celebrate."

Faith rolled her eyes. "I'm going to bed."

"It's only seven-thirty. And you don't have school tomorrow." She lifted an awkward hand as if intending to check her daughter's forehead, but abandoned the pretense. "You haven't even changed out of your clothes."

Deadpan, Faith asked, "Anything else?"

"Here." Millie held out her hand, in which she held her credit card.

Faith accepted and inspected it. "What's this for?"

"Just...just take the bus tomorrow and go pick out a nice outfit for yourself. Nothing too bright or showy. Just a little something for dinner tomorrow night. The Tuffins are taking us out to celebrate."

"I don't need something new, Mother. I've got enough boring junk to wear."

Cutex-stained lips pursed, Millie glowered at her daughter. "I'm trying to be nice here!"

"Yeah. Great job. Thanks."

Millie spun on her heel, then stomped down the orange shag carpet stairs. "*Walt*?! You talk to her. She's doing that damn pouty thing again!"

Faith shut the door. She dropped the credit card on her desk, then flounced back onto her bed and switched off her bedside lamp. Rolling over on her side, she tucked her hands beneath her cheek and faced the window. Gradually, stars appeared in the cloudless fall sky.

Not even eight o'clock on a Friday night. And not just any Friday night, but the night of the first dance of the school year.

"Don't be silly," her mother had said two days ago when Faith asked if she could go. "That's so beneath you."

"I don't have any friends, Mother. People think I'm a freak or a snob or something because I never do any fun stuff like the other kids. And in two years, I'll be a freshman!"

Her mother had stood in the kitchen, breaking green bean pods into thirds, prepping dinner. The more Faith had pestered her, the more severe the "snap" of the pods.

But it did not matter. Every time she asked, her mother would counter with a variation of the same argument: "you're better than that."

Better than what? Up until three years ago, they had lived in a small Brooklyn apartment. Since relocating to New Rochelle, they had lived in a middle-class neighborhood, drove a middle-class car, and wore JCPenney clothing. Not exactly Manhattan or Beverly Hills.

Watching the stars come out in full, Faith tried to get herself under control. It was just a dance. No one would miss her. No one would even expect her. But as she failed to bring about a better attitude, she heard her parents arguing downstairs. About her and her less than enthusiastic response to the letter. Of course. What else?

She covered her ears with her pillow to block out the noise. In a way, she felt guilty. Guilty she had not been more gracious over the news. Guilty that she hated her mother, her house, her school, and even her own bedroom. Twelve years old and not one poster or record to "distract you from your goals." Just lace curtains, colorless furniture, dull framed prints of family or spacious landscapes, and a pink crocheted bedspread that scratched her skin when she lay atop it. Like right now.

For a moment, she fantasized about sneaking out her window and walking the several blocks to the school gymnasium. About how it might feel to be free and fearless. She imagined grooving to the rock'n'roll music and the joyful vibe of her laughing schoolmates as they drank punch and danced to the latest hits. The cool kids. Kids who did not have to be at Austin Jones's piano studio tomorrow morning at 10 AM.

"Can't get lax now," Austin had said this afternoon after Millie had called him with the news. "It's more important than ever to keep sharp and committed. Congratulations, kiddo. I'm so proud of you."

The fighting subsided shortly after it had started. No doors had slammed. That was a good sign. A sign that her father had talked her mother off the cliff.

She replaced her pillow and slid off the bed, disgusted at herself that she lacked the courage to make good on her fantasy. Who was she kidding? She was neither free nor fearless.

The only two things she would accomplish by sneaking out her second-floor window would be a trip to the emergency room with a broken ankle and a lecture from an hysterical Millie, who would suffer such embarrassment from the ordeal, she would feign a migraine to get out of dinner with the Tuffins. So instead, Faith kicked off her shoes and went to her closet for a nightgown.

Another knock at her door stopped her in her tracks. She envisioned round two.

"You still awake, kitten?"

Her father's gentle tone chased away her apprehension. She tossed the nightgown on the bed and opened the door wide so he could come in.

He flipped the wall switch, flooding the room with artificial light.

Faith squinted at the brightness and rubbed her eyes.

Hands in pockets, he looked at her expectantly, yet with the hallmark patience that made him the preferred parental figure in her life. "Anything you want to talk about?"

She stared down at her bare feet and slowly shook her head. Millie did not even let her paint her toenails. Somehow, that thought brought the full weight of her life down upon her. She rushed to her bed and buried her face in her hands, sobbing.

Walt sat down beside her and pulled her to him. Nestled into his chest, her sobs grew to such intensity, her mother came to the door and asked if everything was okay.

Assured he could manage just fine, Millie left without argument, probably grateful she did not have to deal with another one of her daughter's emotional outbursts.

Faith was grateful her father did not pressure her to talk. In truth, she had no words to describe the myriad feelings jumbling around inside her.

"It'll be all right," he whispered, rocking her gently in his arms. "Whatever it is, it's gonna be okay."

She nodded and, by sheer force of will, pulled herself together. He reached over to her nightstand and plucked a tissue from its box. Faith wiped her eyes and blew her nose.

"I'm here if you need me," he promised before he left, switching the light off and closing the door behind him. "Goodnight, kitten," he said from the other side.

Faith changed into her nightclothes, peeled down the scratchy crocheted bedspread, and lay down between her soft, cool, cotton sheets. As before, she rolled over on her side, again fixing her eyes on the stars through her drawn lace curtains.

She wished she had a radio.

A year ago, a Juilliard acceptance letter would have thrilled her. And indeed, both of her parents were over the moon at their daughter's prestigious accomplishment when they received the letter yesterday afternoon. But for Faith, the notification felt more like an omen foretelling a bleak and boring future. So much for attending a normal high school. At this rate, Faith feared she might wind up the second coming of Myra Hess. And wouldn't that just tickle Walt and Millie Peterson?

No. Something had to change.

CHAPTER 6

"*I*'M HUNGRY," POLLY MOANED, HOLDING *her belly.*
With downcast eyes, Ronnie patted his sister's shoulder. "I know, my darling. I am too."

Every so often, he stole a glance at her, a rush of love and devotion he rarely experienced—and never outwardly acknowledged—flooding him. Ronnie owed Polly his life.

A less-spirited Polly Nock would have never defied her parents in the middle of an air raid. Her stubborn determination and mirthfulness had saved both their lives. As for Paul, Ronnie had made his peace with his brother's horrific death. Had he stayed at the school, he would have been dead anyway. Like every other member of their family.

The official death toll of the South Hallsville School bombing reported by the press stood at seventy-seven. Rubbish. Hitler's airborne henchmen had murdered hundreds that morning. Had the rescue and recovery efforts lasted more than a week before they called it quits and spread quicklime out all over the area, they might know better. And maybe he and Polly would have been able to make it the few miles away to the temporary mortuary over at the Municipal Baths on Romford Road to say a proper goodbye to their parents, their brothers, and their sister.

Instead, they hid like fugitives amongst the rubble and bombed out buildings. From blackout wardens, shelter wardens, home guard, and the many volunteers ever on the lookout for orphaned or missing children. It seemed the only way.

Polly began to weep. "We're going to starve, aren't we?"

"Haven't I taken care of us so far? Haven't I kept us together?"

She pushed out her bottom lip and nodded. In her hands, she clasped her ruined teddy bear.

He scanned their surroundings for some hope of a more suitable place to stay. The nights had grown markedly colder. He wagered snowy weather would arrive soon. But he had lost his sense of time and space. Their lives had become one of focused survival. Every night, the bombers reappeared. Every night, more damage. Every night, he had to protect his sister from fire and debris.

He could not remember the last time either of them had bathed. They both reeked of soot and sour body odor. His teeth felt furry. Polly's undergarments frayed, as did his trousers and shirt. Both without coats. It seemed their circumstances only deteriorated.

A part of him was still frozen over the loss of his parents. As if he could not move past the moment he beheld that crater at the school. Another part of him worried where their next morsel of food might come from. Still another part doubted he could do anything to help his sister, and wondered if she might not be better off taking a chance on finding shelter in a stranger's home.

He daily broached the idea with Polly. Although wanting them to stay together, she needed more than he could provide—which was nothing.

Each time, she answered the same way. "Don't you leave me, Ronnie Nock. Wouldn't Mam want us to stay together?"

At this point, he knew nothing of what anyone might want. He only knew his empty stomach and the stone upon which he laid his head to get what little sleep he managed.

"I think she'd want you fed and properly washed."

"I'm going where you go. And if you make me leave, I swear I'll run away and find you."

Tomorrow, they would need to find better accommodations. This makeshift cave he had dug out of the rubble and dirt had been a short-term solution to a long-term problem. But he had no money. No means. Just fear, his wits, and his obligation.

"I'm cold," Polly whined.

He tugged her closer and wrapped her in his arms.

"Maybe when you go to get the food tomorrow, you could find a blanket?"

"It depends on who's around. You know that."

Over the last few weeks, London had rallied against German aggression. And Ronnie Nock had become a thief.

The capitol was burning, holed out, and littered with bodies. Ronnie had heard in passing that one bomb actually hit Buckingham Palace a few days after the school bombing. Having taken the harsh brunt of the Luftwaffe's punishing raids, the mass of working poor residents of Canning Town huddled together in dogged determination. Though many had left, those who remained did what needed getting done to survive. Without complaint.

Some, more jaded residents, who had started out certain their government would assist them, had grown disillusioned. Rest centres were woefully unequipped. They smelled of urine, feces, vomit, and sweat, and they lacked adequate water. For the first couple of nights, Ronnie and Polly had used them for shelter. But when well-meaning adults started asking questions about where their parents were, Ronnie knew he had to either move on or risk getting separated from his sister.

Helping an orphaned little girl was one thing. Taking in her soon-to-be fifteen-year-old brother was a burden. Many siblings shipped out to the north had been separated. Before he would submit to such measures, Ronnie had to give it a go. Polly was all he had left.

Some East Enders had managed to keep their homes and businesses. Others had trekked the eight and a half miles to the Public Assistance Board to get new ration cards, identity cards, a bit of money, clothes, food, and temporary shelter.

Ronnie and Polly had attempted that trip a couple of days after the bomb claimed their family. Instead of receiving assistance, they were treated as scroungers. They were classed as "immigrants" of London instead of "natives," and were denied help due to lack of a parent. Without registering with the PAB, money, clothes, and other resources were not only scarce but problematic to obtain. So he stole what he could, as little as possible, to keep them alive.

Polly screamed each night away as the bombs continued to fall. As for Ronnie, he spent his time encouraging her to buck up and be brave, nobly suppressing his own terror. James and Mary Nock had taught their children well the "we, not I" community creed. Duty, not sentiment, no matter the crisis.

In the darkness of their tiny, makeshift shelter of bricks and stone, Polly coughed and shivered inside his embrace. The whirring of bombs warned them of another air assault.

"Ronnie?"

"Yes, my darling?"

"Maybe it would be better if the bombs get us. You think?"

The comment froze him solid.

She snuggled closer. "I'd rather be in Heaven, with Mummy and Daddy. Wouldn't you?"

His first instinct was to tell her how he really felt. That there was no Heaven. There was no God. Their mother had lied to them all these years. If God was real, He would not allow war. But he did not want to make her feel worse by killing what little hope she clung to.

"I think we need to honor Mam and Dad by staying alive. They died trying to get us to a better place. I think we should find a way to survive."

A bomb struck the area, close enough to catch a few projectile pebbles against their bodies. Polly screamed, pressing her head against his chest, covering her face with the remnant of her teddy bear.

He held her the entire night. Neither of them slept.

"I'm scared, Ronnie. What's to become of us?"

"I'm going to take care of you, Polly. And tomorrow, I'm going to get you

food, some new clothes...and a blanket. I promise."

***

Ben begged his mother to set aside soul cakes.

Lynda bustled around the kitchen, plating and scooping food onto serving platters and bowls while gathering apples for her husband. "We can't wait too long. Daddy's out filling the water barrel."

Careful not to snag any of the accoutrements of his sailor outfit, he slid his guitar over his shoulder by the strap, kissed his mother's cheek, and urged, "Put them in a bowl and let me have them. We'll hand them out."

Intrigued, Lynda halted mid-task, grinning. "What're you three on about, then?"

"Go sit with Aunt Grace. Hurry now. The bonfire's started. I've got to get ready. We're up in five minutes!" He trotted off toward the stairs.

She called after him, "And you'll help Jorie with his costume?"

"Yes!"

A heady spirit of excitement permeated the Grant household that evening. Not only was it their weekly Saturday Night Carpet Concert, a tradition since Ben had started playing guitar while Chris was still quite young, but this weekend's concert fell three days prior to Halloween. As a surprise, their Uncle Godfrey and Aunt Grace had arrived from Sydney to stay through Christmas.

Outside, carved turnip lanterns lit the perimeter of their backyard. A bonfire raged at the far end, placed strategically to avoid nearby homes or dry brush. Closer to the house, George had roped his two oldest sons into helping him erect a small stage—a departure from their normal living room venue. Ben had questioned whether they might get complaints of disturbing the peace. George had assured him they would be fine. And the neighbors were welcome to join if they wished. Their mother had prepared enough food to feed the Royal Air Force.

Several tables with chairs sat before the stage for the audience. Closer to the house, a separate table held various meats and side dishes. An apple dowking station sat farther out near the bonfire, along with other traditional All Hallow's Eve games. After the concert and dinner, they would spend the night grouped together, singing, playing, and telling ghost stories to the kids.

Lynda sat between her sister and her husband, who relaxed in his chair with a cigarette. "Any idea why Ben's so secretive? He's claimed all the cakes. I've none to set out."

George patted her shoulder and exhaled a stream of smoke. "I'm sure it's part of the act. All three little nippers have been sneaking about."

"I can't believe how they've grown," Grace interjected. "We need to plan more visits. And you need to come to ours, as well."

Before Lynda could promise they would make it a point to plan a trip Down Under, she spied two shadowy figures sneak out from the house toward the stage. A sailor and a pirate, both creeping along the outside of the perimeter of lanterns to avoid detection. Both carried guitars. And for a moment, she fretted over the absence of a third figure.

A rustling from inside the house drew her attention. She turned to discover her youngest standing at the back door, the bowl of soul cakes in hand. Fidgeting excitedly, he waved her way, careful not to upend the bowl as he did. She smiled and waved, then turned back at the sound of two acoustic guitars playing a simple, haunting, upbeat tune.

George had rigged a foot petal to operate the stage lights. A simple on or off toggle. For now, the lights remained off.

The duo of guitars impressed her. Ben's playing was solid, though he had never learned to play for any other reason but composition or basic accompaniment. The real star was Chris, whose skillful, effortless fingering drew the adults forward. Rapt, they gently bobbed their heads and tapped their feet.

Grace leaned over to whisper in her sister's ear, "They're grand!"

Lynda preened, nodding in time with the music.

Ben activated the stage lights. As the singing began, a loud whistle originating from the direction of the road caught their attention. The adults turned to find neighbors gathering at the front of the house, outside their stone fence, cheering on the boys. George waved them over.

The guitar intro ended with Ben and Chris singing the pre-chorus in unison, then repeating it as a round.

... Hey, ho, nobody home ...
... Meat nor drink nor money have I none ...
... Yet shall we be merry ...
... Hey, ho, nobody home ...

They stopped the round, played a few bars, then sang the chorus in harmony.

... A soul! a soul! a soul-cake ...
... Please good Missus, a soul-cake ...
... An apple, a pear, a plum, a cherry ...
... Any good thing to make us all merry ...
... One for Peter, two for Paul ...
... Three for Him who made us all ...

After the chorus, family and neighbors started cheering and shouting their approval. The boys focused on their playing. Then, Chris stepped up to the microphone to sing the first verse.

> *... God bless the master of this house ...*
> *... The mistress also ...*
> *... And all the little children ...*
> *... That 'round your table grow ...*
> *... Likewise young men and maidens ...*
> *... Your cattle and your store ...*
> *... And all who dwell within your gates ...*
> *... We wish you ten times more ...*

As Ben and Chris harmonized the chorus again, Jordan stepped out from the house and began to distribute the soul cakes to those who had gathered to enjoy the entertainment. Ben stepped forward to take the second verse.

> *... Go down into the cellar ...*
> *... And see what you can find ...*
> *... If the barrels are not empty ...*
> *... We hope you will prove kind ...*
> *... We hope you will prove kind ...*
> *... With your apples and straw-ber ...*
> *... And we'll come no more a-souling ...*
> *... 'Til this time next year ...*

With exaggerated gratitude, Lynda thanked Jordan as she accepted a cake. She whispered in his ear as he passed, "You're the most handsome Batman I've ever seen!"

"Thanks!" Jordan stopped and hugged his mother, which drew endearing *awws* from the others but delayed his prearranged cue. From the stage, the boys repeated the chorus and the guitar interlude without missing a beat, but protested in unison, "Mum!"

She held up her hands and waved an apology, then took the bowl of cakes and sent Jordan off with a loving swat of his backside. He ran toward the stage, his Batman cape flowing behind him as the adults chuckled in admiration.

Ben stopped accompanying Chris momentarily while he adjusted the mic for his little brother. The crowd fell silent as all three siblings continued on together, with Jordan taking the last verse.

... The lanes are very dirty ...
... My shoes are very thin ...
... I've got a little pocket ...
... To put a penny in ...
... If you haven't got a penny ...
... A ha'penny will do ...
... If you haven't get a ha'penny ...
... It's God bless you ...

From Jordan's solo, the boys did three-part harmony for the final chorus. More neighbors had gathered by then, some bringing guests of their own. They remained quiet throughout the performance.

George leaned into his wife, speaking low. "You thinking what I'm thinking?"

Eyes sparkling, she shook her head. "Tell me!"

"They're a trio."

"Isn't little Jorie good? And Chris—I know he practices all the time. His school marks are proof he's not studying. But George, he's...he's got it, doesn't he?"

George's face grew more serious. "The lad's damn impressive, Lynda. And Jorie's doing complex harmonies at seven? You know what this means."

"Is there anyone you can speak to?"

He joined in the applause as the song ended. Neighbors from all over had arrived to enjoy the entertainment. Some brought pots of hot food. Others brought buckets of ice with drinks or bags of crisps. Kids scampered off to play or enjoy the bonfire.

The boys played two forty-five-minute sets, until only cold remnants remained for them at the buffet table. But they did not care. They played folk tunes and modern rock selections, as well as a sampling of Ben's personal compositions.

"I'll do it," George told Lynda later that night, after everyone was spent and had retired.

Cuddled into his embrace, she lifted her head off his shoulder and looked up at him. "You promise?"

"As of this moment, I'm a manager. And it's a family affair."

***

Beth pinched her forehead, unable to recall the item in the box she had just wrapped. It was either the watch for Kelley's Christmas present or a small set of tools she intended to box up with other kitchen odds and ends. When she could not remember, she moved on, placing the gift near the others she had wrapped in anticipation of Kelley returning home with the tree. It probably did not matter too much. Everything would end up in the same place in a few months.

She went to the kitchen and opened the fridge to find something for Farin's lunch. Leftovers everywhere. It seemed she never got the right size turkey. Of course, this year she deserved a pass. It was not her fault her father did not show. And frankly, no one had missed him.

Farin colored contentedly at the kitchen table, swinging her legs and humming along to the Christmas carols on the stereo.

"So, what'll it be?" Beth asked, arm resting atop the fridge door as she contemplated the meals she would make to incorporate a good five pounds of leftover turkey meat. "Turkey sandwich, grilled cheese, or peanut butter and honey?" Inside, she willed Farin to pick anything but the grilled cheese. After yesterday, she needed a break from the stove. "Or there are tons of leftover hors d'oeuvres."

"Olives."

"You need more than olives."

"And cheese and crackers."

"Only if you promise to eat some of the veggies with it."

Farin stopped in place. She looked at her mother as if she had been asked to lick a toilet.

"If you wanna help Daddy and I set up the Christmas tree tonight, you need proper nourishment."

Farin slid off her chair and stood beside her mother. She pointed to the carrot sticks and the dip. Beth figured that would suffice.

She used a paper plate for the improvised lunch while Farin stowed her coloring book and crayons. Glancing at the clock, she hoped Kelley would not stay too long at the office before coming home with the tree. Usually, they all picked it out together. This year, they had convinced Farin it would feel like a first present to have Daddy come home with it on his own.

They had promised to decorate it together tonight over pizza and soda.

While Farin snacked on her hors d'oeuvres, Beth switched the album on the stereo from Ray Conniff's *We Wish You a Merry Christmas* to *Christmas with The Chipmunks*. "Have you gone through the Sears catalog and circled what you want, hon? I haven't had a chance to look."

"Can I do it after we put up the tree?" she asked around a mouthful of cracker.

"Of course you can."

"Can we see Santa tomorrow?"

"I've already told him we're coming," Beth chirped, grabbing some tea and sitting at the table beside her daughter. She brushed back the child's unruly auburn curls. "You know, we need to get that hair ironed out."

Farin slumped. "Oh Mommy, I hate that iron. Can't I keep my hair?"

"Of course you'll keep your hair. But those curls make you look like a wild child without parents who love you and keep you well-groomed."

"Somebody mention groom?" came a voice entering through the garage door. On his shoulder, he half-hefted, half-dragged their tree.

Beth and Farin rose from the table in unison.

"Daddy!" Farin squealed, running to hug his legs. She ducked pine branches and sat down atop his foot, wrapping her legs around to avoid slipping off.

"Need some help with that?" Beth fussed, failing her feeble attempt to prop up or carry any part of the tree.

"I think Farin and I've got it." He kissed her cheek, then carried the tree into the living room, dragging along a giggling child for the ride. "Can you get the stand and some water?"

Beth moved ahead of them and laid out an old sheet, then centered the stand and loosened the screws. "Did you get a fresh cut?"

He hoisted the tree off his shoulder and momentarily rested the trunk on the sheet. "Just like you wanted. And I had them cut a few bottom branches off so we have room to arrange the presents."

"Oh Kelley," she cooed, standing back for a proper look. "It's beautiful. And so full!"

"I figured we should have the best tree on the lot, what with this being our last Christmas in Seattle."

Farin unwrapped herself from her father's leg and stood up, the smile erased from her face. "Daddy, will they have Christmas trees in California?"

He stroked her curls, then cupped her chin. "You bet they will."

"Yay!" She clapped her hands, twirling in place while singing "Jingle Bells" with the Chipmunks.

Together, Kelley and Beth set up the tree, secured the trunk, and added water. Then, Beth arranged the tree skirt and dressed the area with the few presents she had wrapped—including the mystery present labeled for Kelley.

"Can we decorate?" Farin asked, hopping up and down.

Beth wished she had Farin's post-Thanksgiving energy.

Kelley sat down on the couch and raised an arm, beckoning his wife beside him. As usual, Farin wiggled herself in between them. He kissed her forehead and gave his wife's upper arm a squeeze. "Mommy and Daddy are gonna rest a few minutes. The tree should settle a bit as well."

Deflated, Farin rested her elbows on her thighs, head in her palms. She stared at the tree as though she feared it would wander off before they could hang the lights. Minutes later, she had fallen asleep between her parents.

"Someone didn't get a nap today," Beth said.

He grinned down at her. "The excitement's worn her out."

She sifted her fingers through her dark hair. "I get that."

"So...did you talk to your dad and find out why he didn't show?"

"I've been busy. He hasn't called. Besides, we both know why he didn't show. He was either at the bar or passed out drunk at home. Either way, I'm sure neither of us will lose any sleep over his absence. I only invited him because you made me."

"Made you?" He gave a hearty laugh. "I just think you should let him know we're moving."

"I don't know why that matters. We see each other maybe twice a year—and yesterday's absence mercifully cut this year's visits in half. Good riddance to him and this forsaken place, as far as I'm concerned."

"It's your decision, of course. He's your father."

Beth stroked Farin's hair as they switched to a happier topic. It was nice to have a lull in the day's activities. She foresaw precious few of them before their spring move.

The plan she had envisioned included a little packing each day. Just enough to keep it from overwhelming them all. Leave the necessities for the last couple of weeks. Kelley would arrange for movers. She would notify the utility companies of their departure date once they had it locked down. Two days ago, they had received word that they got the house. The day prior, Joseph had called Kelley to let him know they had secured their office space.

Not fifteen minutes in, Farin awoke from her power nap completely recharged. And thus began their evening. Pizza, tree decorating, Kelley and Farin harmonizing to Christmas carols, hot chocolate before bed while they watched Christmas specials on TV, and then a few adult eggnogs after Farin settled into bed. Kelley relaxed, enjoying an after-dinner pipe.

A busy time, for sure. Who had thought it a good idea to plan a move during the holidays?

Oh well. Soon, it would be finished. Beth would start the better half of her life once and for all. She had told her husband in no uncertain terms that she wanted a bikini for Christmas.

If he could find one in Seattle...in December.

CHAPTER 7

BOBBY WANTED SO BADLY TO tell his mother to lay off the wine. She had consumed two bottles already and would certainly go back for a third. And what difference did it make if it was "just wine, Bobby," or her usual, gin?

"It's Christmas Eve," she would laugh-slur in defense, oblivious or unconcerned about his feelings on the matter. "You really should lighten up. You're too young to be so cynical—and I'm too old to be lectured."

He knew how it went. For three years, she had slowly but steadily descended into someone he did not understand. At first, it had made him angry. Lately, she downright frightened him.

"C'mere." She motioned from the couch, all smiles in anticipation of the most popular day of the year. Her Marylin Monroe do was an uncombed mess, her dressing gown wrinkled from days of wear, her blue eyes glazed and twinkling in the dim light. "Come sit near Mummy and enjoy the tree."

Bobby withered in his chair, shoulders slumped, head lowered. He wanted to protest, but did not want to make her angry.

She scared him when she got angry.

Grudgingly, he relocated into her arms. She cuddled him closer than he would have liked. Held tight against her chest, he noted with marked displeasure the smell of cigarettes, body odor, red wine, and Chanel No. 5. These, coupled with the mixture of pine needles from their tree and what seemed a permanent stench of ant spray permeating the house made him nauseous.

"You know, Santa's coming tonight. We'll need to be off to moonlight soon. You know that jolly old elf won't stop if you're awake. Fancy sleeping in Mummy's room?"

The suggestion alarmed him more than her growing speech troubles. He cringed inside her embrace. "I'm not a baby anymore, Mom. I'm eleven and a half. I can sleep in my own bed."

She released him with a flourish and a bark of disgust. "Suit yourself. You're too heavy for me to carry back into your room, anyway."

He did not know whether to get up and go back to his chair or remain in close proximity. As a compromise, he scooted a few inches away.

Neither spoke again for several minutes. He suspected he had hurt her feelings. When she jerked herself off the couch and stumbled into the kitchen for that third bottle, he knew it.

"Lemme help," he offered, joining her near the sink where she struggled with the corkscrew.

"Stop!" She yanked the bottle away, nearly flinging it across the room. "I can do it!"

He winced and backed off, deciding to grab himself some punch from the refrigerator. When he peeked inside, he could not find the pitcher.

"Mom? Where's the punch?"

"I threw it out. It was poisoned," she answered matter-of-factly, as if it were the most natural thing on the planet to routinely throw out food and drinks for fear that someone had tampered with them. "You're welcome."

Somehow, she never questioned the booze.

The cork gave way with a sucking burst. "Yay! Pop goes the weasel!"

Bobby shut the refrigerator door and grabbed a glass of water from the tap.

Given a choice between home and school these days, he would choose school. Christmas vacation was usually a happy time, where kids enjoyed the two-week break from their studies until after the New Year. But, to his relief, this school year was not all that bad. His teacher did not treat him like a dunce or make him feel stupid. Though he had no real friends yet, a couple of fellow misfits from the other sixth-grade class periodically sat with him during lunch. His determination to portray a positive attitude instead of moping around all day at school might pay off after all. And if not, at least while he was away, he did not have to deal with his mother's weird mood swings.

"Think Dad'll call tonight?" he dared to ask as they settled back into the living room. He considered building a fire in the fireplace but decided against it. He worried about having an open flame around his mom.

Sarah sighed in dramatic fashion. "How many times do I have to tell you, Robert? If it's nine o'clock at night here, what time is it in London?"

He frowned at the condescension but dutifully and immediately calculated the time. "Five o'clock in the morning."

She sipped her wine. "Exactly. Which means Santa's already been to England and you'll be left out if you don't get to bed soon."

He did not have the heart to tell her he no longer believed in Santa Claus. Or much else, these days. Especially her insistence that the house was infested with ants. He had seen none.

"Guess you're right." He got up, walked his glass to the sink, then returned to kiss his mother goodnight. "See you in the morning, Mom."

She turned her head before he got her cheek and kissed him on the lips. The gesture made him cringe. He passed it off as an accident and went in a second time, making sure he got her cheek.

"Sleep well, my angel," she slurred, winking up at him. "I'll check on you soon. Be sure to go to sleep straightaway. Don't want to miss Chris Cringle's visit!"

While brushing his teeth, Bobby thought about the last time he had spoken with his father. He had sounded preoccupied with something but had promised he would come to America for a visit in the coming year. Unlike previous promises, he had sounded different. Determined. It had filled Bobby with hope—much more so than anticipating the new bike he knew his mother had gotten him as his "Santa" gift. He already had two bikes. What he wanted was an auto racing set, a build-your-own transistor radio kit, and some Legos.

But what he really, really wanted more than anything was his dad.

The slamming and swatting started around 10 PM. Thus, the mysterious ant invasion of Santa Barbara continued, with Sarah Lockhardt its sole combatant.

Most nights, as he lay in bed trying to sleep, worry flooded his mind. He loved his mother. He hoped she would get better. There were times before, times when they had had fun and did things together. She had been happy. She had been normal. She had made him feel safe.

But no more. Over time, she had gotten worse. Sometimes, she hinted that she was aware of her peculiar behavior. Her excuses ranged from her isolation, however self-imposed, to blaming his father for ruining their lives. It frustrated him. He wished she would go to the doctor and get some help. Instead, he would wake up tomorrow and choke on insecticide fumes as he walked down the hallway to discover a third bike. From "Santa."

"Oh Bobby!" she would feign surprise, animated and aghast, as if magic truly did exist. As if Santa Claus was real. "He knew exactly what you wanted, didn't he? How exciting!"

He checked the clock on his wall before extinguishing his bedside lamp. Ten thirty at night here meant six thirty in the morning in England. Maybe his father was just getting up. Maybe he would be so excited about Christmas and so eager to talk that he would miscalculate the time and call early. To be on the safe side, Bobby tried to stay up and listen for the phone.

The slamming and swatting stopped just past midnight. The garage door opened twice. A bit of shuffling and commotion as, he was sure, his mother set up his "Santa" gift. Then, quiet. She did not check on him before she went to bed.

And the phone did not ring.

***

Things were unraveling daily. Every villain in the East End felt it.

The Chapel Street job back in August had ultimately been ruled an accidental overdose. No worries there. But news had reached him over the months from various acquaintances. Things beyond what he learned during brief calls from ever-changing locations. Rumblings of increasing concern amongst even the most loyal of their group. Rumors of Ronnie Kray's worsening paranoia. Of the Kray twins turning their ire inward.

Ronnie had paid Jack "the Hat" McVitie £500 to dispose of Leslie Payne, a former business partner who knew too much about their dealings. When McVitie failed, there followed his much-witnessed murder at the end of a blade, by Reggie Kray, who had unraveled under grief and alcohol since his wife's suicide. Whispered concerns spread through Firm members. If Ronnie and Reggie could off McVitie, one of their own, they could off any of them.

The twins had become a reckless pair, relying on continued fear tactics to keep anyone from grassing. It had worked so far. But every fault line eventually broke.

At least he was not in the middle of the fray.

What had started off as instructions to lay low while the business on Chapel Street was sorted was now an imperative to stay as far away as possible for an indeterminate amount of time. Henry had escaped to Spain. Freddie had taken over as his liaison with the twins. But even though the money kept coming in to sustain him, uncertainty over his precarious situation left him restless. Would they ever let him go back to work? If not, what would become of him?

Ultimately, these questions would work to his advantage. He would see to it.

He located the open café at which Freddie had told him to wait. Outside was a sign welcoming all in for a complimentary Christmas Day tea. Inside, the establishment bustled with activity. He managed to find an empty booth among merrier groups of people all wishing each other the best of the day.

A server produced a cup of tea the moment he sat down. He sipped at it while awaiting the call. Why Freddie chose an establishment over the red telephone box a block away, he did not know.

As with previous dealings with Henry, the wait extended well past the agreed upon time. To avoid overstaying his welcome beyond the owner's season-inspired act of goodwill toward men, he ordered a second tea and some food.

"And a happy Christmas to you," the proprietor greeted with a cheerful smile, delivering his full English breakfast.

He lifted his chin at her. "Cheers."

The woman wiped her hands on her apron, then laced her fingers in front of her. "On your way home to family, then? Don't stay out in the cold too long. I hear it may snow. But wouldn't that be lovely on such a day as Christmas?"

He grunted a noncommittal response and arranged the napkin on his lap.

Ignoring the rude and clear signal that he did not fancy a chat, she patted his upper arm. "Enjoy, then. Let me know if you need anything else." With that, she pivoted to enquire after more conversational diners.

He shot his hand out as she passed. "Wait."

She turned with a start, the warm smile still covering her face. "What is it then, love?"

"I'm expecting a call."

"Oh!" She brightened. "The wife?"

He thought quickly. "My brother."

"I see. Well, the telephone hasn't rung all morning, I'm afraid. Gimme your name and I'll be sure to keep an ear out. Hope it's soon, though. In about an hour, we'll be closing. The husband and I are due at my sister-in-law's for dinner and all the festivities, you know."

He rattled off his name and that of his "brother," then thanked her for her time and turned his attention to his meal. After consuming the grilled tomato slices, he went for the beans.

Four months. He had effectively abandoned his room at the lodging house, thus forfeiting what few earthly belongings he had. No worries there, though. He had had little to start with. What mattered to him, he carried on his person at all times: a picture of his ex-wife, a handmade drawing made by his son when the lad was three, and a bit of tattered, brown, decades-old fabric. Anything else he left behind, he could easily replace. And he would.

All he needed was the go-ahead. He had already acquired a passport.

When the call finally came some five minutes before the café closed, Freddie sounded unusually guarded. "It's a long winter for you."

"I've survived worse," he grumbled into the phone."

"You still at that place we arranged for you over in West Ham?"

"No. I'm local. Best you don't know."

"Agreed."

"And about the other?"

"Still on about America?"

He huffed a discontented sigh. "Last time, you said you'd ask again. You said they might change their minds."

"Yeah, I asked. They're thinking about it. What with bloody Christmas and all, they've got other things on their minds. Gotta make it nice for their mum, don't they?"

"Listen, Freddie. I'm in touch with this bloke. One of Arden's heavies. He'll make the introductions if the boys give the okay."

Freddie's voice deepened. "You been talking to someone?"

"Only about wanting to get to New York."

"The boys have their own contacts over there. No going outside the Firm. Understand?"

He had said too much.

Adopting a bit of false contrition, he apologized for the momentary lack of judgment and promised to button his lip.

"Don't bollix things up. You get me? You heard what happened to Jack the Hat."

He bit his lower lip. From the corner of his eye, he spotted the woman who had brought his breakfast. She stood a few yards away, watching him expectantly as she wiped down the counter. Though still smiling, her body language told him he had best end his conversation. Glancing around, he realized all the other patrons had left.

Freddie barked into the line. "You still there?"

"Yep. And I did. A lot of talk about it on the streets."

"Nasty business, that."

Voice lower, he asked, "They find the body?"

Freddie erupted in laughter. The sort of laughter that warned him to let it go.

"So, nothing else, then? No one sniffing around, asking about that business in Belgravia?"

"Nah. Quiet as a church. Just stay put. And quiet. I'll be in touch after New Year's. They should have a decision by then. If they haven't gone barmy by then."

Before they hung up, he asked, "So Freddie, you think if they won't send me, they'd let me go on my own? With things heating up at the Yard and all, wouldn't it be better if I were gone for good? I'm useless to them right now. I wanna help them expand. Like they said they wanted."

"What are you, a mercenary?" Freddie laughed again, his tone less congenial.

He watched the woman stow her dish rag. She wiped her hands on her apron, then removed and hung it on a wall hook. When she headed his way, he knew it was time to go.

"They're closing here."

"I've gotta go anyway," Freddie said. "Family. How about you? Any plans for the day?"

Freddie knew his situation. The question was an arrow. And it stuck. "None."

"Better you stay anonymous anyway. No worries, now. Just a couple more weeks."

One way or another, he decided, Freddie was right.

***

Faith hated to admit it, but she could not wait to get back to school. Not because she relished the homework, but because the thought of seeing Mr. Beam made her heart skip a beat. The most handsome teacher in middle school. Just one week to go before they returned. She felt she might not manage another breath until then.

"You know he's as old as our dads," Vicki Ford teased. When Faith protested, Vicki gave her arm a tepid slap with the back of her hand. "Stop. Don't move. You're gonna make me poke you in the eye with the mascara brush."

They sat cross-legged in the middle of Vicki's bedroom floor. She had convinced Faith to sneak out and go to a couple of New Year's parties with her. And why not? Each girl's parents had made plans and would not return until well after midnight. As long as they were careful, who would be the wiser?

"Maybe we should use the fake lashes," Vicki suggested. "That'd be more dramatic. Make you look older. More experienced."

Faith said she was up for anything. "And teach me so I can do it myself."

"By next year, you'll be a pro."

"Let's just get through tonight."

Things had changed this school year. And Faith had Vicki Ford to thank for it.

The Juilliard acceptance letter had inexplicably put her off her game— much to the concern and confusion of both her parents and her longtime mentor/piano teacher. For weeks, she had eschewed practice. The more her mother pressured her, the less she wanted to go. Walt had finally stepped in and told Millie to back off. Slowly, Faith had come around until she no longer fought going to the studio.

At least her budding professional life had gotten back on track. Even if her personal life had Walt and Millie pulling out their hair.

"You got a picture of Mr. Wonderful?" Vicki asked, attaching the fake lashes to the edges of Faith's lids.

Chin up, eyes closed and relaxed, she answered as best she could while trying not to move her face. "Mr. Beam. It's his first year. I won't have a picture of him until the yearbook comes out."

Vicki shrugged. "So take one yourself. Or better yet—have someone else take one of the two of you."

"I'd have to use my dad's camera. I'm sure he'd love that."

They belly-laughed at the certain doom Faith would face by stealing her father's camera to take a picture of a teacher, an older man with whom Walt Peterson's only child had fallen hopelessly in love.

Over the weeks, she had overcome her fear of crawling out her window. She had also run up her mother's credit card to the tune of nearly a hundred and fifty dollars. Worse, her purchases included not only some new mod clothing, but a radio, a lava lamp, and a groovy leather jacket.

Her father had tanned her hide over the shopping spree, something he had never before done. Her mother had tried to return the items but failed since Faith had purchased everything on sale. So instead, Millie had grounded Faith to her room for a month.

Like that mattered. The punishment exempted her piano lessons. And it was not like she had any friends she hung out with...yet.

In the end? Totally worth it. Faith listened to her radio nonstop once Walt had convinced Millie to let her keep it. She turned it on the moment she came home from after-school practice each day. It stayed on until she left again the next morning. Same with the lava lamp. And the jacket? She wore it at all times. She even slept with it.

Had it not been for that act of rebellion and its subsequent punishment, Faith might never have felt emboldened enough to start sneaking out of her window. Her first, clumsy attempt had nearly sent her to the emergency room after all, but Faith had gone with the fall and rolled in an inelegant fashion to avoid putting all her weight on her feet.

Vicki handed Faith her mirror. "There. Whaddya think?"

Faith scrutinized, then smiled at her reflection. Her first time with full makeup. Millie Peterson would not approve. "I love it. Look at my eyes!"

"Blue eye shadow's so groovy."

"And can I borrow that one miniskirt for the party?"

"Of course!" Vicki rummaged through her makeup box. "And I have the perfect shade of lipstick for it. It's so cool."

Fourteen-year-old Vicki Ford had witnessed Faith's comical first attempt at sneaking out her window. Although they had not spoken in the three years they had lived next door to each other, just an occasional wave of acknowledgment when they passed each other on the sidewalk, Faith's act of nonconformity and the resulting near-accident had impressed Vicki and started them talking. They had since become inseparable, despite the fact they had little in common.

Vicki would start high school next year, though Faith would start the year after. Faith was generally a good student, while Vicki struggled. Vicki wore makeup, something Millie Peterson had forbade before Faith turned fifteen. For the most part, Vicki's parents gave her the freedom to hang out with her many friends. Faith's mother resented every time she left the house.

Classically trained by a string of long-haired, symphony-loving musical elitists and raised by sheltering parents, Faith knew little about the modern music to which she had instantly gravitated. Conversely, Vicki dug rock'n'roll and turned up her nose at the mention of Mozart. Posters of all the latest bands, including the Who, the Stones, Big Brother & the Holding Company, the Byrds, and more covered her wall. No scratchy pink afghan for Vicki Ford.

Visually, they were plenty different as well. Vicki was tall, unlike Faith. She wore her shoulder-length dark brown hair meticulously styled into a Priscilla Presley bouffant, while Faith's wild red locks usually lay unkempt to spill about her shoulders and down her back. At least outside of practice or her parent's stuffy dinners in Manhattan. Vicki's close-set green eyes gave her a cat-like appearance, while Faith's, also green, were more rounded and sometimes overly expressive. Vicki polished her long nails with colorful acrylic. Faith kept her nails on the short side to optimize her playing.

Yet despite these things, along with the slight age difference that only mattered during awkward high school years, the girls hit it off.

They decided on potato chips and soda for their pre-party dinner, ignoring the meal Vicki's mother had left warming in the oven for them. When they went downstairs to grab their less-than-nutritious alternative, Vicki pulled out the casserole, switched off the oven, then dished out and disposed of enough of it to make it look like they had eaten.

"I never thought of doing that, Vick. It's brilliant."

"That way Mom won't have a fit. I do it all the time. Grab a couple extra sodas and meet me upstairs. I just need to dirty a few dishes."

Faith munched and daydreamed of Mr. Beam as she waited for Vicki to dirty and rinse their dishes. There were several cute teachers at school this year. She had been in a couple of their classes before, though she had only recently noticed them "that way." However, none were like Mr. Beam. He taught English and turned her into goo every time he smiled at her.

Just another couple of months to go before she officially became a teenager. And while she did not fool herself into thinking Mr. Beam would ever pay attention to a younger chick like herself, she sure paid attention to him.

"All right," Vicki said upon her return. "You ready?"

The girls replenished their makeup after they ate and then dressed for the party, which started at nine.

"But we don't wanna get there until at least nine thirty."

Faith reached behind her to zip up her skirt. "Why not?"

"Because that's not cool. You always show up to a party as late as you can. That way, all the guys see you come in. They're always looking to see who's coming in."

Faith nodded. It made sense. "You sure your friends won't tease you for bringing me along?"

Vicki winked at Faith through the full-length mirror as she assessed her own attire. "It's a kegger, Faith. Nobody's gonna care."

She joined her friend at the mirror. They remained there for some time, primping and admiring their appearance. "I can't believe I'm going to my first party."

"You'll have a blast. It'll be the first of many, I'm sure. If you stick with me."

Faith hoped her new, and only, friend was right. And who knew? Maybe one day, she and Mr. Beam would go to a party together.

CHAPTER 8

*"*C*AN YOU GET US SOME tea, Ronnie? Or water?"
He brushed Polly's tangled mass of blonde hair aside and felt her
forehead. If anything, the fever had worsened. "Can you sit up?"*

*She tried, but collapsed back onto his lap, barely able to cover her mouth
as she coughed. "My chest hurts."*

*Ronnie refused to think the worst, yet noted the blood on her hand after
her coughing fit. She had been declining for weeks now. Gently, he lifted her
head off his lap, repositioning it upon the now-tattered pillow he had stolen
for her two years ago. "Comfortable?"*

She gave a slight nod. "Thirsty. Cold."

It was late August. A warm August. Polly should not be shivering.

*Four years now since the war began, they still battled hunger and fear.
By day, they still hid from all manner of authorities and a close-knit
community ever watchful for orphaned or missing children. By night, they
hid from German bombers. It was not ideal, but it was livable. At least until
they could find a place of their own once the war ended. Until Polly fell ill.*

*They had each other. Little else. Yet despite age and gender differences,
Ronnie found he had much in common with his younger sister. They both
enjoyed radio shows, preferred sausage rolls to Spam sandwiches, hated
Nazis, and dreamed of one day living in a big house, each with their own
rooms.*

*And, although Ronnie never told Polly, he even cried himself to sleep
some nights. Nights when it seemed the war would go on forever. When self-
loathing over his lack of strength would not snuff out the despair, or the
memories of their lost family. Sentiment was not something to indulge.
"Never complain; never explain," their mother had taught them. But even as
they lay awake at night, discussing dreams for a brighter future, Ronnie
wondered if dreams ever really did come true.*

*"Right, then." He pulled her blanket over her body, then added his as
well. "I'm off to find you something. Be back straightaway."*

*He slipped out of their secret shelter, into the warm late afternoon. He
marched down Barking Road to find something, anything, that might help
his sister.*

*The Blitz bombing campaign had lasted fifty-seven consecutive nights.
Though bombers still punished England beyond that time, Brits had pulled
up their collective bootstraps to reconstruct their everyday routines.*

Stronger, determined, and employing all the ingenuity they could muster. At least that was the message they received from the government via the propaganda films he and Polly would see on the few occasions they managed to sneak into a cinema.

Early on, they had relocated to the Canning Town Library, a fifteen-minute walk from their former home. It had suffered damage but remained largely intact. Ronnie worked various day jobs when he could find them. Though they could not find Polly an open school—which would have helped them fill her belly—the library provided access to a wealth of knowledge. They were both avid readers.

When he could not find day work, he and Polly played among the unstable masonry, electrical wires, and broken pipes that had become their neighborhood. Partly for exercise. Partly to get their minds off their circumstances. Their old playmates had either died in the bombings, left with their parents for safer accommodations, or had relocated as part of Operation Pied Piper. Sometimes, they encountered other kids, but Ronnie avoided mingling with strangers who might rat out their hiding space or try to commandeer it for themselves.

He stole what they needed, a skill he mastered over time but wished he had not needed to develop. He begged for money. He fought boys his own age who competed for what little they had. Together, he and Polly became adept at slipping in and out of their shelter without notice. Without alerting any adults. But it had become problematic over the last few days, as Polly's worsening condition prevented them from roaming the streets by day, when people entered the library or its adjacent Public Hall for various reasons.

A large group of men huddled outside a neighborhood pub, speechless as they leaned toward the door. Ronnie quickened his pace. Maybe it was important news. He needed to know.

Weeks and months more or less melted into a fog of terror and survival, but he had maintained his keen mind. Loitering near pubs or restaurants as these men did, he would get updates on the war efforts. Sometimes, a generous stranger would buy him a pint.

Last night before returning to the library with a National Loaf and some Household Milk he had nicked from a battered home nearby, he had overheard on a radio broadcast that the Allies had entered Paris.

"Any news, then?" Ronnie dared to interrupt.

Several men shushed him, still harkening toward the bar. Ronnie peered through the window and saw the bartender reach over to turn up the radio volume.

Though not a spiritual person, he found himself praying that Hitler would finally start getting back some of the hell he had served.

Then, they heard it.

...Paris has been liberated. A communiqué just received from General Koenig—

Cheers erupted from the group, followed by more shushing. The men leaned in as close as possible without eliciting complaints of loitering from the bartender.

...announces that it has been liberated by French forces of the Interior...

Ronnie ran. He needed to tell Polly the good news.

On his way, he nicked a hot tea and a few dry biscuits from one of the British Restaurants. He spared barely a glance at his ill-gotten gains as he hastened his return. After four years of living like animals, he had found some of the hope he had lost amongst the rubble and death permeating the East End.

Now, to get his sister on the mend.

He slipped inside without a sound, listened for strangers, then sprinted up to the second floor. "Polly! I brought your tea...and news!"

The sight that met him turned him to stone.

Polly lay listless in the exact position she was in when he left. She coughed weakly, but lacked the strength to cover her mouth. "Come," she beckoned weakly. Her voice sounded wet and raspy.

The joy over the news he had heard on Barking Road evaporated. He set the tea and crumbling biscuits on a shelf, then moved closer. Sitting cross-legged beside her, he cupped his hand beneath her neck and tried to lift her closer, back into his lap. She winced faintly, shaking her head. "Come here."

He inclined his ear toward her. This time, he did not need to feel her head. The fever had clearly ravaged her.

"I..." She started and stopped. "I...I want Mam."

Ronnie swallowed hard. Though twelve now, the little girl who had lost her mother still existed, as if that horrid moment had frozen her in time. "I know, my darling," he soothed, stroking her damp, matted hair.

"Take me, Ronnie. Take me back."

His eyes narrowed in concern. "We can't risk it. You're too sick. Once you're better..."

She moaned, then coughed. A thin line of blood trickled down a corner of her mouth.

Despite frail protests, Ronnie maneuvered Polly into his lap. Stretching, he retrieved the tea, which had cooled to room temperature. "Here. Sip this. It'll sort you."

Polly strained to move her lips to the tin cup. Hefting her into position, Ronnie poured some of the liquid into her mouth. Most dribbled down her chin.

"Take me. I want Mam."

As he began to realize what was happening, he rapid-blinked, banishing the threat of tears before they could surface. He needed to get her help. Get her to hospital. Even if it meant they ended up separated. Anything to save her.

"Somebody!" he shouted in panic. "We need help in here!"

"It's okay, Ronnie."

"Anybody!"

Her face paled. Her breathing shallowed. "She's there, Ronnie. I see her."

All cries for help unanswered, he cradled her in his arms. He cursed himself for not insisting she go to a temporary home where they would have better cared for her. In the end, he had not kept them together at all. And when Polly died that evening, the liberation of Paris meant less to him than his own life.

He wrapped her in her blanket and carried her back to the ruined South Hallsville School, barely aware of his surroundings, impervious to anyone who might notice. Numb.

Once there, he found a small metal shovel, perhaps abandoned along with the rescue and recovery efforts that made his former school his family's final resting place. He chose an area at the edge of the hardened quicklime, then began digging through dirt and debris. Hours later, he had holed out an adequate space.

Ronnie sniffed, then cleared his throat. He remained stoic as he laid his sister in the makeshift grave. "This is as close as I could get you, my darling."

He employed the shovel again, this time to cover her up. The dawn broke as he finished securing the area. And instead of offering a prayer to a God he did not believe in, he made two promises.

The first was to Polly. "I swear on my life. After the war ends, I'll get the house we dreamed of. Even if I have to build it with my bare hands."

The second promise, he made to himself. He would never again cry, give into sentiment, or let himself love another soul. Loving meant loss. Loss meant pain. He would never feel either again.

***

Conserves Records was bleeding red. It had been for months. Good thing their accountants had mastered the art of book cooking. Good thing their artists remained blissfully unaware. Though Conserves remained optimistic that their few mid-chart hit makers like Billy Stagger & the Swingers, Crimp, and Julie Dwight would finally strike pay dirt, they rarely produced anything that rose higher than the Top 100.

Ross's phone had not stopped ringing all morning. Top brass had begun fretting over their forthcoming earnings report. He did not know why. At their behest, the entire document was a ruse. What they should worry about was the fact that EMI continued to breathe down their neck, pressuring them to sell.

Still a self-professed baby to the industry, Ross had learned the music business in a baptism-by-fire manner. This included endless mergers & acquisitions, expansions, buy-outs, and consolidations. Rock'n'roll had solidified itself as the era's dominant genre. Since artist production and success dictated the viability of any record company, a strong A&R team, coupled with their contacts with radio station program directors made or broke a label—especially now that DJs had been stripped of their authority during the payola investigations.

But regardless of what Congress said or did, the pay-to-play scheme lived on. The ins and outs of their fragile legal strategies knew no end. And when asked about his place in the industry, Ross expressed gratitude to have started with a smaller label. Anything larger would have eaten him alive.

In these early months of 1968, the recording industry was downright ravenous. Just not for Conserves Records' offerings.

Inwardly, Ross sought what every other mid-lifer with a family legacy of financial success wanted: to prosper in his own right. And although he considered himself a loyal man, he did not see it happening if he did not find a better situation. The only question was, where? Did he stay in entertainment? Or retreat to the less exciting, but infinitely more stable, world of corporate law?

"It's like any other business, except when it's not," he had stated earlier this morning, lingering on a conference call with a colleague well after the other participants had hung up. "There are successful businessmen and unsuccessful businessmen. Successful businessmen know their industry."

"I don't entirely disagree," the colleague had said. "But we *all* know the industry. Anyone who doesn't won't last long. It's more than that."

Ross had considered the response. "You're right. It is more. It takes knowledge, but I think it takes instinct, too."

"Bingo."

"Similarly, while most aspiring artists can sing, few have that intangible vibe or whatever you want to call it. That something that draws people to one entertainer but not to someone else equally talented. An *it* factor, if you will. And that *it* factor is the difference between a group like the Gentrys and, say, the Beatles."

His colleague agreed. "And yet, even those with that *it* factor need the right person to find and back them. A champion. With contacts and a helluva lot of luck."

"Which circles back to the instinct of the businessmen surrounding the artists."

"True. There's a fair amount of *it* factor to the business as well. Record producers and managers like Sam Phillips, Berry Gordy...and, of course, Epstein—God rest his soul."

With that, Ross had ended the call, claiming a full schedule. Something not completely untrue.

His working lunch in the conference room with the top brass included deli sandwiches from Lindy's and three bourbons. Not the most productive, or memorable, but it accomplished two things.

First, it pacified the powers that be with regard to the coming quarterly report. The A&R department announced some promising finds. With creative accounting and a fair amount of what Conserves referred to as Ross's "magicianry," the company would survive another year or so.

Second, it temporarily calmed Ross's nerves. Something he needed a good bit of since returning from last year's extended business trip. Those he worked closest with had noticed. So had Josephine. Initially, he had made feeble excuses for acting in a manner those around him labeled as "off." But ever since his mother's sudden death a week into the New Year, no one questioned him. In a way, dying was the best thing Evelyn Alexander had ever done for him.

By late afternoon, Ross realized he either needed to lie down or have another drink. His head pounded from his mostly liquid lunch. He buzzed his assistant, Jackie, to get him a glass of water and some aspirin. While he waited, he called Josephine to let her know he intended to knock off early.

He heard the concern in her voice. It added a measure of guilt to the throbbing in his head. Those in his circle worried about him. He had parlayed that worry into a buffer between what they knew he had been through and what they did not.

"Here you are," Jackie said, breezing in with his water and pills. She handed him the glass and dropped the tablets in his cupped hand.

He swallowed the pills with the entire glass of water, then handed it back. "I appreciate it. And if you would, please let G know I'll be taking off a little early today."

Jackie rested a comforting hand on his upper arm. "I'm sure they'll understand, Mr. Alexander. If there's anything I can do..."

Ross moved past her to hold the door. "Thanks. That'll be all for now."

Into his briefcase, he shoved several folders containing various contracts. He would work on them tonight after Josephine retired for the evening. A little time with his bride would certainly ease his hangover.

He snapped shut his briefcase, patted his pocket to ensure he had his car keys, then headed out. Before reaching the door, his phone rang. He considered letting Jackie take a message but, with the elevated temperature amid the Conserves Records' higher ups, he opted to take this last call.

The voice on the other end left him stunned. It took Ross a moment to recall having foolishly handed over his business card last August.

"So, it appears Pink Floyd's Syd Barrett's gone mad," he said, as if no time had passed between them. As if nothing had happened. "So much for sex, drugs, and rock'n'roll."

Despite his throbbing head and their possibly sinister past, the glib assessment elicited a subtle tug at the corners of his mouth. "You know what they say. The show must go on."

"Indeed. Seems they're going with some chap named David Gilmour. I guess time'll tell."

"I guess it will."

"How've you been, then?"

"Busy. It's not easy bailing water on a sinking ship."

"Still? You haven't righted that vessel yet?"

He set down his briefcase and took his seat. "Not my responsibility. I just make sure what they do is legal."

"Or *appears* legal."

Ross bobbed his head side-to-side. "Or appears legal."

"I nose around a bit. I'd say you're doing a proper job."

"They're calling me 'the magician'."

A hearty laugh filled the line. "Well done, you."

Ross could not deny he had enjoyed their numerous conversations throughout their limited association. They had connected intellectually. They shared the same humor. For a cabbie, the man seemed ever-eager to better himself. He was an engaging conversationalist, highly knowledgeable on a number of topics. Even entertainment, in which he seemed to have taken an active interest as they had gotten to know each other. "What about you? I never saw you again after..."

He hoped his former driver would finish his sentence. Maybe clarify details previously unshared, or assure him after months of incertitude. He wanted to believe he had misconstrued the goings-on. That it was all just a coincidence. An accident after all. And perhaps it was. But the man skirted the issue as if there wasn't one, leaving him confused and suspicious. What had really happened on Chapel Street that night?

"I did make some changes," the man said, "thanks in part to your words of encouragement."

"Anything you care to share?"

"For one, I've moved."

"I thought you might," Ross said. He glimpsed Jackie peeking in through the sidelight beside his office door. She raised her hands, as if confused to see he had not yet left. He waved her off with a thumb's up. "Did you move southward, near the coast? You'd mentioned Cornwall at some point."

"Too small, I decided. Big dreams require big cities, then, don't they?"

"So you stayed local? What about the wife and son?"

"Again, time will tell. But no, I didn't stay local. In fact, I'm an ocean away from that business."

Ross sank back into his reclining office chair. "Are you...did you move to California?"

The man chuckled. "I don't know if I'm ready for that much sun. Actually, this is a local call. I'm in New York. And I believe I may just owe you a drink."

***

Weeks after the move, Beth O'Conner feared she might never finish unpacking. Her immediate focus had been getting Farin settled, hoping to mitigate the stress accompanying such a significant change in her young life. In that vein, Beth had also declined Carol Williams's multiple offers of assistance. Beth wanted their world to remain small at first. No help. No visitors. No new people in their orbit. Just the O'Conners slowly adjusting to life in the Golden State.

But two weeks in, as Kelley and Joseph officially opened their practice, Beth felt the pressure. And an overwhelming sense of loneliness.

She endeavored to make real progress without her husband's input and help. Every day, she fretted over the placement of each item she unboxed—all the while feeling the pull of the ocean. It seemed their possessions had multiplied by three, as if they conspired to keep her away from the beach. Soon, it became clear they would need to sacrifice some of their belongings or go back on their promise to let Farin use the attic as a playroom.

At week three, she relented and begged Carol Williams to bring her daughter over. She was drowning.

"I'm afraid Kelley's gonna have to build that treehouse sooner than he may have wanted," she flustered, opening the screen door wide to welcome

Carol and her daughter, Marci. "You were right. It is that small. And please don't say I told you so."

Carol walked straight to the kitchen to set down the bags of groceries, cleaning supplies, and the lunch she had picked up on their way over. "You okay, Beth? You look frazzled."

"I am frazzled." She smoothed back the baby hairs that had loosened from her long, dark ponytail. "I need more space."

Carol visually inspected the area. "I'm sure it's not as bad as you think."

"It isn't?" she asked, grateful for the conflicting perspective.

"Nope. First, we'll clear these boxes off the kitchen table. Next, we'll eat. I'd wager you need sustenance. And when we finish our nice, leisurely lunch, we'll roll up our sleeves and get to it. I've arranged a beer and pizza delivery to the office tonight. Apparently, the men have their first big case. Let them stay late. We'll do the real work, here."

Beth threw her arms around the woman. "You're an angel, Carol Williams. That's what you are."

Carol squeezed her tight before letting go. "Hardly. But first things first. You haven't met my daughter, Marci."

Bending down to talk to the child at face level, Beth apologized for her frantic behavior. "I'm not usually like this, honey. Moving a whole house can be hard."

With one hand, Marci pulled awkwardly at the ruffles of her pink dress. With the other, she clutched her doll.

Beth smiled, willing herself to calm down. "Forgive me? I hope so, because I have a feeling we're going to be very good friends. I make exceptional chocolate chip cookies. Once your mom and I finish getting our house in shape, I'll show you. How does that sound?"

The young girl smiled, her cheeks a soft crimson.

"I hear you have a birthday coming up in a few days. You'll be five, yes? Did your mom tell you I have a little girl your age? She just turned five in January."

Marci nodded.

"Her name's Farin. She's upstairs in the attic, and I'm sure she'd love to meet you."

The word attic evoked a less than enthusiastic response. Wide-eyed, Marci recoiled and peered up at her mother.

Beth stood, emitting a soft chuckle. "Oh no, honey, it's not scary. Farin's playroom is up there. She has her phonograph up there and her dolls, too. You'll see. It even has a couple of windows. You can see the ocean." She nodded at Carol for support. "I don't think I'm making a very good first impression."

Carol put her arm around Marci and headed toward the stairs. "C'mon, sweetie. You'll love it. And you'll love Aunt Beth, too…eventually." She glanced back over her shoulder and winked.

Beth followed behind, accompanying them so she could make proper introductions. Then, she stopped short. Carol Williams had a way about her that assured Beth that Farin would think nothing of meeting them both for the first time. Truth told, Farin had shown symptoms of boredom lately, despite having her music and her playthings.

With a shrug of resignation, she confronted the table. She moved and stacked boxes, emptied the grocery bags, and stuck the lunch fixings in the fridge to keep them cold until served. Carol had thought of everything, right down to the paper plates and plastic utensils. Juice for the girls. Wine for them. Maybe organizing the house would not be so bad after all.

"I should have had you over days ago," she confessed when Carol returned. "I can't thank you enough."

Carol waved her off. "Let's uncork that bottle and chat a bit before lunch so we can decide what our priorities will be. The girls're fine upstairs. I'm thinking once we tackle the kitchen, the rest will be a breeze."

"You read my mind." Beth rummaged through a couple of boxes, unsuccessfully searching for their corkscrew.

"Allow me." Carol reached inside her purse and produced a pocketknife with a folding corkscrew. "Joseph gave me this the first year we went camping. I've never used it before today."

Beth sat at the kitchen table and let Carol do the honors. "You camp?"

Carol nodded. "Sometimes. We try to take trips or vacations whenever we can. Of course, they've been more child-focused since we had Marci."

She thanked Carol for the wine, which they drank from plastic cups. "Kelley always wanted to take me camping, but I've resisted for some reason. I wonder if Farin would like it."

"I'm sure she would. You three should join us. We're going to Yosemite for Memorial Day weekend."

Beth brightened. "Maybe we will."

"Talk to Kelley about it tonight when he gets home. He'll be thrilled—especially when he comes home all full of beer and pizza and sees our progress."

Carol beckoned her out of the kitchen, opting for the more comfortable living room sofa. They cleared the coffee table clutter, set down their drinks, then plopped down on the thick, soft cushions. "In fact, Joseph and I have been talking about a trip to Disneyland. Not exactly grown-up entertainment, but I think it'd be a wonderful thing to go before the girls start kindergarten. What do you say?"

Beth picked up her plastic glass and toasted Carol. "I say, this is the most relaxed I've felt in months. Maybe years."

"Good! Look Beth, you're here now. You've got the house. The house you wanted. No reason to stress out about anything. This is the time to be thankful. It's working out. We'll have this place in order in no time. Or hell, maybe not. Maybe we work today and tomorrow we play hooky. For Pete's sake, spring's just days away. Let's go enjoy that beach! The girls would love it. And you, my friend, need a day off."

Beth looked around her home with fresh eyes. For the first time since their arrival, she saw beyond the clutter and unopened boxes. Kelley had not once pressured her to finish getting things together. Farin had not whined or complained about the transition. The move was everything they had dreamed of—and more.

She drew in a deep breath, then released it slowly to steady her nerves. "Yes. We'll work today and go to the beach tomorrow. A day in the sun would be heaven. Let's go tell the girls."

When Beth moved to stand, Carol held out her hand. She winked again. "There's plenty of time, hon. Right now, we're going to finish our wine and discuss Marci's party. You're all invited. And I expect you to bring those chocolate chip cookies."

CHAPTER 9

"COME ON THEN, BEN," LYNDA whisper-shouted, grabbing her startled son by his strumming arm. "Hear for yourself."

Ben slumped in frustration, his mind still stuck inside the song he was trying to finish. He propped his pre-war Martin acoustic up against his bed and followed his mother. Halfway downstairs, she stopped and held a finger to her lips. She motioned for Ben to listen.

Jordan sat alone in the drawing room, playing with the Spirograph he had received for Christmas. He bobbed his head to the radio, singing along to "Rosie" by Don Partridge, adding a bit of harmony here or there.

Lynda beamed down at her son. "Isn't he something?"

Ben nodded patiently. "He's good, Mum. For eight. He sure is."

When Jordan caught them looking, Lynda flustered and rushed her oldest back upstairs. "You know, Ben, you should take some of your songs and work up an act. Daddy's been talking to his contacts."

He plopped back down on his bed. "Dad'll let us know when the time's right."

She gave him that look of hers.

"I'll talk to him on our way to London next week. But Mum, I need to finish these songs or I won't be ready."

"Right, right." She waved and bustled toward the door. "Sorry, son. You're right. Daddy'll know best."

"Jordan'll have his time. I'm sure of it. Dad knows what he's doing."

She turned back before heading downstairs. "He does, doesn't he?"

Ben considered his mother's sad, hopeful expression. With an irritated sigh of resignation, he snatched up his guitar and followed a few steps behind. "Jordan!" he called past her.

"Yeah?" he called back.

Lynda clapped her hands together as Ben passed her on the stairs. "Turn off the radio."

Jordan stopped drawing and looked up. "Why?"

"Time for practice."

He did not need to hear it twice. Jordan hurried to the radio, switched it off, then quickly gathered his papers and pens, stowing the Spirograph in the credenza with the other games while Ben pushed back the coffee table so they could both sit on the rug.

Lynda went behind Jordan and reorganized the games, then retreated to the kitchen to fix them a snack.

"I want you to learn these songs, understand?" Ben instructed, pointing to the stack of sheet music he had brought with him. "Not just the ones on the radio."

Jordan nodded, his eyes fixed enthusiastically on his brother's.

"This isn't a game, now. We promised we'd take it seriously, remember?"

He crossed his heart and held up two fingers.

"We're going to put something together for Dad. You're still a bit young yet, but you won't be for long. So are you in or out?"

"In!"

"Okay. And I'll talk to Dad about getting you your own guitar."

"But...Chris plays guitar."

Ben frowned at him. "More than one of us can play guitar. Besides, even if you don't want to play professionally, you should learn so you can accompany yourself when you practice."

Jordan cocked his head. "Won't I practice with you?"

"Yes, but I won't be here forever. I'm older."

Lynda returned with sliced apples and milk. She placed them on the coffee table with a few napkins. "Don't worry. Ben's not leaving anytime soon."

Ben gave her that look of his.

"Well? You won't. You're only fifteen. I'm not ready to let you go yet."

Twenty minutes into their impromptu practice session, Chris returned from who knew where with a boy they had not seen before. Disheveled. A bit reserved. On the skinny side of healthy. In need of a bath. Lynda noticed him staring at the apple slices and wondered when he had last eaten.

"This is Elliot," Chris said matter-of-factly, bounding upstairs to his room, taking the steps two at a time.

"Hello, Elliot," Lynda greeted. "I'm Chris's mum."

"Nice to meet you, Mrs. Grant." His eyes flicked downward.

"And this is Chris's older brother, Ben, and our youngest, Jordan."

The boys waved casually, keeping their primary focus on the music.

Elliot lifted his chin their way.

"Won't you sit down?" Lynda gestured to the sofa. "Fancy some apples? Can I get you some milk?"

He nodded sheepishly. "Thank you, Mrs. Grant. I'd love some milk." He reached for an apple, but pulled back when he glimpsed his dirty hand.

Lynda called from the kitchen, her voice gentle and knowing. "The loo's over by the stairs, if you want to wash up."

Guitar in hand, Chris trotted back downstairs. He surveyed the room. "Where's Elliot?"

Ben stopped playing mid-strum. Impatient, he scratched the side of his face and looked at his brother. "The loo."

Chris grabbed some apples and plopped down onto the sofa. "What're you two up to?"

"Practicing!" Jordan exclaimed.

"Or, trying," Ben muttered.

"Ben's teaching me his songs!"

"And Jorie's doing a lovely job learning them," Lynda encouraged, returning with Elliot's milk.

Chris gave Ben that look of his.

"What?"

He shook his head, disgusted. "You'll teach the baby but you won't teach me?"

"Hey!" Jordan protested.

Ben glared at his brother. "You're never here."

"I'm here now, aren't I?"

"Fine. Wanna have a go? The sheet music's right here."

Chris leveled bitter eyes upon him. "I'm not your chore."

Ben stabbed the rug as he spoke. "Dad told you months ago he'd manage us. And what've you done since? Where've you been? Started any fires lately? Pulled any new birds?"

Lynda stepped forward, ever the mediator between her two eldest sons. A ready admonition died in her throat when she spotted Elliot out of the corner of her eye, hovering unobtrusively in the hall outside the loo.

"As a matter of fact," Chris snapped, reaching in his back pocket for a crumpled piece of paper, "I've done a bit of writing myself. You're not the only one in this family with talent."

Ben lifted challenging brows. "Yeah? Let's hear it, then."

Elliot inched into the room, head down, holding his left arm with his right hand like a safety blanket.

Chris inclined his head at his friend, unconcerned or oblivious to the fact that their fighting had made him uncomfortable. "Where's your bass?"

"At my place. I thought we were just getting your guitar."

Chris addressed Ben. "We need your bass."

Ben began strumming. "You know where it is. Just be careful."

Lynda, Ben, and Jordan arranged themselves on the sofa while Chris retrieved the bass. As he waited, Elliot snacked ravenously on apple slices and drank an entire glass of milk in a single gulp.

Without a hint of nerves, the boys played three songs they had written over the last week. It turned out they had met the day after the return from Christmas break. Elliot had transferred from a school up near Manchester. Due to their shared love of music, they hit it off immediately, and had gone to Elliot's place to practice almost every day since they met. Instead of lighting fires or wooing girls, Chris now spent his time working with his new friend.

Ben's sullen resentment toward his usually irresponsible brother dissipated as he listened. He found himself tapping his foot and bobbing his head to the music. Though arguably primitive, the songs were not bad at all. But more than that, he was impressed by their musicianship.

When Chris and Elliot finished, Ben and Lynda applauded enthusiastically. Jordan jumped up from the sofa and loudly cheered.

Elliot offered a grateful nod for their response.

With a self-satisfied scowl, Chris handed Elliot his guitar, then grabbed Ben's bass and returned it without a glance at his family.

Lynda stood and hugged Elliot. "That was grand," she said, breaking away. "I know Chris's father would love to hear you two play. Won't you stay for dinner? It's bangers and mash with onion gravy."

Elliot's eyes widened.

Before he could respond, Chris hastened back. "Have fun practicing," he spat, yanking open the front door. "C'mon, then, El."

Deflating, Elliot nodded at Lynda. "Thank you, ma'am. I need to get back."

"Wait!" She followed behind them, hand outstretched. "Chris, can't you lads practice after dinner?"

Still scowling, Chris kissed his mother's cheek but stared daggers at his older brother. "I'll be back by nine."

Ben stood and joined his mother. "You two really were good, mate. I mean it. Keep up the great work...and if you fancy writing a few songs together, let me know."

"You could be in the band!" Jordan added, his mouth full of apple.

Once again, Chris gave Ben that look of his. "Yeah, sure," he scoffed, then to Elliot, "You ready?"

Elliot nodded, doubled back to grab a couple more apples, then followed Chris out the door.

***

Sarah Lockhardt stumbled down the jetway on wobbly, stocking-sheathed legs, sobbing. She leaned against her son, who walked step-for-step beside her, holding her close. Were Bobby any younger, the trip from LAX to Heathrow would have been unendurable.

"I must look a fright." She huddled in his arms, dabbing her eyes with the handkerchief she clutched in her hand.

"You're fine, Mom. Just a little ways more."

"I can't believe they don't take better care."

"It's over now."

"What must people think?"

He patted her arm. "We'll be at Grandpa's soon. You're fine, Mom. Beautiful."

His tender words evoked more tears. Not due to her father's sudden passing, which had prompted their journey, or the horrific flight across the Atlantic. Sarah was overwhelmed at her son's resolute patience.

Something was not right, and had not been for years. But no one could know. If they did, she could lose her son. He was all she had left.

"I don't think I can bear Customs right away."

He nodded. "Okay. We'll wait."

"I should like to speak to someone in charge. They need to know. They need to do something about it."

"I'll do it, Mom. You rest."

"We're in terminal three, son. Gate thirty. Are you sure you can manage?"

When they reached the gatehouse, Bobby helped her to a seat and scanned the concourse signage. He pointed off to the left. "The airline's office is over by baggage claim, next to Customs. I can talk to someone once we meet our driver. That way you can settle in."

Every instinct told Sarah to protest. What if he got lost? What if someone kidnapped him like Frank Sinatra Jr.? The thought of organizing a sizable ransom while traveling abroad nearly undid her. "You're a big boy now."

He stood straight and tall.

"You know to watch for sunshine."

His eyes narrowed.

"Ropes," she corrected, shaking her head. "Kidnappers."

"I'll be fine, Mom. I just wanna get you to Grandpa's so you can relax."

"I'm sorry he died on your birthday." The weeping began again. She could not help herself. Her tear-dampened handkerchief provided little assistance.

Bobby sat beside her. He moved in close and whispered, "People are looking. We need to keep us together, remember? Now try. Try hard. I'll help you. You can lean on me."

She scanned the obtrusive faces of the dozens of strangers meandering the concourse. Some averted their eyes. A few wore expressions of concern, as if wanting to approach them to help. Or worse. What if they wanted to take Bobby away and put her in a home?

Mustering every ounce of strength she possessed, she grasped her son's hand. Two suited businessmen approached, ostensibly to offer assistance. Bobby waved them off.

"You can do this, Mom."

Jaw set, she hoisted herself upright out of the chair. After faltering a bit in her heels, they managed to get through the concourse and Customs. At last, they met up with their waiting driver.

"Get the luggage situated," Bobby instructed the man, still supporting her small frame. "I'll get her into the car, but then I need to run over to the airline office."

The driver did as instructed, then climbed inside the limousine and waited dutifully for the young man's return. He spied Sarah through his rearview mirror. "You all right, Miss?"

"My son's handling everything," she answered proudly, chin raised as she steadied her breathing.

Minutes later, Bobby returned, and they were on their way.

Sarah relaxed into the soft leather and exhaled for what felt like the first time since leaving their home. "You told them?"

He nestled into the seat opposite her, his back to the driver. "Yes, ma'am."

She leaned back against the headrest, eyes closed. "Thank you, son. I don't know what I'd do if you weren't here. How in the world did they get ants on a plane? Do you think they followed me?"

"Please don't start crying again, Mom. Want me to fix you a drink?"

Sarah nodded, emitting a mournful squeak.

The commute to Oxfordshire felt infinitely longer than she remembered. Her father had always insisted that the destination eclipsed the inconvenience. Easy for him to say.

The Palladian estate had been in their family for generations. Old money. Twenty-five acres of immaculate gardens amongst the verdant countryside. Not the largest of its kind, but its eight bedrooms had adequately housed her grandfather, her father, and her to such an extent they saw the wait staff more than one another. And, if one grew bored, there was always the croquet lawn.

But, to her bitter disappointment, no pool. Ever.

Bobby stared out the window, head resting on his hand. "Mom, do you think we can see Dad while we're here, like we did after Grandma died?"

She bit her upper lip. "We're burying my father, Bobby. I have a million matters to handle. Just...let me rest for a couple of days. We'll see."

He said nothing further, but his lips curved downward as he watched the passing scenery.

She studied him a moment, her heart aching at his obvious sadness. "Hey."

He glanced at her.

"We'll see, okay?"

Bobby stared back out at the countryside.

Lies. All of it. But she protected those lies with every ounce of sanity she had left.

She had told Bobby she had not heard from his father in months. That he was still in England. That the man had always provided for them, ensuring their comfort and safety.

In truth, Robert Wellingham had always supplied the money. Right up until last week's heart attack. As for Bobby's father, Jameson had moved to New York months ago. He had told her he intended to relocate to Southern California as soon as he found the means. What little money he possessed was filthy and bloodstained. As far as she knew, he had yet to find a job.

Sarah Lockhardt would rather her son pine for the father he thought he had than hate the one he did.

During the rare conversations to which she had consented, he begged for reconciliation with his family. What she never told Jameson, or their son, was that she wanted that, too. More than anything. Her fraying mind scared her. Too afraid to say anything. Too afraid to ask for help. She was tired of pretending. Tired of being a thirty-three-year-old single mother. Tired of the ants she knew she imagined but could not stop seeing everywhere.

Did she love her estranged husband? With every fiber of her being. But she had taken her stand. Moreover, she was right. His life choices had left her none.

They had last seen each other three years ago after her grandmother's funeral. She and Bobby had defied Robert Wellingham's wishes to meet Jameson at the newly installed Joy of Life fountain in Hyde Park. She had suspected, at the time, that he had chosen that spot not just because it was new, but because it depicted a happy family. That he had wanted to manipulate her feelings. And it had worked. Another of the secrets she kept.

Not only was it the last time she saw Jameson, that trip was also the last time she would see her father.

"Are we gonna move here now, Mom?"

"I don't know, son. I don't know anything right now."

"It's okay if we do."

She lifted her head and looked at him. "Is that what you want?"

His shoulders rose, then fell. "I just want you. And Dad."

The idea had never occurred to her. In fact, she had believed until the phone call three days ago that they had been disinherited. But in the years prior to his death, Robert Wellingham must have had a change of heart.

As the limousine pulled onto the tree-lined road toward the house, she envisioned a life in the country. Then, reality set in. The upkeep. The maintenance. Such a grand property required more than Sarah could manage. In her heart, she knew she would never again visit her homeland.

"Mom?"

She gazed down at the damp, wrinkled handkerchief still clutched in her hand.

"Mom, don't cry."

***

Faith spent the summer of '68 planning. Yes, she fulfilled her commitments to Austin Jones. Yes, she played her part as the budding virtuoso her parents expected her to be. But she hated them. All of them. So, she planned. In five years, she would be gone.

Five years. It seemed a lifetime away. So until then, she would sneak out when she could and pretend the rest of the time. Why? Because she had to. She would never forgive Walt and Millie Peterson for what they had done.

It had happened shortly after summer vacation started. Gossip had sprouted like weeds throughout New Rochelle. Adults knew. Kids knew. Everyone knew. Mr. Beam was out. Out as a junior high teacher, out of town—maybe even out of the state of New York.

And it was all Faith's fault.

She and Vicki had been shopping at the enormous new downtown mall that had finally opened that year. One of Millie's rare concessions, for sure. After all, Millie Peterson did not like Faith's friend—for no reason other than, "she rubs me the wrong way." Yet for some reason, that first Saturday after school ended, her mother had not only let her miss a lesson, she let her go to the mall with "that neighbor girl." For a few hours that day, Faith had wondered if she and her mother had turned a corner.

Back in May, New Rochelle had made national news when an arsonist had torched the high school. This had forced over three thousand students into two intermediate schools for a split session schedule, with the displaced students sharing time. At one junior high, some high schoolers would attend morning classes, and the junior high kids would attend in the afternoon. At the other, vice versa. Faith had felt as terrible as anyone else about the fire but was disappointed when, for her school, she still had to get up early. The one bright spot in her day was English class.

When the news broke, Vicki had sworn Faith to secrecy. They concealed the fact that Vicki knew the arsonist, a sixteen-year-old boy from NRHS. As lenient as the Fords normally were with their daughter, Vicki did not need that kind of heat. And Faith did not want to lose her only friend.

So, they hung out together and shopped. Like normal teenage girls.

Then, just after they had finished lunch at Burger King and were standing in line to see *The Secret Life of an American Wife* with tickets they had purchased by way of an obliging adult willing to aid a couple of underage girls into an R-rated film, it happened.

A group of kids about their age had congregated nearby, snickering and whispering. One of the braver ones had dared to approach. With a cocksure strut and a jutted chin, he had walked up and asked Faith, "So, do you only do older guys?"

The girls had frozen in place.

Mouth agape, eyes fierce beneath a furrowed brow, Faith finally found her words. Or rather, her word. "What?!"

When he repeated himself, she had kneed him hard in the groin, then fled the mall with Vicki close behind her. Confused and mortified, they abandoned their day out and escaped to the privacy of Vicki's bedroom.

Calls from Vicki to better-connected friends soon solved the mystery. Mr. Beam had been seen after school a few days before end of term, talking with a student. Rumor had it, they had been standing close to each other in a darkened hall. Too close. The subsequent discovery of a note hidden in his desk from that same student had sealed the English teacher's fate.

No inquiries had been made beyond the school notifying the girl's parents, who had agreed not to press charges on one condition. In exchange for a quick and quiet exit from their daughter's life, the parents had agreed not to involve the authorities.

"Oh my gosh, Vicki," Faith had exclaimed in horror. "That was me!"

It was Faith who had stood with Karl Beam in the hall that day after school, discussing a missing assignment that could impact her final grade. She had worn her leather jacket to appear older and hipper than she was. She had dared to stand close. She had hoped he felt as she did. She had even dared a little awkward flirting, though she had never before tried. But the busybody who had spied on them left out that Mr. Beam had stepped back when she stepped forward.

Likewise, Faith had put the letter in Mr. Beam's desk drawer. She had been too embarrassed to give it to him in person. He had obviously never found it.

Dear Mr. Beam,

You're the grooviest teacher in all New Rochelle. Probably the world. My days are bright every time I see you in class. I could listen to you every day for the rest of my life. Every song on the radio, I think of you. Especially "Young Girl" by the Union Gap.

Summer's coming soon. Do you have any cool plans? I don't, but I hope we can see each other. I'll do everything I can to keep my promise and write you that poem. Maybe I'll write you a song, too. Maybe someday, you'll write one for me.

Yours with Love,
Faith Annelisa Peterson

Everyone believed the rumor. So, Karl Beam was gone. Faith hated herself nearly as much as she hated Walt and Millie Peterson.

That afternoon, in a last-ditch effort to calm her friend's hysteria, Vicki had given Faith her first shot of whiskey. She had stolen it from her parents' liquor cabinet. At first, Faith had gagged on the bitter, burning taste. The second shot went down better. After the third, she was numb.

Drunk, humiliated, and heartsick, Faith had cried for two hours straight—right up until the moment she ran to Vicki's bathroom and lost the remnants of her Whopper Jr. and fries.

"Do we know where he went?" Faith pleaded as she vomited, head in the toilet while Vicki knelt beside her, holding her hair back. "Can I talk to him?"

"Nobody I talked to knows where he went. Someone said they knew his address but that the place is empty now. Did he ever talk about his family?"

The more hopeless the situation, the harder she cried. "I hate them!"

"I know. I'm sorry, Faith."

"I'm gonna kill my mother! This is all her fault! Bet me!"

Faith had spent that night at Vicki's, having appealed directly to her father to loosen the leash. It was just next door, after all. And instead of planning the murder of Millie and Walt Peterson, she took a hard look at the direction of her life.

"They have it all planned out for me," she had complained, once freshly showered and changed.

"Do they ever ask what you want?"

Over time, the effects of the whiskey had worn off. Vicki had lent her a spare nightgown and had plied her with aspirin, saltine crackers, and several glasses of water.

The answer was no. Her parents had never asked her what she wanted to do with her life. She existed merely as a ticket into the world they longed to live.

That night, she had fallen asleep listening to "Think" by Aretha Franklin.

The next morning, despite the hangover Vicki's home remedies attempted to prevent, Faith began to take charge of her future. Walt and Millie Peterson would just have to deal with it.

CHAPTER 10

"So that's it, yeah? You think I don't know?"

"Know what?!"

"You've been Fanny Flirt-eyes all bloody night!"

"You're drunk!"

"I may be drunk, but I'm not blind!"

A loud SLAP was the last straw. The couple had argued nonstop since he had picked them up at the club several blocks back. At first, Ronnie said nothing. None of his business. But he drew the line at violence.

He slammed the car to a full stop, sending both passengers tumbling toward the closed fold-down seats opposite them. "You drunken barmy bastard, get out of my cab!"

The man ignored him. He righted himself in his seat, then began pummeling his female companion.

Ronnie threw the cab into park, hastened out the driver's side, then jerked open the rear door. As the woman shouted and screamed in protest against the man's punishing blows, he reached in amongst their flailing limbs and bodies, grabbed the man by the collar, and yanked him out onto the pavement.

"What the hell are you doing?" the man slurred. "Take your hands off me!"

Ronnie balled up his fist, then brought it forward full-force, connecting with the man's jaw. He pulled back a second time but stopped short when he realized the first punch had done the job. The man's body slacked. He lost consciousness. Letting go of his collar, he watched the brute crumple to the ground, then kicked him hard in the stomach for good measure.

The woman sniffed back tears as she gathered herself together.

"All right?" Ronnie asked, propping his arm atop the car and leaning inside.

Her lips puckered into a pout. She nodded, but shuddered as she grabbed a 10-pack of Woodbine cigarettes from her purse.

He shut the door, then climbed back inside his vehicle and continued on, leaving the man on the side of the road. "Where to, then?"

Still shaking, she exhaled a cloud of smoke, then rattled off an address in Bethnal Green. "Thanks for the help. He gets that way when he drinks."

Two blocks down, Ronnie made a left at the intersection. They traveled in silence for the ten-minute trip. She attempted to fix her dress and makeup, her hands trembling as she fingered her elegantly coifed hair back into place.

The longer he stewed over what had occurred, the angrier he grew.

When he slowed to a stop in front of the two-up two-down Victorian terrace house on Hadleigh Street, the woman groaned from the back seat. "Please don't tell my brother about this."

A small group of suited lads, roughly his age, congregated outside the front door, laughing and smoking. They turned around as Ronnie pulled alongside them to drop off his fare. One of them bent forward and peered in through the windows, then smiled and stepped forward to open the rear door.

His smile disappeared as he beheld the disheveled wreck of his sister in the back seat.

Ronnie understood the man's unvoiced frustration all too well. Had any bloke taken a swipe at one of his sisters, he would have done him in.

Burying Polly was the hardest thing he had ever done.

Each subsequent night, Ronnie relived the second saddest day of his life. In his dreams, he left her improvised grave, dodged parachute bombs and planes as he flew of his own volition into German territory, and murdered Adolf Hitler with his bare hands.

The isolation of living as a stowaway in the Canning Town Library soon overtook him, so he grabbed the only remaining possession from his pre-war existence—the sad remnant of Polly's disintegrating bear—and made his way into the city to register for service. He had been obligated to do so nine months earlier, on his eighteenth birthday, but had neglected the duty to his country in deference to the obligation he had to his sole surviving relative.

With the liberation of Paris, he believed the war would end soon. He hoped the government would immediately conscript him into service so he would not miss his chance. He hoped they would send him to the front line. Maybe his dream would become reality. The Nazis had stolen everything from him. He longed to take a little back.

But fate had other plans for Ronnie Nock.

His registration in late August triggered a whirlwind of activity. On September 19th, they called him up by ballot according to the last digit of his registration number. But instead of the distinguished military uniform he had coveted, the Ministry of Labour and National Service promised him only Hobnail boots, gloves, a safety helmet, and blistered feet. For while Mother England had turned other boys his age into heroes, she had chosen to turn Ronnie into a human mole.

For the duration of the war, he worked the coal mines as a Bevin Boy. It was unforgiving labor, but provided a respite from the hand-to-mouth existence of street living. For that, Ronnie was grateful. He went down into the mines a boy, but emerged a man.

After the war, Ronnie returned to Canning Town along with hordes of evacuees. The time had come to heal. As a community. As a nation. And especially, as a man who sought to make his place in the world.

Thirty thousand Londoners had died; an additional fifty thousand had been wounded before Hitler finally took the coward's way out by way of a cyanide pill and a bullet to his brain. Nonetheless, London emerged victorious. It bustled with activity. A celebratory air replaced the choking stench of oil and soot. Reconstruction began immediately, despite a desperate shortage of building supplies.

Indeed, shortages impacted all areas of British life. But the hopelessness of the average resident still bound to their ration cards spelled opportunity for any budding entrepreneur with a penchant for the creative acquisition of goods by less-than-legal means.

Ronnie still possessed such talent, and nearly succumbed to his streetwise ways. But the fading memory of his parents, who had instilled in him the determination to make an honest living, however difficult, changed his mind—at least for a while.

"What's this, then!" The young man threw down his cigarette, angrily stomped it into the pavement, then demanded, "Where is he?"

"I'm fine!" The woman exited the taxi, waving frantically, her purse dangling and dancing from the strap slung across her forearm. "It was just a row, Tony. He didn't mean it."

"Where, Lizzy, eh?"

"Gone! I told him to bugger off already! Just leave him alone!"

Tony's nostrils flared as he shook his head. He turned back to the rest of the group and jerked his chin. Without a word, the men dispersed.

"No!" Liz yelled in wide-eyed protest. She rushed to her brother, urgently patting his chest. "N-n-no, please! Call 'em back!"

He ignored her pleas. Instead, he stepped to the front of the cab, twirling his index finger.

Ronnie rolled down the driver's side window.

Tony moved his sister aside and leaned against the frame. "You see what happened, mate?"

The sister screamed, demanding Ronnie keep his mouth shut.

"Stop it, Liz!" Tony turned and shouted. "Get inside with Mam!"

Sobbing into a closed fist, she reluctantly did as her brother had instructed. When she shut the door behind her, Tony turned back and stared expectantly at Ronnie. He did not repeat his question.

"I saw the whole thing. Wanker throttled her right there in my back seat."

"Yeah?" He straightened his stance and told Ronnie to get out.

Ronnie rolled the window up, cut the engine, then exited the cab.

Tony drew a fag from his pack, struck a match to light the end, then offered Ronnie one. When he declined, Tony shrugged and pocketed the pack and the book of matches. "And you drove?"

"As a matter of fact, I stopped. If you'd asked before you sent your mates off, I'd have told you to look for the bastard over in Mile End. He may still be passed out there on the road where I left him."

A grin played at the edge of Tony's lips. "That you, then?"

Ronnie held up his right hand to display its reddened knuckles.

The man paused, then slid his hand into his trouser pocket and pulled out a neatly rolled-up wad of money. Squinting his left eye, he held the cigarette between his lips, then peeled off several fivers, folded them in half, and handed them over between two fingers. "This should do it for the fare."

"Cheers, mate." Ronnie pocketed the money.

Tony nodded, looking him up and down. "How long you been driving?"

Ronnie grinned. "Since I picked up your sister and that bellend. She was my first fare."

He lifted his brows and exhaled smoke through his nose. "This may be the luckiest night of your life."

***

"Dear God. Please forgive us. And if anyone's angry, please tell them singing's a good thing. Angels sing, too. We mean no harm."

An unseasonal rain shower interrupted the otherwise temperate July afternoon. It had given the fields a fair soak, ensuring a stern lecture when he returned home with damp, muddied Levis.

Jordan had left the house after lunch to play with some mates from the village but had promised to return in time for dinner. Not that he relished the thought. Ben was by no means the most accomplished cook in the family. He could manage a grill okay, but it was the two younger Grant children who had inherited their mum's culinary skills.

The descending sun's position told Jordan he should have already started back. Problem was, he could not move. He knelt frozen in place, hands positioned palm-to-palm in prayer as he huddled upon the chalk and grass of Wain Hill, dead center upon the cross that had been carved into the landscape long before he was born.

"Please don't let them chuck our lovely home into the Lyde." He paused, squinting open one eye. He peered all about the area, scanning his surroundings, past the dense woodland all the way down to the Ridgeway to ensure no one had come upon him, be they human or spirit. Detecting no looming presence—real or otherworldly—he continued. "And please bring Mum and Dad back soon. With presents. Amen."

His friends had gone inside when the rain started, but Jordan did not want to return home. Not with his mother gone. So he had wandered off, bypassing Holy Trinity Church, straight for Wain Hill. A longer walk from Chapel Lane, but at least there were not any graves. Well, except for maybe the nearby barrow from whence Bledlow got its name.

If anyone knew his fears, they would laugh at him. He was eight years old. Almost a man, like Chris and Ben. Too old to be afraid. But he was, nonetheless.

A clap of thunder in the distance shook him. He swatted away a swarm of flying ants, then decided the fear of looming darkness outweighed his fear of returning to a house that might well lift off the ground and end up in the river. It was time to go home. Ben would kill him if he stayed out any later.

He stood and hooked his fingers into his belt loops, then hiked up his sagging jeans. It was a long walk home. He would never make it before sundown now, no matter how he tried.

To steady his nerves, he began singing "I Whistle a Happy Tune" from *The King and I*. But as he started his downhill trek, he heard Ben in the distance, calling his name.

His eyes bulged. He could not tell if his brother was mad or worried. Probably both. He swallowed, then scrunched his lips to one side. Time to face the music. "I'm here!" he called back at last.

"Get down here—now!"

He left the clearing and bounded down the twisting, turning paths until he met Ben near the bottom of the hill. His brother did not look happy.

"I've been looking for you for two bloody hours!"

Jordan lowered his head. "I'm sorry."

"It's too late to be up there. You said you'd be back for dinner. Besides, Dad heard a rumor there may be some kind of big cat prowling about. Maybe a cougar or something. You could've been eaten alive."

Cougars and ghosts. Was nowhere safe in Bledlow?

Arms akimbo, Ben stared off at the sunset. He shook his head. "I've been 'round to all your mates' houses. If we don't get back soon, the whole village will be out searching. Tomorrow, you're in for the day."

"No! You can't do that!"

He grabbed Jordan's upper arm and stomped off. "Mum left me in charge, so stop whinging."

Jordan jerked free but kept pace. "We can't stay in the house!"

"Why not?" Ben halted his gait, frowning in confusion.

He ground his teeth. "I can't tell you."

"Tell me."

He hesitated. "Well...because Mum's not there."

Ben continued on with a scoff, pushing Jordan slightly ahead to keep an eye on him. "It's only a couple of days. It's not like they've abandoned you."

Chris caught up with them at the church. Out of breath from his own frantic search, he bent forward, clutching his knees. "Right then," he panted. "Where was he?"

"The cross," Ben snapped, side-eyeing Jordan. "He's staying in tomorrow."

Jordan crossed his arms and pushed out his bottom lip.

"Nutter!" Chris shouted. "What were you thinking? Be glad he gave you a day. I'd have given you a right bollocking."

"It's your fault anyway!" He balled his fists at his sides. "You're the one who said!"

Chris sucked in his lips, trying not to laugh. He failed.

"Stop it!"

"Make me!"

Ben moved between them. "Enough!"

The laughter subsided, but Chris leveled a knowing stare at his younger brother. Eyes narrowed, Jordan seethed back at him.

"What did you do?" Ben demanded of Chris.

Chris's shoulders lifted in an innocent shrug.

When Jordan lunged forward, Ben caught him by the waist, then turned to Chris. "I already sorted this."

Chris stomped away with an indignant snort. "Brilliant, Ben. You sort it. Sort it all. I'm off, then."

"Let the neighbors know he's all right," Ben called after him.

Chris lifted his hand without turning around.

Once out of earshot, Ben bent down to Jordan's eye level. "So, what are you two on about? What happened?"

A shiver ran down Jordan's back. It was nearly dark. The temperature had started dropping. He bit the inside of his cheek, glanced at the church graveyard, then shivered again. "Chris made me promise."

"Look. I can't do anything if you don't say it."

"Fine." He dropped his head back, curving his shoulders downward into an exasperated shrug. "After Mum and Dad left this morning, Chris told me."

Ben rattled his head. "Told you what?"

"That he hoped I'd given Mum a proper kiss goodbye because…"

"Because…?"

"Because Mum won't be home to protect us. And we might not be here when she gets back."

The more Jordan explained, the more confused Ben's expression. "Why wouldn't we be here when they get back?"

"You know." Jordan urged with big eyes. "The big secret."

"What *big secret*?"

Jordan twisted his lips. "I already know. Chris told me before. The ghosts. See? I know. I've known since I was six."

Ben laughed despite himself. "What ghosts?"

"The ghosts of all the people who had funerals before Dad turned the old chapel into our house. Chris says the ghosts are mad because we're sinners and musicians and they want to pick up our house and toss it in the river."

Ben sat back on his haunches, propping his forearms on his knees. He stared blankly at his younger brother. "There's no such thing as ghosts. Chris was just having a go at you."

Adamant, Jordan shook his head. "Nuh-uh! I've heard them! Just last night, I heard—"

"You heard the wind, numpty."

"You're numpty! They're real!"

Ben stood and draped his arm around Jordan's shoulders as they walked on. "Ghosts aren't real. And even if they were, I'd save you. I'll never let anything happen to you, all right?"

"Promise?"

"Promise."

Jordan was too cold to argue. Plus, his stomach was empty.

They walked the rest of the way in silence as night settled upon the village. When they reached their house, a loud, mournful moan came from the bushes near the gate.

"Get ready for a right bollocking!" Ben shouted. He abandoned Jordan and took off running.

Chris sprinted out from his hiding place and raced toward the backyard. Ben followed in heavy pursuit.

Jordan glanced up at his bedroom window and froze in place. For a second, he thought he saw a shadow. Hopefully, their house would not end up in the River Lyde before morning.

***

In *A Wrinkle in Time*, Madeleine L'Engle explained the scientific concept of a tesseract. Her fifth-dimension tale of space and time "wrinkling" to travel from one place to another was precisely how Jameson Lockhardt regarded his quasi-dual life between Britain and America. A taxi driving "made man" in London; a seeker of fortune in New York. As if his past and future folded in upon one another, enabling him to pass quickly, and exist easily, between the two.

A wrinkle here, a wrinkle there.

At least until May. For within months of Jameson's arrival in the United States, Scotland Yard finally made their arrests. This included twins Ronnie and Reggie Kray, Freddie, and several Firm members. And while the charges levied upon them all involved the murder of two East End villains, the supposed suicides or accidental overdoses of music producer Joe Meek and Brian Epstein were not even a blip on Detective Nipper Read's radar.

Henry was safe in Spain. Jameson was free.

But from that moment on, Jameson knew things would change. He would have to travel the long road through his present circumstances. No more financial support. No more direction. And no wrinkling back and forth across the pond.

Ah, well. Science had never been his forté anyway.

Perched upon a dirty stool in a dark, rundown, sparsely filled Manhattan bar mere blocks from Madison Square Garden's new location on Pennsylvania Avenue, he nursed his second scotch. Alone as usual, even in public. Save periodic interactions with the bartender offering refills, no one bothered or approached him. Jameson liked it that way. Still, he would have preferred it if Ross had accepted his invitation for a drink before heading home.

"Can't do it tonight, I'm afraid."

"Josephine?"

Ross had confirmed. "She's getting annoyed over my frequent absences."

"I suppose we have spent our fair share of time together this summer."

"I've enjoyed it. However, I should pay my bride a little more attention. Rain check?"

"Certainly. Have a good weekend, my friend."

Rejecting the prospect of spending the night isolated in the compact, dreary, yet fully furnished apartment he had found in the Village Voice shortly after his January arrival, he opted for a walk, a meal, and a couple of drinks. It was probably for the best, he assured himself. The time had come to make some decisions about his future.

Jameson had arrived in America amongst the turmoil and transition of a nation to which he bore no allegiance. Sure, he kept abreast of local events as well as those back home. He was well aware of the Civil Rights movement and its escalating tensions. Though not reflective of his personal philosophy, the evolution from beatnik to hippie via drug-addicted malcontents like Ginsberg, Kerouac, and Kesey were not lost on him. Still, the US did not corner the market on social unrest. Hippies were essentially self-aggrandizing, next-generation beatniks who would likely become the very thing they claimed to protest.

During rare moments of social interaction with fellow patrons at the various diners and bars he had come to frequent, he eschewed all conversation involving the United States' involvement in an unpopular war, the current climate of insurrection, and its growing social unrest. King had been assassinated in Memphis back in April. Two months later, Bobby Kennedy had met the same fate over in Los Angeles. Those things mattered nothing to Jameson.

And that, he decided, underscored his greatest challenge.

What *did* matter to him? What were his long-term goals? Who was he, if not the man he had abandoned back in England? How would he survive, let alone thrive, in a country whose citizens increasingly stood for nothing except their misplaced, anarchistic rebellion against their perceived oppression? Such phantom enemies were rarely encountered by those who most fervently embodied the "causes" for which an entire generation currently fought. Most of these self-styled activists had never experienced real war anywhere near their front doors, or understood the professed ills fueling their self-righteous rage.

Maybe Jameson had missed his calling. Should he have stayed in England and gone into politics instead of fleeing to a nation in which he could not even vote?

Tough questions for someone approaching forty-three. Most men his age were closer to the end of their careers than the beginning. But that mattered little at this point. What mattered was that he find himself. And while he had initially believed he would end up a reformed family man, reconciled to the wife and child who had left him nearly a decade ago, he now realized he had been naïve. He had placed all his eggs in Sarah Lockhardt's basket. And she had broken every one of them.

So many calls. So many pleas. So many rejections. Maybe it was time to give up and file for divorce.

"Would ya look at that!" a nearby patron exclaimed from a few stools down. "Turn that up, will ya, barkeep?"

Jameson glanced up to the bulky black-and-white television set suspended in the far corner of the bar. He had come to recognize the face of CBS news correspondent Walter Cronkite. Tonight was night three of the Democratic National Convention, held in Chicago—another topic he refused to discuss with his fellow New Yorkers. Obviously, his future did not lie in politics after all.

The bartender climbed the ladder he kept near the television, increasing the volume just in time for Cronkite's recap of the previous night's uproar. More fighting over Vietnam. Bitter feuding over delegates. Pure tosh, all of it.

At least if Ross had met him for drinks, they could have discussed something—anything—more interesting than this.

Jameson envied Ross Alexander. Even respected him on some level. Although arguably gullible, he was not an unintelligent man. He knew his mind. He worked hard. Moreover, he was loyal. Loyal to his wife. Loyal to his employer. And apparently, loyal to his friends. Even friends who manipulated him in order to secure an alibi. A better man might have felt guilty about having proven that. And perhaps Jameson should.

The bar crowd swelled as the night wore on. When it got to the point where people sat upon the stools flanking him, he signaled the bartender for a final drink. But when the patrons began heatedly debating Edward Kennedy's withdrawal from a long list of potential presidential candidates, Jameson gulped down the remainder of his glass, dropped two bucks on the bar, and left.

He thought about seeing a movie, but decided to call it an early night. It would take him an hour to walk back to his apartment anyway. Money was not an issue, yet, but it was getting tight. Tight enough to walk instead of catching a cab. Worse, his previous sources of income currently resided at Her Majesty's pleasure. No help for him there.

As he approached the intersection at Fifth Avenue and West 23rd Street, kitty-corner from the Flat Iron Building, a brand-new Pontiac Bonneville pulled up beside him and stopped at the light. Windows down, its mop-top-haired, heavy eye-shadowed driver unabashedly sang along with the Fifth Dimension's "Stoned Soul Picnic" blaring from her radio. The driver's oblivious whimsy evoked within him a rare half-smile. What a difference a few blocks made. If he had to choose between political debate and musical abandon, he would choose the latter every time. Not that he had ever been prone to any type of abandon.

In hindsight, he counted himself fortunate to have narrowly escaped being dragged into yet another scheme to cement him into the life he had excelled in but never enjoyed. "Murder, Inc." they had called it. Ronnie Kray had always been enamored with the American mafia, fancying himself the ideal person to revive the murder-for-hire enterprise—but in

London. During Ronnie's last visit to America a few weeks before his arrest, Jameson met with him to discuss his future with the Firm. Jameson was in, if he wanted. Great money. But hard terms.

Jameson, however, was not a natural born killer. He had learned this the hard way. Fortune had smiled on him the day Nipper Read got his men, a mere month after having received the offer. Jameson knew of no one else who had gotten out of organized crime alive, still able to maintain the respect of their peers. No price on his head. No suspicions. His life was a clean slate.

So, what was next?

At some point, he might have to submit to the idea of having a boss. Jameson did not relish the idea of punching clocks, or being accountable for his every move. Better to start a business of his own, if he could.

"*Ooo! Surry!*" the driver sang, shooting her arm out of the Bonneville's open window, twirling her fist in the air as if working an invisible lasso. "*Ooo! Surry!*"

The song ended as the light changed. The Pontiac motored on down Fifth Avenue as the DJ reminded his listeners of the song title and group name. Jameson crossed the street, already tuned out. His future lay out there, somewhere. He needed to find it, soon.

CHAPTER 11

BOBBY HOPPED OUT OF BED an hour before his scheduled alarm. The clothes he had chosen the night before lay draped across his desk chair. All new. Everything was new.

Showered and dressed in twenty minutes, he crept down the hall. He inclined an ear to his mother's door, relieved when he heard nothing. Probably still asleep. He had heard her roaming around until well after midnight, so maybe she would stay in bed until later this morning.

Unlike most other nights, when he would lie awake for hours fretting over problems without solutions, Bobby had heard his mother last night because he was too excited to sleep.

Seventh grade! He felt liberated. One of the older kids now, he could finally ride any one of his three bikes instead of getting dropped off by his mother. That meant no more awkward calls from the car to come back to kiss her goodbye. FREEDOM!

He strolled into the kitchen whistling a tuneless melody and grabbed a box of Trix and a bowl. A glance around the counter told him his mother had not made his lunch. Even better. Her lunches made him feel five years old again. Today, he would make a man's lunch. Whatever that looked like.

Still whistling, he opened the fridge door to grab some milk for his cereal. No lunch in there, either. Or sandwich meat. Or lettuce. Or cheese. Or condiments. Until that moment, it had not occurred to him. She had not food shopped in weeks. Since their return from London, she had spent her time finalizing business matters surrounding his grandfather's estate. Then, it was clothes shopping at La Cumbre Plaza, which she had mercifully left almost entirely up to him.

Folding back the carton spout to sniff the milk, he nearly retched. He coughed and gagged from the stench of soured, curdled milk—if one could still call it that—as he poured the contents down the sink, then closed and dumped the waxed cardboard container in the trash.

Okay. No breakfast. That was okay. He was too excited to eat anyway. But what about lunch?

The sound of movement down the hall shifted his otherwise upbeat demeanor. First-day jitters assaulted him. Wrestling them into check, he left the kitchen to see if his mom was okay or if he should just hop on his bike and go.

Before he reached the hallway, she emerged, by all appearances ready for the day. Bedhead notwithstanding, she was fairly well put together. Crisp dress. Stockings. For a moment, he was overjoyed. She rarely looked so good first thing in the morning.

Then, he realized she might want to drop him off.

"We need groceries," she mumbled, skipping her typical morning greeting. "Have you seen my purse?"

"You don't have to go now."

"I forgot to go yesterday. There was so much going on with the estate, the sale, and having to deal with two countries. It's just…"

"It's fine, Mom. Why don't I make you some tea?"

"But your lunch. I didn't make it. There's nothing here. It was all—"

Poisoned, I know. "I'll make do." He stepped toward her, gently touching her forearm. "Really, Mom. Don't go just for me."

Her eyes flickered in confusion, as if trying to compute a complex math problem. "But…did you at least have breakfast?"

"Of course I did!"

"Are you sure?" She swept past him into the kitchen for a look around. "Where's your cereal bowl?"

He stood in the doorway, scratching his upper lip with his index finger. "I washed it and put it away already."

Sarah's demeanor lightened. She turned to him. "You did?"

"I didn't want to leave you with any dishes."

With a grateful smile, she glided into the living room, quick-pinching his cheek as she passed. "Such a helpful boy, my boy." A moment later, she whirled back around. "But that doesn't get you lunch."

He waved her off. "It's cool. It'll be a busy day. I probably won't have time to—"

"Nonsense! Students need lunch, Bobby. Everyone eats at school." She rushed back to the kitchen and rummaged through the fridge, then the pantry, then every drawer and cabinet. "They'll think I don't feed you. We have to find something. Something that won't kill you. Do they provide milk? Oh, of course not. We must find something, or they'll take you from me. It'll look like pictures."

He glanced down, biting his bottom lip. So much for the good mood.

"Help me!" she demanded, slamming the utensil drawer.

Bobby hastened forward, pretending to join the search, then went to his mother and held her. "It'll be okay, Mom."

She dissolved into tears. "I'm sorry."

The sound of his alarm clock ringing startled them both. He must have forgotten to switch it off before leaving his bedroom. He shushed her as he pulled away, whispering, "I'll be right back. Don't worry. It's okay."

When he returned, she had regained her composure. She stood in the living room, purse tossed onto the couch, hand outstretched. "Here. This should buy you lunch."

Bobby stared at the offering, his expression pained and hesitant.

"Not enough?"

"Mom, that's twenty bucks. Lunch won't be anywhere near that much. There's no way they'll make change."

Sarah looked away, staring either at or past the living room window. He could never tell which. Then, she turned back, brightening. "I'll drive you to school! We'll stop at the market, get you something quick to eat, and get change. We both know you didn't really have breakfast, anyway."

Everything inside him deflated. "But Mom..."

She searched his eyes until he detected a flicker of understanding. As if she could read his mind. The prospect shamed him.

"Wh—you...you don't want me to drive you, do you?"

Bobby peered down at their thick shag carpet, which probably had not seen a vacuum since July. His mother had enough trouble. He was being stupid. Selfish. It was not her fault. She was doing the best she could.

Lifting his chin with a crooked index finger, she said, "Bobby, we both know Santa messed up last Christmas. You have not one but three bicycles in the garage. You can ride one of them to school. I'll go to the market while you're gone. We won't have a repeat of this morning. Now go brush your teeth."

Relieved, he bounded down the hall. The morning had flown by until his early day became a race to beat the first bell.

A cursory brush, followed by a bit of mouthwash and a final combing of his hair, and he returned. He grabbed his satchel and sprinted for the door leading to the garage. Before he reached the handle, Sarah stopped him.

"Here," she said, her voice gentle and full of what sounded like regret. She held out her hand again.

At first, he shook his head, intending to remind her of their previous conversation. But instead of a twenty-dollar bill, her small hand clutched a wad of what looked like singles. He had no idea where they had come from, and did not want to ask.

"This should be enough. And they should be able to make change if you need it. Or have them give you credit if they can't. Call me if I need to come down. I'll get this sorted, Bobby. I'll be better prepared from now on. I promise."

He hugged her tightly, then accepted the balled-up wad of cash, which he shoved into his front jeans pocket.

When she winked at him, she appeared confident and more in control. Almost clear-eyed. It reminded him of earlier days. Better days. And maybe this day had recovered as well.

He kissed her cheek, then rushed out the door into the garage. He chose his newest bike, the smooth-shifting 10-speed with the magenta frame, dual handbrakes, and steel racing rims.

His mother watched from the doorway as he lifted the garage door, doubled back for the bike, then temporarily employed the kick stand while he closed everything up.

"Bye Mom!" he called, lowering the garage door. "See you after school!"

Maybe this year, he would not only make new friends, but also find a girlfriend. Anything was possible once a guy reached seventh grade.

***

Farin sat on the front porch swing, arms folded, pouting as she waited for her father. She had left her lunch box inside. Who wanted a pale blue Holly Hobbie lunch box, anyway? She had wanted the red Pussycats one. Or the Beatles. Or even Elvis.

Holly Hobbie. That was for babies. Even Snoopy would have been better than Holly Hobbie.

"Sorry, hon," her mother had said after breakfast while clearing and rinsing dishes, all happy and smiling, as if it did not even matter. "They were out of the Pussycats, so I picked the one with the little girl wearing a dress. Besides, you're too young for the Beatles. They looked like they were meant for boys anyway. Just use this for now and we'll replace it as soon as we can. I'll look again today while I'm out. Deal?"

"But *Mommy*—"

Across the table, the top of her dad's newspaper folded downward. "C'mon now, Farin. It's not Mommy's fault."

Maybe not. But it was her mom's fault that her head hurt. All that straightening and pulling her hair into a bun. It was so tight, her face felt like it would rip in two.

She scratched near its center, careful not to mess it up. Otherwise, her mother might insist on redoing it.

"There you are." Her father walked out onto the porch. The creaky screen door swung shut behind him. "What are you doing out here?"

"Waiting." She pushed out her bottom lip.

He looked like he wanted to laugh. "Where's Holly?"

She peered at him without answering.

Arms stretched wide, he yawned, glancing skyward. "What a pretty day. Isn't it pretty?"

Farin kicked her legs out, then in, repeating the movements until the porch swing moved. Beneath her, she felt her leotard snag on the wooden bench. Her eyes bulged.

"Those shoes still giving you trouble? Mom told me they gave you blisters."

She shook her head. "Mommy said to wear them around the house so I'd get used to them. Look!" She lifted her legs so he could see. "They feel better now."

"Terrific!" He sat down next to her, encircled her in his arms, and gently rocked the swing.

The snagged leotard had started running, but she was too angry over Holly Hobbie to tell her mother. Instead, she cuddled into her father.

"You nervous about starting school?"

She shrugged.

"Big day for a big girl."

She nodded into his chest.

"You'll meet a bunch of new kids."

"Why can't Marci go?"

He squeezed her shoulder. "Marci's going, just not to your school. She's going to one closer to her house."

"Not fair."

"You'll still see her on the weekends and when we all go out. Nothing's changed." He sat forward, lifting his arm so she could sit up. "What's this? Are you crying?"

She pinched her quivering lips but shook her head.

"You sure?"

She wiped her eyes.

He shot her a mischievous look, then whispered in her ear, "Wanna take a brown bag for your lunch instead of Holly?"

She nodded, fighting the sudden tug of a smile.

He winked, then headed inside. "Leave this to me."

Her mother met him at the door, clutching the brown bag lunch.

"Now look at this!" He opened the screen door. "Mommy saves the day!"

With a flourishing flip of her wrist, she handed it over, cutting eyes at him. "Softy."

Farin hopped off the swing, eyes alight. "Thank you, Mommy!"

"Uh-huh." She looked at her father like they shared a secret. Then, refocusing her attention, she arched an eyebrow and finger-beckoned her daughter. As Farin approached, she stepped aside. "C'mon, you. Let's change those tights."

"Don't be long," her father called after them. "I'm starting the car."

They went upstairs for new stockings. Her mother even said she would make it so her hair no longer hurt her head.

"Mommy? Can you talk to Aunt Carol?" Farin sat as still as she could while her mother changed her hair from a bun to a braid.

"About what?" she asked out of the side of her mouth, bobby pins pinched between her lips.

"About Marci going to school with me."

Beth spoke to her through the vanity mirror. "I thought Daddy explained that."

Farin squinted at her. "You heard us?"

She waggled her brows. "I hear everything."

Her stomach dropped at the thought.

"I'll ask Aunt Carol to stop by after she picks up Marci from school so you two can play a bit before dinner. How's that?"

"Okay. But can you still ask about school?"

"You know you'll make other friends, right? Dozens, in fact."

"I want Marci."

Her mother finished her hair, grabbed a new pair of tights, then bent down to help her into them. "This isn't like the lunch box, honey. Aunt Carol and I don't make the rules. Kids go where the schools tell them to. If we lived closer, it'd be different. Do you want to live closer? We wouldn't be near the beach."

Wide-eyed, Farin shook her head. "No! I wanna stay by the beach."

Beth stood and looked her over, nodding her approval. "Okay, kiddo. You're all ready."

"We're not gonna move, right Mommy? I wanna stay by the beach."

"Me too." She gave Farin's nose a playful flick.

Outside, her father honked the horn.

"Time to scoot! You have everything? Your bag? Your lunch?"

Farin nodded. As they trotted downstairs, she asked, "Mommy? Why aren't you taking me to school?"

Her mother opened the screen door with a sigh and waved to her father. "Because the first day of school is a really big deal. Most mommies cry. You'll see. And the last thing you want is for me to cry while you try to meet all those new friends, right?"

Farin gasped. "Don't cry, Mommy! I'm a big girl."

Her mother bent down to hug her. When she stood back up, Farin suspected she would cry anyway. "Now go. You don't want to be late. I'll be there this afternoon to pick you up."

Climbing into the front seat, Farin heard "People Got to Be Free" by the Rascals on the radio.

"All set?" her father asked before pulling out of the driveway.

She propped her elbow onto the armrest and rested her head in her palm.

"You okay?" He side-eyed her as he shifted the car into reverse.

"Mommy said she's not taking me to school on the first day because she doesn't wanna cry. Is that true?"

"Mommies sometimes do that."

Farin made a face. "You're not gonna cry, are you, Daddy?"

"I'm not," he assured. "And neither are you."

"Can we turn up the radio?"

"Ready to sing?"

"Daddy, I'm always ready to sing."

***

Chris and Elliot never discussed Elliot's home life. Chris had met Mr. Lawrence a few times working out in the garage, but had never even glimpsed his mom. No one at their house talked much. Of the four kids, Elliot was the oldest. Then there was a sister, a brother, and another sister. Elliot watched them an awful lot.

But not this weekend. This weekend, the boys were on an adventure. The Lawrence family's odd aloofness had been the key that had opened the door, so to speak.

Finagling tickets had started earlier in the month. The Doors had appeared on *Top of the Pops* in early September. The boys had watched in open-mouthed wonder as they had performed "Hello, I Love You." The following two nights, the band would play the Roundhouse, and Chris had been determined to go.

"We can take the train to London. I'll tell my mum I'm staying with you."

It had taken little to convince Elliot. One of the reasons the boys got on so well was their shared love of rock'n'roll and their plan to one day start a band. Inseparable mates since the day they met, they practiced every chance they got. In fact, Chris believed they had become quite good. Even Ben had said so.

That Saturday, they had taken the train into London. But when they got to the venue, they learned the concert had been sold out. They tried to buy a couple of scalped tickets, but went away disappointed. The cost was greater than they could scrape together. Older customers could easily pay the inflated asking price.

"I guess that's that," Elliot had said, frustrated as they sat with their backs against a long wall of billboards on Chalk Farm Road amid dozens of other failed seekers, debating aloud whether to try to slip in via the stage door.

"What about tomorrow?" Chris had suggested. "We'll try again."

"Don't bother," a nearby eavesdropper had chimed in.

Elliot stood and stretched. "Let's get back. No use standing 'round for nothing."

Chris had resisted. There had to be a way. And when he overheard a couple of blokes discussing their alternate plans, he found one.

"We're going to Frankfurt," he announced on the train back to Bledlow.

Elliot stared blankly at him.

"Can I tell my parents I'm spending the whole weekend?"

"We're not going to Germany," Elliot insisted. "You're barmy, mate."

"Oh yes we can. And here's how."

Chris spent the week between the Roundhouse and Frankfurt concerts plotting their trip, constructing an alibi, and stealing enough money for the various transport and concert tickets as well as food. They could never rent a room without an accompanying adult, but Chris doubted they would sleep much anyway.

"We're really doing this?" Elliot asked that next Thursday.

"Yep," Chris said. "We leave tomorrow."

Being a middle child had presented many disadvantages over the years, but sometimes, it worked in his favor. Between Ben's budding career and Jordan's *wunderkind* status as the family favorite, no one would miss him. And if they discovered the £100 he had nicked from his father's money stash in the garage, he would have still seen the Doors. Some crimes were worth the punishment.

"You'll be practicing with Elliot the whole weekend, then?" his mother had asked as she helped him pack a bag. "Fancy some fresh cakes?"

Normally, he would have refused. How embarrassing to have your mum pack you snacks for a weekend kip-over with your mate. But the train ride from Calais to Frankfurt alone was six hours. Add in an hour and a half ferry from Dover to Calais and it made for a long day. An expensive day. Plus, the trip back. So, Chris accepted his mother's generosity.

"Ring us Sunday night," she had pressed. "Your father can bring your school bag 'round so you'll have it for class Monday."

Stuffing the cash into his bag, Chris rolled his eyes but nodded in agreement. Better to avoid another fight about school.

He had not attended more than three days this term. Why did it matter? His future lay outside academics. Besides, he could read, write, and do sums in his head. He read the odd novel now and again. Who cared if he finished traditional education? He had his guitar and an entire world to learn about. As far as he was concerned, school was out. Permanently. The only thing he would miss was the girls. But he would pull more birds with a guitar than a certificate, anyway.

A tinge of guilt nagged at him as they left. Not because he had lied about his plans, but because of the money. He comforted himself by promising to replace all of it once he and Elliot were big-time rock stars.

They headed out Friday afternoon, riding the train to the Port of Dover, where they bought tickets for a morning ferry, then sought a place to sleep. The port was bigger and busier than Chris had remembered from previous trips with his family.

"What if someone asks where our parents are?" Elliot whispered after the second time security ran them out of a hiding place.

"They won't," Chris said, more determined than confident.

For the most part, they wandered the night away, keeping clear of potentially curious adults. By morning, they were exhausted, and the cakes Chris's mum had packed were long gone.

"Sure we can do this?" Elliot asked as they queued up to board the ferry.

Chris slapped his back. "We've come this far. And tonight, we're gonna see the Doors."

They chose a bank of seats near a family to blend in, then slept atop their bags the entire trip across the channel.

Once at the Calais Ferry Terminal, Chris became overwhelmed. They were already a long way from home. Half their journey still lay ahead. And, like the Port of Dover, the terminal was massive and unfamiliar. He did not even speak French—or German, for that matter.

"Which way do we go?" Elliot rubbed sleepy eyes with his free hand, clutching his bag with the other. "How do we get to the train from here?"

Chris bit his lip and looked around. He did not want Elliot to think he was a coward. This had been his idea, after all. So he pretended, and focused on the concert. "Let's ask someone."

The first five people they approached did not speak English, but a sixth gave them directions. They walked the forty-minute trek to the train station but got lost twice before they arrived.

"We can always go back, mate," Elliot had offered.

He flatly refused.

It surprised Chris that so few adults paid them any attention. When formulating his plan, his biggest fear had been getting caught traveling alone in a foreign country. But for the most part, people ignored the two youths with their unkempt appearance and canvas bags.

The train ride from Calais to Frankfurt passed quickly because they slept through most of it. More problematic was getting from the train to the concert hall. On top of the language barrier, Chris had forgotten the address. But thanks to an accommodating twenty-something who understood their awkward hand gestures and probably recognized familiar words like "Jim Morrison," they made it in time to secure tickets and find food before the concert started.

Chris never told Elliot that, prior to their arrival, he had no idea whether they would find themselves facing another sold-out venue.

"How's the cash?" Elliot asked as they stuffed themselves with bratwurst and bread rolls. "All right, then?"

Chris swallowed a huge mouthful, chasing it with his Afri-Cola. "Tight, but okay. Tickets are sorted. Train and ferry were round-trippers. The rest's food. We'll be back in England tomorrow, anyway."

The answer satisfied Elliot. They finished their meal, then joined the queue waiting outside the *Kongresshalle* for the doors to open.

Several older boys passed marijuana joints down the line. Chris and Elliot looked at one another, wordlessly daring the other. Chris indulged, then passed it on. Elliot tried it as well. The smoke made him cough when he exhaled.

Amongst the German chatter of fellow fans, Chris discerned some English. He glanced back and saw a scrawny bloke with a couple of kids who looked about their age. He nudged Elliot. "Hear that? I think they speak English."

Elliot peered down the line. "So?"

"Maybe we can get a ride back to the train after the concert. Hold my place. I'm gonna ask."

Minutes later, Chris returned with the two boys in tow.

"This is Elliot," he told them. "El, this is Todd Dalton and Lance Turner. Lance's brother brought them over in his van. They were on the same ferry as us!"

"Hiyah." Elliot leaned sideways to chin-lift an acknowledging greeting at Lance's brother.

Chris waved the brother up, defying the groaning protests of others in line.

They chatted as they inched forward in the queue, occasionally accepting another toke off a traveling joint. Lance's brother, Clifford, bought them all fizzy drinks before they took their seats.

Though separated at first, Chris managed to charm the two German girls beside Clifford in the back row to take their closer seats, leaving the five of them together in the last row.

"Are those drumsticks?" Chris asked Lance, who sat between his brother and Elliot.

Lance smiled. "I play a bit."

"They're always either in his pocket or his hands," Clifford interjected, mussing his brother's moppy black mane.

"We play, too," Chris said, chest out, trying to appear taller and less lanky as he bragged. "Elliot's a bass player. I play guitar."

"How old are you two?" Clifford grinned curiously.

In unison, Chris and Elliot blurted out their rehearsed lie, "Fourteen."

Clifford eyed them doubtfully, then grew serious as he peered past them. "Todd, what is that?"

Sitting in the aisle seat, Todd Dalton held a plastic cup of what looked like Kool-Aid. He took a drink. "Some bloke gave it to me."

"What *bloke*?" The light air surrounding their conversation dissipated as Clifford pressed the boy.

Todd shrugged. "Dunno. But it's free."

Clifford pushed past Lance, Elliot, and Chris, but Todd had downed the drink before Cliff could stop him. His eyes narrowed as he scanned the crowd. "Point out this bloke."

Todd stood and stared out at the crowd of people. "I didn't really see him."

Clifford swore under his breath, then waved the boys into an impromptu huddle. "Look, you lot. I don't know how Chris and Elliot got here without a chaperone, but I hereby elect myself leader of you misfits. Now, I don't want to go to jail over this, got it?"

The boys groaned in protest. "You're not our mum! This was supposed to be fun!"

"Oi!" he semi-shouted, staring down each of them in turn. "Not one of you should be here, and we all know it. So, here's the ground rule. There's only one. Wanna smoke a little? Fine. But this is important. Do NOT drink anything unless I give it to you myself. Got it?"

Todd jutted a defiant chin. "Why not? Look at me! It's not poison, then, is it?"

Clifford set his jaw as the house lights lowered. "Any of you take another free sample and I'm herding the lot of you back to London tonight."

Elliot and Chris traded glances, lifted their shoulders, then sat down.

Concertgoers all around them continued to pass joints. Chris and Elliot participated, as did the rest of their group. Even Clifford partook a time or two, while continuously glancing down to the end of the row at Todd.

Chris thrilled as Canned Heat, the Doors' opening act, took the stage.

The crowd cheered. The discordance of bumped cymbals sounded as drummer Frank Cook sidestepped into his kit. Chris came alive at their energy, vowing to remember this night as long as he lived. It was worth every risk they had taken getting here. He even glimpsed Robby Krieger offstage.

But before Canned Heat finished their opening act, the boys understood why Clifford Turner had taken the lead. For all Chris's effort to steal and lie his way into seeing the Doors in concert, he only watched Jim Morrison and his bandmates perform their first three songs.

His mind had thickened by then. He felt curiously tall. Every movement, whether his or someone else's, seemed to happen in slow motion. He barely discerned Todd's sprinting out of the seat with a loud shout and rushing the stage. Soon after, Clifford corralled all four of them out of the *Kongresshalle* and into his Commer FC.

Every so often, as they navigated out of Frankfurt toward the A560, Lance's brother shouted over his shoulder for them to help keep Todd inside. To Chris, the six-hour drive felt eternal as they raced out of Germany, through Brussels, and headed to France. Instinct told him the scene should have him panicked. He just could not reason why.

"But the train," he asked outside Ghent. He nudged Elliot, who sat bleary-eyed and half-conscious beside him. "Mate, where's the train station?"

A spontaneous burst of laughter escaped Elliot, something Chris had never experienced. Moments later, he and Lance scrambled forward again to block the van's side door as Todd insisted he wanted to fly home, which he did repeatedly when not staring at his hands.

Elliot swayed as he addressed Chris. "I think we passed the station."

"Hey mate," Chris slurred toward the front of the van. "Where's the station?"

"Bugger the station!" Cliff shouted, head forward, eyes on the road. "Just keep Todd inside. I'm getting you back to London before you lads get us a first-class ticket to the Old Bill."

Clifford swore, then mumbled something about things going all to pot every time he let his brother talk him into one of his adventures.

Chris's lids grew heavy. He envied Lance. Ben would have never taken him to Germany for the most epic night of his life.

CHAPTER 12

*I*T WAS LIKE CINDERELLA, BUT *not. Maybe Cinderella with an East End twist.*

"Say yes. Say you'll go," one of them coaxed.

Ronnie declined. "I spend all day in London. Why go back at night?"

Another one piped up. "Because it's Friday night, mate. Because you've never once gone out with us. Because it'll be fun. Remember fun?"

Actually, no. Ronnie did not remember the last time he had had "fun." Further, these fellow drivers were acquaintances, not friends. He could not even recall their names.

Ronnie had survived a war that claimed his entire family, had worked in England's coal mines until his lungs were compromised, and had spent six years after war's end learning the Knowledge—painstakingly walking the London streets until he had memorized her every road, every alley, and the best route to every address. Tireless work for a man without an education and few choices. Yet, what Ronald Nock lacked in opportunity, he made up for in raw ambition.

Notwithstanding the cozy relationship he had developed with some lower-level members of the East End's gangland community, he had abandoned his former criminal ways. No more stealing. No more fighting. No more bobbies busting him over his many petty crimes. And no more living on the streets. He now slept in a proper bed each night in his rented room, worked an honest job, and saved every halfpenny he could in the hopes of one day buying a small home of his own. He had, after all, promised Polly.

The last thing he needed was a foolish night of drinking and pulling birds.

"My mum said there's some ladies' ball over at Town Hall," a third suggested.

"A ball?"

The 1952 London Season had started. Not exactly something he would categorize as "fun." Besides, Ronnie had had his fill of events involving the Royals over the past few months. With King George's death and funeral, and the subsequent fanfare surrounding Queen Elizabeth II's ascension to the throne, he had carried more than his fair share of tourists to the various iconic locations throughout London in their hopes of catching a glimpse of any member of the British monarchy. "Cheers, lads, but no thanks."

"Aw, c'mon, Ron. Take a chance, then."

Indeed.

He agreed to go, but insisted he drive himself so he could leave as soon as he got bored. Watching from a distance while pretentious debutantes filed in and out of posh ballrooms with their flowing taffeta gowns and their timid, nose-in-the-air escorts would surely get him home in no time.

The event took place at Town Hall. No sooner had the cabbies parked their cars than the scenario Ronnie had envisioned materialized. Dozens of bejeweled young women in full-length gowns, coifed hair, and white gloves emerged from chauffeured cars and limousines, their mardy escorts waiting to link arms and lead them inside.

Ronnie groaned as if in physical pain. "That's it for me—"

The others shushed him, then produced a brown bagged bottle of liquor and passed it around.

He took a swig, passed it to his left, then pointed at the parade. "This all there is, then? We sit here, watch, and get pissed? This is what you lot deem fun? I've been in this cab all bloody day."

"Look at that one with the ruffles!" one said.

The others gawked and commented on the ugly ones, the pretty ones, the heavy-set ones, the dresses, the potential suitors, and the various things they might do if any one of them could trade places with those suited gents.

Ronnie passed bored and went straight into annoyance. When the bottle came back to him, he took a greedy gulp before handing it over to the next fellow.

Then, he saw her.

He could not pin down exactly how the blonde with the strapless gown— one among so many others—had caught his attention. She had tripped slightly as she exited her Bentley, then had struggled with her wrap. He could not take his eyes off her. Awkward and beautiful, but she possessed something, an understated softness in her countenance.

The intangible "something" about her drew him forward before he realized he had exited his cab.

"What're you doing?" one of his fellow drivers called after him.

"Where are you going?" asked another.

"Come back here before they see us!" demanded the third.

But on he went. He strode toward her, eyes fixed, as the girl's driver exited their vehicle to lend his assistance.

The warnings of his comrades fell to background noise.

The woman arched and craned her head around to peer down the back of her dress, then thanked her driver as he helped fluff out her train. Ronnie got close enough to hear their short exchange.

"I'm so clumsy. Thank you, Ulfred."

"Certainly, miss."

She glanced briefly toward the Town Hall doors, then back again. "I think he's coming."

The driver finished his task, then straightened and stepped unobtrusively back to the car.

She squared her shoulders, at once the visual embodiment of London society. A man younger than Ronnie descended the steps, his suit tails flapping behind him as he rushed to collect his date. He took his place beside her, offering his arm. When she nodded her acceptance, her eyes darted away from the hall, as if embarrassed by the pomp and circumstance.

Ronnie knew she had seen him. He parted his lips to say hello, but no words came forth.

A moment later, the escort whisked her inside the hall.

He stood in the middle of the street, staring at the doors as if awaiting her return. Behind him, he heard the jeers and laughter of his so-called mates.

"See? What did we tell you?"

"She's a right beauty, that one."

"Go on, then, Ron! Go in and chat her up—we dare you!"

Though too far away to be sure, he believed her eyes were blue. That would doubtless describe half the girls inside. But this one...this one was different.

One of the lads rushed forward and roughly put his arm around Ronnie's shoulders. "She looked right at you! What're you gonna do about it?"

Ronnie shook his head. "Nothing."

"What?"

"There's nothing to do. She's inside and I'm out here."

"So go inside, you nutter!"

He did not respond to the ridiculous suggestion. Even if he did not look dirty and disheveled after a long day's work. Even if he could possibly fit into such a different world than from whence he had come. Even if she had marched outside and invited him herself, it could not happen. He had nothing to offer a woman...least of all, himself.

His heart had long since died. It lay in two pieces, in a grave below the sad remains of the now-tarmacked South Hallsville School on a street gone so long now, too few remembered it.

Arm still crooked around his neck, the first gent laughed as he addressed the others. "Willie Wandought here is shook!"

The cabbies laughed and taunted him.

"Plonker!"

"Poof!"

At first, Ronnie tried to control his temper. But as they continued, pride won the battle over reason. These gobbins wanted him to make a move? They would pay for it.

He grabbed the bottle and took an impressive gulp, wiping his mouth with the back of his hand. "Right, then. What's the wager?"

The boys laughed and spoke over one another. At last, they came to a consensus. "You have to get inside and get her to dance with you."

Ronnie scraped his upper lip with his bottom teeth. He had gone to dance halls a time or two, but was nobody's Fred Astaire. Still, he had come this far. And he needed the money. "A century."

They gasped collectively, then went silent as they traded looks.

"Blimey, Ron. That's a lot of dosh."

"Your game, my rules. Besides, I need a dinner jacket."

The drunkest among them took the bait. "All right, then. A hundred quid. Don't worry, lads. He won't get in the door."

Ronnie raised an eyebrow. "Fancy another go for just the door?"

His confidence killed the additional bet.

He left the boys and casually strode across the street toward the hall, avoiding eye contact with the two men guarding the entrance doors. Keeping his stride as he passed, he ducked down the side of the building as his fellow cabbies gawked.

A small group of escorts stood outside, smoking. To Ronnie, they all looked the same. Same height, same build, same age, same pampered expressions. As he approached, all but one finished their cigarettes, crushed them out with the toes of their shoes, and returned inside. The one who remained turned his nose up as Ronnie walked by.

He never saw Ronnie's fist before it found its target. Without a word, the boy dropped to the ground, unconscious. Not the most honorable moment of Ronnie's life but, after all, he did need the money. He could not rent a room forever.

Changing in the dark side street was less than optimal, but he managed. He stripped the unconscious young man of his suit, switched clothes, then dragged him a few yards down. Likely, he had little time before the boy came to, so he rushed inside and wandered the maze of corridors until he finally found the ballroom.

Hundreds of white dresses and penguin-looking suits danced in a regal sort of undulation that left Ronnie overwhelmed. Any minute, security or police could arrive to drag him off. He needed to find the girl and get that dance.

Standing against a wall, he scanned the girls' faces as they twirled inside their escorts' arms. As seconds turned to minutes, he feared he might not find her. Worse, he feared he would go away all mouth and no trousers.

"Hello," came a soft voice from beside him.

He whirled around to face her, fearing she may be flanked by authorities. But fear morphed into elation. It was her. Somehow, she had noticed him first.

"I'm sorry to be so forward, but..." She stared at him quizzically, her blue eyes sparkling. With a slight shake of her head, she asked, "Do I know you?"

In an instant, his confidence returned.

He glanced around the room to ensure he had not yet been caught, then smiled her way. Hand across his middle, he bowed and said, "Not yet. But give me one dance, and I'll tell you anything you want to know."

***

Ross never heard him say it, but he got the impression Jameson needed money. He had not asked him about his situation, but his friend had not once offered to pick up the check the last three times they met for lunch. Occasionally, he would reach across the table in some feigned attempt to grab the bill, but he never put up a fight when Ross inevitably insisted on paying.

Pretense aside, Jameson had visually flourished in the nine months since moving to America. He wore suits at all times, exuding assertiveness in his walk and manner. He had slimmed down and firmed up to the extent that Ross wondered if he had spent time exercising at the YMCA. Or if he had himself a girlfriend.

Equally astonishing was that Jameson seemed to have absorbed his surroundings like an igneous rock. It seemed only his British accent separated him from natural-born New Yorkers. Notably, he knew the subway and theater schedules, the best restaurants in the city, and the bars with the most generous pours.

The man had a chameleon-like way about him. Proficient in every topic they discussed. Even the entertainment industry. This impressed Ross, reinforcing his belief that Lockhardt was a learned man. More and more, it felt like talking to a colleague instead of a friend or acquaintance. Jameson would doubtless break through whatever financial barriers currently plagued him.

"And what about you?" Jameson asked, nodding his thanks at the waiter who had delivered their drinks. "The last time we spoke, you'd started making inquiries. Any progress?"

Ross leaned back in his seat, folding his hands atop his lap. "None yet. But it's nearly Thanksgiving. I should've waited until after the holidays to start shopping my resume."

"Anyone at the office suspect you're looking?"

"Honestly? I suspect everyone's doing the same. Polydor's made it clear they won't bail us out. And G's too stubborn to sell to EMI."

Jameson sipped his scotch. "Pride's a destructive force."

Ross toasted the astute observation. "This time next year, no one will even remember the name Conserves Records."

They ordered two specials and another round of drinks. Ross had an afternoon meeting, so he would need to cut short their usual hours-long lunch. They discussed the latest charts, which included none of Conserves Records' artists, and how Josephine had made overtures about Ross getting back into corporate law if he did not find another position soon.

"It's almost too bad I chose law. There's a sweet A&R position open over at GPG right now. Unfortunately, I'm better at spotting contractual loopholes than talent. Otherwise, I'd consider applying."

"Maybe you should forget applying to other companies. Get your own A&R man and start your own label."

At this, Ross chuckled heartily. "Sure. How hard could that be, right?"

"There are worse things than having your own business."

"Not *this* business. Besides, it's difficult. You need ready talent, a lot of capital, reliable industry contacts, and experienced employees."

Jameson tilted his head. "There are ways to get those things."

"Luck and timing, my friend."

"We make our own luck."

Ross considered the comment. Quite a boast for a man who, he suspected, had little means. Then, it hit him. "What about you?"

"Me? What about me? You want me to start a record label?"

"No-no. The GPG job. What if you applied?"

The waiter arrived with their meals. Jameson shook out his folded napkin and draped it atop his lap.

"I'm serious," Ross pressed, moving his drink aside to make room for his plate.

"In A&R?"

"Why not?"

"I've never worked a day in the entertainment business, for one."

"What if I recommended you?"

Jameson scrunched up his face. "How would that work? You haven't even heard back from putting out your own resumes. And didn't you just say you'd apply if you had any experience?"

Ross scooted his chair closer to the table, tossed his tie over his shoulder, and grabbed his fork. "No. I said I didn't have that talent bank. And I don't. But you? You're a virtual savant."

They conversed little as they ate. Ross hoped Jameson would consider the offer. For some reason, it seemed a perfect fit. If Jameson could absorb the ins and outs of an entire industry over periodic mundane chatter with a friend, how could he fail?

When they finished eating, Ross checked his watch and decided they had time for a final drink, though they declined the offer of dessert when the waiter came to clear their plates.

"Any plans for Thanksgiving?" he asked, dabbing the corners of his mouth with his napkin.

"Yes. I plan to avoid Times Square."

"No turkey?"

He grinned over his tumbler as he brought it to his lips. "It's not yet Christmas, mate."

"You've never had a traditional Thanksgiving, have you?"

"I've never had any Thanksgiving."

Ross thought a moment. "Would you like to join Josephine and I? She has some family coming, but I doubt she'd mind one more. It's about time you two got to know each other better anyway, I'd say. Especially with all this talk of starting a record label."

Jameson wagged his finger at him. "You're thinking about it."

"Right now, I'm thinking about how I can persuade you to apply for that A&R position."

He looked him over. "You were serious about that, weren't you?"

"Dead serious."

"And you'd be willing to give me a reference?"

"Without hesitation. You have something, my friend. Not sure what it is, but I'd wager my reputation that you have it."

"Hmm." He twirled his empty vessel in his hands. "It'd be a helluva birthday present, to be sure."

"Your birthday's coming up?"

"It's today, in fact."

"Is it?"

"Forty-three today."

Ross rightly assumed he would once again pick up the check.

***

For months, the Peterson household had existed in a state of cold war. War between Walt and Millie. But mostly, war between Faith and her parents.

"If you sneak out of your room one more time," Millie would shout, "I'll have your father put bars on your window!"

"If you put bars on my window, I'll stop going to practice!"

"If you stop going to practice, you'll never be allowed out of this house!"

"Try and stop me! I'll run away! Or I'll call the child protective authorities—and I'll never step one foot inside Juilliard!"

"Millie," Walt would intervene. "Maybe we should talk about this."

"Talk about what, Walt? You give in to that child every time!"

"I don't need you to fight my battles for me, Daddy!" Faith would scream. "You've done enough!"

"What's that supposed to mean?"

"Forget it! I'm going to Vicki's! Don't freak out. I'm not sneaking—but I am spending the night!"

And so it went.

No one really wanted to know if anyone else would make good on their threats. On the upside, Faith had stopped pretending to be the dutiful daughter. She and her parents had reached an impasse. Neither side would negotiate. So they settled into an uneasy coexistence that made no one happy.

"You can't stay mad, Faith. Not tonight. It's New Year's Eve! Now fix your makeup and grab something cool to wear."

She had brought nothing with her but her leather jacket. "I'll need to borrow something of yours."

"No prob. Take whatever you want!"

Faith had moved beyond the planning stage. Now, she counted the days until she could leave Walt and Millie Peterson in the dust. Tonight, she would usher in a new year and be one calendar digit closer to living her own life. Come on, 1969!

If only she could find Mr. Beam.

She drew out one of Vicki's oversized T-shirts and grabbed a pair of black vinyl, 30-inch-high stretch go-go boots. "What about this?"

Vicki quit teasing her hair mid-stroke. She stared at Faith through her vanity mirror. "That's my dad's T-shirt. I sleep in that."

Faith held the shirt to her shoulders, scrutinizing her look in the floor-length mirror affixed to Vicki's bedroom door. "I dunno. I think it's groovy."

"It's December," Vicki argued. "Are you sure?"

"Don't start sounding like my mom, Vicki. Between the boots and my jacket, I'll be fine. Besides, it's an indoor party, right?"

Vicki returned her attention to her hair. "If you say so."

Faith changed and did her hair. The all-black ensemble suited her, she decided. She combed her red spirals upward, adding a wide, floral headband to make her appear taller, and older.

They arrived at the party at half-past nine. Faith did not know their host, but that was nothing new. She had crashed many parties since the first one Vicki had taken her to last New Year's Eve. Some kids even waved as if they recognized her. So what if she did not know the name of the senior helping them usher in the new year? Vicki did, so she trusted him by proxy.

A couple of Vicki's other friends were quick to direct them to the cups and the keg by way of shouts and hand signals amid the blaring music. Marvin Gaye's "I Heard It Through the Grapevine" ended and "Cinnamon" by Derek began.

The guy in charge of the tap eyed Faith as he filled her cup. "Haven't seen you before. You the new girl?"

She shrugged him off, trying to play it cool. "I don't go there."

"Where're you from?"

"A few blocks away. I go to a different school, though."

"Which one?"

She accepted the drink and took a sip. "Juilliard."

The boy whistled. "Really? Wow. You an actress? You look like you could be an actress. Or a model."

Inside, she thought she might pass out from the excitement. Outwardly, she pretended it was no big deal. "I'm a musician."

"How old are you?"

"Sixteen," she lied, as usual.

"I'm seventeen." He looked her over. "I'm Wayne. What's your name?"

"Faith."

He smiled. "Hi, Faith."

Something about the way he looked at her tied her stomach in knots. She wished she could more easily hear him above the blaring stereo. She also wished she had opted for the sunglasses Vicki had talked her out of, having claimed they would look ridiculous at an evening party. How could anyone believe she was sixteen?

Wayne was cute, if younger than she preferred. Dark hair and eyes. Muscular build. Tall. Beautiful mouth. Of course, he was no Mr. Beam. But what if Vicki was right? What if she would be better off with a boy closer to her age?

When other kids started complaining about access to the tap, Wayne passed his duties to an accommodating alternate, then inclined his chin to a room past the kitchen where several others were playing pool. They grabbed a couple of vacant seats and talked about music, sports—not her most knowledgeable topic—and school. She bobbed her head in time to Steppenwolf's "Magic Carpet Ride."

Wayne was attentive and interested in her time at Juilliard, which she made up since she had not yet started there. Whenever she finished a beer, he hastened to get her a refill. In fact, she had lost count of how many she had. Her lips and head began to feel like a blanket of fluffy granite.

"You okay?" Vicki asked when she and another girl drifted in from another room. "Haven't seen you all night."

Faith hand-beckoned her to lean down, but she still had to yell to be heard over the music. "I met someone."

"Who?" Vicki scanned the room.

She pointed toward the keg. "His name's Wayne."

Vicki's smile faded. "No, Faith. You need to get away from him. He's trouble."

"What do you mean?"

"Just...trust me." Vicki grabbed Faith's upper arm and tugged. "C'mon. Some girls and I are playing beer pong in the other room."

Faith yanked free. "You go on. I wanna stay."

Vicki's demeanor went from urgent to demanding. "I mean it, Faith. Let's go."

"Okay, *Millie*," she mocked, bobbing her head.

Wayne returned with Faith's drink, which Vicki immediately batted out of his hand. "She's had enough."

"Hey!" Faith cried out, angry when a few beer droplets hit her. "What're you doing, Vick? You'll ruin my jacket!"

"We need to go, Faith. Now."

Faith stood but faltered on unexpectedly wobbly legs. "I'm not going anywhere. Got it?"

Soon, Wayne and Faith had teamed up against Vicki. The more Vicki tried to drag Faith away, the more determined she was to stay.

"Fine!" Vicki shouted at last, arms flailing about. "See if I care!"

"Don't bother caring!" Faith yelled at her friend's retreating back. "I don't!"

Wayne stepped forward after Vicki took off with some friends. "Want another beer?"

"Yes!"

She checked her jacket while he was gone. Fortunately, it had not sustained any damage. Using the back of her wrist, she dabbed her face. Without a mirror, she had no idea how her makeup looked.

Wayne returned with a beer for each of them. She downed hers, then grabbed his.

"Hold on there, little fishy. Pace yourself. Otherwise, you'll never make it to midnight."

"Who cares?" She downed his drink as well, then became aware of her protesting bladder. "Where's the bathroom?"

He led her back through the kitchen, then down the hall. "I'll wait outside to make sure Vicki doesn't come back and kidnap you."

She laughed, patted his chest, then stumbled into the bathroom as "Crimson and Clover" blared through the house.

When she reemerged, he was waiting. "Everything all right?"

"It's hot in here," she shouted above the music and various party noises, fanning herself with her hand. "I'm gonna go outside for a minute and cool off."

He moved forward and kissed her. It caught her by surprise, but felt nice. She kissed him back. The feel of his tongue sliding into her mouth surprised and excited her.

"Come on," he coaxed, whisper-shouting in her ear. "I can help you cool off."

She giggled at the unlikely thought. His kiss had done anything but lower her temperature. "It'll be cooler outside."

"Follow me," he said, taking her hand.

That last beer had made her head spin. She followed him blindly, past other kids, bumping against the wall as he stalked down the hall into an unoccupied room. There, he kissed her again.

When she began sweating, she pushed him away. "I'm sorry. I really need some air."

"Relax, little fishy. It's not even midnight." He stripped off and cast her jacket to the floor beside the closed door, then cupped her head to bring her forward for another kiss.

Bleary eyes flitting about, Faith realized they were in someone's bedroom. "Wait. What are you doing?"

"Celebrating," he said, kissing her neck.

"Stop it." She tried to push him away again, but he held her tight. "I mean it! Stop!"

He encircled her back with one arm to pull her closer, then moved his other hand under her T-shirt to touch her breasts.

She struggled against him. "Wayne, don't. Let me go."

He buried his mouth into the nape of her neck, kissing and sucking her skin. "What's the matter, Faith? Do only older guys do it for you?"

Her eyes opened wide. "What?"

"You think I don't know who you are? Now, c'mon, baby. Let's do the new year right."

He maneuvered her around and walked her backward toward the bed.

She struggled against him. "Is that what this is about?"

"Isn't it always?"

She shut her legs tight when he tried to touch her, then fought to push his hands away. In the struggle, he ripped Vicki's T-shirt.

"A little feistier than I'd thought," he laughed. "Must be the red hair."

Before she realized what she was doing, she brought her knee up hard between his legs. With a pitiful yelp, Wayne collapsed where he stood.

Faith grabbed her jacket off the floor and ran.

CHAPTER 13

CHRIS WATCHED ELLIOT STUFF HIS mouth full of a third bag of smoky bacon Quavers, then wash it down with a can of Vimto. It amazed him how much his friend could eat—almost as much as the fact that his mum had started stocking various crisps and fizzy drinks in volume since Elliot had come into their lives.

Once satisfied, Elliot wiped his hands clean of salty, bacony food dust and collected his trash. "Are we gonna watch the show?"

"*No.*"

"Why not? We watch every week. You should be proud of him. Bygones and all that."

Chris's face contorted into a bitter scowl. "Oh yeah? If that were true, we'd have been there to watch the filming instead of being stuck here."

Elliot carried his trash to the kitchen bin. "Only one more week to go."

It annoyed Chris that his friend so casually accepted the punishment. Then again, it wasn't his punishment. Elliot was not the one stuck in his house for four months.

Four months!

"Be glad I'm not taking your guitar!" his father had roared during his domestic sentencing a week before Christmas.

Since September, they had believed they had gotten away with it. All the way to Frankfurt and back without a single suspicion. Even when Chris returned home knackered and pale. Even when he had slept all the next day. Not a word.

Then, Christmas had come 'round. A chunk of the money his parents had set aside for presents had gone missing.

At least Chris had not lied about it once confronted. But had that earned him any leniency? No!

"You could have been killed!" his mother had sobbed. "Or taken from us!"

"What were you thinking?" his father had shouted.

"When are you going to grow up?" Ben had admonished, as if it were any of his business anyway.

Of course, it could have been worse. Elliot had received the lion's share of the fall out. At least Chris had not gotten the strap.

House arrest had nearly driven him mad. He had seen no other living soul outside his family until well after the new year, when his mum had taken pity on him and reinstated both his telly privileges and Elliot's visits. She had figured that receiving coal in his Christmas stocking as his only "gift" was difficult enough, especially after the quiet, non-celebration of his thirteenth birthday days earlier.

How wrong she had been. The manual labor had topped the bill. Worse than having to do all the inside and outside chores on his own to pay back the money he had taken, it had virtually handed his brothers a vacation. Plus, he had to get greasy helping his father with his new hobby: cars.

Miserable, but in the end, he and Elliot still believed their adventure was worth the price they paid. At least the parts they remembered.

Elliot switched on the television despite Chris's groaning. Watching *Top of the Pops* had become a sort of weekly habit for them. But tonight was different. Tonight, Ben would be there to talk about the new song by the Couplers, "Make You Mine"—the first Ben Grant-authored tune to make the British charts.

The song had created a lot of buzz even before the Couplers had decided to record it, and had been submitted by their dad to the annual Eurovision Song Contest.

Championed by their dedicated father, Ben's career was taking off. The hottest new bands competed for his compositions with old-timers trying to reinvent their previous careers as swing artists. He spent more time at London's recording studios and less time at home. The two most devastating casualties of his burgeoning success? Jordan and Ben's fiercely close bond, and the retiring of the family's Saturday Night Carpet Concerts.

Given the attention Ben was receiving both in- and outside of the house, it was a wonder his parents had even bothered to address Chris's excursion to Germany.

"I don't want to watch, El," he insisted. When his friend ignored his wishes, he went upstairs to practice. "Come up when you're done, then."

For the next hour, he practiced his base runs, hammer ons, pull offs, and string bending. Though he would never admit it, he was thankful his father had not taken his guitar. Little else mattered to him anymore.

"So what do you want to do?" Elliot asked when the show ended, and he joined him upstairs. "I gotta go soon. I'm due home at half nine."

Chris tipped his guitar into its stand and laid down on his side atop his bed, propping his head on his closed fist. "Can't you stay over?"

"School night."

"I can't believe you're still going."

"I can't believe you're not. Guess I'm not quite the rebel you are, yet.

As it is, I couldn't sit down right for a week after my dad found out about the concert."

Chris shot him a sideways grin. "Worth every lick, no?"

Elliot nodded. "I just wish we could've seen the whole show."

"Yeah. What was that Todd on about, anyway? Strange bloke."

"You don't know?"

He shook his head.

Elliot plopped down atop Jordan's bed, crossing his legs. "That drink he had? It had something in it. Clifford says it was LSD."

Chris gasped. "Sod off. No way!"

"True!"

"How'd you find out?"

"You don't remember Lance giving me their phone numbers before they dropped us off in London?"

"Mate, most of that night was a blur. All I remember was having to leave, trying to keep Todd from jumping out of the van, and legging it home from Princes Risborough station."

"I've chatted to 'em since. We keep in touch."

"Really?" Chris swung his legs around to sit up. "Where are they? Do they live near us?"

Elliot shook his head. "They're in Bromley. Todd Dalton's parents own a furniture store there."

"What about Lance? Didn't he say he's a drummer?"

"I don't know how serious he is, but yeah. He said so."

Chris set his jaw and stared off at nothing. "Think he'd be interested in starting a band?"

Elliot stood up, chortling. He grabbed his anorak off the floor where he had tossed it earlier and prepared to leave.

"I'm serious." Chris followed him out of his room and down the stairs. "We could ask."

"And how would we practice?"

"I dunno, but it can't be a coincidence that the lot of us live in England but met all the way in Germany, can it? Maybe his brother can drive him! Or, he could take the train!"

Elliot carried his jacket over his arm. "Nice idea, Chris. Clifford's a decent guy, but I can't see it happening."

"Ask him."

"We can't form a group with local kids?"

"We have no local kids!"

"Only because you quit going to school."

Chris sucked his teeth. Out the window, he glimpsed the family car pulling into their driveway. "Just ask him, yeah? Unless you're not serious, either."

"Of course I am. I'm just more realistic than you."

George, Lynda, Ben, and Jordan entered the house chatting excitedly about their trip. Chris tuned them out. Ben's success story was the last thing he wanted to hear.

"You off then?" Lynda unwound the scarf from her head. "You keep warm, now. Shall I have George drive you?"

Elliot kissed her cheek and held the door from closing. "I'm fine, ma'am. I'm not far."

"Are you sure, dear? It's no bother at all."

He thanked her but declined again.

Chris followed him out into the chilly evening in just his jeans and T-shirt. He rubbed his bare arms as they walked to the gate. "Tell me you'll ask."

"You know, Todd's a singer."

"He is?"

"That's what Lance said."

"Is he any good?"

"How would I know?"

"What did Lance say?"

"Ask him yourself, why don't you?"

He scoffed. "Bloody unlikely. I still have a week to go."

"I know. That's why Clifford isn't bringing them up for a visit until next month."

Chris stopped, squinting at Elliot. "He what?"

"I already asked, ya plonker. They're interested. Don't know how we'll sort this, but it looks like they're both in. Maybe you can find a place for us to put on a sort of audition. We can't keep playing in our bedrooms if we're serious, now, can we?"

Stunned, he stood in silence.

"And before I go," Elliot added, "think your mum would mind if I grabbed a couple more bags of Quavers for the walk home? I'm starving!"

***

Bobby watched the wall clock high above the blackboard. Five minutes to go. He bounced his leg, keeping a white-knuckle grip on his yearbook. His first. And as soon as the bell rang, he would put it to good use.

Mrs. Updike's end-of-year recap, information on grades, and her big speech about how proud she had been to be their teacher did not hold his attention. He wanted to get out. He wanted to get signatures. He wanted something in writing. Something that proved he had made progress in the social area of his life.

"Psst," Kerry Iverson called from the desk beside his.

Bobby leaned sideways.

"What're you doing after class?" the boy whispered.

He tapped his yearbook.

"Me too. Hold up and we can sign each other's before we leave."

Bobby nodded. He could not wait. His first signature.

A flurry of activity erupted with the ringing of the bell. Students scattered, chattered, and traded books. Promises to keep in touch and invitations to movies and pool parties filled the air. Mostly, everyone was eager to start the summer of '69. The last summer of the decade.

"Here." Kerry handed his yearbook to Bobby, who traded back his own. "Put your phone number in it. Maybe we can hang out."

Kerry Iverson had not so much as waved to him in the hallway the entire year, but Bobby did not care. "Sure!"

"And I'll give you mine. Call me if I don't call you, okay?"

Bobby nodded, mindful not to appear too eager. He scribbled his number and a generic sentiment into Kerry's yearbook, then passed it back.

"Cool, man. Thanks. Now don't forget. Call me."

When the boy left the classroom, Bobby thumbed through the pages to see what he wrote.

> *Bobby,*
>
> *7th grade was a blast. Keep in touch. Here's my number.*
> *See you next year. Stay cool.*
>
> *Kerry*

The simple inscription galvanized him.

Crossing the campus toward his bike, several more classmates stopped him. They repeated the trading-of-the-books ritual. Many of the notes he read were similar to Kerry's, and most included their phone numbers. He collected a dozen, at least. No one asked or seemed to notice that he had not included his own number. Then again, no one knew his mother.

Emboldened yet perplexed at the ease with which everyone approached everyone else, he found himself asking to trade books with some of the shyer kids. Kids like himself, who might feel like no one had even noticed them throughout the year. Soon, his pristine yearbook was slightly worn from flipping and signing pages. It thrilled him.

But the true test was when he approached Wendy Myers. A half hour ago, he would have never dreamed of asking her to sign. She was too pretty. Too popular. Yet somehow, the idea of summer vacation seemed to have broken through the unmarked boundaries of La Cumbre Junior High School's social structure, leaving most students open to all their fellow Lancers.

Wendy stood by her locker, mingling with a group of girls. Bobby waited several feet away, trying not to stare. She smiled brightly, chatting with exuberance as others approached to exchange signatures. Always fashionably dressed, she wore a pristine white tee beneath tight-fitting overall shorts and a floppy yellow sun hat. Peeking out beneath the brim, her dark bangs and long straight hair accentuated her green eyes and perfectly framed her face. And what a face.

When the others buzzing around her left, he made his move.

He approached cautiously, projecting less confidence than he would have liked. "Uh, Wendy?"

"Yes?" She turned, still smiling. Something in her eyes told him she did not recognize him.

Once inside her orbit, he froze.

She shifted her weight to one foot, pointing into nowhere with a casual, upturned wrist flourish. "Bobby, right? Bobby Lockhardt?"

"Uh..." In his head, he ridiculed himself as he fought to form a coherent sentence.

"Did you...?" She indicated his book. "Did you want me to sign your yearbook?"

He nodded, slack-jawed.

"Will you sign mine, too? By your picture?"

Somehow, he managed not to drop the heavy tome on her foot as they switched. He scribbled a feeble sentiment, signed his name, and even included his number, though he could not imagine her ever using it. She was still writing when he had finished.

He waited patiently as she wrote, drinking in the sight of her. The subtle scent of rose or some other flowery perfume filled him. Not too strong. Just perfect. Like Wendy. The Wendy Myers he had dreamt about for months, prompting him to learn how to wash his own bed sheets in order to avoid an embarrassing conversation with his mother.

When she finished, she closed the book and, once more, smiled that brilliant smile of hers. "Here ya go."

"Th-thanks." He took his book and turned to go, fully intending to rush home and read her note in private.

She reached for his arm. "Wait, Bobby."

Exhilarated at the contact, he looked back. "Yeah?"

"I just wanted to say have a great summer." Her expression softened. "Got any plans?"

He could think of no response. Certainly, no honest one. The question reminded him what a loser he was. Fleetingly, he hated his mother. And his father.

"You live in Hope Ranch, right?" She tucked some hair behind her ear. Again, he could only nod.

"Maybe we'll see each other at the movies or something. Call me if you want. I put my number with my name."

"Have a great summer, Wendy. Thanks for signing." With that, he dashed to his bike and raced home as fast as his legs would pedal.

To his relief, his mother's car was not in the garage. He considered it a good sign. Well, maybe a fifty-fifty chance of it being a good sign. She was either lucid and running errands or had stranded herself trying to buy rat traps—her newest thing. He would not worry unless she did not return by dinner.

He stored his bike, grabbed his satchel, burst through the inside door, and hurried to his room. Home at last, he slid the yearbook out, stowed the bag in his closet for safekeeping until next year, and sat down cross-legged atop his bed.

The yearbook swelled with inked messages, goofy drawings, and dozens of numbers. Until now, he had had none. A part of him wished he had known earlier in the year how easy it would be to talk to them. Another part of him longed for fall. He wondered if, and when, he should call them. Might they think he blew them off by not including his own number?

He flipped through the pages, smiling and laughing as he read. At last, he came to Wendy Myers's message.

Bobby,

Don't be so nervous talking to girls. You're a great guy. Just be yourself. I hope we see each other over the summer and again next year. Call me and maybe we can go see a movie or something if you want.

Love,
Wendy

His heart hammered in his chest. "Love." Did she write "love?" None of the other girls had written "love." And sure enough, there was her phone number.

He set the book aside and went to the kitchen for some water. Though probably a futile search, he checked the fridge to see if he could find an alternative. Inside he found soda pop and juice, along with milk and some fruit. Clearly, his mother was in one of her saner periods. He wondered how long it would last, but would take what he could get.

The pantry was likewise fairly well stocked, so he made himself a sandwich, grabbed a Coke and some chips, then headed back to his room. He had to read Wendy's note again. Had she really signed her name with "love?"

Halfway down the hall, the phone rang so he doubled back to pick up. He set down his snack, wiped his hands on his jeans, and then answered.

"Bobby?"

"Dad!"

"How are you, son?"

Somehow, his father remembered that this was the last day of the school year. He could hardly contain himself. The day could not possibly get any better.

They chatted for several minutes. Bobby told him about his day and how excited he was about vacation. Yes, his grades were okay, though still not honor roll. And yes, as a matter of fact, he had made some friends he hoped to hang out with over the summer.

"Has your mother made plans for your birthday?"

He did not know what made him happier—Wendy's declaration of "love" or the fact that his father remembered his birthday, which up until this minute he had forgotten himself after the excitement of the afternoon.

"I may be out to visit you soon. We'll see. I have a new job, so I may have to send something in lieu. I realize it's been a while. I hope you understand."

Today, Bobby did understand. Or maybe he was just too happy to hold a grudge. Summer was here. He intended to make it the best ever.

***

When Kelley arrived home late that Friday afternoon, Farin was in the attic listening to music, and Beth was lying on their bed, in tears.

"My dad found me," she explained when he laid down next to her and kissed her cheek. "He called a couple of hours ago."

Apparently, Gene St. John had sobered up enough to notice his only child no longer lived in Seattle. It was anyone's guess how he had managed to track down their new number. But as usual, his presence—though merely over the phone—had done her in.

"He yelled and accused me of taking Farin away from him."

Kelley grabbed the tissue box from the nightstand, handed it to her, then stood and kicked off his shoes. They were due to meet Joseph and the family for dinner in an hour. He motioned for her to continue and listened as he changed.

"So I told him he was crazy. I mean, it's not like he's seen Farin more than a handful of times. He doesn't even like children. But he went on and on about us leaving without saying anything. He blamed you, then he blamed me..."

He considered it a positive step when anger eventually replaced her tears. Soon, she was up, animated, and stomping to their closet as she relayed the rest of the conversation.

"I told him, 'Well, Dad, if you'd made it to Thanksgiving last year like you'd said, you'd have seen Farin and learned we were leaving.' But you know how he is. There's no talking to him. I didn't even bother mentioning how much food we ended up tossing out."

One by one, she punished their clothes hangers as she jerked them across the closet rod, searching for something to wear. Kelley thought about offering his two cents but knew that, more than anything else, Beth needed to vent.

They rarely spoke of the abuse in her past. Of the mother she had never known, the frequent beatings, or the drunken groping she endured even before she had reached puberty. She had told him about the horrors of her childhood in increments, rightly assuming the details would so anger him, he might take action that he would later regret, or that might resurface to impact his law career.

In short, it was a miracle Beth St. John had survived. Even more so that she had turned out as lovely as she had.

"So yes, Kelley, I refused to give him our address. He hinted something about wanting to come down for a visit. An extended visit. We can't have him here. We can't subject Farin to it. I won't have it."

When he finished dressing, he sat on the chair near the bureau to tie the laces of his Hush Puppies. He watched her change into a stylish but casual dress. She sat down at her bureau to touch up her hair and makeup. Slowly, the storm inside her quelled.

"If he calls again and asks to visit, tell him we won't be here."

She coughed out a laugh as she combed her long dark hair into a high ponytail. "And just where should I tell him we'll be?"

"We'll think on it. For now, let's get our daughter and have dinner. We'll be late if we don't leave soon."

She stood, closed her eyes, took a calming breath, then exhaled through her perfect lips. "You have no idea how much I need this. It's been a helluva day. And I hated to get upset, what with Farin being so excited about the end of school. It's just, my father makes me crazy."

Kelley pointed out the window in the direction of Stearn's Wharf. "There's a gimlet with your name on it waiting for you."

She smiled and did a little shimmy. "Sounds heavenly. I can't wait." With that, she headed for the stairs. "Farin, honey? Time to go. You ready? Marci's waiting for you."

By the time they reached the restaurant, Beth was again her jovial self. The Williamses had already arrived and had procured a table overlooking the water.

Marci and Farin sat opposite each other, closest to the window. They chatted about what they planned to do over the summer. The treehouse was ready for them to spend as much time in as they wanted. Sleepovers were high on their list of priorities, though it sounded as if there might be some differences of opinion as to how they should decorate. Their simple debate soon became a squabble.

Seated next to Marci, Carol winked at the girls but cautioned them to keep their voices down. "We don't want to annoy the other diners, do we?" She gave them a warm smile, then turned her attention to Beth. "So, did he tell you?"

She shook her head, squinting in confusion. "Who? Kelley?"

Carol nodded, eyes twinkling with glee.

The sound of his name drew Kelley's attention away from his and Joseph's discussion about a case they were working on. When he realized Carol was about to ruin the surprise, he gave his partner's wife an urgent head shake. Unfortunately, she missed his signal.

"It's so exciting," Carol gushed, hand upon her chest. "I've never been."

"Been...where?" Beth glanced at her husband, then back across the table at her friend.

"We should toast. Joseph? Shouldn't we have a toast?"

Kelley patted his wife's knee. He leaned in and whispered, "I was going to tell you before, but it didn't seem like the right time."

Carol raised her cocktail glass. "To Marci and Farin, who just finished their very first year of school, and who love each other no matter how the treehouse is decorated. And to Joseph and Kelley, who spoil us all."

Beth giggled through her confusion. She touched her glass first to Farin's, then Marci's, then to the others. "To the girls, and to our husbands, whatever they're up to."

"You really don't know?" Carol set down her glass.

She shrugged.

Kelley reached inside his jacket pocket for the envelope, then handed it to his wife. He gave her a lopsided grin. "Uh...surprise?"

Inside the envelope, Beth discovered tickets. And not just any tickets.

Cruise tickets.

She gasped. "Mexico?"

"Fourteen days!" Carol blurted before Beth could absorb the details in the accompanying brochure.

Beth threw her arms around her husband's neck. "I can't believe it!"

Kelley held her close. "Now see? We won't be home. And that's all he needs to know."

She buried her face in the crook of his neck. "You're too good to me. To us."

He shushed her. "Never good enough, my darling. There's a brand-new decade coming soon. I promise here and now, it'll be the best of your life. I'll see to it. Everything else is behind you."

She gazed into his eyes. "I love you."

He heard the catch in her voice and held her tighter. "I love you, too. Now take Carol and go fix your makeup. We can't have you crying in your lobster."

CHAPTER 14

*I*T WAS THE END OF *Ronald Nock, tragic war orphan and sometimes petty criminal. Good riddance to him, as far as he was concerned. Like something out of a fairy tale, they had fallen in love. One dance had changed everything.*

Not that their coupling did not present challenges.

Sarah Wellingham had plied Ronnie with questions as they danced that night, as if desperate to know every detail of his life before he no longer held her in his arms. As if the spell would be broken the minute the music stopped, and they would never see each other again.

"Where are you from?"

Canning Town was not the answer she had envisioned.

"What does your family do for a living?"

The question had caught him off guard. When pressed, his answer had saddened her.

"I'm so sorry, Ron. I don't know what to say."

The genuine empathy in her voice had left him emotionally stripped and thoroughly spellbound. He had never discussed his war experience with anyone. Not even in the mines.

"How did you survive? It sounds utterly horrifying."

In the course of a waltz, she had disarmed him. He answered her every question, as he had promised. That included the details of how he had come into possession of the dinner jacket he wore. And maybe their initial contact was more accurate than either of them could have imagined. Instead of becoming insulted or angry, she had laughed. Maybe Sarah did know him, as she had asked outside Town Hall moments before her escort had whisked her away.

Halfway through their dance, she had ceased the interrogation. "It's not a night for melancholy," she had said, her body pressed against his. "I don't want to make you relive the pain. Just hold me."

So he did.

Soon after, Ronnie had recognized the boy he had subdued to gain entry—or, rather, he recognized his trousers and shirt on the boy's person as they entered the ballroom. As he had predicted, the lad had brought the authorities.

Scandal had ensued, but Sarah had asked the police where they would take Ronnie. The next morning, she arrived at the Old Bailey to post his bail.

Overwhelmingly, she carried with her three large bags from the Harvey Nichols department store, containing the finest men's clothing Ronnie had ever seen.

"I can't take these, Sarah. What would you think of me?"

"I'd think you want to accompany me to lunch, Mr. Nock. Now, go change."

So he did.

For the next six months, they met every day. Never at her house, of course. And not because she was ashamed. She simply did not want to subject Ronald Nock to the Wellinghams' cruel scrutiny.

"I have to meet your family, love. We can't keep meeting at parks and restaurants."

"Then take me to your place," she would say, a mischievous glint in her beauteous blues.

Every time she had made the suggestion, it reminded Ronnie that she existed in a world into which he could never fit. "You deserve so much more than I can ever give you," he would tell her as they sat on a blanket in Hyde Park—a blanket she had purchased—and ate the lunch she had provided.

"Don't talk like that, Ron. It won't be like this forever."

"I need to meet your family. I need your father's approval."

One late summer day, as they lay next to each other enjoying a cuddle after another of their park picnics, she finally agreed. "But you must promise you won't let my family run you off. Ever since I came out, they've pressured me to marry. My father has his eyes on a couple of different choices and is quite frustrated over my refusals."

"Is one of them the bloke I knocked out?"

Sarah shot him a coquettish side-eye. "As a matter of fact..."

Ronnie belly-laughed at the revelation. He only wished he could recreate his crime.

"Promise you won't let them discourage you."

So, he did.

Sarah had awoken a desire in him he never thought existed. It went beyond his ability to give the heart he believed had died. She made him want to better himself. To become a man she did not have to hide from her family.

Ronnie needed to become a gentleman. He needed to convince Robert Wellingham he was worthy of his daughter, for he had determined to marry Sarah. So, for the next three months, he dedicated himself to her tutelage. Diction, dress, deportment, desirability.

"And now, my name," he told her shortly before the big day.

"Your name?" she asked, stunned. "Good heavens, Ron. Why would you change your name?"

"Because Ronald Nock sounds like a poor, filthy Canning Town dock worker who could never give Sarah Wellingham all she deserves. Besides, Ronald Nock has a police record."

She nestled into his arms. "I love you. That's not who you are."

"Not anymore."

Even as he pursued his present course of action, guilt harbored inside him. He had never been ashamed of the family he still mourned. He still loved every one of them, and felt their absence every day.

Mary Nock, or Molly as his father had called her, had been a strong, educated woman with high standards and fierce affection for her children.

James had sacrificed a working leg in the first war, and his life in the second.

Paul had planned to attend university. He had wanted to be a doctor.

Twins Oscar and Owen had excelled at sports.

Daisy had been a kind, gentle soul. Molly's pride and joy.

Francis had never even had a chance to distinguish his own personality, but his smile had always lit up the room.

As for Polly, well...he could not bear to think about her.

"Our pasts are so different," Sarah would say on the rare occasions they discussed their war experiences. "I suppose the only heartbreak I've ever experienced was growing up without a mother. She died having me. I've always had my father and my grandmother, though."

Sarah's acceptance of him without judgment bewildered him. But he grew to depend on it—and her. He vowed to pay her back, somehow. Not only with a forever love, but with a life worthy of the woman he had danced with that first night at Town Hall.

"Well, if you're determined to change your name, I'll support you. What'll it be?"

He had given the idea due consideration. "I don't know. It's difficult. I'll always be James and Mary's son."

The declaration sparked her creativity. "James. Son. Jameson."

His eyes widened at the simple brilliance. "Sarah, that's it. It's perfect." He mulled it over. "Jameson. Yes."

She had giggled with delight at their deception. "It's regal."

"Is that my first or last name?"

"Um...first!"

"Okay. Now for a last name."

In the end, they had borrowed her father's name, along with a surname Ronnie had seen somewhere in the Times of London. That day, he became Robert Jameson Lockhardt. A bit of Sarah's family. A bit of his.

Assumed identity notwithstanding, the road to Oxfordshire was a bumpy one for Sarah and Jameson. Family matriarch Vera Wellingham had initially refused to meet him. The nine-year age gap between Jameson and Sarah did not bother her, but his lack of pedigree did. Robert, on the other hand, had eagerly greeted Sarah's would-be suitor...in the hopes of paying him to leave his smitten daughter alone. In the end, neither one of their objections worked.

On pain of disinheritance, Sarah Wellingham eloped with Robert Jameson Lockhardt on February 2, 1953.

***

Jameson dropped a tea bag into the silver hot water pot and left it to steep. His two-thirty appointment had arrived closer to three, sliding into the booth at Ben Frank's as if punctuality mattered little when one considered himself a musical polymath. He dipped his head to consult his watch, then lifted his eyes. "I'll get right to it. I caught your set at the Troubadour last night. You were good. But you can be better. If you're prepared to work hard and improve, we'd like to offer you a contract."

A waitress approached and asked what she could get the newly arrived party to drink. He hesitated and looked at Jameson. Once given the nonverbal okay to order whatever he fancied, he chose coffee, juice, milk, and a three-egg breakfast. Jameson ordered a piece of cherry pie.

"Thanks, man. I lost my day job a couple weeks ago. I've been focusing exclusively on my music ever since. Cash is tight, ya know?"

"Well, as I said, with hard work—"

"Oh yeah, yeah. Absolutely! Hardest working dude on the Strip. Ask anyone. I can really churn out the material, know what I mean? My mind's, like..." He splayed his fingers to either side of his head, "I can't keep up with the ideas. I'm, like, writing all the time. LA's so free and easy. And with everything going on..."

Yes, yes. Jameson knew more than most about "everything going on." The Vietnam War. The draft. The ongoing saga of the Manson Family murders. McCartney exiting the Beatles. Various bands breaking up and forming other bands. Continued fallout over Altamont. The upcoming Isle of Wight festival. Various world catastrophes.

Good thing this dirty, unkempt singer-songwriter was on the job.

"It's like Lennon said—"

Jameson raised a hand, stopping him mid-sentence. "Don't talk to me about Lennon."

"Why not?"

"Because he's a fake and a buffoon."

The singer blinked wide eyes. Lips parted, he raised his eyebrows and scoffed. "Whatever, man."

"No?"

He rolled a shoulder.

Jameson leaned in, flattening his forearms atop their table, fingers laced. "Six years ago. The June, nineteen sixty-four issue of *Sixteen Magazine*. Lennon gave an interview. In it, he said his aspirations were to, quote, 'make a lot of money; to be a real millionaire.' End quote. Then came Beatlemania. Now, he feigns outrage over any fringe movement that makes him appear evolved, or cool, or whatever. So he lies in a hotel bed for a week, without a care in the world, fucking his new wife while the press waits breathlessly outside the door for an interview. In reality, all he does is keep fans like *you*, who swallow his bullshit, at bay while he lives the very life he said he wanted in the first place. A weakling outpaced, out-talented, and outshone by his former songwriting partner."

Jameson paused. He splayed upturned palms to the boy seated opposite him, inviting rebuttal.

None came.

"In any case, I'm here to discuss business, not debate the existential genius of those who've long since carved their names into the annals of music history. Play your cards right and you'll meet plenty of rock journalists interested in cataloging your musical heroes. I'm not that person."

Nate Hayword could not have been older than twenty-three, and had likely never stepped foot out of California. Long, stringy, sun-bleached hair. Handlebar mustache. Unbuttoned shirt over a wrinkled tee. Jeans and boots. He had probably rolled out of bed at the last minute, perhaps having forgotten he had an appointment to meet the man who could change his life.

Solid voice, though. And a promising songwriter. The audience had not only loved him, they had appeared to connect. Those things mattered. Though not someone his fellow A&R men had rushed to sign right off the stage, he had caught Jameson's attention. He had something. And Jameson intended to grab that something before the others realized what they had overlooked.

Animated and pointing Jameson's way, Nate said, "We're gonna save the *world*, man. You know that, right? And we can do it with guitars instead of guns. This thing we're doing? It's bigger than all of us. It's destiny, man. Can you dig?"

Grass and granola. It seemed he would never get away from hippies.

"Well, Nate, you may be doing it under another name. We'll see."

"My name?"

"Problem?"

"It's my *name*, man."

"Whose album would you rather buy: Robert Zimmerman's or Bob Dylan's?"

Nate Hayword broached no additional complaints.

By the time the food arrived, their business had concluded. Jameson asked the waitress to box up his cherry pie, explained their next steps to his newest acquisition, then excused himself to settle the bill on his way out. Nate would have to eat his large meal alone. No time to stay and chat. Jameson had another three world-changers to meet with before returning to stalk the talent base at the usual LA hotbeds. Two more nights to go before his return to New York.

Musically, he had had worse assignments. The Laurel Canyon artists had for years now produced some of the best singer-songwriters in the world. If one forgave the sometimes-ranting lyrics of post-flower children who seemed more focused on wanting to overthrow the American government than falling in love, the vibe was inarguably magical. But even as their momentum grew, Jameson suspected it approached its peak. All "movements" eventually came to an end.

He found it amusing that two of the LA music scene's most outspoken anti-establishment, activist-poets—Neil Young and Joni Mitchell—were Canadians.

A cynical perspective, yes, but it had served him well. In his year and a half as an A&R man, he had discovered some of the chart's greatest new sensations. It did not matter if he liked the music or the musicians. It did not matter that he was in his mid-forties. It did not matter that he preferred classical music and theater over rock'n'roll and concerts. Ross had been right. Jameson was thriving.

And secretly, Jameson quite enjoyed Crosby, Stills, Nash & Young's new album, *Déjà Vu*. A rarity for him since he had never much cared for modern music. Nonetheless, he had found himself drawn to "4 + 20" in particular. Neil Young, he could take or leave.

"Hey, uh, Mr. Lockhardt?" Nate called from across the diner.

Jameson tossed a few bills atop the money for the check, then strode back to the table.

"Do ya think I could get a few bucks advance? I'm a little short on my rent."

"Let's get that contract signed first, shall we? And maybe you'll be there on time. For now, enjoy the meal, and all your assorted beverages."

"Dick," Nate spat under his breath as Jameson walked away.

He pivoted, expressionless.

The young man drooped in his seat. "Sorry, man. But do ya have to be such a dick?"

"This 'dick' singled you out of dozens of kids your age who'd give their left nut to be in the position in which you now find yourself. Perhaps the 'hardest working man on the Strip' should be focused on what material he's going to write for his first album instead of whether or not he's short a few bucks. Struggling makes one more creative, no?"

Nate clenched his jaw and stared straight ahead.

"That's what I thought." Jameson temporarily slid back into the booth. "I realize kids like you think this business is all laughter and getting high and becoming millionaires. And maybe it is to some extent. If you're that good and the timing's right. Hell, many of my counterparts at other labels would eagerly hold your hand, get you drugs, and suck your dick dry if that's your scene. They'll lie and convince you you'll be the next big thing. But you won't get that from me. I don't want to be your friend. I want to see you work for it. Why? Because I want to make money. So Nate, do you want a friend or someone who'll make you sweat blood to earn your shot at the charts? I mean, you say you want to change the world."

Jameson left a speechless Nate Hayword alone with his breakfast—and an enormous piece of humble pie.

***

It electrified Chris that he and his friends had pulled off a parentless adventure in Germany, while Ben still needed a chaperone to set him up at a hotel in London. Well, at least until his eighteenth birthday next month. Ben spent more time in the city now than he did at home. He also made his own money. With any luck, he would move out soon. Chris had already laid claim to his brother's bedroom when that time came.

Lynda bustled about near the front door, inventorying their luggage. "Now Chris, be sure to tell the sitter we're sorry we weren't here when she arrived. That we had to leave early."

He lounged on the sofa, one leg dangling over the armrest. "I know, Mum."

"And don't give her any trouble before you leave for Elliot's. Be a gentleman."

He ground his jaw left, then right. "Which one's supposed to be here?"

Lynda patted George's back as he moved past them to load the car. She primped in the entryway mirror. "Her name's Penelope. Penelope Young. She's new."

"So don't scare her off," George barked over his shoulder from outside.

Ben galloped down the stairs and out the front door. "Or worse."

"Jealous?" he shouted at his brother's back.

With a sigh of patient frustration, Lynda beckoned her middle son to stand up. She placed her hands on his shoulders, holding his eyes with hers. "This is what your father and I've been saying. This sort of behavior's why we can't trust you to watch little Jorie while we're away. And this time, we can't take him with us. So please say you'll behave. We'll be back in the morning. Penelope's parents want her home tomorrow by ten AM. I need you back here before then, in case we're delayed."

He halfheartedly promised not to scare Penelope Young away. What he left out was that practice had been canceled. Even if Lance and Todd had not promised to help Clifford move out of his family home into his own place, Elliot had a cold. This left Chris on his own. And home for the night.

"You'll stay here with Jorie until she arrives? You won't leave early?"

"He's ten now, Mum. He's not a baby anymore."

"Even so." She marched upstairs to say her goodbyes. "Promise."

"I promise."

He waved from the door as they left, then bounded up the stairs two at a time to check on his brother. Bouncing atop his unmade bed, he asked, "What're you doing?"

Jordan sat atop his made bed, pillows propped behind him. He used his knees as a desk as he jotted notes on a pad of paper. "I'm writing a song."

Chris scrambled into a sitting position. "Yeah? Can I see it?"

"It's not done."

"Want some help?"

Jordan shook his head, barely glancing up from the page. "I can do it."

"Hungry? Mum left us snacks."

"She left me and Penelope snacks. You won't be here."

"Maybe I will."

Jordan peeked over his knees. "Mum said you were spending the night at Elliot's."

"He's sick." He stood, grabbed his guitar, then sat back down at the edge of his bed and wiggled his fingers before playing.

"Can't you do that downstairs?"

"Why? It's my room, too."

Jordan slid off the bed and left, taking his notepad and pencil.

Chris laid back and rested his guitar across his middle. Without his bandmates, it would be a long night.

The knock at the door came an hour later. Chris heard Jordan answer, so he stayed put. There followed some light chatter. Then, the sound of the television. Only when his stomach let him know it was time to eat did he finally go downstairs.

Halfway down, he heard Jordan say, "This is my brother, Chris. He was supposed to be gone for the night."

"Oh," came a soft voice. "Okay."

When Chris walked around the staircase into the living room, he stopped in his tracks so quickly, he nearly tripped over his feet.

Jordan laughed at the inelegant entry. Chris's lips pressed into a straight line.

"Are you sure your mum needs me? If your brother's home..."

Penelope Young was stunning.

"Yeah. Mum doesn't trust Chris, so you should probably stay."

She giggled and nodded Chris's way. "Hi. Bit awkward, yeah?"

He formed a roguish grin and brushed past her to sit on the sofa. "Not really."

"Oh. Okay, then." She smoothed down her short skirt, then sat, knees locked, at the opposite end of the sofa. "Jordan, just let me know when you're hungry. I'll fix you something."

"I'm hungry," Chris said, eyes fixed on the television screen to avoid staring at her shiny, waist-length hair.

She tucked several strands behind her ear. "I guess I could make something for everyone. I'm not much of a cook, but I can fry sausages. Hungry, Jordan?"

"Don't care." Jordan lay on his belly, head in his hands, legs bent and dangling as he watched television.

Chris slunk down in his seat until he could reach his brother with his foot. He gave Jordan's shin a kick. "Oi! Penelope's talking to you, numpty. You hungry or what?"

Jordan scampered up and spun around. "You're not even supposed to be here."

"Well, I am. Wanna make something of it?"

Penelope stood and left for the kitchen. After a brief and bitter stare-off, Chris joined her.

"Want some help? I'm a pretty good cook."

She had found a pan and placed it on a burner. "That's okay. I'm not making anything grand. I saw crisps in the pantry, and some bread."

"I asked," he singsonged, hopping up to sit on the kitchen counter.

"How old are you?" She leaned against the counter and folded her arms.

"I'll be fifteen in four months. You?"

"Fourteen in October. I haven't seen you at school, though."

"I stopped going," he boasted, squaring his shoulders. "I'm focusing on my music."

Unimpressed, she knitted her brow. "Your parents all right with that?"

"No."

She bobbed a shoulder, then shifted her attention to arranging their bare-bones dinner.

Studying her, he realized she looked nervous. Her hands shook as she grabbed the crisps and prepped the bread for the sausages. Every so often, she peeked his way, only to jerk her head back when their eyes met. The contrast of her dark hair, dark brows, and emerald eyes aroused him. She had an exotic quality about her he found sexy, despite the fact that she was more than a year younger.

Chris had started noticing girls at a young age. Mostly, he liked them older because he liked to look at their breasts. A few had let him touch them. But over the last year, he had spent so much time focused on practicing and developing a band, he had fallen out of practice in the flirting department.

Much of his post-Doors concert sentence had been spent between practicing his guitar and studying what turned women on. It had all started the day he had discovered an article in one of his mum's magazines about the "language of flowers." He had read it several times, committing it to memory. It captivated him, the things girls got off on.

Symbolism was his newest, non-music obsession. Gems, flowers, astrological signs. Anything. Everything.

As they stood together in the kitchen, Penelope's subtle reactions to his presence intrigued him. The less he said, the more nervous she seemed. Fascinating.

He made it a point to stay in the kitchen with her, and watched her every move. It felt almost like a game between them. Inexplicably, he seemed to be winning.

They ate in the living room, balancing their plates on their laps while watching LWT's *Maggie's Place*.

Penelope sipped her fizzy drink, then set the glass on a coaster. "So...are you any good at the guitar?"

"He's brilliant," Jordan said around a mouthful of sausage. "He's next."

"Next?"

He nodded, swallowing. "Next to leave. Everyone in the world wants Ben to write their songs. He'll move out soon, Dad says. Then, when Chris is old enough to work the clubs, Dad says he'll probably go, too. It makes Mum sad, but he's next."

Chris gave his brother a sideways smile. "Dad said that?"

"Sure did."

He pushed his lips out and nodded. "Good to know."

"So go on, then," Penelope pressed. "Play us a song."

"Right now?" He raised his hands, indicating his plate. "Mind if I finish first?"

She gathered her and Jordan's plates, then disappeared into the kitchen to clean up. Soon, Chris brought his empty plate in to add to the dishes. When he slid it into the soapy water, he brushed her hand. He noticed the slight smile she tried to hide, and the reddening of her cheeks. He also noticed her full, glossed, pink lips.

They turned off the telly and sang UK Singles Chart songs all evening. Jordan nodded off close to midnight. Chris rousted him awake and told him to get upstairs. When Penelope accompanied him to ensure he brushed his teeth, Chris followed.

Jordan fell back asleep the moment his head hit the pillow.

Penelope turned out the bedroom light. "I should've sent him up earlier."

Chris stood close behind her. He whispered, "At least we know he'll sleep."

They went back downstairs. Penelope grabbed the pillow and blanket Lynda Grant had left out for her and made up a bed on the couch.

She tucked the sheet into the cushions. "You don't have to stay if you're tired."

"I'm good. Fancy another song?"

"I'm all sung out." She smiled. "You're really good, Chris. Your dad's right. You are next."

He jutted his chin. "Think so?"

"Oh yes. If your band's half as good, I'm sure you'll be famous rock stars one day."

The question was, should he kiss her or keep pretending she did not want him to?

CHAPTER 15

"Are you excited?" Millie crept into Faith's room, all smiles, hoping to help her get ready. "Your first day at Juilliard! I can't wait to hear all about it."

"Remember, Mom. No parents on campus."

"I know, I know." Millie sat on the bed and crossed her ankles. She picked through Faith's suitcase, scrutinizing her packing job. "You'll call. It'll be fine."

Better than fine. Just how Walt and Millie had pulled it off, she did not know. All she knew was that she was allowed to start earlier than the prestigious school normally allowed. She would not turn sixteen for another six months.

The New Year's Eve party with Wayne had provoked a major shift in Faith's perspective. He had scared her. Her fear had manifested itself as rage. Good thing, since it had enabled her to make a fast exit.

Since then, Faith had retreated into herself, refocusing her efforts on her music. She did not belong in a world of high school proms and football games, anyway. She was a musician. That life was all that made sense. It was a far safer place than the real world.

Boys her age, she decided, were carnal brutes. She wanted nothing to do with them. And friendship? Completely overrated. Not to mention a waste of time.

"Your father and I made reservations for dinner. We should go soon if we're going to get into the city and get you situated before then. You about ready?"

"Almost." Faith grabbed her lava lamp. She wrapped it carefully in a couple of her shirts, then secured it in her bag.

"Walt?" Millie called downstairs. "Can you come and get her things?"

Faith snapped her suitcase shut, grabbed her leather jacket, then scanned her room to make sure she had not forgotten anything. For a moment, her eyes lingered on her scratchy pink afghan.

Walt joined them. He pointed at the boxes near her closet. "You taking both these?"

She nodded. "And the suitcase. But I can get that, Dad."

Millie followed them out of the room, closing the door behind them. She grabbed her handbag and gloves while they loaded up the Fairlane, then joined them in the car. "Everyone ready?" she asked, adjusting herself in the passenger's seat.

Pulling out of the driveway, Faith caught a glimpse of Vicki Ford staring at them from her second-story bedroom window. They made eye contact. Neither of them waved.

The Petersons drove into the city listening to Walt's favorite talk radio show. This suited Faith just fine. It gave them all an excuse not to talk to one another.

Only once, and only to herself, did Faith admit that the idea of leaving her school, parents, and everything familiar made her nervous. Austin Jones had teared up at their final lesson. He told her he believed an exciting future awaited her and made her promise to keep in touch. She hoped he was right and said she would.

It took a couple of hours to get through campus, sign in, and find her dorm room. As her parents signed papers and collected a folder containing her schedule and information on the basics of campus life, she studied the grounds and watched other students mill around with their families and belongings. Everyone looked happy. It was a little weird.

Millie strode into the dorm room ahead of Faith and Walt. She visually swept the space, her bright disposition fading. "It's a bit...small, don't you think?"

Walt maneuvered around Millie to stack the two boxes on the unoccupied study desk furthest from the window. "Looks like no view for you, kitten. Sorry we didn't get here sooner."

"It's fine, you guys. No big deal." Faith hoisted her suitcase onto the bottom bunk, which she got by default since her future roommate had already claimed the top. Its already-made flowery sheets and bulky blankets set her mind to wondering whether they would have a thing in common.

The roommate was not there, but Faith saw a framed picture of who she assumed was the girl with her parents. She looked nice enough. Plain. Sweet. Hopefully, they could live together without hassle. She had zero interest in making new friends, but did not want any drama over it. She wanted to learn, grow, graduate, and get out.

The Faith Peterson Freedom Countdown continued, despite its change of address.

They made it to Keens Steakhouse less than five minutes before their reservation time and were seated right away. Millie paused a time or two as the waiter showed them to their table, kissing the air, or laughing, or promising to call soon. It was the same whenever they went out. Millie Peterson knew everybody.

"Let's toast," Walt suggested when their drinks arrived.

Millie lifted her Manhattan, then glanced beside her. She indicated Faith's soda with stern eyes and a sharp lift of her chin, as if embarrassed she had to urge her on.

"Dad, can we not make this—"

Walt tapped his highball glass four times with his fork as he stood up.

I knew it. Faith exhaled through her nose and stared down at the white tablecloth, wishing she could run back to her dorm room and hide under her roommate's flowery sheets.

"If I could have everyone's attention." Walt turned his head left, then right, smiling as he addressed the roomful of mostly strangers seated around them.

"Dad, they don't care."

Millie shushed her, a pinched expression covering her face. Again, she jerked her chin at Faith's glass.

Grudgingly, Faith reached for her iced Pepsi.

"My name is Walt Peterson. My daughter, Faith, starts Juilliard tomorrow."

The crowd *ooh*'d and *ahh*'d. A few clapped.

Millie preened, glass aloft, soaking up the attention-by-proxy.

Walt continued. "I hope you'll all raise your glasses and join me in toasting her many years of tireless dedication, her uncommon talent, and what her mother, Millie, and I believe will be her stellar future as a concert pianist."

Throughout the restaurant, glasses clinked. Patrons called toward them, wishing her well and congratulating her parents. Faith smiled politely, mouthing *thank-yous*, wishing she were dead.

Dinner was impossible. Each time one of the tables of diners finished, they would stop by on their way out, chatting briefly, shaking hands, and again wishing her all the best. To Faith's shock and embarrassment, some dropped off sealed envelopes of what Faith suspected was cash, which they insisted Faith keep despite Walt and Millie's feigned pleas of, "Oh no, we could never accept this."

When they finally finished and Walt asked for the check, their waiter informed them it had been settled earlier by a guest who had long since finished and left.

By the time Faith returned to her dorm room, having managed to extricate herself from the family vehicle before Millie began sobbing, she was exhausted.

Inside, she recognized her roommate from the picture on the desk. The girl sat on her bed, painting her toenails. Faith acknowledged her with a nod as she beelined for the bottom bunk.

The girl rolled over on her belly, mindful of her wet toenails, and peeked down at Faith. "I'm Yvonne. Yvonne Quale. Don't say it. I'm changing it the minute I'm eighteen."

Faith chuckled a bit, folding her hands behind her head. "I'm Faith. Peterson."

"You're new, aren't you?"

She nodded. "First day's tomorrow."

"Lemme know if you have questions. I know what it's like to be new. But everyone's pretty cool here. This is my second year. I'm dance. You?"

"Piano. And thanks. Right now, I'm gonna try to get some sleep."

Yvonne smiled, then disappeared atop her bed. "I'll get the lights when I'm finished."

An hour later, Faith still struggled to close her eyes, though her roommate had long since turned off the lights. A million random thoughts assaulted her.

She fretted over her first day. Juilliard was, well, *Juilliard*.

A part of her wished she had said goodbye to Vicki, and maybe given her a proper "I'm sorry" for ruining her father's T-shirt that night—a ridiculous reason for them to have stopped hanging out, but it had mattered to Vicki more than Faith had realized at the time.

She wished she knew how to contact Mr. Beam. Every so often, she would hear whispers that he had moved to the city. Did he ever think about her? Well, other than the fact that she had cost him his job...and reputation?

Close to eleven, Faith saw Yvonne climb down from bed and put on her robe.

"You okay?" she dared to ask, immediately chastising herself for not minding her own business.

"Can't sleep either?" Yvonne switched on her table lamp.

Faith squinted and sat halfway up, propping herself on her elbows. "Guess not."

"You cool?"

"What do you mean?"

She shrugged. "I mean, are you cool? Are you a goody two-shoes, or a snitch, or...are you cool?"

"I'm no snitch."

Yvonne waved her up. "C'mon, then. I've got something to help us sleep."

***

After an early dinner, Kelley chased the girls around the house a little before sending them up to play in the attic. He wore an old sheet with cut outs in the eye area so he could see, a goofy expression drawn on the "face" with colored pencil to make it appear less frightening. The girls giggled and squealed as they ran around the sofa and in and out of the kitchen to get away from "Kelley the Friendly Ghost."

When the novelty wore off all of fifteen minutes later, Beth and Carol carried a bowlful of popcorn upstairs. The girls followed behind like mice after the Pied Piper.

Marci helped her mother lay out the thick quilt they played upon. "Your dad's so funny."

"That wasn't my dad." Farin laughed, bringing forward the popcorn bowl and setting it atop the quilt. "That was Casper—I mean, *Kelley*."

When their mothers left, Farin went to her Close 'n Play phonograph and put on Freda Payne's "Band of Gold." Marci and her Dancerina doll grooved and spun around while Farin danced and sang into an old paper towel roll she and her mother had painted.

Pinnacle nights were the best nights. Each Saturday, the O'Conners and Williamses congregated at one or the other of their homes, had an early dinner, then the adults played cards, and the kids played in their playrooms or watched television.

"I like it up here," Marci said as Farin changed the record. "But I miss the treehouse."

"It's too cold for the treehouse right now."

She sat upon the quilt, cradling her doll. "It was fun decorating last summer."

"It was until you tried to paint the walls pink."

Neil Diamond's "Cracklin' Rosie" played next. The girls lay head-to-head on the quilt, staring up at the attic ceiling, which Kelley and Beth had rigged with twinkle lights to look like stars.

"Why do you think that man at the dime store asked us if we were sisters?"

Farin shrugged, then scampered up to prepare for the next record. "I don't know."

"We don't look alike."

"We don't act alike."

When Farin changed the record again, this time to Anne Murray's "Snowbird," she was surprised to hear Marci pipe up, "I like that one." She even started singing.

But as soon as Farin tried to add a harmony, Marci lost her place. Frustrated, Farin returned to her impressive stack of 45s—a growing collection of Top 40 hits that rivaled those belonging to most adults.

"I need a new stereo. Daddy has a bunch of albums, but they won't play on this."

"Gonna ask Santa for one for Christmas?"

She nodded, eyes brightening as she sat back down. "And a lava lamp, the new Partridge Family album, the Carpenters album, and the Osmonds album. What're you gonna ask for?"

Marci sat up and smoothed down the back of her hair, nestling her Dancerina doll in her lap. "I want a Which Witch? game. And a new choker and a tie-dye shirt."

Farin tucked her chin. "Really? Tie-dye?"

"Yep."

"That's really cool, Marci. What're you gonna be for Halloween? A bride, again?"

She shook her head. "This year, I'm gonna be a witch!"

"Really?"

"Momma's already got the cauldron and the hat."

When Farin grew tired of changing out her records, she switched on the radio.

"Did you watch the *Partridge Family* last night?"

"Yeah."

"Keith's cute."

Marci raised a shoulder. "I like Peter better."

"Peter's not a Partridge, silly! Peter's a—"

"Brady. I know, Farin. I'm not stupid."

"I never said you were stupid. But we weren't talking about the Bradys."

"I like the Bradys better, that's all."

Farin frowned and wiggled her head. She hummed along to Diana Ross, then to Creedence. Marci made a restroom run, then returned with a couple of bottles of soda pop to go with their popcorn. They nibbled their snack and listened to music. Occasionally, they would hear their parents downstairs, laughing.

"You never asked what I was gonna be for Halloween."

Marci leaned over for a napkin to wipe the butter off her fingers. "I already know."

"You do?"

"You're gonna be a rock'n'roll princess."

"How'd you know?"

"Because that's what you are every year."

"But this year, my dad's gonna be part of my act!"

"What do you mean?"

Farin's eyes widened as she spoke. "He says he's gonna dress up as my manager."

Marci scrunched her face. "What kinda costume is that?"

"I don't know. But I bet it'll be really cool."

From downstairs, they heard a jovial "*Oh!*" and a chorus of laughter.

Marci sat cross-legged on the quilt, twirling her doll. "Can we go down and watch TV now?"

"Why?" Farin frowned.

"Because I'm bored."

"Bored? How can you be bored? You don't like music very much, do you?"

"I like music. Just not as much as you." Marci gathered up the popcorn bowl, used napkins, and pop bottles, set them aside, then had Farin help her fold up the quilt. "Besides, *My Three Sons* is gonna be on soon."

With a slow shake of her head, Farin switched off the radio and ceiling lights, then managed an armful of trash while Marci grabbed the popcorn bowl in one hand and her doll in the other. "Guess you'll never be a back-up singer, then."

"Witches aren't back-up singers."

***

"I should tell Dad!" Ben shouted.

"Of *course* you should!" Chris countered. "That's the good boy, then, eh? Bloody Prince Charles. Saint Ben!"

"If I don't, Mr. Young will anyway! Wouldn't you rather let Dad prepare himself instead of getting surprised? Do you realize what you've done?"

"We don't even know yet!"

"That's all you have to say?"

They stood in the hallway between their rooms. And, if Ben's threats were not enough, Jordan had ratted on him even before the call.

"This time won't be house restriction, brother," Ben spat. "This is serious."

"It's none of your business."

"It's all our business. I'm trying to help you. This isn't something Mum and Dad should hear from Penelope's father."

Fists balled at his side, he raged. "Why don't you stay out of my life, you tosser?"

"She's thirteen, Chris!"

"*Fourteen!*"

"Whatever!"

"And you made sure to ruin my birthday yesterday, as well, didn't you? Yeah, that's it. 'Happy birthday, Chris! Care to tell us about the night you knocked up the babysitter?'"

Ben opened his mouth to reply, then clamped his mouth shut. He retreated to his room and continued packing.

More than the call from Penelope Young's father an hour ago, demanding to come over and speak to his parents, his younger brother's betrayal still stung. Did no one in this family have any loyalty?

Chris marched back into his own room. Jordan sat wide-eyed atop his bed, covering his ears. "And you, you little troublemaker! Why'd you tell Ben?"

Jordan shivered in his bed.

"Well?"

The sound of the front door signaled that their parents had returned from shopping. Tomorrow was Christmas Eve. But probably not for him. Again.

Chris leaned down close to his younger brother. Through clinched teeth, he seethed, "I hope the ghost comes and swallows you up tonight."

Wide-eyed, Jordan attempted to fight back. He peeped, "Ben says there is no ghost."

"You sure about that?"

He considered a moment, then shrank back and covered his ears again.

Their parents joyfully lugged their purchases upstairs before even removing their coats. "Hide your eyes, boys! You don't want to spoil the surprise Christmas morning!"

Chris shook his head. Sod Ben. He wished he was the one moving out.

"What's going on?" George asked, stopping at Ben's doorway.

When Chris heard his father go inside and shut Ben's door, he cursed under his breath and threw himself on his bed. He did not even pick up his guitar. Instead, he rolled onto his side and glared at Jordan.

Then came the knock on the door.

"I'll get it," Lynda singsonged, unwrapping her scarf from around her head as she descended the steps.

Chris's stomach flip-flopped when he heard the shouting. And not just shouting from Ben's room. Shouting from the front door.

"Chris!"

He closed his eyes and waited.

It sounded as if their guest had managed to get halfway upstairs before his father had intercepted him. Mr. Young's voice boomed, demanding, "Where is he?"

"Calm down, Finn. Let's you and I discuss this, yeah? I confess, I just found out myself. How's Penelope?"

"Penelope's none of your bloomin' business! Now, where's that chav of a son of yours!"

"I'll deal with Chris later. Right now, you and I should sit down and have a chat."

"George? What's going on?"

"Go put the kettle on, Lynda."

"Don't put the kettle on, Lynda! But you'd well prepare an ice pack. Your son'll need it when I'm through with him!"

Frozen in place, Chris could not see his mother, but her voice filled him with remorse. He envisioned her looking up at his father from the foot of the stairs, confused, wringing her hands, and completely blindsided by the disruption to their household less than forty-eight hours before Christmas.

Ben was right. This would be worse than house restriction.

When Finn Young tried to bypass George on the stairs for the second time in his search for the young man who had defiled his daughter, the scuffle drew Ben out of his room. Jordan cried out in fear.

"George!" Lynda called. "Be careful!"

"Dad!" Ben shouted, lunging forward to separate them.

"Calm down, Finn!" George implored the man, their arms tangled amid the struggle. "Violence never solved anything!"

"Shall I call the police?" Lynda sobbed. "What's everyone on about?"

Seeing no other option, Chris rose from his bed and went to his door. When Finn Young saw him, he reached out with both hands, over George's right shoulder, and tried to grab him. Ben stood a step up from his father, blocking him before he could reach Chris.

Jordan buried his head under his pillow.

"Enough!" Ben shouted, startling the adults.

George released his grip on Finn's jacket collar when the man abandoned his attempt to get upstairs. Crying now, Lynda disappeared into the kitchen.

Finn craned his head until he had a clear view of Chris standing in his bedroom doorway. He stabbed the air with his thick, sausage-like fingers. "One day, your family won't be around to stop me, boy. What you did to my Penelope is criminal! You hear me? DO YOU?"

Ben and his father blocked the stairway as they nudged Finn Young down the stairs, one step at a time.

The longer Chris remained silent, the angrier Mr. Young grew. "Nothing to say, then? It's all good when your John Thomas is having its fun, eh? And now? You've ruined my Penelope!"

For a moment, it looked as if Finn would make another lunge for him. Instead, he caught his breath. Unmanly tears pooled in his eyes. Again, he stabbed the air. "You *ruined* her!"

Ben glanced back at Chris as they corralled the man downstairs and into the living room. He sneered, shaking his head. "Happy, then?"

Chris said nothing. He sat down on the top step and listened. Try as he did, George could not calm Mr. Young down.

Penelope had been sick for two weeks. At first, everyone thought it was the flu. But then, she came clean to her parents. She told them everything about that night and confessed her period was late. Tomorrow, her mother would take her to the doctor for a pregnancy test.

Somewhere in the conversation, Lynda served the tea. Ben helped. But that was the best she could do. She sat in her chair near the sofa, sobbing in horror and humiliation. Finally, George told her it might be best if she went upstairs.

Chris sat in place, shoulders hunched, elbows on his knees. Lynda climbed the staircase, head high. When she reached him, she stopped. Arms akimbo, her voice low and deliberate, she said, "I can take a lot from you, Christopher. And I have. Fires. School. Trips to Germany. But this? Compromising a young girl?"

He stared meekly at the floor.

"So that's it, then? Nothing to say to your mother?"

Chris felt her eyes on him. Her disappointment was a living thing. He had never seen her so upset.

"Right then. I'm off to bed. You can deal with your father. I don't even want to see you."

She moved past him, walked to her bedroom, and slammed the door behind her.

"Chris?" his father bellowed from the living room. "Down here, lad, straightaway."

He swallowed hard, stood, and started down the steps like a man condemned.

When he entered the living room, Finn Young bolted up from the sofa and lurched forward, fist drawn. Before his father could stop him, the man's marble-like fist connected with his jaw, sending him backward onto the floor.

George surged toward Finn, but Ben stopped him.

Finn Young marched to the front door, spitting in Chris's face as he passed. "That's for my daughter. Come near her again and I'll bloody kill you. Got it?"

Chris lay on the floor, massaging his throbbing jaw until his vision cleared. Ben helped him up to sit on the couch, then mumbled something about getting him some ice. George sat in his wife's armchair and stared at him, stone-faced.

When Ben returned with some ice wrapped in a kitchen towel, Chris quietly thanked him. Ben nodded, then went to check on Jordan, who had started crying.

"Your mother's upstairs, embarrassed and sobbing her eyes out," George began. "Your younger brother's upstairs, terrified. Tomorrow's Christmas Eve, and you've cocked it up once again. But this time, you weren't content to involve just our family. You've dishonored a poor girl and her parents. You've destroyed this family's reputation, not just your own—not that your personal infamy hasn't long been established throughout Buckinghamshire."

"I—" Chris cleared his throat. "I'm sorry, Dad."

"Do you even know the meaning of those words, son? I wonder...I wonder."

He pressed the improvised ice pack against his jaw and slumped in his seat.

"Somehow, you're going to repay Finn Young's family. First, you're going to stay away from Penelope. Second, you're going to reimburse me the various expenses related to any medical care Penelope needs, which I'll pay for. Third—"

"I'll...I'll pay. My band has some gigs lined up."

George's doubtful laughter sliced through Chris like a razor. "You're not old enough to play venues that pay any kind of real money. You boys're starting out. And, at least for the next six months, you'll be home. Further, you'll be selling that guitar of yours to help Penelope."

Chris bolted up despite the pain. "But Dad! Not my guitar! Without it, I don't even have a band!"

George leaned back in the armchair, nonplussed. "I didn't take your guitar when you decided to quit school. I didn't take it when you lied and took off for Germany. But this isn't about you. You need to realize that."

"But my *guitar!*"

"I'll not argue with you about it. It's done. I'll take it into the city tomorrow to find a buyer. It being Christmas Eve, I'm sure I can find someone willing to give me a decent price. Then, I'll deliver the cash myself to Penelope's father. Come January second, I expect you to either get back to school or start looking for a job. We clear?"

Chris faced his father for the first time since coming downstairs. "I won't let you have my guitar."

George stood up, unmoved by the bitter glare of his middle son. "This is my house. And your mother's. We'll be here long after you've grown and moved on. While you live here, you live by our rules. Until now, you haven't had many of them. That stops tonight." He walked around the coffee table and toward the stairs. "Now, I'm going to try and calm my wife down and see how we might salvage Christmas—if only for Jordan. When I wake up tomorrow, I expect to see the guitar here waiting for me."

Chris watched as his father reached the second floor. Ben stood there. He had heard the entire thing. Instead of brotherly sympathy or an encouraging word, he shook his head again and walked away.

No way would he surrender his guitar. For years now, he had played every day. Hours upon hours of bleeding fingertips and building calluses. He had formed a band. Against all odds and the miles that separated them, they had found ways to practice. Elliot was starting to write some really good tunes. They had started getting requests around Lance's and Todd's area to play parties and birthdays. Chris would not let anyone, or anything, stop the momentum he had built. Life was short. In the last four months alone, Jimi Hendrix, Janis Joplin, and lead singer Alan Wilson of Canned Heat had died. He needed to get into the rock scene while there still was one.

He lay down on the sofa, unwilling to stay in the same room with his snitch of a brother.

The next morning, George did not find Chris's guitar waiting for him. But he did find a note.

> *You can keep your house and your rules. I'm keeping my guitar. Tell Mum I love her. And tell Penelope I'm not running from her.*
>
> *Chris*

CHAPTER 16

*T*HE PRESSURE STARTED SHORTLY AFTER *their wedding. When the baby arrived three years later, it increased. It was not her fault. She had lived a life of neither want nor worry. Naturally, she wanted to raise their son in the same manner.*

"You did promise, Jameson," Sarah had reminded him, the day they brought Bobby home. "I've tried not to keep after you. I know how hard you work, my darling. I really do. But with three mouths to feed...well, it's something we need to consider."

On a good month, he earned roughly £100. With taxes, food, rent, and various essentials, it did not go far. Sarah was right, as usual. He had promised to take care of her. In fact, he had used every bit of the money he had tried to save to that very end. Now, not a shilling remained.

And so, he worked. Harder. Longer. Weekends. Evenings. Special events. He worked until Sarah grew lonely from his time away. Yet, for all his effort, the sacrifice netted little difference.

"Have you considered a change of profession?" Sarah would ask every so often, as they cuddled the baby at night while enjoying their favorite radio shows.

The answer never varied. "Other than the coal mines and a bit of time working the docks, I've never trained for any other profession. I've little formal education."

"No one who spends five minutes with you would believe that. You're so well read. I'm certain you could find an apprenticeship and work your way up."

"Perhaps. But I'm a bit old to be starting over. The time I'd spend on the lower rungs of such ladders would ensure we remain in our precarious condition. What help is that to us now?"

She could have pushed harder than she did. They both knew it. But they had entered their union with eyes open. Jameson was a blue-collar worker. Sarah's family disapproved of him and had effectively disowned her over their marriage.

Night after sleepless night, Jameson plotted ways to better their circumstances. Sarah had turned him into a more refined version of the man he once was. Had it only mattered for the time it took to meet—and immediately suffer rejection by—her family? What future could a new name promise his family? Or was it for naught? Who was he, really: Jameson Lockhardt or Ronald Nock?

The obvious solution tormented his inner thoughts, daring him to take the risk. It was so simple. And the improvement would happen overnight. However, he did not fool himself. The life he had abandoned was a gamble in the best of times.

"Perhaps we should start attending church," Sarah had suggested more than once. "I used to go as a child. We could pray. Get Bobby baptized. Maybe God's trying to tell us something."

The last thing Jameson wanted to do was alienate the wife he loved by confessing his fervent disbelief in a Supreme Being. So he went. Twice. After that, he left the praying to Sarah.

"But we should go as a family, shouldn't we? They'll think I'm a widow. Or that I'm married to a heathen."

"I don't know why, but Sundays are becoming my busiest days. We can't afford to not take advantage. You go. Take Bobby."

"Jameson, how is it that, all of a sudden, Sundays are your busiest days? Don't you want to go to church with us?"

"Maybe that's the answer to our prayers, love. After all, God works in mysterious ways. I'm sure He'd want me to provide for my family."

"God will provide for our family."

"Looks like he has, doesn't it?"

The problem was, Jameson needed to find a way to make at least a few extra pounds to turn his lie into a reality. He fought it as long as he could. In the end, desperation led him back to his old stomping ground.

Jameson Lockhardt did not officially exist beyond the faked birth certificate he had acquired by less than legal means in order to marry. His driver's license still declared him a Nock. It worked well, because only Ronald had ever spent a night in jail. If he intermingled his old and new lives, only Ronnie would pay. Sarah Wellingham Lockhardt's reputation would never suffer. And his son would remain unblemished.

His first stop was Bethnal Green.

Still congregating with the small group of friends or associates outside his mother's house, it seemed as if he had not moved since Jameson last saw him. Still projecting that air of overconfidence, smiling with his lips while keeping a keen eye on his surroundings. Still smoking like a chimney. And still Jameson's best bet for a little side dosh to help his family along.

Tony recognized him the minute he pulled up outside the house and greeted him warmly. He motioned his group to take a walk while they talked. "If it isn't Ronnie Nock. The boys and I figured you'd gone the way of the sea by now."

Jameson exited his black cab and casually leaned against it as they chatted. His long habit of visually assessing his surroundings reemerged, though he had no current reason to worry about police presence.

In nonspecific terms, he told Tony about his marriage and the birth of his son. How he had tried, "for the sake of the missus," to walk the straight and narrow road.

Tony drew a cigarette from his pack and placed it between his lips. He sniggered as he struck a match, cupped his hand around its end to light it, then killed the flame with a shake of his wrist. "All roads lead home, then, don't they?"

"They very well may. She wants me to secure an apprenticeship. I'm thirty bloody years old, Tony. It isn't likely, but we're skint. Not sure what to do."

The man streamed smoke from his nostrils. "A shame, isn't it? It's nineteen fifty-six, and a man can't make an honest living."

Jameson glanced up to find Liz waving at him from the second-floor window. He lifted his chin at her. "How's your sister?"

"The same, I guess. Bad taste in men." Tony looked up to the window and motioned for Liz to step away and mind her own business. "Got herself in the family way a couple months ago. Bloke did a runner. He'll stay gone if he knows what's right for him."

On one hand, he wanted Tony to ask him. He did not want to be on the hook for a job beyond whatever moral compass still had a say in his life's direction. On the other hand, that compass had led him nowhere.

All he had to do was compare his appearance to that of his East End acquaintance. Most days, Jameson donned a modest suit and shirt. Clean but worn, as he had never found the money to replace the fine attire Sarah had gifted him with during their early courtship. But Tony always dressed to the nines. Shiny black wingtips, a proper fitted suit, crisp dress shirt, suspenders, and a fedora.

Tony stepped forward and stood beside him, leaning against the cab. "Still driving this bleedin' thing, I see."

"My lot, it seems. But I'm lookin'."

"My boys and I need a driver now and again. Trouble is, it's hard to find someone fit enough to watch the road but blind to what's happening in his own back seat."

"Someone the Yard wouldn't normally suspect."

Tony tapped Jameson's chest with the back of his hand. "Exactly."

"Someone who wouldn't grass."

The man nodded. He threw down his Woodbine, crushing it with the toe of his polished shoe. "My sister sees a doctor over in West Ham. It's a damn nuisance to get her there, and our mother doesn't drive. Maybe you could look after her on the days she goes. I'd be grateful for the favor."

Jameson stared straight ahead, nodding. "I could do that."

"And if you could make sure she's not sneaking around to see the father, well..."

"Always good to know what's going on in your own household."

"It is." Tony plunged his hand into his pocket and pulled out his ever-present roll of pound notes. He peeled off several tenners, folded them between two fingers, then passed them across. "Petrol's expensive. And she'll need lunch. Gotta keep her strength up."

"Whatever she wants." Jameson pocketed the cash. "I appreciate this, mate."

Tony straightened and stepped back onto the curb outside his door. "You've been good to me and to my family. But it's a short-term gig, Ron. We both know it. By the time Lizzy has the little piker, you need to decide. You in or out?"

He nodded again, determined to find an alternative means of bettering his family before Lizzy delivered. Sarah could never know.

***

Beads of sweat dotted and trickled down Jameson's face. It was useless to keep mopping them up with the damp hand towel beside him. He loathed the sauna. Ross loved them. How his lawyer-friend could relax or feel refreshed after a session of heat and humidity confounded him.

Head back, eyes closed, arms limp beside him, Ross lounged upon the slatted cedar bench, a towel knotted at his middle. "I'm sorry, my friend. That's tough."

"She hasn't filed...yet." Jameson wiped away the perspiration near his stinging eyes. "But I imagine it's just a matter of time."

"I know you'd hoped things would end differently."

"I'd hoped it wouldn't end at all. However, we've been apart so long now, we've become different people."

"Do you still love her?"

"I'll always love her."

"And your son? What about him?"

Jameson shook out the flimsy towel, rubbed down his face and neck, then scraped his lower lip across his upper one to squeegee away the perspiration. "I saw him briefly in LA last summer. He's a good lad. I wish my schedule permitted more visits. I'm sure he understands."

Ross stood to pour a ladleful of water on the hot rocks stacked in the pit at the center of the room, then dropped back onto the cedar bench. The steam rose in curvy billows like a gypsy performing her sultry dance. Jameson was sure the increased humidity would choke him.

"Another ten minutes," Ross said, as if reading his mind from behind closed eyes.

Jameson employed the towel once more in his feeble attempt to mop up the moisture pooling on his face. "You're avoiding work."

"That's the Conserves way, anymore. No one wants to go in."

"You said a year ago they'd be gone by now. Maybe there's hope?"

"I've been as creative as I can be. No. There's no hope. Just a slow death. I've agreed to stay on until they decide to cut and run. G has something against the EMI leadership. Some sort of history or bad blood or something. He'll never sell. I've given up trying to make him see reason."

"It's a funny business, to be sure."

"You're doing well, though. I knew you would."

"I can put in a word, if you..."

"Wouldn't that be ironic?"

Jameson exhaled sharply through his nose. "I'm not long for the place anyway."

Ross blinked and squinted his eyes open, sitting forward.

"I'm not quitting. I'm just...looking."

"But why?"

"It's frustrating to watch bad managers waste good talent while they nurse hopeless cases. They ignore bands who lack stage presence but can write good songs and are willing to take direction, then develop showy bands with better stage presence even though they lack the ability to write their own material. I'm speaking in generalities, of course. A difference in perspective."

Lifting his chin, Ross leaned back again. "Maybe you should start your own label after all."

Their running joke had grown less amusing over time. The seeds of such a possibility had taken root. Jameson wondered if they might grow.

Throughout his adult life, he had watched those around him miss more opportunities than he had ever been given. The longer he struggled to eke out a meager living following someone else's rules, the more it frustrated him. He wanted more. If he remained subject to the will of a superior, he might never obtain it.

Mercifully, they left the sauna, showered, then Ross agreed to a drink. His extended lunch had long since turned into an afternoon off. No point in returning to sit behind his desk pretending to shuffle papers. As for Jameson, he rarely worked during the day anymore. His real job was to frequent clubs in the search of the next breakout artist.

As usual, the music business was shifting. Singer-songwriters were still the rage, but he spied an artistic fragmentation on the horizon. Rock'n'roll was not one thing. Pop. Soul. Funk. Rhythm and blues. Subgenres expanded like surface roots on a giant fig tree. Evidence of a new, post-psychedelic genre of lesser-skilled, vocally challenged garage musicians was everywhere if one bothered to pay attention. American music critic Dave Marsh had labeled it "punk rock" a year ago.

Tough, angry rockers with arguably little talent and even less respect for social mores had started to emerge. They commandeered the typical four-count rock beat, speeding it up with driving, dissonant electric guitars. Vocals had devolved into incomprehensible, unmelodious shrieks of fury. These self-styled anarchists organized themselves into bands of rebels who expressed their discontentment with whatever they deemed "the establishment" in far harsher manners than ever did the California hippies. When leaving their basements and garages, these "punks" played underground venues, and were notorious for their discordant guitar licks, foul lyrics, and violent performances.

The Rockin' Ramrods. MC5. The Stooges. To Jameson, every downstroking guitar note was pure noise—sufficient enough to drive him back to the eucalyptus-scented hills of Laurel Canyon and the "make love, not war" crowd. But whatever this new "punk rock" was, it was undeniably the next big thing. At least, it would be if its poster-children could ease off the heroin.

Ross slid onto a bar stool. "If you hate music so much, why are you staying in it?"

"Because I'm good at it." Jameson nodded at the barkeep as the man dropped cocktail napkins in front of them and collected their order. "And I don't hate music."

"I've never once heard you say you like a song, or an artist."

"I admire strong work ethic."

"Many musicians work hard."

"Perhaps, but how many work so hard after they succeed? It's common to strive for what one wants. It's not about that. It's about what they do once they get what they want."

Ross flirted with a bowl of communal nuts as he considered his friend's response. He popped a few in his mouth. "Okay, but that isn't what I said."

The bartender delivered their drinks, collected the cash Jameson had dropped on the bar, then left to get change.

"I may not like most popular music, but I seem to have an ear for it. Instinct, perhaps. I'd prefer to believe it's less simple than that, however."

"How so?"

"I appreciate talent. I even appreciate a skillfully written piece of music. That doesn't make me a music lover. But not being a music lover doesn't mean I dislike music."

Ross huffed. "Less simple, you say? And here I was feeling relaxed after my sauna."

"Drink up." Jameson touched his glass to Ross's. "And tell me all about your anniversary. Did Josephine like the necklace?"

"What woman doesn't like diamonds? But I think she enjoyed the weekend in Maine even more. I may never eat lobster again."

They drank and talked until well after dark. Mostly, they avoided business. Jameson extolled Dorothy Kirsten's performance as Mimi in *La Bohème* at the Met the week before. Ross told him Josephine adored theater and had mentioned wanting to see the Johnny Johnson revival next month. They made tentative plans to go as a trio.

Ross laughed, then grew serious. "What about a date?"

Jameson peered curiously at him. "I'm not following."

"For you. For the theater. Instead of a trio, why not ask someone to join us? We can make it a double date. Maybe go to dinner before?"

He finished his drink and set the empty glass on the condensation-soaked cocktail napkin before him. At the other end of the bar, the bartender raised his chin. Jameson nodded.

"And don't tell me you're swearing off women, either. I'm sorry it's not working out with Sarah, but that's no excuse to swear off women. You're too young."

He gazed at the gold band on his ring finger. "She hasn't filed for divorce...yet."

***

For two summers, Bobby had battled. To go out. To help his mom. To talk to his father. To see the few friends who had not given up on him over his very strange and very secret home life. And where his mother had her good periods and her bad periods, the good periods were becoming increasingly rare.

Even if he did not understand them, her excuses were real—to her. It frustrated her when all the exterminators in Santa Barbara failed to rid them of the ants running roughshod throughout their sprawling Hope Ranch estate. The local supermarket managers had long ago stopped letting her return all the poisoned food she claimed they sold her.

Sometimes, there was nothing at all in the house to eat. At one point, she had threatened to smash all the glasses in the cupboard because she feared "they" had poisoned the tap water, and Bobby refused to stop drinking it. She was losing weight, not just her mind.

He did not know what to do. She needed help. There was no denying it any longer. But she had made him promise not to tell a soul. Not even his father. No big feat, there. His father rarely called. And almost never visited.

Despite his high hopes for the summer preceding eighth grade, he had not made a single call from the numbers in his yearbook. Each time he had considered it, either his nerves or his circumstances intervened. Both Kerry Iverson and Wendy Myers had called several times, but his mother had beat him to the phone each time.

"Why do you want to talk to my son? Who are you?" she would demand.

He could only imagine they had been stunned by the shocking interrogations.

"*Answer me!*"

Sometimes, she answered the phone screaming.

Eventually, the calls had stopped altogether.

Embarrassment had prevented him from attempting to reach out to them to try to explain. He could have done so during one of the many times his mother confined herself to her room. But what would he have said?

"Sorry, my mom's crazy."

"Sorry, she's afraid I'll be kidnapped."

"Sorry, I'm afraid she'll hurt herself if I leave."

"Sorry, it's hard enough to go to school without her showing up."

So instead, he had stayed around the house. He had read. He had watched television. He had listened to the radio. He had helped around the house. He had found her stashes of money. At least he would not starve. And he had discovered the numbing effects of alcohol.

Bobby returned to La Cumbre Junior High School for his eighth-grade year, humiliated. Most of the kids who had signed his seventh-grade yearbook were ambivalent. Lots of kids traded phone numbers but never connected. But Kerry Iverson and Wendy Myers had made it a point to avoid him. They had looked away when they passed him in the halls. In the classes they shared, they had taken seats as far away from him as possible. And they had whispered about him to others.

They had made him feel like a freak. And maybe he was.

At the end of eighth grade, he collected his yearbook on the last day, just as he had the previous year. But this time, he rushed home before anyone could stop him. There were no signatures, no phone numbers, no promises to keep in touch...no opportunity for rejection.

Like the summer before, he remained isolated. He pacified himself with brandy, and the knowledge that ninth grade would mark his final year at La Cumbre. Maybe high school would be different. San Marcos would have kids from other schools around Santa Barbara. He could make a fresh start. Again.

At least he had seen his father that summer, even if only for a few days.

"I'm in Los Angeles on business," he had announced. "I'll come visit if that's okay."

His mother panicked at first.

"You remember what Mummy said, Bobby."

"I know, Mom."

"Your father wouldn't understand. It's you and me, remember?"

"I remember."

"Tell him he needs to find a hotel. You can stay with him there. I...I can't see him."

In the end, they both pulled themselves together. His mother did so to avoid sending up red flag warnings over her mental state. Bobby did so to avoid having his father discover that he had started drinking quasi-regularly at the age of fifteen.

His father had booked a cottage at the San Ysidro Ranch. For three days, Bobby would have him to himself. At first, he felt awkward and unsure how to behave. It was the first time they had spent alone together since he was too young to remember. Neither of them seemed to know how to connect.

Then, out of the blue on the second night, his mother joined them for dinner.

Sitting together like a real family had thrilled Bobby. His dad came alive. His mom looked resplendent in her silk dress. It even appeared as if she had gotten herself to the salon.

For a few hours, they were the family Bobby had romanticized over for so long. They dined at the hotel restaurant. His father ordered champagne for the two of them, and a Shirley Temple for him. His mother consumed her steak without spitting anything out over fears of strychnine poisoning. And they danced.

"I'd like to propose a toast," his father announced after the waiter delivered their drinks.

His mother smiled radiantly, glass aloft. Bobby lifted his grenadine-infused ginger ale.

"To the Lockhardts. To new beginnings. To a bright future for us all."

Bobby touched his glass to each of theirs, then sucked a generous sip through his straw. His father was everything he vaguely recalled, and so much more. Maybe he would save them. Maybe he would come to live with them. Maybe his mother would recover.

Later that night, after the dinner and the dancing, they returned to his father's cottage. Bobby could tell his father wanted to talk privately with his mother. He wanted to stay up and spy on their conversation, but ended up falling asleep.

The next morning, he awoke to disappointment when he found his mother gone and his father in bad spirits. Whatever magic they had shared the night before had evaporated. For the remainder of the visit, it was just his father and him. The awkwardness returned. And soon, so did Bobby. To his home. Alone.

After his return, his mother did not leave her bedroom for a week. Bobby helped finish off the assorted bottles of booze she stashed around the house.

Later that summer, she forgot to take him school-clothes shopping. He ended up taking some of the money she stashed and slipped off to the mall on his bike. There, he saw some of the kids from school, shopping with their parents. No one had even waved at him.

Life at La Cumbre did not improve during ninth grade. As a freshman, he had become invisible. No one even bothered to whisper behind his back anymore. A couple of other outcasts took pity on him after the Christmas break, but that did little more than give him people to sit with at lunch.

Sophomore year at San Marcos had to be different. He needed hope. He needed friends. He needed to start thinking about what he would do after high school. And he needed to decide whether or not to keep his mother's secrets.

CHAPTER 17

BEN RELOCATED FROM HIS PARENTS' Bledlow home to a London flat in January 1971. Eighteen and successful, the commute had become an impediment. He needed to be closer to the artists seeking his music. It made sense to situate himself in closer proximity to the studios. Thanks to his father's contacts and assistance, Ben was in. And he was "it."

Yet, where he was initially excited about the prospect of transitioning from his boyhood home to a place of his own, Chris's dramatic departure left him feeling guilty for leaving. Their parents were distraught—particularly their mother. Jordan blamed himself for months, despite Ben's semi-regular calls reassuring him that what had transpired was not his fault.

The year passed in a blur. Ben spent most of his free time camping out with bands looking to write their next album, or with those wanting a brilliant one-off single, or in the studio, writing music as the artists recorded. Occasionally, engineers would give him crash courses on how they worked the studio boards. Making music was a complex process. He absorbed their tutelage like a sponge.

"When will you come for a visit?" his mother would ask each time he rang the house. "We miss you. Jorie's been asking for you."

She sounded lonely. Even with their father home now, and even with her youngest still more or less at heel, the abrupt departure of not one but two of her sons had hit her hard. A decade and a half had passed since she had sacrificed her once-thriving career for family. And what did she have to show for it? The slow transition of the responsibilities of wife and mother back to wife, this time without an independent career, would take some getting used to.

It did not help that their father, not yet fifty, seemed to have aged overnight after Chris left. He did not discuss his feelings as readily as their mother, but Ben sensed the regret and anxiety associated with Chris's absence.

"He spends a fair amount of time in the garage, now," his mother had told him when he called on Mothering Sunday with apologies that he could not come home for a short visit. "He's restoring a nineteen fifty-one

Austin A-forty he bought from a gentleman in Surrey. He drove an hour and a half one way to pick it up, then had to tow it another hour and a half back. Such an ordeal."

"I guess that means he's officially got himself a hobby, then, doesn't he?"

"Spends all his time talking about restoration these days. And of course, Jorie wants to be out with him but doesn't really want to work on cars."

"Is he practicing his guitar like I told him?"

"Well..."

It disappointed Ben to hear about Jordan's waning interest in his instrument. He played okay, but lacked the desire to take it seriously. According to his mother, he still enjoyed singing along to the radio. Sometimes, he still sang with her. But the Grant household had diminished by two, leaving a void everyone felt.

"Should I move back, Mum? Is it that bad?"

"Benjamin Alan Grant, don't you think on it! We'll be fine. You have a whole life to live. It's an adjustment, that's all. It was bound to happen eventually. One by one, your children leave. I just wasn't prepared for..."

It tore Ben up to hear his mother cry. Though he told no one, he sometimes wondered if it would have been easier for his mother if Penelope Young's pregnancy test had come back positive. The prospect of becoming a grandmother might have distracted her from the heaviness of losing her two oldest sons. Of course, it would have likely caused more problems than it would have solved.

Like his mother, Ben dealt with his own transition. For years, he had acted as a virtual stand-in father to his siblings. That pressure had eased upon their father's retirement, but it had taken Ben months on his own for him to truly embrace his freedom. When his mother assured him he did not need to move home, he felt enormous relief.

Career on track, he looked to the next step. He saved every bit of money he could in the hopes of buying a home in the following year. Another rite of passage into adulthood. What he did not tell his mother was that he hoped to one day relocate out of England altogether.

Americans had started calling him for material. He enthusiastically obliged but told no one. Not even his manager/father.

"The band wants to meet you." Peter Barrett, manager of the up-and-coming pop sensation Sterling, had called him out of the blue in early July.

"We'd like to fly you over."

"What are they looking for?"

"A Grammy. When can you come?"

Ben spent the summer working at RCA Studio A in New York. The best producers. The best engineers. A talented, hardworking band. And him— on the edge of nineteen and overwhelmed by early success. He had never traveled to another continent. And, while he could never promise anyone a Grammy, the finished work had impressed everyone who mattered.

Money was good. Better than good. But the experience meant more than anything. Work begat more work.

"We need you in Chicago."

"Please get back to London as quickly as you can."

"There's this band recording at Hansa…"

"How soon can you be in Toronto?"

The days of penning lyrics and composing melodies from the foot of a twin bed in his parents' home were long gone. Musicians liked Ben because he understood them. Producers liked him because they got timely results when he was around. Engineers liked him because he understood their technical language and the sounds they worked to achieve. He developed a reputation and solid contacts. No longer in his father's shadow, he had emerged his own man.

His burgeoning schedule had him committed through next spring. Come December, he decided he needed a couple of weeks' rest. And he knew exactly where he needed to go to get it.

When he arrived at the house in Bledlow, his mother locked her arms around him as if she would never let go. "How long can you stay?"

"Until the New Year, if you'll have me."

She shook her fists in excitement. "It'll be a proper Christmas, then!"

He waggled his eyebrows. "And I brought presents!"

His father emerged from the garage in grease-stained coveralls, smiling and wiping his face with a worn blue shop towel. He extended his hand, then brought Ben in for a hug. "It's good to see you, lad. Good indeed. Been keeping up with you in the trades. You make your mum and I proud."

Jordan came running out full force from the backyard.

Ben caught him in his arms, lifted him up, and spun him around. Releasing him with an exaggerated grunt, he stood back and gave him the once-over. "Look at you! I can't believe how much you've grown. It's barely a year!"

For the first two days, he did nothing but eat and sleep. The third day, he felt rejuvenated enough to go for a walk with Jordan up to Wain Hill like they used to in younger years.

The exercise soothed him. Until now, he did not realize how much he missed country living. Not that he could complain. He was right where he belonged. London was an exciting city.

For all the enthusiasm Jordan had displayed over having his big brother home, Ben found him curiously silent as they walked along. They reached the Ridgeway at the foot of Wain Hill at high noon, then began their climb.

"So," Jordan broke the silence at last, "have you heard from him?"

Ben took a beat before answering. Perhaps the question was inevitable. But what good would such a conversation do either of them?

"I try not to ask Mum and Dad. It upsets Mum too much. Well, both of them, I suppose."

"We're still a family, Jordan. No matter what happens. Never forget that."

"I know. But I haven't heard anything. Either nobody knows or they know something and just won't tell me. So...have you?"

They navigated through the thick woodland and headed for the clearing.

"I haven't spoken to him, no. But I hear things now and again. He's staying with the brother of one of his bandmates. They're working wherever and whenever they can. Mostly parties and such. They're still too young to get any proper gigs. I hear they're good."

"But he's okay?"

"I think so, yeah."

"Does he know about Penelope?"

"I don't know. Maybe."

"You know, today's his birthday."

Ben softly nodded.

"Think he'll call?"

"Dunno, buddy. He might. I wouldn't bet on it. Let's just try to give Mum and Dad a happy Christmas. How does that sound?"

They spent the early afternoon seated at the center of the chalk cross where Jordan used to go to pray for the safety of their home. Though still a preteen, Ben liked talking to his younger brother. They had always understood one another in ways their other family members did not. Their eight-year age gap had never mattered. They "got" each other.

"Mum says you're not playing anymore."

Jordan drew in the chalky earth with his index finger. "It's not the same with you and Chris gone."

"I get it."

"You mad?"

He tousled Jordan's blond mop. "Why would I be mad?"

"Because maybe I won't be in music like everyone else."

"That's tomorrow's business. You're eleven. You don't know what you're going to be yet. That's no crime. You'll figure it out when you figure it out."

They made sure to return home long before dinner. Their mother had promised to make one of Ben's favorites: stew and dumplings. Visiting home had made him realize how much he missed her cooking. Since his return, he had stuffed himself at every sitting.

When they returned from their afternoon out, they heard their mother crying in the bedroom. They looked at each other, unsure what to do.

Eventually, she came downstairs, dabbing her red-brimmed eyes. "Don't mind me, lads. I'm fine. Dinner won't be an hour."

Chris. Again. He did not even have to be present to make their mother cry.

***

Kelley twirled Beth on the dance floor to the Stylistics' "You Are Everything," absorbing her radiance as her shimmering gown billowed and swirled around her.

She returned to his arms with an elegant flare, giggling. "I'm dizzy! I haven't danced like this in...well, I've never danced like this."

He held her tight. "Get used to it. You're so beautiful when you smile. So free. This is what you were made for."

"I was made to be right here," she said, snuggling into the nape of his neck.

"Really? So...maybe we should leave early?"

She squeezed his hand. "The night's still young. And so are we."

"I dunno, babe. Thirties. Is that so young?"

"Young enough."

They swayed together as one person, Kelley humming in her ear. "Young enough to discuss having another baby?"

She pulled back and looked at him. "Are you serious?"

"Why not?"

"Farin's eight. Isn't that an awfully big age gap?"

"One man's age gap is another man's built-in babysitter, no?"

She nuzzled back into his neck. "We'll talk about it later."

"That, we will." He twirled her again, then dipped her in grand fashion.

When the song ended, Beth took her husband's hand and led him back to their table. Carol and Joseph had returned as well.

"Should we call the sitter?"

Carol swept her dress beneath her as she sat down. "I called an hour ago. They're fine."

Beth patted her hair. "All this celebrating gets exhausting, doesn't it?"

Joseph inched his chair closer to his wife, draping his arm along the back. "We're celebrating more than the win this time. Kelley and I are considering taking on a partner."

Beth turned to her husband, agape. "Are we doing as well as all that?"

He bobbed his head side-to-side. "So far, so good."

"Better than good," Joseph insisted, reaching for his drink.

Kelley lifted his glass, toasting the air. "Better than good."

"If things continue as they are, we'll start putting feelers out within, I'd say, the next year. Stay tuned."

Carol rested her elbow on the table, her lips pulled to one side. She eyed the men with equal measures suspicion and wonder. "All right, spill it."

Kelley and Joseph traded smiling glances.

She pointed at them in turn. "You know they're planning something, Beth. Look at them. So where are you taking us this time?"

Beth folded her hands in her lap. She stared at them, expectant and playful. "It is about that time, isn't it, Carol?"

"After Christmas, before New Year's. And always a grand announcement during couples' night. So go on, tell us."

Joseph leaned back casually in his chair. "I don't know what you two're talking about."

Carol play-slapped his chest. "C'mon. Don't tease us. Will it be during the girls' Easter vacation, or do we have to wait until summer?"

He shrugged. "Easter vacation's out, sorry. We're looking at a very busy spring. As for summer, well...I dunno."

Beth turned and squinted at Kelley. He lifted innocent hands.

"I'd hate to have to involve my mother-in-law," Joseph continued cryptically.

"What? Why? And you love my parents! Everyone loves my parents."

Their waiter arrived at the table. He bent down to whisper in Kelley's ear.

Kelley patted Beth's shoulder, then stood up. "Be right back."

"Everything all right?"

He extended his thumb and pinkie finger to his ear and mouth, then stalked to the front of the restaurant, nodding cordially as the hostess handed him the phone. "Everything okay, hon?"

"Daddy? Tell her to stop!"

"Stop what?"

"Marci says she's gonna paint the walls pink! Pink! It's my treehouse. Tell her she can't paint the walls pink!"

He sidestepped away from restaurant foot traffic with an apologetic smile. "Sorry," he mouthed to the hostess. Then, to Farin, "Why are you calling the restaurant to tell me this, hon?"

"Because it's *pink*, Daddy! And it's *my* treehouse!"

"It's December, Farin. No one's painting anything for a while. Why don't we talk about this tomorrow over breakfast? Marci's spending the night tonight, yes?"

An exasperated sigh of frustration filled the line.

"I'll make pancakes. For now, you girls need to get ready for bed."

"We already are."

"Good. Mom and I'll be home soon. I love you. Now, put Katie on the phone."

When he returned to their table, he briefed his wife and friends on the crisis unfolding at home.

Beth rubbed Kelley's back as he took his seat. "I can't believe she called for that."

"It's that thing our daughter has with pink," Carol said. "But I think sometimes she likes getting Farin all worked up."

"Most girls like pink." Joseph lifted the bottle of champagne from the ice bucket to refill their flutes.

Beth extended her glass toward the bottle. "Most girls don't turn their Barbies into rock singers."

Kelley smirked. "What can I say? Farin's gonna be a star. Mark my words."

Beth indulged his prediction with a kiss on his cheek. "So where were we? Oh yes. You men were just about to announce where you're taking us all this coming year."

"And what that has to do with my parents." Carol dipped her chin at her husband, arching her eyebrow.

Joseph looked at Kelley. "I guess we've kept them in suspense long enough."

Kelley winked and gave his friend a go-ahead wave.

"Okay. Well, here goes. This year, we're bringing your parents out, Carol. They'll stay at our place for a couple of weeks."

Carol tilted her head. "That's it?"

Joseph nodded.

"That's the big summer surprise?"

"What else do you want? We'll still have the camping trip over Memorial Day weekend."

"And we were thinking of a couple of days in Disneyland before the girls start fourth grade," Kelley added.

Carol grabbed her handbag with a disappointed pout. "Come on, Beth. I need to powder my nose."

"You just said we all love your parents," Joseph called after her, smirking.

Kelley leaned forward. "When should we tell them?"

When the women returned, Joseph ordered more champagne. Carol jerked her head away from her husband when he tried to kiss her cheek. It did not help matters when he found himself suppressing a laugh.

"I'm not ungrateful," she explained. "It's just that it's nice to get away in the summers. I spend all year at the house. And you said yourself, we're doing well."

Joseph gave a thoughtful nod. "Which is why we need your parents to watch the girls while we're in Brazil."

"Honestly, Joe, I think—"

He raised his brows at her and waited.

"Did...did you say Brazil?"

Beth gaped at Kelley. "Seriously?"

He smiled, then leaned over and whispered in her ear. "Can you imagine telling our future second child that he or she was conceived on a beach in South America?"

***

Instead of reprisals over Faith's refusal to return home over Christmas break, she received cash. Nearly two hundred bucks' worth, if she added in what her grandparents sent her. And no guilt trips from Walt and Millie. It was perfect.

"Second trimesters are always hard on your mother, kitten. We're not doing much this year. We didn't even decorate. I'll probably try to find an open diner and grab some food to go."

Whatever. Faith was fine with them having a second child. At least their attention would not focus solely on her. Rather than speculate on whether she would have a brother or sister, she wondered if her mother would give birth to another pianist or something different. Austin Jones also taught violin.

Yvonne Quale's parents had gone to Barbados for Christmas. They had offered to bring her, but she declined. "I want to get some extra practicing in before next term. But have a great time." They had not balked at the suggestion. In fact, they sounded relieved.

"That's the good thing about getting older and living off campus, Faith. Our parents stop freaking out every time we want to stay behind. Practice is always a good excuse."

The girls hung out, shopped, and visited the various museums in town. Yvonne had come in to two tickets for *Jesus Christ Superstar* at the Mark Hellinger Theater the Wednesday between Christmas and New Year. They snuck backstage during intermission and caught of glimpse of Ben Vereen and Yvonne Elliman.

"Are you nervous about the concert?" Yvonne asked later, as they roamed Times Square, munching on street vendor sauerkraut dogs before heading back to their dorm.

"A little. What about you?"

"I get terrible stage fright. Always have. I'm afraid I'll twist my ankle during my tap solo."

"Really?"

She nodded, mouth full of kraut, relish, and dog, then rinsed it down with a slurp of Pepsi. "Recurring nightmare, if you can believe it."

"Hopefully, we can smoke a little before the show. That calms me down."

"Exactly. Glad you've lightened up."

Faith moved her head back and forth in a dreamlike figure eight. "Lighter than air."

They window-shopped another hour. When the tourist foot traffic increased, they decided to walk the half-hour trek back to school instead of wasting what money they had left hailing a cab. Winter weather had never bothered Faith, anyway. She enjoyed the crisp air and any excuse to sport the new leather jacket she had purchased to replace her first, which she had outgrown once she finally got breasts.

Yvonne stuck her gloved hands in her jacket pocket as they strolled down Broadway. "Wanna stop at Columbus Circle and have a bowl before we go back?"

"Sure."

Tourists with cameras milled about the Circle, along with local commuters pacing toward buses or the subway entrance. Horse-drawn carriage drivers passed out wool blankets to their bundled patrons before trotting off into Central Park for a quick tour before the big snowstorm forecasted for the evening.

The girls found a spot not too far into the park where they could indulge in private. When they finished, they continued down Broadway toward Lincoln Center.

But at the corner of West 60th Street, Faith abruptly stopped.

Halfway into the intersection, Yvonne realized she was walking alone. She laughed, doubling back before the light changed. "What's the matter? Too buzzed to walk?"

She stood statue-like, staring across the street at the entrance to the shops.

Yvonne attempted to follow Faith's line of vision, but could not figure out what held her attention.

Suddenly, Faith bolted off across the street, waving frantically. Horns blared as she dodged cars, buses, and taxis. "Mr. Beam!"

The cacophony of horns and shouts caused tourists to turn and stare. For the most part, locals ignored the outburst.

"Mr. Beam!" Faith yelled again, sprinting to catch up as he walked in the opposite direction to which she and Yvonne had traveled. "Wait up! Please!"

He turned around as the space between them decreased, visibly curious to see who had called his name. She held her side, panting to catch her breath, as she looked at him. His eyes widened in recognition and, Faith sensed, fear. He said nothing at first.

She could not tell if her sudden presence had delighted or disturbed him.

"F-Faith," he stuttered, glancing left, then right. "What are you doing here?"

"Walking." Inside, she cursed her clumsy response. "I mean, walking back to my dorm."

"Dorm? You mean you finally made it?"

She brightened. *He remembered!* "Yes!"

"Congratulations!" He smiled broadly, showcasing those beautiful white teeth of his. "I knew you could do it."

His hands remained buried in his camel topcoat's pockets as they spoke. When she attempted to go in for a hug, he took a casual step back.

"What's the matter, Mr. Beam?"

"Nothing, nothing. I'm just surprised to see you. How've you been? You look well."

"I..." She wanted to tell him she had been looking for him for years, that she was sorry she had caused so much trouble, that she still thought about him every day—that she loved him. "Where've you been? Are you still in New York?"

The longer they stood there, the more uncomfortable he seemed. He stuttered when he spoke. Every few seconds, his eyes darted around as if expecting someone to show up.

"What's the matter, Mr. Beam?" she asked again, numb from weed and rejection.

"Faith, I—"

"I'm sorry about what happened at school. I never meant to..."

"Shhh." He withdrew a gloved hand and patted her shoulder.

The thrill of his touch sparked her every nerve. She hitched her breath.

He had not changed a bit since she last saw him, save the shock of gray contrasting his otherwise thick, black hair at the sides of his temples. Every bit as handsome as she remembered. Tall. Dreamy brown eyes. Slightly thick around his middle. Not at all like her stick-thin father.

He leaned slightly forward, leveling sad eyes upon her. "Where are your parents?"

"Home, in New Rochelle." Her heart beat so hard she felt it might burst. "Won't you please talk to me?"

Mr. Beam straightened, again scanning their surroundings. He consulted his watch, then stuffed his hand back into his jacket pocket. "I'm not really supposed to talk to you."

"That was three years ago," she pleaded. "I never even got to say goodbye. At least let me buy you a coffee. It's the least I can do."

He grinned despite himself. "You don't drink coffee, do you?"

"I could start," she suggested with a coy shrug.

They stood together for what felt to Faith like blissful eternity as Karl Beam considered her offer. Across the street, Yvonne waved to get her attention, then impatiently lifted her arms. Faith shook her head and held up a finger.

"Please, Mr. Beam. I've missed you so much."

Her proclamation drew a troubled expression. He cleared his throat. "You know, hon, I really don't think it's a good idea. Just talking to you like this could get me in trouble. It's not your fault, so don't keep blaming yourself. I just...can't."

Faith tried not to fantasize about all the ways she could rid the world of Walt and Millie Peterson for good. They had done this to him. He was scared. Too scared to even talk to her.

"Please."

When he exhaled, she watched his foggy breath in the cold air. It took every ounce of restraint she could muster not to kiss him.

"Faith, I'm gonna have to say no. I'm sorry. It's great to see you. You know, I've often wondered how you are. And you look terrific. I just...I just can't risk it."

"My concert!" she blurted out as he turned to leave.

He stopped and faced her.

"I'm in a concert at Juilliard at the end of March. Will you come? Please, Mr. Beam?"

He looked down, shoulders slumping. "Faith..."

"Don't say no. At least say you'll think about it." From across the street, she heard Yvonne shout her name. Faith gritted her teeth and jerked her head at her. "Just a second!" She faced him again. "I've gotta go. But please say you'll at least think about it. Even if it's a lie."

With a tilt of his head, he pushed his lips out and squinted. "You win. I'll think about it. But I can't promise anything."

"Thank you!" She squealed, lurched forward, and stole a quick kiss.

Before he could respond, she raced back across the street, again prompting all manner of honking protests as she dodged traffic.

He had said he would think about it. That was enough for today.

CHAPTER 18

OZENS OF JOYFUL WELL-WISHERS SQUEEZED into the tiny Bethnal Green terrace home the day Lizzy and the baby left the hospital. Brightly colored, handmade "It's a Girl!" banners drawn on long sheets of white butcher paper by her close mates and neighborhood children hung throughout the living room and kitchen. Champagne flowed. Cigar smoke hung thick in the air. It was a day to rejoice. And, for Jameson, a day of decision.

Tony took him out back to chat privately. He slipped him a final payment for his services, which included a handsome bonus. "You done a right good job for us, Ron. You've earned every bit."

Jameson pocketed the cash, eyeing their surroundings for prying eyes. "Cheers, mate."

"Like I said, we can always use you if you're interested. But no more fence-straddling. You're in, or you're out. Now, I can always find a little extra on the side, but if you want the steady dosh..."

Jameson had thought about it every day for the last six months. Everything inside him told him to thank Tony for the short-term gig and walk away clean. For the sake of his marriage. For the sake of the man he believed Sarah had made him. But the lure of security was powerful.

"What're we thinking, Tony? If I'm in, I need to know what I'm in for."

"Aw, mate. You know. A little of this, a little of that. There's loads more opportunity than sitting in your car. More opportunity and more money. You know. Like you've been doing all this time."

"But no guns, right?"

"Whoa, whoa!" Tony tittered in protest, hands raised and open, as if pushing back an invisible foe. "Who said anything about guns?"

Jameson eyed him expectantly.

He jerked his head left, then right, ever watchful for witnesses to his conversations, then leaned in conspiratorially and whispered out of the side of his mouth. "Ron, you know the reality of this place as well as anyone. If you're not willing to get your hands dirty..."

Tony had a way of saying things halfway, then leaving those around him to fill in where he trailed off. It was effective. It let one make their own decision. No one could ever accuse him of heavy-handed tactics. The man was subtle. And smart.

As for Jameson, he knew all about getting his hands dirty. Moreover, money was a great motivator. He had had his taste of ease and comfort. Could he so easily walk away and expect to support his family on principles?

In the four years since they had married, Sarah rarely complained about having left her regal, carefree life on a lush, green country estate for the barren, gray slums of London's East End. She never made Jameson feel like a lesser man for it, or like she believed her father had been right about him all along. Yet over time, their impoverished existence had stolen her smile.

Tony had helped Jameson buy it back.

The additional cash had done more than pay the bills. It had enabled him to give Sarah a night at the theater for her birthday last October. Their first proper night out since they had married. The first time she had worn one of her fine, if dated, dresses in ages. And instead of spending Bobby's first Christmas as paupers who could barely scrape together enough to finance a satisfactory meal, they had a tree and presents. He had even replaced tenfold the money he had saved up before they wed.

"Oh darling," Sarah had cooed one night as they lay together after putting the baby down. "I wish you could take some time off for a holiday. You've worked so hard all winter. We barely see you. I worry."

"Soon," he had promised. "Where would you like to go?"

"How about Spain?"

"Anything for you, my love."

"Anything?"

"Anything."

"What about another baby?"

He had smiled at the idea. "A girl, perhaps?"

"Oh love, girls are infinitely more difficult than boys. They're endless baubles and bits. Bobby needs a brother. Someone he can do a bit of rough and tumble with. Bother girls."

More children meant more responsibility. He could not let Sarah down.

Jameson had long ago decided against involving himself in politics. It was useless to condemn the government for the poor state of the docklands and its surrounding neighborhoods. Pointless to expect them to help improve their standard of living. Rationing had only recently ended in full. The newest invasion into their lives was the forced relocation of residents by way of "slum clearing" and the rebuilding of low-income housing. The docks had started closing. Railways suffered cutbacks. Loss of industry further devastated the area. And the government? Useless.

East Enders had survived the war despite taking direct hits from the enemy. Despite little help from Mother England, with her disorganization and rationing what little goods and services came in. And now, they would continue to take care of their own, without government intrusion.

Even if that meant getting their hands a little dirty.

"Count me in," Jameson told Tony. "But I won't top anyone. I've got a family."

Tony secured his fat cigar between his teeth and shook his hand. "We all have family, Ron. Look at Lizzy there, with her little girl needing someone to look after her. We're careful. We may have to get a little physical now and then, but..."

Jameson gave him a curt nod. "Okay, then. Tell me where to start."

His cabbie duties continued enough to maintain appearances. That way, Sarah would not question where he spent his time or wonder why they were not paying taxes. But as he had anticipated, it was not all driving. Tony had sounded impressed with his ability to move products they nicked off various lorries and out of appliance stores.

"You've done this before," he observed.

"A time or three, yeah."

"There's a lot more where this came from."

And there was. More money. More perks.

By March of 1957, Jameson saved enough to upgrade their living situation. He moved his wife and child out of their impoverished terrace home in Stepney into a semi-detached over in Bush Hill Park. It was not Mayfair, but it put some distance between himself and his most painful memories. Plus, it renewed Sarah's hope in him. They were finally going in the right direction.

When he started bringing home some of the items that had "fallen off the back of a truck," her elation outweighed her skepticism. Sometimes, he feared she might question him about their curious run of good fortune. She never did.

But Jameson's greed grew proportionate to Sarah's happiness. A cavern lay between the former debutante's old life and their present circumstances, however improved—not unlike the life he lived with her as Jameson Lockhardt vs. his real job, which still knew him as Ronald Nock. It would take more than a holiday in Spain, a new washer, and a Hoover to replace what she had sacrificed.

Whoever said crime did not pay had never experienced the self-policing, isolated world of London's gangland. But even petty crime, thievery, and manipulation had a ceiling.

Jameson vowed to break through it.

***

Chris awoke to Clifford kicking at his makeshift bed. "Oi! Move it. You know the rules. Up by ten, no matter how late you play. There's nowhere else to sit in here, is there?"

He sat up with a loud groan, stretching.

"And rent's past due."

He snagged his jeans off the arm of the couch and dug into one of the pockets. "Here. There's enough for me and for Elliot."

"Cheers, mate. Looks like you hooligans are starting to turn a profit. Good on you. Fancy paying my lop of a brother's share?"

"Where's all his money go?" He slipped his feet into the scrunched leg holes, then stood to slide them on.

Clifford tossed Chris's blankets aside, then plopped down on the couch to eat his beans and sausage breakfast. "Crap food and rugby. Thinks he's the next Mike Burton, that one."

He did not follow rugby enough to understand the reference. "But he plays drums."

"Exactly."

When he finished folding his bedding, he dropped it to the side of the couch atop Elliot's. "You don't think he'd leave the band to—"

"Ever seen my brother play rugby?"

Chris shook his head.

"Right, then. Trust me. Nothing to worry about, there."

He hoped so. Despite their youth, they had come a long way in the last fourteen months. Sure, they struggled to develop a unique sound to distinguish themselves from more experienced bands. Older bands. But they had worked hard to secure every gig they could find. Lunch shows. Dinner shows. Festivals. Parties. Anyone who would give them a shot.

Elliot's songwriting had greatly matured. Todd's good looks and strong vocals appealed to club owners interested in attracting female patrons. Chris had become quite adept on his axe. It would sure set them back if they had to find another drummer—especially when their drummer's brother now housed three out of the four of them. Chris hoped he had not left home for nothing. Or worse...that he might have to return a failure.

The sound of running water let Chris know he would have to wait to relieve his bladder. At least Elliot took short showers, unlike Clifford or Lance. Probably the natural result of living with a large family sharing one bathroom.

He went to the kitchen to make himself some beans on toast while he waited. The kettle still had boiling water in it, so he fixed himself a cuppa. He ate standing at the small kitchen counter, dreaming of the full breakfasts his mum used to make them on weekends.

Sometimes, he considered calling. So far, he had not. He did not want to hear his father yell. Or, his mum cry.

Ben had become a semi-regular guest on the weekly entertainment shows like *Top of the Pops*. Chris avoided watching whenever possible. The buzz in music circles concerning his older brother had increased throughout Greater London to the point Chris hesitated to use his last name. Their father's influence and connections had paved the way for a stellar career...a luxury Chris would never know.

Instead, he and his fledgling bandmates did the hard work. They hustled by day to drum up gigs throughout Greater London, then played or practiced each night until dawn. Todd's parents had indulged their only son—the youngest member of the band—by letting him and his friends use their warehouse as a practice venue. In exchange, Lance often volunteered to help Todd make deliveries. As the oldest, outsiders often mistook Lance for the mature one. At least he had a driving license.

Elliot strode out of the bathroom wet and naked, save the towel he had wrapped around his waist. Chris bid him a quick "good morning," then raced to commence his morning ritual before Clifford beat him to it.

"Where are we tonight?" Elliot asked when Chris returned. He sorted through his clothes for something clean, occasionally drawing his head back with a wince when he caught a whiff of a particularly foul-smelling T-shirt. "Is that festival this weekend?"

Chris finished the last of his toast and his tea. "It's the Woodvine party tonight over in Chislehurst. Festival's next weekend."

"Lance get the lorry?"

"I think so. He's working with Todd today, so he'll ask."

"I hope so. It's murder trying to drag our gear on the bus."

"If we keep getting steady gigs, maybe we can pick up a van of our own. Which reminds me. I paid Cliff the rent for us both."

"Cheers, mate. I'll repay you tonight."

"Just put your portion in the savings box. We'll have our own transport in no time. Then, we can find some real gigs. Maybe a residency in one of the coastal towns. Maybe even Ibiza."

"We have to do something. We're going nowhere playing parties."

"It's all experience, mate. As long as someone's paying us to play, I'll be there. And you'll be there with me."

Elliot had taken Chris in the night he had walked out on his family. He had smuggled him into his room so his parents would not know he was there. The next morning, he had told Elliot he was moving on, out of Bledlow, to somewhere beyond his parents'—and Ben's—reach. Without questioning Chris's plan, Elliot had packed his bass and a bag of essentials, then announced he would join him. No excuse. No big upset in the Lawrence family that Chris could see, but Chris did not ask why he would so easily up and leave. He was just relieved he did not have to set out alone.

"I have a date tonight." Clifford walked his breakfast dishes into the kitchen. He lifted the plate to his chin, slurping the last spoonful of beans into his mouth. "You lot need to clean up the place. It may feel like a doss-house around here, but it's not going to look like one."

"You should bring your bird 'round Chislehurst, Cliff. You haven't seen us play in weeks."

"Oh yeah? Improved any?"

Chris scoffed. "Got your rent, didn't you?"

"I did. And if you're doing as good as all that, maybe you lads'll find your own place."

Elliot and Chris exchanged concerned glances.

"That's what I thought. Now, don't get all pinch-faced. I'm not kicking you out—yet. But this place better be right before you piss off to Chislehurst."

The boys divvied up a list of chores. Chris took care of the flat while Elliot borrowed Cliff's car to transport the wash to a nearby launderette. Clifford watched the small black and white telly in his bedroom, then prepped for his date. Neither Chris nor Elliot complained.

Clifford's small Bromley flat felt even tinier once they moved in, but he had taken pity on them, having left their homes with nowhere to go. Or maybe less pity and more opportunity to offset his rent with roommates. He had made it clear from the jump that if they wanted to live with him, it would not be a free ride. When Lance joined them a few weeks later, the cramped space bulged with piles of clothes and instruments. Clifford had taken it in stride. Always smiling and happy, like Lance.

Chris finished cleaning in time to shower before Cliff needed the bathroom. Elliot returned with clean clothes later in the afternoon. Todd and Lance arrived with the van soon after. By 7 PM, they had loaded up their equipment and were headed for Chislehurst.

Barely on the road, Todd produced a bottle of whiskey. "A bit of the merry, anyone?"

"Aw, go on then, Todd," Lance complained, peeking over his shoulder, then back at the road. "You bleedin' alkie."

"You're just pissed you can't get pissed along with the rest of us." Todd chortled at his cleverness. He took a greedy gulp, then passed the bottle to his right, waving his free arm Lance's way. "Carry on, driver. Don't mind us."

Chris refused to let his younger bandmate best him. He swallowed twice as much liquor before handing the bottle to Elliot.

Elliot brought the bottle to his lips, then tipped it high but, as usual, only drank a drop. He snatched the screw cap out of Todd's hand, secured the bottle, then stowed it next to him. "We don't party until the party's over."

Todd made a face. "You'll be a boring rock star."

"At least I'll be alive to enjoy my success."

"Okay, Dad."

Elliot took the bottle and climbed into the van's passenger seat next to Lance.

"Nice try." Todd produced a second bottle. Like before, he opened then upended it for a healthy gulp before sharing.

The bitter alcohol felt warm as it traveled to Chris's belly. Before they reached Chislehurst, he could barely feel his fingers. Ah well. He could play guitar in his sleep—and, certainly, drunk.

***

It irritated Josephine. Period. They had not discussed it, but Ross knew. Husbands always knew. A better man would insist they talk it out. Instead, he worked. Josephine buried herself in church and various humanitarian causes. It worked out fine, until it stopped working.

He had made reservations for Tavern on the Green, but Josephine had changed her mind at the last minute. "It's such an ordeal to travel into the city anymore. And the crime? Best case scenario, the car's stolen. Worst case scenario, one or both of us ends up in the hospital. We can celebrate here. I'll cook."

"I'll not have my bride cooking on our anniversary."

"Then let's go somewhere local. Somewhere casual. Why on Earth do people have to get all dressed up to celebrate their most intimate evening?"

Lately, she had seemed...well, "off."

Ross canceled their reservation while Josephine changed into something comfortable. He waited until she finished before deciding just how casual she meant. When she emerged wearing a simple, pretty dress and heels, he opted for khaki slacks and an Oxford button-down shirt with a sports jacket.

"There, now. Isn't this better?"

Josephine waxed congenial while they supped at one of Greenwood Lake's most popular pizzerias. To Ross, the lack of formality made their anniversary feel commonplace. It disappointed him. But maybe they would make up for it later in the evening, once they were alone.

Neighbors and friends dining nearby stopped to congratulate them on their eighteen-year milestone. The Alexanders were staples in their community, starting back before Ross was born. More recently, Josephine's charity work with the hospital and other noble causes had set her apart as one of Greenwood Lake's most beloved residents.

It also kept her busy. Even busier than her husband's career.

They finished their unglamorous anniversary dinner with no champagne, no toast, no dessert, no flowers, and no dancing. He had planned out every romantic detail with Tavern on the Green management. Instead, they had consumed half their combination pizza and a bottle of red wine.

Maybe his gift would spark a little intimacy.

When they returned home, Ross told Josephine to change while he prepared a celebratory drink. "We're going to have a glass of bubbly. I insist. After eighteen years of marriage, we're not going to get complacent."

She leaned her head to the side to unhook an earring. "You think this is about being complacent?"

"I don't know what it's about, but I think it's time to find out. Now go. I'll get everything together. And I still have your present."

The faint smile as she retreated to the bedroom renewed his hope for a better end to their evening. When she joined him in the living room fifteen minutes later wearing a new silk peignoir with matching high-heel slippers, the tension between them eased.

They sat atop the fur carpet in front of the fire Ross had prepared before they went into town. He toasted their union, then kissed her deeply. "Whatever it is, Jo, I'll fix it. I love you. And I'll go ahead and apologize now to get it over with."

The warmth in his words thawed her icy demeanor. "I do love you, Ross. And I love the earrings. They're beautiful. Thank you."

He beheld his new set of cufflinks. "And these are spectacular."

"They sort of match your gift to me, don't they? The gold and pearl?"

"You think?" He held the two jewelry boxes side by side. "You're right. Very similar."

She sipped her champagne, set down her glass, and then snuggled into him to watch the fire. "I suppose we can still read each other's minds."

If only. "Tell me what's wrong, Jo. This isn't us."

"I know."

"Are you tired? Are you stretching yourself too thin?"

Ross felt her stiffen in his arms. He swallowed another mouthful of champagne, though he suspected this would prove to be more of a whiskey conversation.

"I'm not stretching anything too thin."

"Okay. Then what?"

She moved from his embrace, picked up her glass, and walked it to the sofa. "I need more than this."

The sudden gut punch commanded his full attention. "What? Are you...are you saying—"

Josephine massaged her temple. "Nothing like that. I just need something more. Times have changed so. Women don't just stay home anymore, isolated and alone, while their husbands work all day, then schmooze into the evening. It's nineteen seventy-two, for Pete's sake. I'm bored. We can't have children. No one needs me. What is this life about if not helping others? We've been so blessed, Ross."

He joined her on the sofa, beckoning her closer. "I need you, my love. And I've never complained about your commitments."

"Not directly, no."

"Well, I'm sorry if I've given the impression that I devalue your hard work and dedication. I don't. If anything, I envy you."

Their conversation hit a pause. They refilled their flutes and cuddled on the sofa, watching the crackling fire singe, blacken, and consume the stack of white oak logs.

"Is it my activities after work? Am I spending too much time away?"

She looked at him with downcast eyes. "That's part of it, I suppose."

"Is there more?"

Turning away, she again stiffened inside his embrace.

"Tell me."

"First, tell me why you're still working for G when the company's virtually bankrupt. You said you'd leave a year ago."

He exhaled through flattened lips. "You want me to go back to corporate law. Is that what's bothering you?"

"I don't want you to do anything you don't want to do."

"But what I'm doing is making you unhappy."

"What you're doing is fooling yourself about what the real problem is."

"So, I'm the problem?"

The weak snort she emitted told him their evening might not end as he had hoped. But inside, he knew. What he could not figure out was his refusal to admit it, if only to himself.

Jameson Lockhardt had become his best friend. Despite all misgivings. Despite every red flag and every alarm warning him to remain wary. It was not a simple matter of his bride wishing her husband spent less time away from home. It was a matter of who he spent his time away with.

"It's just...something about him, Ross."

Maybe they really could read each other's minds.

Her voice was small and concerned. "Why him?"

Such a direct question demanded an honest answer. He gathered his thoughts, hoping he could give her one. "I'm forty-five years old, Jo. And professionally, I'm miserable."

Until he had said it out loud, he did not realize how true a statement it was.

Josephine slid to the far end of the sofa, placed her flute on the end table, and kicked off her heeled slippers to rest her feet on his lap. "Tell me more. And rub my feet while you're at it."

He grinned and complied. "I don't want the sedate life of a corporate lawyer in who knows what boring business. At first, it was a whim. I grant you that. But I've grown to like the entertainment industry. I may not live the lifestyle of its executives or even my colleagues, but I enjoy what I do."

She rested her head on her index finger. "Then what's the problem? And how does a taxi driver from London suddenly fit into the equation?"

Ross closed his eyes, momentarily neglecting his foot-rubbing duties while he considered what he could, and could not, tell her. "It's complicated."

Josephine wiggled her toes to get his attention. "Try me."

No doubt about it. A whiskey conversation.

Twenty minutes of clumsy, flimsy attempts to nail down the last six years of his life left them both frustrated. Additionally, during the more frustrating moments, he rubbed his wife's feet a bit too hard.

"But why follow us here from England, Ross? It's creepy. It makes no sense."

"It wasn't like that. He wanted to reconcile with his wife, but it looks as if they're headed for divorce."

"Okay. Fair enough. But...now he's this mega-successful A&R man looking to help you find a place with GPG? And you're suddenly best friends?" She wriggled her shoulders and stared at the fire. "I don't like it. I don't like him. There's something I can't put my finger on. He's dangerous."

Ross swallowed hard. He had married an uncommonly astute woman. "Look, Jo. We're a couple of old dogs playing in a young dog's field. Neither of us do drugs, or drink excessively. We take fewer chances but make smarter choices. That makes us the oddballs. We get each other. That's all I can say. Now, finish that champagne and let me show you how glad I am you've stuck with me for the last eighteen years. Come to bed. It's late."

Her features transformed into the playful bride who could still take his breath away. "Can I wear my beautiful new earrings?"

"*Only* your beautiful new earrings."

CHAPTER 19

JAMESON USED WHAT LITTLE TIME he spent in his office observing his superiors. He watched their interactions with their subordinates, noticed their subtle flirtations with younger females—as well as some men—and regularly saw them partake of various drugs. Whatever one needed or wanted, they had it. And they liberally shared it with one another.

It was disgusting.

Everything he needed to know about running a company, he learned here. It boiled down to a simple philosophy: whatever the average music industry professional did, he needed to do the opposite.

He would give himself another year to raise the funds. Armed with a keen mind, tireless will, and the experience Ross had warned him he would need, Jameson intended to build the most successful record label the world had ever seen.

"Too bad about the dry spell," one of his low-rise, bell-bottom-wearing colleagues with platform shoes had sneered earlier as they passed near the water cooler. "Maybe the well's running dry, eh?"

"There're plenty of acts out there," he had countered. "It's not about quantity. It's about quality."

"Whatever, man."

Whatever, indeed.

He had developed a new strategy in anticipation of starting his own company. It would not do for him to pilfer established acts from GPG or anyone else once he left. The London music scene had taught him that much. To avoid a hostile end to their business relationship, he began carrying two sets of business cards—one with his professional information on it, and one with his personal information.

Part of this new approach toward his temporary employment netted him the unintended consequence of improving his rapport with management. He had become more amenable when they suggested he check out potential acts they might want to sign. Rarely anymore did he point out the various reasons one or another aspiring sensation would miss the mark. He no longer insisted he would only pursue authentic, hardworking acts. If GPG wanted flash over substance, why stand in their way?

As his success rate of finding viable artists tapered off in a year-over-year comparison, his coworkers warmed up to him. Astonishingly, mediocrity endeared him to the masses.

It soon became a game. Jameson forced himself to smile around his colleagues. Or laugh at their idiotic jokes. Sometimes, he participated in small talk. His superiors remarked favorably on his new "team player" persona. He even surprised them by providing catering trays from Katz's Deli for March's monthly meeting.

No matter the negative perception he had of those around him, he paid attention. More to the accountants and lawyers than those in lesser positions. Every nugget mattered. What rang true. What he could discount. He jotted down in a notebook any terms or subjects he intended to research in his regular visits to the New York Public Library. For the more complex legal issues, he would ask Ross.

The meeting lasted two hours. By the time people began filing out of the conference room, Jameson had four handwritten pages of notes.

Chic Cabello, the label's Executive Vice President, stood up from his place at the head of the table and called them all back. "And before we leave today..."

The attendees grumbled as they returned to their seats.

"I know, I know. Any volunteers?"

Jameson leaned left to address the young brunette seated beside him. "I usually avoid these meetings. What did I miss?"

The low-rise, bell-bottom, platform shoe-wearing sneerer from the water cooler sat opposite him. His upper lip curled into an elitist frown. "Chic's looking for the next Itzhak Perlman."

"C'mon, now," Chic prodded, visually assessing each of his employees in turn. "Who's it gonna be?"

The mention of Itzhak Perlman piqued Jameson's interest. He scanned the faces of those seated around the table, curious at the pained expressions as Chic pressed for a volunteer.

"You can bring a date," he coaxed. "Maybe go to dinner first, on GPG?"

Jameson eased back into his chair. Whatever the assignment, he was out.

Most times, he refocused his attention on less carnal matters. Sarah had left him over a decade ago. He had had no steady female companionship since. At first, he had avoided women because it felt like infidelity—and due to the lingering belief they would one day reunite. Later, because he did not want to inadvertently entangle someone in his unpredictable, often dangerous, lifestyle. Since moving to New York, he had spent every moment trying to build a future.

In truth, he was lonely. Something he would admit to no one. This weakness of character displeased him. And so, whatever the allusion to Itzhak Perlman, if it included anything having to do with a date, he would have to pass.

He called Ross the moment he returned to his office. "I know it's Friday, and short notice, but can we meet for a drink after work? I have questions."

"What kind of questions?"

"Questions I'd rather not ask over the phone."

"Ah. Business questions."

"Exactly."

"I suppose we can have a quick one. I promised Josephine I'd be home at a reasonable hour. Her sister's coming for dinner."

"I won't keep you. And I'm buying."

They made arrangements to meet at McManus at 3:30 PM.

Jameson finalized a few calls and worked out what acts he intended to catch over the next few days, then slid his notebook into his briefcase. As he stood up to leave, Chic stepped inside and closed the door.

"I need your help."

An image of Itzhak Perlman slammed into his brain.

"I...I don't date," he mumbled awkwardly before he could think of a more eloquent excuse.

Chic Cabello was a beringed, shade-wearing pimp of a man with long wiry hair, a fake tan and bad skin. A nice enough gent, though, when he was not all coked up. A rare occurrence these days.

"Fuck the date. You don't need a date. But I need you there. Everyone else in A&R has gone but you. I can't get any takers. Sorry, buddy. It's all you."

Chic produced two tickets, which Jameson reluctantly plucked from his hand. When he looked down at the venue, he groaned. "You really are looking for the next Perlman."

Unmoved, the man wrinkled his nose and sniffed, then headed back to his office. He called over his shoulder, "What I'm looking for is something nobody else has."

Jameson could not argue the logic, no matter how much he dreaded his task.

He checked his watch, then paced back to his desk and grabbed his phone's receiver. Thankfully, Ross had not yet left.

"I'm going to have to take a rain check. Say, Tuesday night?"

"Sure. Everything okay?"

"Yes and no. I may finally have an assignment that won't end up with my nursing a pounding migraine the next day. But I think Chic's lost his mind."

***

Faith peeked out from behind the stage curtain at the crowd of people milling about, chatting and taking their seats. No sign of Mr. Beam. Yet.

The good news was, her parents—stage monster Millie Peterson, in particular—were not allowed backstage. That meant no pulling her hair into a high, tight pony tail with her curls cascading down around her head and shoulders. No poking her in the eye with makeup brushes or the end of a mascara wand.

The bad news was, they had shown up despite Millie's ginormous pregnancy belly. Faith just hoped her mother's water would not break during the show. It would be just like her to go into labor in front of the whole world.

Faith had long since grown accustomed to the obligatory formal attire she had to wear for the various concerts in which she had performed over the years, but she hated it. Today's monstrosity was a sleeveless, full-length, black silk evening gown with a high, ornate neckline of silver sequins. Silver drop earrings. Black stilettos. So much elegance it made her nauseous. She wanted her leather jacket.

She wanted Mr. Beam.

"Miss Peterson," the stage manager scolded in her direction. "Get away from that curtain."

She stole a final peek at the crowd, but still only noticed Walt and Millie.

"*Now, Miss Peterson!*"

Faith grabbed the folds of her gown and hurried backstage to join her fellow performers. When she realized she forgot to put on her lipstick, she made a brief detour to the communal dressing room she had shared with the other girls. One last check to ensure her powdered face and false eyelashes looked right, and that no random hairs had managed to escape the bun Yvonne had helped her with before getting chased out of the area by the director.

Being on stage had never bothered her. The bustle and contained chaos of the myriad performers and stage crew comforted her. She enjoyed the sound of tuning instruments and the humming and trilling of vocal warm-ups. The barking of clipboard-wielding stage managers did not rattle her. Still, she had for years now longed to substitute leather jackets and electric guitars for penguin suits and cellos.

As promised, Yvonne had set her right an hour before she left for the concert hall. She had smoked enough to keep her mellow, but not too much that it would negatively affect her ability to play. Hopefully, Yvonne had stayed for the show. The thought of handling her parents all by herself after the performance bothered her far more than any stage fright.

Which Millie would approach her? The "oh my darling, you were perfection!" Millie, or the "you really tanked on that second bar" Millie? Faith never knew. Adding in the mid-life crisis pregnancy factor, it was a crap shoot.

The stage manager rapped his clipboard with the end of his pen. "Okay, people! Five minutes to curtain! If you haven't already checked in with me, do so immediately. Everyone should be sorted into groups by now, according to time slot. Orchestra! Start making your way on stage."

Faith remained stage left long after the other soloists retreated to the green room as directed. She stood in the wings near the prompt corner but out of the stage manager's sight, where she had the most promising view of the audience without the glaring assault of spotlights. Mr. Beam had to come. He had promised he would try.

The orchestra opened with Handel's Concerto grosso in G Major, op. 6, No. 1. House lights down and coupled with the harsh brightness of the spots, it proved impossible to get any decent visual. She slipped away unnoticed, then used the crossover to get stage right, hoping for a clearer view. It did not help.

"What are you doing here?" The stage manager had temporarily left his post at the prompt center to stalk after her. "What's wrong with you tonight?"

"I-I'm looking for someone."

He pulled his lips to one side and shook his head. "Honey, we're all looking for someone. Now get back to your group." The man stomped back along the crossover, swearing under his breath and mumbling something about "herding cats."

The performance could be heard through the green room speakers. Faith listened intently, as if she could pick out Mr. Beam's applause at the breaks. Intermittent glances at the wall clock frustrated her. She soon found herself nibbling at one of her cuticles.

A fellow soloist sat down beside her at the table. "Nervous?"

"I don't get nervous," she snapped, pulling her hand from her mouth and resting it in her lap. She instantly regretted her tone. "Sorry. I didn't mean it like that."

"No problem. I get nervous all the time before I go on stage. Are you parents here?"

"Unfortunately."

"That explains it." The boy chuckled and stood up as he heard his name called. "Welp, that's me. Gotta go."

"*Merde!*" Faith called after him, employing the French alternative to the non-good-luck good luck wish she and her fellow artists preferred over the more traditional "break a leg."

He kept his stride but raised his hand as he disappeared into the hallway.

Eyes glued to the clock and ears tuned to the speakers, she waited. At last, she heard her name. She shut her eyes, took in and held a deep breath, exhaled slowly, then stood and grabbed the folds of her gown. A chorus of "*merde!*" from her fellow musicians filled the green room as she exited. She glanced at her reflection as she passed the mirror beside the door.

The marijuana she and Yvonne had smoked before leaving for the concert hall had started to wear off, leaving her to face the piano, her parents, and the possibility that Mr. Beam had missed her big night, completely sober. As she walked on stage amidst the gratuitous applause at her introduction, her mother's critical shrieking echoed inside her head. Variations of insults that the woman had never, in fairness, actually spoken.

She swept her dress beneath her to take her place upon the bench, then sat up straight, pushed back her shoulders, and poised her long, slender fingers above the keys. This was it. And just in case Mr. Beam was somewhere in the crowd, she would perform tonight as never before.

He had only ever known her as an awkward, lovesick schoolgirl. Now, having just turned seventeen last month, she was a woman. The countdown she had started years before had almost reached zero. Soon, she would be free. Karl Beam needed to see her with fresh eyes this evening. Not just for her musical talent, but as a woman. A woman he might one day love as much as she loved him.

Faith put her entire being into her music. Keenly aware of her facial expressions, her body's gentle swaying as it became part of the performance. The intensity. The whimsy. The emotion of Brahms' 6 Piano Pieces, op. 118.

Several minutes later, she finished, softly hitting the last few sweet and solemn notes. When they evaporated like mist into the air, the crowd erupted into cheers and applause. Faith slid up from the bench, then did a deep curtsy that would rival that of any princess. She smiled in appreciation as she lifted her head.

Scanning the crowd, she saw him.

An initial rush of elation turned immediately to crushing blow as she watched the gentleman seated beside him put his arm around him in what no one would mistake for anything other than an intimate gesture. Mr. Beam leaned into the man, momentarily resting his head on his shoulder.

She froze as they locked eyes. He stopped applauding, allowing his hands to fall at his sides as his smile dissolved. Eyes narrowed in recognition and concern, he shook his head and mouthed, "I'm so sorry, Faith."

By force of will, Faith maintained her smile as she exited the stage, giving the audience a final nod of appreciation. Once out of sight, she rushed to the bathroom, sobbing.

***

"Sir, you can't go back there," barked the rippled muscleman guarding the backstage entrance. "Crew members and performers only."

Jameson handed over his GPG business card. "I'm here to speak with the director."

Something about his British accent had a tendency to disarm the average American. This goon was no different. Without further objection, he stepped aside, hitching his head toward the door.

Once Jameson reached the backstage epicenter with its bustling post-performance activity of excited chatter, occasional tears, and traded accolades, he watched unobtrusively from the sidelines.

He had enjoyed the evening's festivities far more than he had anticipated. Far more than a typical work night, in fact. Pounding rock'n'roll music performed in smoky clubs, most often by amateur wannabes, could never compare to the thrill of classical music. Why, in all his time in New York, had he never before attended a Juilliard performance?

The program had included some of the most accomplished young musicians he had heard in some time. He had found himself riveted in his seat, even through intermission. The rapturous sound of the orchestra, the various trios and quintets, and the solos had enthralled him. And though he had not discovered the next Itzhak Perlman, and still did not understand why Chic Cabello had demanded someone from GPG attend, one of the fine young musicians had caught his eye.

"Can I help you, sir?" asked a passing crew member.

Jameson fixed his eyes on his target several yards away. "I've found what I came for."

It appeared the girl's parents had somehow talked themselves past security as well. Far from enthusiastic, she seemed annoyed at their presence. Upset perhaps. She appeared to have been crying. Jameson wondered why. Her performance had been flawless.

The mother, large with child, fussed over her daughter's hair, picked at and straightened the dazzling silver neckline of her dress, and lifted the bottom of the girl's gown to glance at her shoes.

"Austin couldn't make it but he sent his congratulations. He knew you'd do well." She turned to her husband. "Walt? Did you hear all that applause? I think they loved our Faith more than any of the others. Isn't it just wonderful?"

"Of course they did!" The father puffed out his chest, adjusting the high waistband of his dress slacks. "I wouldn't have expected anything less."

Several students, the director, and various personnel dared to interrupt the exchange as they passed by, congratulating the girl on her magnificent performance. Hands folded beneath the wool overcoat draped across his arms, Jameson quietly studied the girl's reaction. Praise did not appear to faze her. He appreciated the refreshing absence of ego.

Hers was an amusing blend of hostility and feigned patience as she endured her chirping mother and more docile father. Quite the difference from the poised, self-possessing disposition she had portrayed on stage. An obviously skilled performer beyond her impressive talent.

"Don't you guys have to get home, Dad?"

"We're fine, kitten. We'll be out of your hair soon. If you're up for it, we've got reservations at Keens to celebrate."

She exhaled sharply, rattling her head in frustration. "Celebrate what? It was just a performance."

Every so often, the girl craned her neck to peer past her parents, past fellow performers, toward the stage door. Her parents, the mother in particular, chattered nonstop, oblivious to their daughter's inattention.

When they finally convinced her to accompany them to dinner, Jameson slipped away, unseen.

He beat them to the restaurant and headed straight for the bar, where he ordered himself a scotch and waited. Not twenty minutes later, they arrived.

The mother smiled brightly as they were seated, waving like a newly crowned beauty queen to the many people she seemed to know while her husband followed behind, sparing an occasional nod left or right. The daughter brought up the rear, no longer poised, or even annoyed. Shoulders slumped, head down, she followed meekly, possibly resigned to spend the next hour or so in the company of people who clearly enraged her.

Jameson relocated himself to the bar stool closest to their table. He ordered another scotch and watched them through the long, semi-obstructed bar mirror. A time or two, he thought the daughter caught him staring. Curiously, she neither looked away nor appeared disturbed by his subtle intrusion into their conversation.

When they had received their drinks and placed their order, he made his move. He extracted his wallet from his trousers back pocket and slipped out two business cards—one from GPG and one of his personal cards. The tone of the conversation would determine which one he gave them.

He slid the cards into his breast pocket, then approached them with a slight bow and an outstretched hand. "I'm sorry to interrupt, folks. The name's Lockhardt. Jameson Lockhardt."

"Walt," the father replied, accepting the man's greeting with a hearty shake. "Walt Peterson. This is my wife, Millie, and our daughter, Faith."

Jameson nodded at Millie, then lingered as he and Faith exchanged formal nods across the table.

The glint in the mother's narrowed eyes as he shook her hand told him she was curious.

"I'm an A&R man over at GPG records. I was fortunate enough to have attended the Juilliard concert this evening. I must say, I was quite impressed with Faith's solo. What a talented young lady you have here."

Millie wiggled a bit straighter in her chair. She visually swept the restaurant. "Are you...are you dining alone this evening, Mr. Lockhardt?"

Walt stood, gesturing to the empty seat between Faith and her mother. "Absolutely. Please, join us."

Jameson accepted Walt and Millie Peterson's offer, temporarily returning to the bar to grab his drink and tip the bartender. Their server appeared with another menu. Jameson waved his hand and ordered—verbatim—the same meal Faith had requested.

She glanced his way as the waiter retreated to put in the extra order for their table. When he caught her eye, he winked. A rebellious half-smile tugged at the corner of her lips.

"So..." Millie singsonged, lacing her fingers and resting her elbows atop the table. "An A&R man. What's that?"

"It's short for Artists and Repertoire." He set down his drink and leaned back in his chair. "In a nutshell, I discover and nurture talent."

Millie's brows raised, one higher than the other. "You don't say."

"I'm sure you've talked to a dozen like me already, Mrs. Peterson."

"Actually, no. Faith's still young yet, and only started Juilliard a couple of years ago."

"You don't say? How long has she trained?"

They talked through dinner, dessert, and after-dinner cocktails. Walt and Millie Peterson were more than proud of their musical prodigy. If Jameson read them right, they virtually relied on her for their future prosperity. What a cruel position in which to put one's children. It made him wonder what grand plans the Petersons might have in store for their second, unborn child.

For her part, young Faith participated little in their conversation. Every time she tried to ask him about the bands he had signed—specifically, the rock'n'roll bands—her parents became agitated and changed the subject. Eventually, she had given up.

What a shame to see such a talented, beautiful girl treated as a commodity. Not that his intentions were so dissimilar.

He insisted on taking care of the bill. Walt lodged a courtesy protest, though both men knew it was merely for show. As they stood and donned their jackets before heading back out into the chilly evening, Jameson dug out his GPG business card and handed it to Millie.

"What's this?" she asked, pretending she did not already know.

"It's my card, Millie. Clearly, you and Walt are in no hurry for Faith to begin her career. Especially before she graduates. But you're obviously invested in her future. I'd like you to keep my number until you're ready for her to consider her next step."

Faith's wide eyes darted between her parents, then briefly met Jameson's.

Millie passed the card to her husband, then slid the strap of her handbag over her forearm before pulling on her gloves. "Thank you, Mr. Lockhardt. And thank you for a lovely dinner. So unexpected. What a treat!"

Walt perused then pocketed the card. He shook Jameson's hand once again. "Yes, thank you for your interest, and for dinner. Maybe once our girl's graduated, we'll speak again."

"As we said, Faith's on track to be a concert pianist," Millie boasted.

Jameson gave a slight bow. "Yes, you mentioned that. And I understand. In any case, hold on to my card and feel free to call. Maybe we'll meet again at a future show."

The Petersons filed out of Keens one by one, Millie in the lead. Jameson tapped Faith on the shoulder as she passed. When she looked his way, he slipped her his personal card.

"When you're through letting your parents run your life, give me a call. This is my private number. You're good. Better than good. We should talk about it."

Walt held the door for his daughter. "Coming, kitten?"

Before she left, Faith shook Jameson's hand for her parents to see. She turned her back to them and whispered, "I'll call you next week. Or maybe we can have lunch?"

Jameson smiled hugely, revealing his prominent upper canines. "It would be a pleasure, my dear. I'll free up my schedule."

When she smiled back at him, the first honest smile he had seen from her, something electric passed between them that both startled and intrigued him.

CHAPTER 20

"*WHY ARE YOU SO ANGRY?*"

"*Leave me alone!*"

"*Calm down and we'll discuss it!*"

Sarah threw the half-washed plate down into the sink of warm, sudsy water, toweled her hands dry, and stomped out of the kitchen.

Jameson did not follow her. Why even try? Whenever his wife was in one of her moods, there was no talking to her. He snatched the newspaper off the table and retreated to the living room to catch up on current events. Maybe they could finish their conversation when Sarah was more rational.

Granted, these days he spent more time away than at home. And yes, he understood the frustration. Men worked. Plain and simple. He could not tell the boys he had to knock off early to help with household chores. Had he not provided all the newest appliances for their home to make her life easier? Did she not have more clothes, more luxuries, more nights out than before he had started freelancing with the various gangland firms?

Ungrateful—that was what Sarah was.

When he heard the washing machine start, the built-up tension in his shoulders eased. Their arguments had developed into a predictable routine. First, one of them would react negatively to something the other said. Next, they would discuss it until someone got frustrated. If they could find no common ground, it devolved into shouts and accusations. Then, Sarah would huff and walk out. But once she started doing the laundry, they were on the road to reconciliation.

Bobby padded out of his room, rubbing his eyes. He climbed onto the sofa and sat close to his father, peering at the newspaper as if he had already learned to read.

Jameson looked at him, then resumed his reading. "Isn't it time for bed, son?"

"Mummy said to come say goodnight."

He gave a curt nod. "Right, then. 'Night."

The child gazed expectantly at him. At first, Jameson ignored him. But when Bobby kept staring, he glanced down. "Aren't you off to bed?"

"Mummy always gives kisses and hugs goodnight."

The request, however normal, made him uncomfortable. He paused a moment, then awkwardly put an arm around his son, giving him a soft squeeze.

The gesture satisfied Bobby. He hopped off the sofa and headed for his bedroom without another word.

If only Sarah was so easily placated.

Jameson heard them chat briefly, followed by the closing of Bobby's bedroom door. When Sarah returned to the living room, he assumed they would make up and maybe watch a bit of telly. Instead, she stood before him, arms at her sides.

The top half of the newspaper bowed over as her scowl drew his attention. Apparently, the washing machine stage of their rows had not worked tonight.

He attempted to read her expression so he could figure out what she wanted him to say. When that failed, he asked, "What?"

She hip-shifted her weight to one leg and crossed her arms.

"Sarah, I can't read your mind. What is it?"

"Tell me."

With casual precision, Jameson folded his newspaper into fourths, dropped it atop the coffee table, then laced his fingers across his lap.

"I won't let this go." She jutted her chin ever-so-slightly, at once the regal debutante of her earlier days.

There came no reply, even when she repeated herself. How many times did they have to orbit this topic?

"I'm waiting, Jameson. You always outlast me. You always wait until I give up. No more. I've had it."

The sustained silence did not improve his wife's mood.

She uncrossed her arms and pointed toward the kitchen. "How much of our life is a lie? A London cabbie doesn't make enough to afford this house, these things...why won't you tell me where it all comes from?"

He stared blankly into her eyes.

Something between a scream and a scoff burst from her lips. "I'm your wife, Jameson! I deserve—no, I demand an explanation!"

"Demand?" He chuckled. "Yes, you're my wife. You might want to remember yourself. Especially after all I've done for you in the last few years."

Slack-jawed, her eyes widened. "Done for—?"

"Honestly, my dear. I don't know why you keep bringing this up."

"Because I don't want to wake up one day and have to tell my son his

father's been taken into custody. Especially since I wouldn't know why."

He waved her off. "No one's going to jail."

She wagged a trembling finger at him. "Mark my words. Whatever you're involved with, it isn't right."

"You and Bobby have food, correct? And clothes? A decent roof over your head? Your life's a damn sight better than you give me credit for if you have enough time on your hands to worry about my business."

"And what business is that?"

Her dogged inquiries had started before Christmas. He had no idea what triggered them. All he knew was that he was tired of enduring the same, endless interrogation.

Some of gangland's wives knew about their husbands' activities. Most did not. This was, in part, to maintain their plausible deniability and, in part, to avoid arguments such as these. But Sarah was not content to revel unquestioningly at their unexplained good fortune. She had not come from poverty and was, therefore, not easily impressed. Whatever he had gained in terms of their standard of living, she had grown up with infinitely more.

"Whatever it is, you need to get out."

Her insistence dumbfounded him.

"I mean it. I want you out."

"Maybe you should finish the laundry and let me do what I do. You're right. You are my wife. And I'm your husband. I'll provide for us. You needn't worry about how I get it done."

"It's nineteen sixty-one, Jameson. Women aren't content to turn a blind eye while their 'stronger, smarter' spouses carry on doing who knows what behind their backs."

"So, you think I'm having an affair on top of everything else?"

The circular argument lasted well into the night. When she grew too exhausted to fight any longer, she stomped into the bedroom, grabbed a couple of blankets and his pillow, then dropped them unceremoniously on the sofa before going to bed. Complete with the slamming of the door. She even neglected to transfer the wet clothes to the dryer.

He awoke the next morning stiff and out of sorts. A glance at his watch had him up and scrambling. Ten o'clock. He had a half hour to make his forty-five-minute commute.

Curiously, the kettle was not on the stove as usual. The soapy dishes from last night now soaked in cold, dirty water. Sarah was punishing him by sleeping late and not preparing the tea or breakfast.

Angry now, Jameson stormed out of the kitchen, through the living room, down the hall past his son's unusually silent bedroom, and to his still-closed bedroom door. He grabbed the handle and shoved open the door. "We're not going to have another day of this incessant—"

Their bed lay fully made and unoccupied. Bureau drawers had been left half-closed. And empty. The wardrobe door was open, revealing a tangle of hangers that no longer had clothes on them.

Jameson hurried to Bobby's room and went inside, only to find a similar scene.

When he returned to their bedroom, he tabled his shock and panic and searched for a note or letter of some kind that might explain. A wave of nausea assaulted him as his searched ended in failure.

Then, he returned to the kitchen. There, he found the note.

Jameson,

I can no longer do this. I love you, but I hate the deception. I'm afraid for you. I'm afraid for us. I've taken Bobby with me. We're going to America. This has been a long time coming, not something I've done lightly. I'll let you know when we're settled. I won't keep you from your son.

Sarah

P.S. You should have told me. I found out anyway. I just hoped you'd tell me yourself.

As he crushed the note in the palm of his hand, pangs of abandonment that Jameson had not known in fifteen years assaulted him. Sarah Lockhardt was the love of his life. A love he had vowed never to feel. He had to find a way to bring his wife and four-year-old son back.

***

Jordan surged with excitement over the view from Ben's studio flat. So many people out walking the streets. So much movement. Such a change from the slower pace of Bledlow's country living. "I can see Tower Bridge!"

Ben joined him at the large window. He tousled his hair. "I thought I might take you for a tour later. Filming's not until tomorrow. Today, let's have some fun. What do you say?"

Jordan had never visited Ben in London without his parents, and had never before seen his place. On his twelfth birthday earlier that month, he had received an invitation from his brother to stay with him for a few days and accompany him on the set of a *Budgie* taping, where Ben would make his acting debut.

"But I thought you wrote music."

"I do write music."

"Then why are you going on *Budgie*?"

In truth, Ben had no idea why his agent had booked him on a local television series. He would play a character incarcerated at the same open nick as the series lead. Ben could not even say it was a "small role." He had only one short line. As he passed Budgie in one of the prison's corridors, he would lift his chin and say, "all right then, Budgie?"

It was silly. But it was exposure. At least that was how his agent had sold him on it.

"But I thought...isn't Dad your agent?" Jordan asked, overjoyed as he continued admiring his brother's view.

"Dad's my manager. An agent's different."

Jordan shrugged. "Sounds like your agent doesn't understand what you do."

On that point, Ben could not argue. His career path had, for months now, seemed to be veering off course. For years, George Grant had successfully directed his oldest son's career. Yet once the demands on his time grew, his small world had expanded. Heavy demands for material. Travel. Deadlines. Having an agent made sense. But as his younger brother so aptly observed, he did not seem to understand that Ben Grant did not want to be an entertainer.

"But those looks! The birds'll really go for a handsome bloke such as yourself. A flash of that smile—did you have to pay for those pearly whites? You've got the whole package. Why not capitalize on it, yeah?"

And what could it hurt? He had built himself a solid reputation among the music industry's inner circles. His compositions regularly hit the charts published in *Record Retailer*. With several appearances on various television and radio shows such as *Top of the Pops* and Radio 1's *Johnnie Walker Lunchtime Show*, his popularity grew outside those industry circles. The only frustration was that his agent seemed determined to turn him into a celebrity. After committing to the *Budgie* appearance, Ben wondered whether it was time for a change.

They unpacked Jordan's small bag, made him a bed on the floor next to the fold-out sofa where Ben slept, then set out to see the sights of London. They spent the day playing Frisbee in Hyde Park, eating at Quaglino's buttery, and watching the newly released *Steptoe & Son* at the cinema.

"You should get a dog," Jordan told him later that night as he lay atop his improvised bed, watching London's brilliant cityscape through the enormous window of the artificially lit flat.

"A dog? Why?"

"Because you're lonely."

"I am?" Ben frowned at the ceiling as he listened. "What makes you think I'm lonely?"

"You have to be. Mum and Dad and I are home. Chris is...wherever he is. You don't even have a girlfriend, or at least you've never mentioned one. Aren't you lonely?"

"Not really." He rolled over on his side, propping his head atop his closed hand. "There's no time to be lonely."

"There's always time to be lonely. People can be lonely in front of the whole world, I'll bet."

Ben peeked down at his brother. "You think so?"

Jordan linked his fingers behind his head.

"I wouldn't mind having a dog. We always wanted one. But I travel too much now. It wouldn't be fair. Or convenient."

"I'd take care of him while you're away."

"Yeah? Sure you aren't really asking me to ask Mum if you can have a dog?"

"If I had one, would you visit more?"

Ben knit his brows. He opened his mouth to respond, but could not find the words.

On several occasions since his relocation to London, their mother had told Ben how much Jordan missed him. How often he asked when he would come home for a visit. Until tonight, Ben had suspected his mother had used Jordan as a decoy for her own questions.

"I don't come 'round enough, do I?"

The boy stared up at the ceiling.

"But we had a good time today, didn't we?"

"The best."

"You realize it's just work, right? I'm not avoiding you or Mum. I'm not staying away on purpose. I'm not Chris."

"I know."

Ben rolled onto his back and stared at the ceiling again. Animated shadows from the traffic below wove in and out of themselves, indiscernible as they danced, fluttered, then ran across the ceiling until disappearing altogether. "Why don't you play your guitar anymore?"

"I don't have anyone to sing with. Well, Mum sings with me. But she treats me like a baby most the time. Like some doll."

"Really?"

"It's not her fault, but yeah. She's lonely. Better than when Chris first ran away and you moved here. But still lonely."

"I've never heard you say anything like that before."

"I'd never say it to her face. I don't wanna hurt her feelings. She needs me. I'm the only one left."

Ben chewed the inside of his cheek.

"You're not the only one who grew up, Ben."

He stared over at the lights of Tower Bridge. "I guess not." Jordan's words stung him, however unintentionally.

"Ben?"

"Yeah, buddy?"

"Do you think the next time I come out, I could go with you to work at the studio?"

"Sure. I just thought visiting a television taping would be more fun for you."

"It will be fun. I can't wait until tomorrow. I just...I want to see you do your real work."

He chuckled. "You've seen me write dozens of songs."

"But you said you're learning how to do the studio stuff. How to make sounds and do recordings."

"Is that what you wanna do when you grow up? You wanna be an engineer or a producer?"

"Nah. I just wanna watch you do it."

Ben rolled over and smiled down at him. "Tell you what. Keep up with your guitar and I'll bring you in some time to lay down a few tracks. Maybe we can press a copy for Mum to have. For Christmas or Mothering Sunday. You know, to show her you're growing up. That you're not a doll. That might help her adjust. Like you said, you're growing up, too. Would you like that?"

"Sure!" His eyes sparkled in the reflected artificial city lights pouring into the flat.

"So you do want to be a singer, then? Follow along in the Grant footsteps a bit?"

He bobbed his shoulders. "I dunno."

"Well, what else might you wanna be, then?"

Jordan turned toward the window. "I just want to be with you."

***

"At least give me a shot, Mrs. Ostberg!"

"I wish I could help you, Bobby, but we conducted the auditions weeks ago. If you wanted a part, why didn't you read for something?"

His shoulders hunched in disappointment.

"Nerves?"

"Sorta."

Zelma Ostberg bounced her foot when frustrated or deep in thought. Standing or sitting, she would gaze off into the middle distance, squint her eyes, push out her lower lip, and rapid-bounce her left foot. "And we've already cast the understudies as well," she muttered under her breath.

"Maybe I could audition just for you, and you could decide if—"

She cocked her head to the side, giving her warmest, most understanding smile. "Sweetheart, it doesn't work that way."

Bobby held his books tight against his chest. Students filled the hallways with their usual after-school jumble of chatter, locker-slamming, and the sharp, high-pitched screech of bustling rubber-soled sneakers against polyurethane-sealed wood floors. Fortunately, no one paid attention to his conversation with the drama teacher. No one witnessed her rejection of his plea. He remained in all ways invisible to those around him. Which was one reason he so badly wanted to audition. Maybe if he participated in school activities, he would find a way to fit in.

"I can always use more stagehands. How're you with a paint brush?"

The negotiation ended with Mrs. Ostberg offering Bobby a supporting role...for Mrs. Ostberg herself. He could help her make and keep the practice schedule, coordinate with set designers, and oversee the creation of posters and fliers advertising the production. Sort of like a marketing director, she said. It was clearly a concession.

Bobby's failure to excel in the various San Marcos High School extracurricular activities had started early in the year, with sports. He had tried out for football, basketball, track, and baseball. Humiliations, all. Not only was he physically uncoordinated, he did not possess the requisite strength or endurance to keep up with the jocks.

Next came the more intellectual pursuits. Chess club. Yearbook. The school newspaper. None of these choices interested him, but he had nonetheless made an effort. He needed to find his crowd. His people. But nothing seemed to fit.

The greatest failure he could possibly endure came when he could not find his place even amongst the school's artistic clique. He could not sing or play an instrument. When it came to dancing, he had two left feet. And now, the drama teacher had essentially relegated him to the position of paper-shuffler.

Mrs. Ostberg laid a gentle hand on his shoulder. "Don't take it too hard, hon. Not everyone's a George C. Scott. And there's always next year. You could try out next fall."

His brows arched in sorrow. "But I just wanted to audition."

She bit her bottom lip, again looking away in thought. Her foot bounced rapidly, as if pumping critical information to her brain.

"Please?"

"Bobby, there's just—"

"I could read the part of Donald, or one of the G-men! Not a big part, just...something."

For decades, high schools across the nation chose either *You Can't Take It with You* or *Our Town* as their go-to stage productions. This year, San Marcos had decided upon the former. Bobby had read the script, seeking the part with the fewest lines.

"I didn't realize acting was such a passion with you, Bobby. Is this something new? Why all of the sudden—and two weeks after auditions ended?"

He did not want to tell Mrs. Ostberg the truth. That he did not care a whit about acting. He just needed something that might make his father proud of him. A distraction during his off hours away from school. An excuse to stay out of the house.

High school was supposed to be different, but it was more of the same. It seemed the more Bobby endeavored to find out who he was, he only discovered who he was not.

Mrs. Ostberg pursed her lips and motioned for him to follow her. She marched purposefully to the auditorium, the click of her heels echoing in the hall. "This is an exception, you understand?"

He followed closely. "Thanks, Mrs. Ostberg!"

"I'm not promising anything."

"I understand."

"If it doesn't work out, it doesn't work out. No arguments, no self-pity. And the offer to be my assistant still stands. Got it?"

"Got it!"

They slipped in through the back entrance of the auditorium. Ms. Ostberg switched on the footlights and a spot for the center stage. "See that 'x' over there?"

He nodded.

"You stand there. You'll read the part of G-man two."

Bobby stacked his books atop an offstage stool while Mrs. Ostberg disappeared into the darkened auditorium.

"Don't be nervous," her voice echoed from the shadows. "It's just you and me."

The good news was, he did not feel nervous a bit. The bad news was, he read his few lines like he would a grocery list or newspaper story.

"Let's try again. Take a deep breath. In...then out. Get inside Jim's head. How does he feel about confronting Grandpa Vanderhof? About the snakes? About the potential danger of the suspected Communist making threats to blow up the White House?"

Arms at his sides, Bobby closed his eyes and shook out his wrists. He exhaled a deep breath through his open mouth. He tried it again.

And again.

And again.

He read the part of G-man two, Jim. Then, the part of G-man three, Mac.

"Want me to read Donald's part?"

"Donald's black," Mrs. Ostberg called from what sounded like somewhere midway up the auditorium.

Bobby's face flushed, embarrassed to have missed that detail.

She worked with him for close to a half hour, then said she would give him her decision on Monday and sent him on his way.

He analyzed her facial expression and body language for some clue as to what she might decide. But Mrs. Ostberg gave him nothing to go on. Not even that far-off look or the tapping of her foot.

As he trudged across campus to get his bike, he derided himself for the poor performance, and realized his mother would have started worrying that he had not arrived home at his usual time. He picked up the pace and semi-jogged toward the parking lot.

Most of the kids had left long ago. The lot was virtually empty, save a couple of vehicles parked near the front, including Mrs. Ostberg's light-yellow VW Bug.

The bike rack was empty. His vinyl-coated chain lock lay on the ground. The lock itself, missing.

Bobby swore under his breath as he marched back to the office to try and find someone to whom he could report the incident. Not only would he have to walk home, he had lost the best of his three bicycles. And who knew what consequence that would bring when he finally arrived home?

The office was locked. He would have to make his report Monday morning.

He ran his fingers through his hair, dreading the long walk ahead of him. As he set out, he realized he had forgotten his books in the auditorium. It seemed his day could get no worse. Hopefully, his mother had gone to the liquor store to replenish her stash. While other San Marcos students would gather tonight at various parties and hang outs, Bobby would spend his Friday night sneaking vodka and enduring his mother's creepy behavior.

After a moment's consideration, he decided against returning to the auditorium, trusting his books would still be there on Monday. Unlike his bike, he could not imagine anyone would swipe his history or algebra books. He slipped on his windbreaker, plunged his hands inside the pockets, and began walking. The two-and-a-half-mile trek would take about an hour. His mother would be furious with worry by the time he got home.

He trudged down Hollister toward Puente Drive, shoulders hunched as he catalogued the day's losses. Mrs. Ostberg had warned him against self-pity. What did she know, anyway?

As he neared the final parking lot on the campus' east side, he heard someone jogging up behind him. "Hey, Bobby," Isaac Fett huffed as he breezed by.

A group of about ten boys loitered near the three cars parked along the fence separating San Marcos from the bordering neighborhood. Based on their impatient calls, it appeared Isaac was holding them up.

Bobby ignored the greeting. He and Isaac had not exchanged more than a few awkward pleasantries in years. Until fifth grade, they had been good friends as well as next-door neighbors. But Bobby figured people changed as they got older. Social circles often redrew themselves. Especially when a friend's mother confronted his parents, accusing their son of stealing a thousand dollars cash from her purse. Not only had Isaac not stolen the money, there had been no thousand dollars in cash to begin with. Isaac's parents stopped letting him visit after that, and did not let Isaac invite Bobby over either. Their friendship eventually dissolved.

A few yards up, Isaac stopped and doubled back. "What's up?" he asked, falling in beside Bobby as he walked on.

Bobby continued at pace. "Just heading home."

"Where's your bike?"

"Stolen."

"Really? Bummer!"

The comment did not require a response.

The boys in the parking lot shouted over one another, beckoning Isaac to hurry. He held up his index finger, then looked at Bobby. "Need a ride?"

The idea tempted him. Unfortunately, Bobby knew the group Isaac hung out with these days. The one group he had not attempted to join as part of his high school assimilation plan: the stoners. "No thanks."

One of the boys broke off from the group. He trotted over to join Isaac and Bobby. Adam Utely. If San Marcos High's football quarterback was its most popular jock, Adam Utely was its most famous pothead. Probably because he got more girls. Musicians always got the prettiest girls.

"Hey," Adam greeted. "You about ready? We gotta go."

Isaac introduced Adam to Bobby, who had yet to break his pace as the trio strode past the parking lot and neared the light at Puente Drive.

"Bobby Lockhardt?" Adam echoed, stopping in his tracks. "Aren't you the one related to Jameson Lockhardt?"

The recognition prompted him to stop and turn around. "Yeah."

Adam bobbed his head as if impressed. He flipped his long, stringy hair back over his shoulder. "That's cool, man. We should hang out some time. I could give you a tape of some of my songs. Maybe you could pass it along."

As soon as Adam suggested hanging out, Isaac made a face. Bobby pretended not to notice. "I don't really see him a lot," he told Adam. "He's all the way in New York."

Adam gave him an unconcerned frown. "We should hang out anyway. In fact, we were all just heading down to shoreline. Wanna come?"

Before Bobby could decline, the sound of screeching brakes startled the boys. They spun around, only to see Sarah Lockhardt's Buick Electra come to an abrupt stop just beyond the open gap in the median. The vehicle's front driver's side wheel crashed into and came to rest atop the cement border.

Sarah barreled out of the car, slammed the door shut, then marched across the westbound lane to the sidewalk where Bobby, Isaac, and Adam stood in open-mouthed shock. "Where have you been? And where is your bike?" she shrieked.

Bobby did not care about being grounded. He rarely went anywhere, anyway. What he did care about was that Monday morning found him not only embarrassed as he encountered the jeers and whispers of classmates who had heard about his mother's meltdown outside school grounds, but humiliated to find that Mrs. Ostberg had made her decision. Instead of a script, he received a clipboard with blank scheduling sheets for him to fill out.

"Sorry, Bobby," the note clipped to the top read. "But I'd still love you to assist, if you're available."

CHAPTER 21

"I F WE DO THIS, WE'RE gonna do it right."

"Absolutely. Partners down the middle—fifty-fifty."

"No. That, I can't have."

Jameson adjusted himself on the settee. He looked uncomfortable. A rare state for a man who exuded such confidence. Even as one of countless cabbies back in London, Jameson had stood out. Ross had known instinctively his friend would one day find, nay create, a successful future. And despite Josephine's misgivings, Ross did consider Jameson his friend. His closest friend. But even that friendship had its limits.

"Is it a matter of money?"

Ross rose from his seat, gesturing for Jameson's empty rocks glass. "That's not it at all."

"You'd stated earlier that you'd had concerns about raising capital."

"I'm less concerned about capital than...other matters."

He tried to convince himself that this caveat to their proposed partnership would appease his bride. She often, and in no small way, voiced concerns about their unlikely friendship. Maybe she was right. But now, as they discussed in earnest expanding that relationship to one of business, he anticipated a downright battle in his household of two.

As he freshened their drinks, he became aware of how empty their home felt with Josephine away for the evening. Betty had whisked her off for dinner and "girl time." Ross could not help but feel that inviting Jameson over in her absence might be construed as a betrayal of sorts. But he had his reasons. One day, she would thank him.

Ross returned Jameson's glass, then eased back into his chair, crossing his legs. He did not expound on his statement. Too rarely did he have the upper hand with his associate-to-be. But here, in the comfort of his domain, a roaring fire in the fireplace to combat the still-cold evenings of early spring, he found it. Even as they sat in full corporate attire well after the close of business. He had spent his entire life in this house. On the chance that he was, indeed, about to strike a devil's deal, he needed to surround himself with all things familiar.

Jameson scrutinized his friend with cautious eyes, sipping his drink.

"I'm not entirely sure it's wise to revisit matters of ancient history."

"I can't go into business with someone who doesn't trust me. And who I can't trust."

"Is that it? A matter of trust? Or is it curiosity?"

"Perhaps both."

They fell silent and nursed their drinks.

Inside, Ross's heartrate surged. He wondered whether Jameson would finally share the details about that night in Belgravia. For five years, he had wondered. Speculated. Feared his own unwitting involvement. Tonight, he would brook no excuses. If they intended to go into business together, they needed all the cards on the table.

Jameson excused himself to use the restroom. This gave Ross enough time to engage the mini-cassette recorder he had prepped and hidden close enough to capture at least Jameson's end of the conversation. More instinct on Ross's part. Or maybe, paranoia.

Upon his return, Jameson strode more purposefully, stood straighter, projected more confidence—however manufactured. He sat on the settee, draping his arm casually along its top. "So again, it comes back to London."

Ross gave a curt nod. "I'm afraid so."

"What exactly do you want to know?"

"I want to know if I have anything to worry about. I want to know what happened."

"Why would you have anything to worry about?"

"I'm a lawyer, Jameson. I can think of a dozen reasons why my being in your cab that night might come back to haunt me."

A faint grin played at the corners of Jameson's mouth. He picked up and held his glass without taking a sip. "Are you suggesting you want a more favorable agreement than fifty-fifty? Is that what this is about? A negotiation?"

The question elicited a bark of laughter. Ross twirled his glass in both hands, gazing at the amber liquid, which seemed to glow in the reflected firelight. "As I said, I can't have that."

"You were vague."

"As are you."

Again, Jameson fell into quiet contemplation. Ross knew he had the man on the ropes. It was now or never.

"As an attorney, you surely understand plausible deniability. Details may do you more harm than good."

"They might also prevent me from making a monumental mistake that endangers my life and bride."

Jameson ran his thumb across the lip of his glass.

"I'm sorry, my friend. This is what I need. I confess, I'm eager to move forward. If we can raise the capital—"

"—which we can."

"Then I say it's a go. But not until we clear the air."

Jameson stared at him.

"Did you kill Brian Epstein?"

His features flattened, save the tilt of his head and a noncommittal lift of his brows.

"Is that a yes?"

"You're asking me to confess to murder."

"I'm asking if a murder took place."

With each inquiry, Jameson hesitated before answering. "And if it did?"

Ross's hands began to tremble, prompting him to set his glass on the end table near his chair. "If it did, I have more questions."

"Such as?"

"Such as *why*."

"Why, indeed." Jameson rose and stalked to the fireplace, propping a forearm upon the mantel. He stared into the flames. "I've asked myself that question numerous times."

Bile rose from Ross's stomach to his throat. He swallowed hard, then grabbed and downed the contents of his glass, cursing the burn as it mingled with the acid it chased back.

"And if I tell you, you'll join me?"

"On two conditions."

Jameson regarded him, expressionless.

Ross rattled his head, clearing the fog of drink and fear long enough to slip back into his role as attorney...and friend. He leaned in, stabbing the end table with his fingertips as he ticked off the deal breakers. "One, I want the truth. The whole truth. And two, I want to be an employee, not a partner."

"Why on Earth?"

"Because I see things as they are."

"And how are they?"

"Bluntly? You're a brilliant man, clearly bound for success in any endeavor you choose. Able to face all that comes with that success. But if you're capable of murder, you're capable of anything. I don't want to end up bearing the responsibility of your indiscretions."

"Then why consider embarking on any business relationship at all?"

The question sent Ross back in his seat. Ever since they had begun toying with the idea of going into business together, he had questioned his own motivation.

Admittedly, the potential coupling intrigued him. Jameson was driven. Self-made. Ross arguably lacked many of the qualities that drew him to his friend. Standing on the periphery of such danger was exciting. Like a voyeur, near enough to participate in the excitement, yet far enough removed to avoid repercussions.

And why not enjoy some excitement for once in his life? Had he defied his father's hopes for his future only to live the constrained existence he could have just as easily achieved by dutiful compliance?

Jameson straightened his stance, filled his lungs, and returned to his seat. "How long will Josephine be out?"

Ross consulted the mantel clock. "Another couple of hours or so, why?"

He gulped the remainder of his drink, then raised and jiggled the empty glass of ice cubes as if it were a call bell. "Because if we start now, we might just finish before she returns."

Ross nodded. "Okay."

"First, get me another drink. In fact, you'd might as well bring the bottle."

On his way back to the bar, Ross glanced in the direction of the concealed cassette player. Hopefully, it had enough recording time left.

***

Farin peered out at her seated classmates, affecting what she called her "stage smile." She had practiced it for weeks. Head high, she defied her stomach's nervous knots.

Standing in the back by the storage cabinets, art supplies, and the portable record player Farin had brought for their end-of-year classroom party, Mr. Ramos nodded his encouragement as Lorrie and Tracy joined her at the front of the classroom. He had rearranged all the desks into a semicircle with an aisle down the middle, and had even helped the girls string up white sheets they had painted earlier in the week to resemble stage curtains.

"You'll be great," he had whispered as they passed each other in the aisle after his introduction. He strode to the back of the room. "Go get 'em!"

Most of her classmates cheered and applauded as she took her place. Some of the boys jeered and made fun of her. But who cared? Boys always made fun of the girls. Even for doing nothing.

"I'd like to see you get up and sing," Mr. Ramos chastised the notorious "band of three" cynics, as he had labeled the trio of troublemakers early on in the year. "Shannon? Teddy? Ozell? Knock it off or I'll have you go up and do back-up vocals."

The hecklers shrank in their seats. They crossed their arms upon their desks and lowered their chins atop them. Though silenced, they leered at the girls as they took their places.

Mr. Ramos was the best teacher ever. Every Friday during third grade, he had brought his guitar to class. After lunch, they would sit on the floor in a circle and sing songs as if they were at camp, except that there was no fire, and they sat on a large rug instead of dirt or logs. Mr. Ramos played and sang, urging the kids to sing along. And not sissy kid songs, but actual songs. Top 40 radio songs. They sang Elvis, the New Seekers, Bread, Don McLean, Three Dog Night, Elton John, and many others. Any song the kids requested as long as it sounded good on an acoustic instrument. He challenged them to sing harmony and do rounds. It was glorious. But as the year ended, Farin grew sad. She did not want a new teacher next year.

Today, though, she was excited and self-assured. Today, she wore her stage smile like a shield against all negativity. Even against the "band of three." It was her turn to shine. Not only had Mr. Ramos agreed, he had loved the idea.

She only wished her parents could have come to watch her first public performance.

Tracy Austurias trotted up and stood to Farin's right. She beamed at their fellow students despite the earlier squabble with Farin over a minor wardrobe snafu. "I didn't have anything black," Tracy had explained apologetically. "My dad wasn't gonna go out and buy something new just for this."

"But you could've put your hair up, like we said," Farin had complained.

"I didn't even want to do this, Farin. You're the one who talked me into it."

Fair enough. Neither Tracy nor Lorrie had seemed overly enthusiastic about being her backup singers. They had only agreed because they had been friends since kindergarten. It seemed no one at Franklin Elementary School besides Farin wanted to be in show business. Tough crowd. But at least her friends had rallied. She wished Marci could have joined them. Then again, Marci would have never agreed. Friend or not.

Lorrie Cockrell trudged up to stand at Farin's left. Like Tracy, she had neglected to wear the agreed-upon, pseudo-synchronized attire. But at least Lorrie's mother had obligingly tucked her daughter's wiry orange hair into a manageable bun before sending her to class.

Once they had assembled together on their makeshift stage before their classmates, Farin nodded at her teacher to start the music.

"All year, Mr. Ramos has played for us," Farin told their captive audience as the music started. "He made it fun. And since this is the last day and we're gonna miss him next year, Tracy and Lorrie and I wanted to sing a song for him. And for all of you."

The band of three frowned. They shot condescending eye rolls but remained quiet. The rest of the class looked on, seemingly unmoved. Mr. Ramos stood in back, smiling brightly. He gave them two thumbs up.

The Staple Singers' "I'll Take You There" began. Lead singer Farin sang along to the record. She bobbed her head and moved to the rhythm as Tracy and Lorrie began an awkward two-step beside and behind her. Arms bent, snapping on the 2 and 4 beats as they had practiced, it took a few seconds to synch their steps. They eventually mastered the simple choreography. As the girls joined in with a semi-on-key "lyin' to the races," Farin fell in with them, stepping side-to-side as she sang.

The class watched, disinterested, at first. Farin had expected as much. Mr. Ramos had warned her when she had first approached him with her idea.

"Are you sure you wanna do *this* song?" he had asked, scratching his dark, fuzzy beard.

She failed to understand the problem. "What's wrong with it?"

"Nothing's wrong with it, per se."

His doubtful reaction had puzzled and, frankly, hurt her. Only a month before the end of the year, and she had set her heart on performing. He had told her she could.

"I love the song, Farin," he explained. "It's just that it's a little...ambitious for a nine-year-old, don't you think?"

"It grooves, Mr. Ramos! Besides, we've already started practicing!"

Ultimately, he had relented, but warned that her fellow classmates might not possess the maturity to appreciate the tune. Farin did not care. She just wanted to sing.

Lorrie and Tracy were troopers. As Farin belted out the soulful lyrics, the girls' simple, four-word repetition of the song's title sounded good. It kept their feet moving in time even as they struggled with their coordination. Not exactly Cleotha and Yvonne Staples, but they did great.

Before long, the class was drawn in by the unexpected participation of none other than one of the band of three. Ozell Washington began to clap along in time with Lorrie and Tracy's snapping fingers. Farin worried at first that he was making fun of her. Then, he stood up beside his desk and sang back at the girls, pointing periodically as he echoed the call-and-response.

More kids joined in. Ozell grooved to the music and sang with Lorrie and Tracy, evoking smiles. They began to perform more enthusiastically.

When the song ended, the entire class jumped up and cheered. When they took their bow, Farin caught a glimpse of the window portal of their classroom door. She saw a few teachers from other classrooms peeking inside. But more than that, she saw two familiar faces.

"Daddy! Mommy!" Farin had squealed as Mr. Ramos waved them in.

They had come after all, but said they had stayed just out of her line of vision in case their presence made her nervous.

She ran to them as the class's applause ended. The other kids gravitated into various groups to chat as Mr. Ramos turned on his radio and announced a quick break while they set up refreshments for their end-of-year party. Several complimented Lorrie and Tracy on their impressive performance.

Farin's dad lifted her into his arms. "You were fantastic!"

Her mother petted and patted her back as her father set her down.

Mr. Ramos approached, an earnest grin stretched across his face. "You've got yourself quite a talent on your hands," he said, shaking her dad's hand. He winked at Farin. "Good job, kiddo. You killed it."

Farin's eyes sparkled with excitement as she glanced up at her father, then Mr. Ramos, then back to her father. Her friends beckoned her to join them, but circumstance pinned her in place. Things had worked out better than she had planned. Performing in front of a group of peers had exhilarated her. She wished she could bottle her joy. At the very least, she would live off its memory for the whole of the summer. She could not wait to share her success with Marci.

This was the best day of her life. So far.

***

Elliot stomped into their backstage dressing room. Well, a dressing room according to the pub owner. In reality, it was little more than a dank and dusty storage room.

He threw the cash down atop a stack of unopened liquor boxes. "That's it, then."

Todd grabbed and counted the pound notes. "Where's the rest of it?"

"Exactly," he spat.

Chris sat on the floor, too spent to get up and too sweaty to inflict his own scent on his bandmates by moving around. "What happened?"

"What happened?" Elliot echoed with marked disgust as he snatched up the money and shoved it into his jeans pocket. "What do you think happened?"

Stupid question.

Seaside towns. Resorts. Pubs. Lunch shows. Dinner shows. Private shows. The band played them all, up and down the coast, inland, and throughout Greater London. After a year and a half on their would-be circuit, few venues hassled them over their age anymore. Youth and aspiration drove them to work seven days a week, two shows a night during the week, three on weekends and holidays.

The girls loved them—especially Todd and Chris. Even as they struggled through their awkward teenage years. Most boys their age found puberty frustrating. Pimples. Voice changes. Obvious and often uncontrollable physical reactions to the opposite sex. But the members of Mirage, as they called themselves, plowed through. They learned to conceal acne flair-ups with longer hair and a bit of stage makeup. They wore constricting jeans. Though this remedy produced sometimes painful consequences, it worked well enough.

Love-struck females flooded their shows. This brought in lads who eagerly bought them drinks, hoping to get lucky even as the ladies swooned for the band. The increased revenue ensured repeat bookings. The more they played, the tighter their show. Everybody won.

But something needed to change.

"We need a manager or an agent or something," Lance suggested, absently drumming the top of the backward-facing chair he straddled.

Todd marched out of the room. No one tried to stop, or help him.

Somehow, the youngest and prettiest of the group had emerged as Mirage's enforcer. A role he had to play far too often for anyone's comfort. Pub owners loved them. But some did not want to pay them.

They all lived at Clifford's now. And everyone complained about it. The neighbors. The landlord. The band members. And mostly, Clifford himself. They packed into the one-bedroom flat like clowns in a VW bug. Five testosterone-heavy males, four of whom would prefer bringing their post-gig dates back to their own place instead of insisting they satisfy their lustful appetites at the girl's house. Or a van. Or an obliging though filthy unoccupied bathroom at whatever venue they played. Not to mention the toll it had taken on Clifford's love life.

"Here," he had said a couple of weeks ago. "Take it."

Lance had accepted the keys with stunned gratitude. "You sure?"

"Positive. Take the van. If it'll get you lot out of London to play more, I'm all for it. The sooner your band breaks, the sooner you'll all piss off and get your own place."

"I'll pay you for it," Lance had promised. "Out of our earnings."

Clifford had scoffed. "Bloody likely, that. Every pound you make already goes back into petrol or instrument upkeep."

Frustrations aside, Clifford steadfastly supported their efforts. He provided them shelter, even when they came up short on the rent. He made sure they did not starve when they did not have the dosh to eat. And although he complained, he had not once hinted he would throw them out. Not even when he had to insist that he and whatever girl he dated go back to her place instead of his.

Secretly, Chris marveled at the relationship between Lance and his brother.

Todd stormed back into the storage room, slapping down the rest of the money atop the same stack of liquor boxes. He ran the back of his hand across his mouth. "Right," he said, spitting on the floor. "Time to go."

"We're square then?" Elliot asked, swiping the bills off the box and shoving them in his pocket with the rest of the money for later distribution.

Todd nodded. "And we've been invited to return when the Thames dries up."

Chris's lips pulled to one side as he stood, exhausted from the evening's two sets of adrenaline-fueled covers and originals, mostly penned by their bassist. "Sod him, then. I just want to go home and take a shower."

Todd dug into his front pocket. He pulled out a short metal-bowled pipe and a baggie of weed. "One for the road?"

Lance yanked open the nearest box of liquor. He pulled out one of the bottles and looked it over. "Imperial Pilsner," he announced, distributing them amongst his bandmates as Todd prepared the pipe.

They toasted each other, then sat on the hard floor, backs against the pub owner's boxed inventory, to enjoy a private party before heading back to their Bromley flat.

Chris downed his bottle in one continuous glug, belched, then gestured for another before accepting the pipe passed his way.

Todd lay back onto the floor, knees up. "Where are all the birds?"

"Back door, as usual." Elliot crossed his legs at the ankles and nursed his beer, waving off the offer when the pipe came his way.

Lance hoisted the box of beer, relocating it to the floor in the middle of their group. He sat down, cross-legged, and took a long swill from his bottle. "Anyone see a box of nuts or crisps or anything? I'm starving."

"We could find an open restaurant."

Todd rose when the pipe came back his way. "Anyone remember where we're at tomorrow?"

"I barely remember where I am right now," Lance said.

Chris yawned and stretched. When he caught a whiff of his own stench, he made a face and lowered his arms. "We're off tomorrow."

Halfhearted cheers and chatter erupted at the prospect of their first night off in as long as any of them could remember.

"I think I'm gonna check out that new group at the Speak." He peeled the condensation-soaked label from his bottle. "See how they're doing."

"They should be coming to see us," Todd countered. "Not the other way around."

Chris shook his head. "That's not how it works, mate. We'll do ourselves no favors by pretending we're Roger Rock Stars and shunning the competition. That's not the rep we want, is it? The more visible we are, the bigger the draw."

Elliot nodded in agreement. "I'll go with you."

Chris touched the neck of his pilsner to his friend's.

"Not me." Todd arched his back. "I'm gonna sleep until dark, then call that one girl. What was her name?"

The boys spouted a chorus of possible names, to which Todd shook his head. "No, that's not the one."

"Anyone need the van?" Lance asked. "Thought I'd head up to Mallory Park."

The boys groaned in protest.

Elliot chuckled softly. He finished his beer and set the bottle aside. "Which one is it, then?"

"MCD. British Formula three. Round eight. But if I need to, I can take the train."

Todd lifted his hands. "It's your van, mate."

"It's *our* van," he corrected. He sucked his teeth and thought a minute. "You take it, Todd. See that girl. I'll take the train."

For the next hour, they smoked up Todd's stash and killed off the box of Imperial Pilsner, the empty bottles littered about them. Elliot began to nod off as they discussed the upcoming two-month Hamburg residency Clifford had helped them score for the fall.

When the pub owner entered the room, they barely noticed.

"What's this then?" he shouted, lumbering toward them. "I thought I told your singer to take your money and piss off!"

Infused with a sudden burst of energy, the boys scrambled and stumbled to their feet, racing past the man. The empty beer bottles strewn about the floor skidded and shattered in the commotion as they left.

CHAPTER 22

*T*ONY DID NOT INTERRUPT HIS *close acquaintance's sorrowful tale. He listened, stance open, arms crossed, head down, soberly nodding. Periodically, he sucked on his cigarette, the exhaled smoke streaming dual trails from his nostrils.*

They congregated, as usual, on the narrow cement curb outside Tony's mother's house. Somewhere between rageful and distraught, Jameson paced the length of his cab, venting as he raked his fingers through his uncombed mess of blond hair. Dress shirt tucked unevenly into his trousers, his clothes hung wrinkled and unwashed upon his person. His face, unshaven.

Tony, by contrast, was impeccable in his sharp, single-breasted suit and perfectly slicked-back mane of black. His ever-present band of shady colleagues had temporarily dispersed so the pair could talk in private. They heard Liz's baby upstairs, fussing to be fed or changed.

"So all I've done," Jameson concluded, talking as much with his hands as his mouth. "It didn't matter a whit. She's taken my son and gone to bloody America."

Tony tossed down his fag, crushing it with the toe of his polished Oxfords, then stuffed his hands in his trouser pockets. With a contemplative squint, he glanced up, then down, Hadleigh Street. "And the note said she knew?"

"It did." Jameson's cheek muscles rippled as he ground his teeth.

Tony faced him, knowing and expressionless. "How?"

The question was so obvious, Jameson could not fathom that he had not asked it himself. His facial muscles relaxed until his lips parted.

Tony clapped his hand on Jameson's shoulder. "I'd start there."

Indeed, he would. And he knew exactly who to contact.

For eight years, Jameson had walked the East End tightrope. Ensconced in gangland's criminal enterprises, but only enough to bring comfort to an otherwise impoverished existence. Safe blowing. Payroll snatches. General thievery. It hurt no one. But the more successful his endeavors, the more trusted he became in their circles. He was stealthy and sure, and never took more than his cut. More importantly, he never grassed when one or another of his less careful colleagues was dragged down to the Yard for questioning.

As his good reputation flourished, so had his worth. Many firms had tried to recruit him as one of their own. He had resisted the brotherhood of an organized group, convincing himself that by maintaining a freelance status, he could avoid the risk and inevitable violence that came with such membership. This way, he could avoid admitting he was one of them. He could tell himself he still possessed the respectability Sarah's social tutelage had given him as the husband of a former London debutante. Not that anyone on the East End knew his personal life.

Ronald Nock still lived, albeit anonymously, in the shadows of a double existence.

Or, as Tony had pointed out, perhaps not so anonymously after all.

It took a couple of months and the calling in of several favors to solve the mystery of who had informed his wife of his extracurricular activities.

"Looks like you'd been followed," Freddie announced the day they met at the Crown and Anchor to discuss his findings.

The declaration shocked and angered him. "She had me followed?"

"Calm down, J." The man slid his short, stocky frame upon a bar stool and held up a finger to the bartender. "It wasn't her. It was her father."

Freddie was a fellow freelancer. Another maverick of gangland who refused to be bound to a single affiliation. But unlike Jameson, Freddie did not shy away from wet work. Or cleaning up the wet work of others. He occasionally assembled his own firms, though never as long-term ventures. Tony had introduced them soon after Jameson had made his decision to leap into a less reputable way of earning a living.

"Her father?"

"He's got powerful friends."

Jameson held his head with his hands as the barkeep delivered Freddie's stout. Freddie thanked the man with a sharp nod, paid for his drink, then gestured for another round for the two of them.

"He's got money, Fred. And a legacy as old as England. I don't know about friends."

"Money buys all the friends a bloke needs, J."

"J." Freddie's subtle way of letting Jameson know that his new name, and his other life, were no longer a secret. In fact, his secrets seemed to be exposed on every side.

"Any idea who he hired?"

Freddie sucked his teeth. "The ol' bastard doesn't even know. Friend of a friend or whatever. No one from 'round here."

Every ounce of angst Jameson had suffered since his wife's abandonment settled in his gut. He fell silent and nursed the drink Freddie had ordered him, trying to devise a definitive response to whoever it was that had given Robert Wellingham the goods on him.

Freddie sat, arms folded atop the bar, and casually sipped his stout. He looked straight ahead at the bottles of alcohol lining the wall before them. "I wouldn't."

Jameson gave him a quizzical side-eye.

Freddie did not meet his glance. "It won't bring her back, mate."

He gave the man's warning due consideration and found he could not argue.

The bearer of his bad news did not linger. Freddie finished his second stout, slid off his stool, and left two quid for the bartender before he headed out the door without another word.

That night, Jameson drove to Piccadilly Circus, parked on a side street, then walked the London streets until dawn, not unlike he used to do so many years ago when learning the Knowledge. His life's journey swirled in his head. Once again, he had come to a crossroads. Did Sarah want him to go after her? Had she left England hoping he would follow, thereby ensuring he would abandon his life of crime?

Dare he confront his father-in-law and demand to know where in America she had taken his son? No. Too risky. If Robert Wellingham knew the truth, he could stitch him up. The last thing he needed was to lose his freedom. Better to let the man believe he had achieved his ultimate goal of decoupling his daughter from the cockup who had ruined her life.

After an exhausting, endless night, he returned home to Bush Hill Park. Too tired to think anymore and too wound up to sleep, he stepped inside the door and beheld his surroundings. An hour from the action in Bethnal Green. He no longer needed that distance. Or the expense.

He washed up, had some toast and beans, then headed back out in his cab. By noon, he could barely see from lack of sleep.

Freddie's words echoed in his mind. "It won't bring her back."

Then what would?

The answer that screamed into his brain was the same answer that had prompted every move he had made since he had first met Sarah Wellingham: money.

He slept that entire night, less from any sense of peace than of sheer fatigue. The next morning, he packed his clothes and left Bush Hill. For good.

Jameson had faced devastating life circumstances before. Until Sarah, he had perfected the art of living single. Losing his wife and son felt curiously different than losing his brother to a bomb or his parents and siblings to an explosion. Somehow more personal and agonizing than losing Polly. This pain, this emotional pain, was a foreign thing to him—and nothing he wished to endure.

Death, desertion. Either way, he was alone. Again.

He found a lodging house with a vacant room in Shoreditch, paid a couple months' rent in advance, then headed out for a night of drinking. He settled in at the taproom at the nearby Grave Maurice. Shoulders slumped, making zero eye contact, he kept to himself. He knew the reputation of the pub's clientele.

A part of him wanted to be seen. To send a message. Another part of him wondered if he should remain innominate, even to those he recognized or had done previous business with.

Late the next morning, he awoke to a massive hangover and a pounding on his door.

"The twins want to see you," Freddie announced with a growl. With that, he turned on his heel and stomped away. As he retreated, he barked over his shoulder. "And get a bloody phone. Today."

Jameson did not ask how Freddie had found his new place.

The twins. The Kray twins.

As it turned out, Sarah Lockhardt's departure from England, and her husband, could not have occurred at a more ill-fated time. He knew instinctively his life was about to take a difficult turn.

***

Ben could tell his date was impressed when the Marquee Club's doorman, cloakroom girl, and manager greeted him with smiles, promptly ushering them inside ahead of the usual Saturday night queue stretching down Wardour Street. Stephanie Edwards linked her slim arms around his. She cuddled into his shoulder as manager Jack Barrie personally walked them down the long corridor to their table near the stage.

"Uh, Jack? Actually, I'd rather sit somewhere less visible tonight, if that's all right."

"No worries, Ben." Jack gave him a cheeky wink. He led them away from the stage, back toward the entrance, then stopped before a more intimate table that would not find itself illuminated once the stage lights came on.

Ben thanked him. He moved behind Steph to hold her chair for her. First dates always made him nervous. Tonight's made him more guilty than anything else.

"I've never been to the Marquee," Steph confessed, scooting into her seat. Her eyes sparkled as she scanned the room with its black walls.

"Never?" Ben took the seat beside her. The seat with the best view of the stage.

"And everyone knows you," she marveled, placing her small handbag on the table. "You must come here an awful lot."

"A bit. What would you like to drink?"

The club filled steadily ahead of its scheduled act's 7:30 PM show. Ben and Steph made small talk. And he tried.

The date had been his mum's idea. "She's a lovely girl, Ben. Your age. From Bledlow even! You need to find someone. Can't stay a bachelor forever. Give her a ring, then. I'm sure you'll get on."

The problem was, lovely girl or not, Ben felt no matrimonial pull. He was not yet twenty. Work consumed most of his time. It would be unfair to get involved with someone to whom he could not devote the necessary time or attention.

Unfair. The perfect word. Guilt niggled him. His mother's suggested date was nothing but an excuse to visit the Marquee Club this evening.

Tomorrow's regularly scheduled Sunday chat with his parents would discharge his duty. First, he would relay the pertinent details of his first—and only—date with Bledlow's most eligible female. Second, he would update them on the London band scene. Specifically, their middle son's band.

Steph sipped her Pimm's No. 6 Cup. "I've never seen Mirage play."

She chatted away as Ben visually scoured the room for his brother. "Neither have I."

"You haven't? But I thought...?"

No sign of them. He checked his watch, then glanced at Steph when her unsubtle "ahem" registered in his brain. "Sorry, darling. What was that?"

"Are you okay, Ben? Is it something I said?"

He willed away the tension in his shoulders and regarded the pretty blonde beside him. She had taken great care preparing for their date. Trendy, large-plaid miniskirt. A yellow turtleneck with matching knee-high socks. Low heels. Perfect hair. Flawless makeup. All things his mother had taught him to notice. "It's important to compliment a woman, son. Make her feel special."

Ben had done nothing to make Stephanie Edwards feel special. "I'm sorry. I'm being rude."

She gave him a patient, if weak, smile. All lips and no teeth. "It's all right."

"No, it's not." He scooted his chair closer to hers. "I'm afraid I made a mistake bringing you here."

"Why? Because your brother's in the band and you're here checking up on him?"

He stared at her, dumbstruck.

She patted his hand. "It's okay."

Her understanding disarmed and recentered him. They chatted in earnest over drinks. As it turned out, Steph knew the Grant family well, though mostly by reputation. Only recently had she met Lynda in a shop and struck up a conversation. From there, the woman had endeavored to play matchmaker. Steph confided that she, too, had no immediate desire to settle down. "But I didn't see any harm in a date. I thought it'd be fun."

"And then I ignored you."

"Only at first."

"I can imagine what you'll tell my mum."

"The night's still young. Buy me another drink."

Ben soon relaxed into his date. The best date he had ever had. He and Steph discussed his career, her new job as a secretary in one of London's most prestigious law firms, and the perils of being the oldest child in a large family, something they had in common.

"It's like being a second mum," Steph said.

"Or dad," Ben agreed.

They toasted their glasses and laughed.

No spark of romance ignited between them, but there was a connection. The thrill of finding a new friend. They exchanged phone numbers. Ben offered to help Steph whenever she decided to move from Bledlow to London.

The music started before Ben realized Mirage had taken the stage. Steph tapped his shoulder, chin-pointing toward the stage. "Here we go."

Ben dragged his upper teeth against his bottom lip as he took stock of his brother. How did he look? Was he healthy? Happy? Did the family estrangement show?

In the two years since Chris had left home, they had not seen each other. Ben heard the occasional rumor of rebel behavior, a growing reputation with girls, reviews of his progression as a musician. But until tonight, he had avoided his gigs. He did not want to fight. Circumventing a probable public confrontation seemed more likely if he showed up on a date—and sat at the back of the room.

"He's very good," Steph whisper-shouted into Ben's ear.

He nodded, eyes glued to the performance.

For all the ribbing Ben had given Chris, doubting his commitment to do the hard work necessary to establish himself, he could not deny his brother exceeded his expectation. Turned out, Chris did not need George Grant's connections after all.

Mirage wove into their set a mixture of original material and covers by Jimi Hendrix, the Doors, the Rolling Stones, and the Who. They possessed a confidence on stage that belied their youth. Long hair, unbuttoned shirts, tight jeans. Chris had matured over the last twenty months away from home. Visually, at least.

Mirage was impressive. And not just their performance. Their original songs, penned by bassist Elliot Lawrence, were quite good. Lynda Grant still professed a soft spot for the young lad, and always asked after him when she interrogated Ben about whether or not he had seen or heard from his brother. It would thrill her to hear that Chris, Elliot, and Mirage were paying their dues, making good music, tightening their style, and entertaining London's club goers. It thrilled Ben, too.

Toward the end of their set, Chris stepped up to the mic. Girls squealed amidst the cheers of the crowd. He winked and shot them a roguish grin. After introducing the individual members of the band, he shielded his eyes with his hand, guitar pick pinched between his thumb and index finger, and looked out over the audience. "Before we break, we're gonna do a little tribute to a great songwriter who came here tonight hoping to stay anonymous."

The crowd murmured and scanned the room for a famous face.

Steph's eyes bulged. She clutched Ben's forearm. "How'd he know?"

Ben looked askance at the manager standing just inside the corridor. "I should've told Jack not to tell him I was here."

"My brother," Chris spat in a condescending manner the crowd missed. "Ben Grant."

The audience whistled and applauded as they continued to search the smoky venue for the famous songwriter.

Steph nudged him. "Should you stand up?"

Ben raised a hand but remained seated. He nodded appreciatively, then pointed back to the stage in the hopes of redirecting the attention.

Drummer Lance Turner counted off, then Mirage exploded into a mimicking version of "What I See," a recent hit for up-and-coming pop sensation Laura Dempsey. Oblivious to the ill intent, the crowd ate up the parody. When it ended, the band exited the stage to rousing applause.

Ben stood and took Steph's hand. "Come on."

"Where are we going?" She grabbed her purse, mince-stepping to keep up.

Ben checked in with Jack, then led Steph backstage to where the band rested between sets. When he asked where Chris was, the band informed him their lead guitarist was currently unavailable.

***

"I'll give it another year—for Kelley's sake. After that, we should probably give up."

Carol Williams upended the near-empty Coppertone bottle, gave the vessel a vigorous shake, then squeezed. With a trumpetous raspberry, a generous dollop of lotion splattered into her hand. "I thought for sure Brazil would do the trick. And who knows? We've only been back a couple of weeks." She motioned her friend closer to rub the excess lotion into her shoulders.

Beth swept her ponytail forward and off her shoulders. "I'd know. Trust me. I knew I was pregnant with Farin practically the moment I conceived. Besides, my cycle started the day we got home."

"Well, whatever you do, don't obsess over it. That'll only make it more difficult." Carol rubbed the orange blossom-scented lotion into her friend's tanned skin, then lifted a still-greasy hand to shield her eyes against the late summer sunrays. She squinted at the girls playing in the strand. "Not too close, now!" she called. "If you wanna go swimming, you'll need to dig up your fathers first!"

The comment drew Beth's attention. She shielded a squinting eye for a glimpse of their children, then laughed at the sight she beheld.

Carol shook her head. "I don't know why they let the girls bury them."

"Every time."

"I think they just love burrowing down enough to escape the heat."

"At least it's not too deep."

"Maybe instead of school clothes, we should have bought new vacuum cleaners. I don't know about you, but all that sand's freezing up my motor or gears or whatever."

"We should implement a garden hose policy. No coming inside until they're sprayed off." Beth laid belly down atop her beach towel. "Mind getting my back?"

In some ways, the women had brought the lazy sensuality of Brazil home with them to Santa Barbara. It had been their first trip without the girls. No responsibility to ensure everyone was fed, bathed, groomed, dressed, or in bed at a reasonable time. No moderating the bickering. No booking the occasional babysitter. Just the beach, romantic evenings, dancing, and making love. Pure bliss.

Upon their return, they had little time to rest before rushing the girls off for a few days in Disneyland, as promised. They returned home three days ago, avoiding the House of Mouse's busy Labor Day weekend crowds. A hollow victory. The holiday weekend mall traffic was only marginally better. It seemed all of Santa Barbara had left school clothes shopping to the last minute.

Carol stretched out atop the beach towel next to Beth's and adjusted her sunglasses. "Slim pickings. We'll need to go back in a couple of weeks."

Beth grunted an agreement. "Farin needs a couple more pairs of shoes. And tights. She's always snagging her tights."

When the heat of the sun battering their bronzed bodies became too much, they relocated to the shade of their low-set chairs beneath their beach umbrella.

Beth watched Kelley and Joseph emerge from their shallow, sandy "graves" with playful roars. The girls scampered away, squealing with frightful delight as their fathers chased them down the strand and eventually into the salty waves.

"Don't let them go in too far, Joe!" Carol called to her husband.

The men waved an acknowledgment.

"I'm not cooking, tonight," she said. "The sun's done me in. How about we all go out for pizza? Sort of a night-before-school dinner? The girls'll love it. And we won't have dishes."

When there came no reply, Carol turned and looked at her friend. Beth sat still, her face a mixture of sadness and deep thought as she stared out at the ocean. Carol frowned. "You okay?"

She nodded softly. "Can I tell you something?"

"Of course. Anything."

"I don't know if I want another baby."

Carol touched her forearm. "But I thought you said—"

"It's Kelley. He's desperate for a second child. But honestly, Carol, he's so attached to Farin, I'm afraid he'll either break her heart by shifting his attention to a new baby, or ignore the baby by continuing to shower all his love on Farin. Not to mention another eighteen years of parenting. I'd be in my fifties by the time he or she graduated high school!"

Carol did not immediately respond. She watched through narrow, contemplative eyes as Joseph and Kelley lifted their children onto their shoulders before wading deeper into the sea. "There's no trouble at home, is there?"

Beth scoffed out a giggle. "It's nothing like that. I know I shouldn't complain. I've got everything I ever wanted. And so much more. I have a wonderful husband. A beautiful, healthy daughter. A cozy home walking distance from the beach." She faced Carol. "The best friend I could ask for."

Carol gave Beth's arm a tender squeeze.

"Kelley's been talking a lot about getting Farin into vocal training, dance lessons...he's convinced she's going to be some big star someday. Worse, he's convinced her."

Carol rested her head against the back of her chair and closed her eyes. "Maybe he's right. Farin is talented. Lessons can't hurt. And who knows? She certainly has the drive."

"It's just...he spends enough time away. He and Joe work so hard. I can't imagine seeing less of him. What about when he starts dragging Farin around to talent shows and concerts? What then?"

"Simple. You go with them. If nothing else, Farin'll need someone around to straighten that hair of hers."

Beth nestled back in her chair as the ongoing battle of the auburn curls relaxed her. "I know, I know. I'm obsessed with those things."

"Sorta like that thing you have against wearing black. See? You'll be the stage mother she never wanted."

Her smile faded. "Not if I have to stay home with a newborn."

Carol rolled her head along the back of the chair. "Seems you've thought a lot about this."

"I just don't want to end up alone."

"Kelley would never."

"Fair enough. But what if he takes it too far? What if he comes home one day and announces he's giving up the practice to be her manager or something?"

Carol lifted her head and looked at her friend. "You're not jealous of their relationship, are you?"

Beth's eyes widened. "Oh, no-no! Nothing like that."

She leaned back again, shutting her eyes. "This is what Joe would call a 'first world problem,' hon. Try not to think about it too much."

Beth stared off again to watch the rise and fall of the Pacific Ocean's steel-blue waves. Maybe she was right. It would not be the first time Carol Williams had talked her down from an emotional ledge. In truth, Beth had always been a worrier. "Maybe I'm just tired. It's been a long summer."

"That, it has."

Sighing, Beth tilted her head back. "If Kelley does abandon me to take Farin on a world tour, promise we'll go back to Brazil."

Carol reached across and patted Beth's hand. "I'll book our flight before you can pack your English-to-Portuguese dictionary."

CHAPTER 23

THE TWO QUALITIES JAMESON MOST appreciated about Faith Peterson were her anger and her passion. Both, he witnessed at that first encounter at Keens. And both, he now hoarded Ebenezer Scrooge-style. Only somewhat frustrating was her intention to buck her parents' will that she pursue a future in classical music. Classical music was so much more dignified. Rock'n'roll was a dirty business, dominated by Jews, gays, and misogyny. Not that Faith lacked the grit and talent to make a go of it.

Jameson supposed it had to do with her youth and rebellious nature. The latter fueled the passion he so loved. In fact, it evoked within him a desire to step up his own personal calendar. If only he had met Faith two decades earlier.

If only their relationship did not subject him to the possibility of criminal charges.

Their affair began days after the Juilliard concert. Jameson had expected Millie Peterson to reach out. Both parents had appeared eager to exploit their then-only child's talent in order to increase their social standing and fatten their bank accounts. Millie, in particular, acted with breathless zeal to protect her daughter—not from the advances of hormonal young men who threatened to corrupt her in her youth, but from veering off the predestined course upon which her parents had set her. The control they exercised upon Faith's life was shocking. That the girl possessed the gumption to use the private card he had slipped her as they all left the restaurant that first evening had, in no small way, impressed him.

"Hello, Mr. Lockhardt," her message had begun. "It's Faith Peterson. We met the other night at Keens. You said to call you when I was ready to stop letting my parents run my life. So, here I am, calling."

She had not left her number. Instead, she suggested they meet at an off-campus diner. She left the address, a date, and a time she would be there.

He had found her lounging in a booth, sucking down a Dr. Pepper through a plastic straw. When she saw him, she smiled and waved, no hint of nervousness over meeting him without her familial chaperones.

The leather caught him off guard.

"I ordered for us both," she announced as he slid across the vinyl bench, opposite her. "It seemed we liked the same food. But if you're not a poultry man, we'd better grab our waitress."

He had suppressed a grin. "Chicken's fine."

"I love your accent," she blurted.

"I love your talent."

"And you work for GPG?"

"I do."

She rummaged through her jacket for his card, then eyed it with interest. "Why does your card say 'Lockhardt Sound' on it?"

Her query amused him. "You're observant."

"So, are you for real? Or are you a perv?"

A *perv*? No one in his life had accused him of such a thing. The question evoked a bark of laughter. "I assure you, I'm no 'perv'."

"Then why the second card? And why give it to me when you gave my mother your GPG card?"

"Because I'm looking to start my own label."

They talked over lunch, then Faith excused herself with apologies when she had to leave for a class. They agreed to meet again for dinner. She said he had intrigued her. She had most certainly intrigued him.

That night, he escorted her to the Cattleman on Fifth Street, where he talked owner Larry Ellman off the piano and into letting Faith participate in their famous nightly sing-along by way of providing the accompaniment. By the end of their evening, which lasted well beyond her Juilliard curfew, the establishment had swelled with cheering patrons. Impressed by her talent and ease with the audience, Ellman had offered her a job, which Jameson politely declined on her behalf.

When Jameson hailed a cab to return her to campus, Faith kissed him full on the mouth before climbing inside. "This was the best night of my entire life. Thank you, Mr. Lockhardt."

Jameson had never found himself so physically aroused. By the time the sexual revolution had started in Britain, he had been a married man. And not even that until twenty-seven. He had engaged in few physical encounters since Sarah had left. Determined to remain faithful, he had ignored the occasional spark of tension between him and a member of the opposite sex. Faith Peterson's kiss changed everything.

Still, he did not want to be a "perv." More specifically, he did not want to be arrested.

"She approached me," he had defended when Ross spotted them one Saturday evening at a fine midtown restaurant where he and Josephine had ventured for a rare evening in the city. "In any case, she's very talented."

Ross had scrunched his nose at the comment. "I've no doubt, but this isn't England. Here, the law of consent is eighteen."

Jameson continued to see Faith no less than three times a week.

"I love your smell," she would coo in a guttural post-coitus purr as she snuggled her sweat-soaked body against his. "Let me stay the night. Just this once."

"We can't take that risk, my dear."

As the weeks passed, Faith acted like an addict to a drug. She pressed to see him more often, begged to spend the night—sometimes, the weekend. Each time, he refused. And the more he did, the more she wanted. It progressed beyond any promise or understanding that he might help start her career by signing her to his new label, which she had inspired him to pursue more diligently. She desired a legitimate relationship, something he outright refused. He was a married man, even if his wife would not agree to reconcile.

Six months in, they celebrated their half-year "anniversary" at a clinic on the West Side. A GPG colleague had recommended a Dr. Lionel Childs who, he claimed, practiced the utmost discretion. Jameson hoped so. He had finally developed a business plan for Lockhardt Sound. He had secured a tentative "yes" that Ross would come on board, subject to Josephine's agreement to relocate. The only remaining obstacles were the decision on locality—New York or LA—and the enormous funding he would need to make real his dream. For reasons too numerous to count, neither Jameson nor Faith could afford a pregnancy.

When Lionel Childs delivered the news that it was a false alarm, Jameson bought Faith a new leather jacket to celebrate. Faith had no money, but found another way to celebrate. She was as eager to please as he was to be pleasured.

As they cuddled in bed that evening, the phone rang. Jameson grew uncomfortable when he identified the caller.

"Are you all right?" he asked, throwing off damp sheets and spinning his legs around to sit on the side of his bed, his back to Faith. "Is there anything the matter? How's Bobby?"

"He's fine," Sarah slurred, clearly half in the bag. "Bulging orange bells."

Jameson squinted at the floor. "What's wrong, my darling?"

Behind him, he felt Faith vacate the bed.

Sarah paused a beat, then continued on with what sounded like strained deliberateness. "We're fine. He keeps asking about you for Christmas. It's not my idea."

"I wish it were."

She said nothing.

"I don't think I'll make it this year, love."

"Again. Typical."

"I'm working on some financing options."

"And you're still determined to base the company in Los Angeles?"

"I am."

The line fell momentarily silent. "You've never asked me for money, Jameson. Not in all the years we've been married. Don't ask now."

"I wouldn't dream of it."

"So, when shall I tell your son to expect you?"

"Hopefully, spring."

Out of the corner of his eye, he spied a fully clothed Faith lift her bag off the coat hook next to the front door. She opened the apartment door quietly, then backed out into the hallway. He caught a glimpse of her sad expression as she closed the door.

Six months. Maybe six months too long. She had grown too attached. They both had. He needed to end it.

***

"We need more money."

"We need a plan."

"We need a manager."

"We need a record deal."

"We need proper passports."

"We need to add a keyboardist."

"We need to get the van repaired."

Every one of Mirage's band members had ideas. Some, they even agreed on.

One thing about which Chris and Todd agreed: they needed to expand beyond the club circuit. Sure, it had helped them hone their skills and pay their proverbial dues. It had built their fan base. But they needed forward momentum. A plan to transition from clubs or at least incorporate recording and, hopefully, radio.

"Maybe we should book a studio and lay down a couple tracks," Elliot suggested. "It'd give us something to shop around."

"Where's the dosh for that?" Todd countered. "We spend more than we take in traveling across the channel and driving 'round to gigs."

"If we could budget more into maintenance," Lance defended, "the van'd be fine."

Oil leak notwithstanding, they clattered and sputtered along the A1 through France, Belgium, and Holland toward Hamburg, Germany. A drive they had come to know well. On the upside, it was another residency—through the holidays, no less. They would not have to return to London for two months. This pleased Chris, especially after the unannounced, and unwelcome, visit his brother had made to the Marquee back in August.

"It hasn't been two years since we started," Elliot reasoned, declining with a wave the joint the boys passed around. "This is what bands do. They play. Everywhere."

Todd exhaled his toke, coughing into his closed fist. "Exactly. Everywhere. As in everywhere. We need to cross the bleedin' pond!"

"America? We've only started making a name in England and Germany the last few months. America's huge. We're not ready. Besides, we've no one to introduce us around."

Frustrated, Todd stood, bending forward enough to avoid banging his head, then balanced amid the motion of the vehicle as he waded through and climbed over equipment and bandmates to sit in the passenger's seat next to Lance.

Elliot moaned, stretching his arms wide. "How much farther?"

"About five hours," Lance and Chris answered in unison.

Lance peeked over his shoulder and grinned at Chris, who shrugged and said, "I've bloody memorized every bump in the road."

They stopped in Eindhovan, Holland for snacks and petrol, and to stretch their aching limbs. Lance lifted the bonnet to check the oil level while the others used the facilities. When they piled back inside, he announced they would need to shell out money for a quick repair, or the van would not make it back to London. The boys groaned and argued over each other for some time, but eventually agreed to the unavoidable. Lance promised to ask Cliff for a loan—another one—to help ease their financial strain.

Chris grabbed his new-to-him '58 Hofner Senator guitar. He tuned the instrument by ear, then began strumming. His fingers soon warmed up. Before long, all four teens joined in for an impromptu acoustic practice. By habit, Lance drummed along, using the steering wheel. The others sang and added harmonies.

Later, Elliot and Chris worked on a few tunes that Elliot had started while Todd and Lance shared another joint. It filled the time as they neared Hamburg. The late afternoon sun faded to dusk.

Elliot lifted his hands to play air piano as Chris strummed the bridge to one of their newer songs. "See? Right there, mate. I hear it in my head. It'd be perfect." He hummed and sang a "da-da-da" filler to help communicate his vision.

Chris nodded, as he always did, at the suggestion. "Maybe when we get back to London, we'll have a look around. See who's available."

"Our stuff's...I don't know, expanding," Elliot urged, stretching his legs to work out a spasm. "We can't just be some cover band. We need to play more of our own stuff. And we need some keyboards. Other bands are doing it. If our sound was fuller..."

"I still say we need proper passports. Our BVPs are rubbish if we're ever going over to the States."

Elliot looked askance at their lead singer. "We know."

Todd held out the half-smoked joint to Elliot. This time, he accepted. He took a deep toke, then passed it to Chris.

"You tossers may think I'm mad. I don't care. What happens when some posh manager comes in, catches one of our sets, and wants to sign us? We'll be a sight better off if we're prepared, won't we?"

Chris caught Elliot's glance. "He's got a point."

"Yesss!" Todd play-shouted from the passenger's seat, raising his arms in victory. "Finally! Someone understands."

"We'll have to look into that when we get back to London, too," Elliot told him. "I don't know if I can do it without my parents. And we all know they won't help. I wonder if we can get a forged passport."

Lance piped up, "I can—"

"—ask Cliff!" Todd, Elliot, and Chris finished the sentence synchronously.

Stoned and tired from the long trip, they burst into a laughing fit as they passed into Hamburg's city limits. Poor Cliff, always having to save them.

Lance snort-laughed. "We'll pay him back someday. He knows it's temporary."

"The tab grows every month!" Elliot said. "And that's with us all paying rent."

Their hearty laughter lessened when the van's engine began knocking. When the vehicle died, it stopped altogether.

All color drained from Lance's face. "What the bloody...?" He turned the key off, then back on, trying to ignite the engine. "N-n-n-n-no," he pleaded. "C'mon, then. Start."

Elliot peeked inside the front cab. "I thought you added oil."

"I did!"

"Did you put enough in? How low was it?"

Lance exited the van, swearing. He checked the road behind them, then had the boys get out and help him push the vehicle to the side of the road.

From there, they waited in the freezing temperature of the early November evening for what felt like an eternity. Each time a car passed, they tried unsuccessfully to flag it down. Who wanted to pick up a group of long-haired teenagers in desperate need of showers and clean clothes?

Thankfully, one of the people who passed them must have called someone to assist. A hook and chain tow truck arrived and got the van to a repair shop a couple of blocks from their hotel. The boys had crammed inside with the driver, smashing themselves together and on top of one another so as not to impede the man's ability to navigate his truck. It was 1 AM before they checked into their hotel.

By the time they readied themselves to pass out asleep, Elliot had finished a new song in his head. He called it "Oil," and pestered the others to give it a listen before he would allow them to rest.

Elliot Lawrence had written dozens of songs for the band, but this one felt different. Each of the band members said as much. As they listened, they understood exactly what Elliot had intended. They bobbed their heads and imagined how their own instruments would mold the driving melody.

They practiced the song through the night, until the early morning illuminated the edges of their drawn window curtains like a glowing frame. Exhausted, they finally stopped to sleep. That night, they debuted "Oil" to the Hamburg crowd.

In no time, it became the centerpiece of their residency and an indisputable fan favorite.

***

Bobby lay atop his bed, eyes fixed upon the room's textured popcorn ceiling. His stomach rumbled and growled, protesting its empty state. Thanksgiving. But his mother had forgotten to get a turkey. In fact, she had not shopped for food in over a week.

He thought about leaving to get some take-out, then remembered McDonalds would be closed by now, even if it were not a holiday. Besides, he did not relish the idea of leaving the solitude of his bedroom. His mother surely lurked somewhere in the living room or the master. She rarely slept anymore, it seemed. At least while he was around.

Rolling over on his side, he stared sullenly at the car keys on his nightstand. The black leather keyring with the gold-plated Porsche emblem tempted him. He wanted desperately to leave. Take a drive in the birthday present he had received from his dad back in June. The greatest gift a guy could get.

Maybe he would go and never return. But that was just fantasy. He did not have the heart to hurt his mother that way. Even if she did scare him so much he hated to stay home.

She was not getting better. He had to admit, if only to himself, she never would.

Bobby sat up on the side of his bed, then felt under his pillow for the pint of Wild Turkey he had snatched from his mother's stash. He twisted his mouth to the side and softly chuckled. Wild Turkey. Happy Thanksgiving, Bobby.

For a long time, Bobby had assumed his mother was a drunk. Like Kerry Iverson's dad back in seventh grade. Everyone knew Kerry's dad was a mean drunk. Conversely, all anyone knew of the reclusive Sarah Lockhardt was that she was "strange." At least if she were a lush, he could maintain some hope she would get better.

In reality, she drank far less than he originally thought. She would buy bottles of alcohol, but Bobby rarely saw them after bringing in the bags from the car. He assumed she drank them so quickly, they never lasted long once she got them home.

Then, he had found her stash. He paid closer attention after that. To his amazement, she only drank on special occasions, or when she felt particularly agitated. Usually, in anticipation of talking to his father.

A knock at his door startled him. He slid the bottle back under his pillow.

"Bobby? Are you awake?"

"Yeah, Mom."

She opened the door and peeked her head inside. "Are you okay, my darling?"

He stood up. "I'm okay. How about you? Are you hungry? Maybe I can find an open Denny's or something."

Sometimes, his heart ached for his mother. Especially when she appeared sad and frail. Like now. She stood in his doorway in a beautiful, worn, silk peignoir set. Who knew? Maybe her periodic odd behavior scared even her. He had never thought to ask.

She stepped inside, glanced down at the floor, then met his eyes. "I'm sorry, son. I can't tell you how sorry I am."

"It's okay, Mom."

"Not really, though, is it?"

He bobbed a shoulder. "Should I try to find us something?"

"You know I hate it when you drive at night. That car's too much for a sixteen-year-old boy." She chewed at her thumbnail. "Tell you what. How about we go to the store tomorrow and you can grab everything you want? Just fill the house with whatever you want."

And then you'll throw everything out because it's all poisoned.

"How does that sound?" she urged, mustering a pained smile.

"Sounds great, Mom."

"I'll let you go to sleep now. Sweet dreams, son."

He bit his cheek. "Mom?"

She turned back. "Yes, love?"

"Mind if I try to call Dad?"

She jerked her head to consult his bedside clock. She began scratching her upper arm.

"I know it's late," he acknowledged, his tone calm and soothing. "But Dad's usually out late scouting acts anyway. I can try, at least, right?"

Sarah's features softened, as if unable to counter gravity. She walked away without answering. Bobby decided to take the lack of opposition as a yes.

He went to the living room and grabbed the avocado-green rotary phone off an end table, then walked it back, stretching its lengthy cord as far as it would go, just inside his bedroom door.

Sitting cross-legged on the floor, he pulled the cord beyond its length, just enough to clear and shut his door. He hesitated before picking up the receiver, listening for any noise that would indicate his mother had left her room again to wander the darkened house. She did that a lot these days.

Hearing nothing, he lifted the handset and dialed the phone number from memory. He glanced behind him at the clock. Eight thirty Santa Barbara time meant eleven thirty in New York. Hopefully, his father would be home, and awake.

Bobby's face lit up at the sound of his dad's voice. He cheered excitedly, "H—"

Before he could speak his greeting, the phone died. He scrunched his brow and hung up, then picked up again. No dial tone. He rapid-tapped the switch-hook. Nothing.

He had probably stretched the cord too far. Maybe he had ruined it. He hoped not. His mother would have his hide if she had to stop by the grocery store *and* Radio Shack tomorrow.

Quietly, he stood and opened his door enough to avoid snagging the cord on its bottom corner. Once free, he swung the door open wider.

Sarah stood before him, fierce-faced, nostrils flared. "What do you think you're doing with that phone?" she demanded, erupting into shouts and flailing arms.

He stepped back, wide-eyed, his heart racing in his chest.

"Answer me!"

Bobby stumbled back, tripping over the phone's base. A muted gong from its innards sounded at the contact. He caught himself before he fell to the floor, but landed against the side of his bed.

"Who are you trying to call?" Sarah dogged his movements, crossing his bedroom in a smooth but steady stride as if gliding just above the flooring, like something out of a horror movie. "Your father? Is that it?"

"I asked you!" He raised his arms, afraid she might strike him.

She bent down until their faces were inches apart. "And what were you going to tell him, Bobby? What were you going to say? Were you going to talk about me?"

"No! I promise! Mom, please!"

She stood straight, clutched angry handfuls of her own hair, and shrieked in agony. Bobby lay petrified against his bed, too frightened to move.

It took hours to get her into bed. That and half a bottle of wine, into which he slipped a sleeping pill from the bottle he kept stored on the top shelf of his closet. He had learned long ago that, sometimes, she needed help coming down and going to sleep.

At least this time, he had avoided her fists when the initial outburst started.

By the time he washed her wineglass, replaced the phone base, and double-checked she had fallen asleep, it was nearly midnight. Far too late to call New York.

He returned to his room, locked his door, and switched off his lamp. For a long time, he sat in the dark, waiting for his pounding pulse to stabilize. Hot stinging tears spilled from his eyes. He rubbed them away with an angry swipe.

In a single, rageful movement, he snatched the keys off his nightstand, squeezing them tight in his fist. He should go. Drive to New York. Make his father listen. Insist the man keep him. Anything to get away from his mother. She needed help he could not understand, let alone provide.

"*Bobby*?" came her frantic call from the other room.

He fused his eyes shut.

"Please, Bobby, help!"

He opened his eyes in bitter resignation, dropped his keys, and stood up. "Coming, Mom!"

On his way out, he grabbed a second sleeping pill, just in case she again tried to convince him to spend the night in bed next to her.

CHAPTER 24

*E*VERYONE CAME THAT NIGHT. POLITICIANS. *Press. Actors George Sewell, Victor Spinetti, and Edmund Purdom. Actresses Barbara Windsor and Adrienne Corri. A beautiful night filled with beautiful people.*

It was spring, 1965. The politically volatile Profumo Affair of '63 had dimmed in the minds of UK citizens. Scandals involving top Tory and Labour party figures and their alleged involvement in shocking accounts of homosexual relationships with a certain high-profile, club-owning East End villain had handed Labour a victory in the last election.

Not that social and sexual mores had not evolved. Post-war austerity had given way to a thriving society. Fashion, art, music...London had become their epicenter. Mini-skirts, mopeds, cropped hair, and the Union Jack illustrated the general disaffected air of success portrayed in Vogue Magazine by models like Twiggy and Jean Shrimpton. Streets teemed with teenagers casting aside the meager lives they had endured as youngsters. They embraced the culture depicted in the store windows along King's Road and Carnaby Street.

Britain owned the decade.

Yet, if one ventured outside the colorful fashion and excitement of Soho's boutique-lined streets, away from the bustling prosperity of mid-60s Swinging London...if one stepped into the bowels of the East End, a very different England existed. But not here, tonight. Not at the West End's El Morocco. Here, glamour and celebrity reigned. And so did twins Ronnie and Reggie Kray.

Not only had they won their court case, they were untouchable. And that was the problem.

Jameson moved inconspicuously through the smoky club, a suspicious glint in his eye. Donning black suits and bow ties, he and other Firm members blended into the gaiety of the celebration. They congregated for whispered conversations on the customer's side of the bar, ever mindful of business, then casually dispersed, only to reassemble in another area of the bar or among various tables, like choreographed dancers in a Busby Berkeley production.

Leslie Payne sidled up to him from nowhere. He leaned in to whisper in his ear. "Would you please handle that, Ron?"

Jameson followed the man's line of vision. The sight that met his eyes was as nauseating as it was commonplace. But before he could respond to the request, Payne disappeared into the crowd.

Bypassing the band and the crowded dance floor, Jameson strode toward the entrance. Teddy Smith intercepted him, hands raised in a defensive flutter. "Now, Ron."

"Get them out of here," Jameson said calmly, pointing to the group of young men Teddy had ushered into the club.

"They're requested," Teddy argued.

"They always are."

"You wanna tell the Colonel, then?"

The Colonel. Ronnie Kray's nickname, which long preceded Ronald Nock's assimilation into the Firm. At least the term eased the confusion when discussing one or the other of them.

"Get them out of sight. It's the last thing we need. Especially now."

Teddy and the twins had been acquitted days ago of the charge of demanding money with menace from club owner Hew McCowan for his Hideaway club. As good a reason as any to celebrate with a lavish party filled with British notables. Many guests believed, or claimed to believe, the brothers were innocent. Yet here they all were, laughing and reveling in the very club at the center of the controversy. McCowan had sold them the West End club after all. The twins had promptly renamed the Hideaway, "El Morocco."

And so it went. East End gangsters-turned-celebrities and their newest in a long line of clubs, with all its red velvet and chandeliers. Eleven days ago, famed photographer David Bailey had shot Reggie Kray's wedding photos. Judy Garland, among others, had sent a note congratulating them on their victory. To the uninitiated or willfully ignorant, the twins were merely club-owning philanthropists.

Jameson moved past Teddy to the starry-eyed group of young men gathered inside the entrance. They craned their necks to see who they might recognize among the crowd.

"This way, gentlemen." Jameson lifted his arm, herding them away. Passing Teddy, he instructed him to let the Colonel know his personal guests had arrived and where he could find them.

Payne caught his eye before he moved from the main room. He gave

Jameson a wink and a nod. Jameson dipped his chin in response.

For four years, Jameson had ridden his employer's growing wave of criminal success. In that time, the Yard had nicked him twice for grievous bodily harm. Under the name Ronald Nock, of course. He had been acquitted both times. Witnesses for the Crown had either misremembered or recanted any evidence they had originally given. Just like the twins' most recent victory.

Over the years, he had learned to launder money, and how the protection racket worked. In fact, he had performed dozens of jobs from intimidation to fraud. Anything to keep the money coming in. Earning trust had been no easy feat, even though the Krays had sought him out, but he had done it.

Jameson appreciated the Firm's organization. The sense of order. The simple creed of their profession. He sampled various areas of criminality like hors d'oeuvres to find his ideal bite. Club management appealed to him. But they had asked so much more.

Enforcement was not his preferred role. Though by no means physically weak, he lacked the requisite brute force it demanded. Bribery, especially of the myriad cops, judges, and politicians on their payroll, was his preferred brand of villainy. Money collection and driving? Easy. Extortion, he could get behind. Truck hijacking, so-so. But fists? Razors? Not so much.

When Ronnie Kray bolted to his feet and shot him a lethal, expectant scowl of disapproval after having been informed of his guests' whereabouts, Jameson and other Firm members froze in place. They remained stone-faced, careful not to project fear or make eye contact. Even the hardest of their group feared the Colonel's black, piercing eyes.

Reggie Kray excused himself from the table he shared with his young wife, Frances Shea, the twins' mother, Violet, and celebrities Spinetti, Corri, and Purdom. Reg intercepted his twin, Teddy in tow, before the man could make a scene. Reg put his arm around his brother's shoulder, chatting and ushering him out of view. A moment later, Reg returned to his table without incident. And without Ronnie. Another crisis averted. For now.

The day Jameson learned that Sarah had settled in Santa Barbara, California, he knew his next move was America. Like his wife, he needed a change. Maybe it was better she had left when she did. This world he had become a part of could not last forever. Especially when one of the twins was a paranoid schizophrenic who grew increasingly unpredictable and had a taste for young boys.

Tomorrow, the Colonel might break Jameson's nose for interfering in his procurement of guests, who would likely end up back at his Cedra Court flat for one of his regular orgies. Who knew? At least for tonight, it appeared the attractive East End club owners would content themselves with their victory over the Yard.

"Here." He turned to find Payne beside him again. This time, he had brought Jameson a flute of champagne, which he accepted.

"Cheers, mate." Jameson downed its contents as if it were a shot of whiskey. "Let's hope the El Morocco doesn't go the way of the Barn, eh?"

Payne sipped his champagne. He eyeballed their surroundings, his free hand in his suit pocket as he rocked on his heels. "Their recipe for every temporary success, eh? Buy a club, mismanage it, and then move on to the next."

Jameson said nothing.

"I always liked you, Ron. You're a smart bloke."

He absorbed the compliment, maintaining a watchful eye on the room at large.

"I mean it. Men who value brains over brawn are a rarity in our line of work. Especially those who lack a more formal education. Most enjoy the violence and thuggery of it all. No mind for business."

This was not the first time Payne had sought him out to chat. In truth, Jameson preferred him to many of their fellow Firm members, even though he did not trust him. Even though he knew Payne was loyal only to himself.

The man had a keen mind. He encouraged the twins to temper their impulsive spending and often ill-advised generosity in favor of building out their legitimate club and gambling interests. As the financial brain of the operation, Payne despised violence, as well as the boys' tendency to allow otherwise well-heeled patrons of their gambling establishments to carry debt so they could later blackmail them. During their fleeting discussions, Jameson suspected Payne had grown disillusioned with his involvement and might be planning to make a move. Jameson worried the man would try to recruit him away to start another venture. Both of them would surely regret any such betrayal.

Jameson sidled up to the bar to trade his empty champagne flute for something harder.

Payne followed him over. When it became clear Jameson would not indulge in any hint of disloyal conversation, he clapped Jameson on the back. "Good to see you, Ron. Cheers for the help." With that, he adopted an affable smile and wandered off.

With the Krays' newfound invincibility came new dangers. The twins grew careless. Firm members feared them. Loyalties, feigned and sincere, were prone to shift. Jameson felt it in his bones. With any luck, he would soon have enough to make his own move. The twins were looking to expand into America. It might prove the opportunity he sought.

At least he had not had to kill anyone.

***

The worst mistake Faith made in her life was coming home the weekend of her eighteenth birthday.

Yvonne had begged her to stay on campus. "We'll celebrate. Just the girls. No parents, no judgments, and no guys. C'mon, Faith. It's been forever since we partied together!"

It had tempted her. She needed a weekend out. Especially since she had not yet received Jameson's decision about taking her with him on his upcoming trip to England. But when her father left a message that her passport had arrived, she had decided to hurry home and pick it up before they realized she had lied about needing one on the off-chance Juilliard planned a performance out of the country.

Sometimes, Walt and Millie Peterson were so gullible.

She caught the first train to New Rochelle after her final class Friday afternoon. The twenty-four-minute commute gave her enough time to decompress from a busy school week without dwelling too hard on the fact that, as of midnight tonight, she would be eighteen. And free.

For five years, she had smoldered over the humiliation of what her parents had done to Mr. Beam. She had counted down the months, weeks, days until her parents could no longer rule her life. Five years. She checked her watch and smiled. Only eight hours left.

She had tried to reach Jameson before leaving campus, but his secretary had intercepted the call and said he was in a meeting. He had worked a lot lately. Probably to finalize his plans to leave and start Lockhardt Sound. Maybe he was giving them notice. What better birthday present than to be the first artist signed to a new label? By her boyfriend!

"Let me get your suitcase for you," Walt said when he picked her up from the station.

She pulled back. "I can get it, Daddy. Stop fussing. You're just like Mom."

"Nonsense!" He reached for and secured the solitary piece of luggage, then opened the car door for her.

He seemed strange. No smile or upbeat chitchat. None of the usual "kitten" this, "kitten" that. Not even the token kiss on the forehead. Maybe he and Millie were fighting.

"How's Hope?" she asked as they pulled out of the parking lot. "She walking yet?"

"She's trying," Walt said.

"Has Mom called Austin yet to set her up for lessons?"

He scoffed as if agitated. "Don't be silly. She's far too young. It'll be a couple of years before we think about putting her in any music lessons."

Faith rolled her eyes and stared out the window. Faith. Hope. Her parents sure did like their unsubtle affirmations. At least Walt and Millie would have no more children. Who knew what they might name a third. Chastity? Love? Prudence? Or maybe the old standby cliché to Faith and Hope—Charity? The thought elicited an audible groan.

"What's that?" Walt asked.

"Nothing."

The silent drive relieved as much as annoyed her. Every so often, she would steal a sideways glance at him and wonder. He stared ahead at the road, expressionless. One hand on the wheel. No radio. No drilling her about her schoolwork or her grades. The absence of sound was nice, if a little weird. But if this was any indication of the weekend, maybe she would go home, grab her passport, and head back to Manhattan. Maybe Yvonne was still available. She did not want to celebrate her eighteenth birthday in a tomb.

Then, it hit her. She fused her eyes, deflating as her stomach flip-flopped. What if Millie had planned a surprise party? What if she had convinced Walt to pretend he was preoccupied or mad or something to throw her off the scent? Faith hoped not.

"Is everything okay, Dad?"

He glanced her way. "Why wouldn't it be?"

She shrugged.

The lack of follow-up response told her something was definitely up.

They pulled into what looked like a freshly shoveled driveway. Faith scanned the street to spy any familiar vehicles parked amid the seamless snowbank running its length. When she looked next door, she caught a glimpse of Vicki Ford taking out a bag of trash. They exchanged a tacit wave as Walt got Faith's bag out of the car. He marched past her and into the house.

Vicki gave Faith a quizzical head-tilt. Faith raised her hands, then followed her father inside.

Baby toys and washed but unfolded clothes littered the living room, alleviating her worry over the possibility of a surprise party. Hope played quietly in the wooden playpen they set up in the center of the room. They had pushed aside the coffee table to make it fit.

With Millie nowhere in sight, Faith beelined for the kitchen to check the mail. Clean and dirty baby bottles littered the counter. Plastic cereal bowls filled the sink. A small pile of bibs lay stacked on top of the table. The various scents of baby—from spit up to old diapers—permeated the air.

In general, the Peterson home was a wreck. Seeing Millie's perfect home reduced to baby madness filled her with joyful satisfaction.

She found her passport in the junk drawer and quickly stowed it in the secret inside pocket of her leather jacket, then returned to the living room to see her sister.

Hope smiled at her when she sat down next to the playpen.

"How ya doin', little sis?" Faith slid her hand through one of the wooden slats, grabbed a rattle, and gently shook it. Hope gurgled and drooled as she reached for the toy with a mostly steady hand.

Upstairs, she heard their parents fighting in restrained, hushed tones. No wonder her dad had been so quiet on the ride home.

"Sorry, kid," Faith told her sister. "It's all on you, now."

Walt came stomping down the stairs with Millie in tow. She wore a ragged, stained housedress. Her hair looked like it had not been combed—or colored—in weeks. When Faith caught her mother's eye, she could tell whatever the matter was, it was no ordinary fight.

"Humiliated us, that's what you've done!" she shouted as they reached the bottom of the steps.

The outburst startled Hope, who began to cry.

"See what you've done?" Millie shouted again.

Faith scrambled to her feet as her mother lunged past her to pick up the baby. She looked at her father for some clue as to the cause of her anger. But Walt turned away, as if unwilling to even look at her. "What's going on?"

Millie gasped in disgust as she roughly bounced the fussing ten-month-old on her hip. "What's going on? *What's going on?* Walt, did you hear your firstborn?"

Walt said nothing. He disappeared into the kitchen, then returned with a fresh bottle. He eased Hope out of Millie's arms, and then cleared a place on the sofa to sit down and feed her.

Arms folded, Millie glared at Faith. "Did you think we wouldn't find out?"

Faith mentally inventoried her many transgressions. Which one had her parents found out about? Her grades were fine, though they could be better. She had skipped a few classes over the last semester. Sometimes, she would stay out past curfew with Yvonne or Jameson. Or had they found out she smoked pot?

She glanced at the wall clock. Seven hours left.

"It ends *now*, Faith. Today."

Faith raised her arms, squinting in confusion. "What ends? What're you talking about?"

Millie marched out of the room, muttering and swearing under her breath.

"Dad?" Faith shifted a pile of clean clothes to the far side of the couch, then sat down. "What's she upset about now?"

Again, her father turned away, focusing all his attention on the baby in his arms.

When Millie returned, she held in her hand the business card Jameson Lockhardt had given them the night they met. She stomped forward, tore it up, and tossed the pieces in Faith's face. "I mean it. *Today!*"

The realization of the source of Millie's angst only temporarily shocked Faith. She bolted up, jutting her chin. "Or what?"

"Is it true?" Walt asked, devoid of emotion. "Have you been seeing that man? That man who's older than I am?"

Faith softened as she turned to her father. "Daddy, I—"

"Don't deny it!" Millie shrilled.

"Millie, the baby," Walt scolded as Hope rejected the remainder of her bottle and began fussing again.

Faith's arms stiffened at her sides. "You can't tell me who I can see and who I can't."

"Is that so?" Millie seethed, her eyes angry slits. "I guess we'll just see about that, won't we? I'm sure the police will be happy to look into a complaint of statutory rape!"

Faith paled. "You wouldn't!"

"Wouldn't I?"

Her head swam, desperate for a solution. "If you call the police, I swear I'll cut off my left hand."

Millie gasped in open-mouthed shock.

Bolder, Faith inched forward, a challenging sneer overtaking her features. "I'll never play another note."

Walt stood and put Hope on his shoulder to burp her. "Your mother and I've decided to stop paying your tuition. You can transfer to New Rochelle High. We've already spoken to Austin. He'll resume your lessons."

Faith went numb. She stared at them in turn. "What?"

With a self-satisfied tilt of her head, Millie crossed her arms and lifted a single brow.

"You can't do that. I'm not coming back."

"You're not staying at Juilliard," Millie spat.

"*Fine*! Take me out of Juilliard! I don't care! I hate the piano! And I hate both of you!" She tromped toward the door, where her father had left her suitcase.

Millie raced past her, blocking her departure. "Oh no, young lady. Don't even think about it."

"Get out of my way!"

"I will not! Now, go up to your room while your father and I discuss this further."

When she tried to leave, Millie pushed her away. She wanted to push back, then decided on a more subtle approach. Snatching her bag, she stomped upstairs. And waited.

"I don't know why I'm helping you," Vicki whispered later that night as she assisted Faith's escape by bringing over a ladder and a hammer to ply away the nails Walt Peterson had pounded into the outside of her bedroom window.

"I'm surprised you're still at home," Faith told her.

"I decided to live at home while I'm in college."

"If I had cool parents like yours, I'd stay home, too." Faith passed Vicki her suitcase, then hoisted one leg up and over the windowsill. "I'm sorry I ruined your dad's T-shirt, Vick."

Vicki softened, as though she had waited years to hear those two words from her former best friend. "It's okay. I heard about what happened. That Wayne's a real asshole. Sorry you had to go through that."

They descended the ladder without making too much noise. There came no sound, no alarm, no lights, no parents racing into her room to stop her.

Jameson would know what to do. Besides, he had promised to make her a star.

She helped Vicki return her dad's ladder, hugged her goodbye, and headed off on foot toward the train station. When she checked her watch, it read midnight.

***

Standing outside his childhood home unsettled him. As if he had come to knock on the door of strangers, to beg them to let him in so he could take a nostalgic tour inside the place where he had learned to walk, sing, and play guitar, where he had celebrated fourteen happy, and one not-so-happy, birthdays...where he had once had a family.

He blamed his grudging return on Todd's obsession that the band all get passports. Lance had his. Elliot's and Todd's were in process. Only Chris held them back. From what, no one knew. They did not even have a manager, let alone a single reason to believe they would travel to any international location. Least of all, America.

Chris stood poised to knock when Jordan happened around from the backyard.

"Chris!" He sprinted to greet his brother but stopped short of racing up the front steps to go in for a hug.

"How's it going?" he asked casually, as if impervious to his younger brother's warm welcome. As if it did not put a chink in his armor of indifference. Head to heel, he sized him up, then whistled. "You've grown a bit, haven't you?"

The boy pushed out his chest. "I'm almost as tall as you."

"So you are. Sounds like your voice is changing, as well. You're what? Thirteen?"

Jordan's eyes sparkled with excitement. "On Monday. Come to my party! Mum's having it tomorrow because of school. Ben'll be here. Maybe the three of us can do another concert!"

He hooked his thumbs into his belt loops. "Sorry, mate. We've got a gig tomorrow. In fact, we're playing tonight as well. I need to leave straightaway."

"Then what're you doing here?" Deflated, Jordan glanced up and down the road, scanning the area. "Where's your stuff? Are you moving back?"

Chris peered at the familiar neighborhood homes. "I need to pick up a couple of things."

"Well, in any case, Mum'll be happy you're here!" Jordan bounded up the steps and lunged for the door.

He moved in front of his younger brother. "Wait."

Jordan stopped mid-motion. "What's the matter?"

"It—it's nothing. Just...is Dad here?"

He hiked his thumb over his shoulder. "He's in the garage. Want me to get him?"

"No, don't."

Jordan made a face. "You can't pick anything up if you don't go inside."

Chris gnawed the side of his cheek. "You don't know where Mum keeps our birth certificates, do you?"

"Why do you need your birth certificate?"

"I just bloody do. Do you know where they are? You could get it and bring it out to me. Dad and Mum wouldn't need to know I was here."

Jordan scratched his head. "I'm not sure."

"Can you check?"

Reluctantly, he agreed. But as he reached for the doorknob, the door flew open. Jordan stumbled inside the entryway.

"Chris?" His mother stood before him, stunned with amazement.

Head down, he twisted his lips to one side. "Hi, Mum."

She pulled him inside, locking her arms around him. Her body quaked softly in the embrace. Awkwardly, he put his arms around her. "Don't cry, Mum."

"I can't believe you're here," she sobbed into his shoulder.

Standing against the coat rack at the foot of the stairway, Jordan shot him an I-told-you-so grin.

Chris peeled away his mother's arms. "I can't stay, Mum."

"What?" She pulled up the bottom of her apron to dry her eyes. "You just got here!"

"I know, but I have a gig tonight. I need to get back."

"He came for his birth certificate," Jordan said from behind her.

Lynda whirled around to Jordan, then back to Chris. "Your birth certificate?"

Chris nodded, shoulders hunched. "I need a passport."

Panic filled her sorrowed eyes. "You're not leaving England?"

She argued him inside for a cup of tea.

Jordan stuck close to his brother while their mum put the kettle on and prepared a snack. He chatted about all the local goings-on, voiced complaints about his teacher, and confided how boring the house had become without him and Ben.

For Chris's part, his senses were overwhelmed. Their house looked smaller. It smelled like every moment of his life. Like tea and cakes, with a hint of old car and sweat. He supposed each home had its own smell. A combination of its occupants' habits, favorite foods, and personal body scent. Sitting on the sofa with Jordan beside him made him uncomfortable, yet it was the most natural thing in the world.

Until his father returned from the garage.

George Grant had become an amateur mechanic. Though he still loosely managed Ben's successful career, he spent most of his free time these days restoring old cars, then selling them for little more than he had put into them. It kept his hands occupied, and also kept him out from under his wife's feet.

He slipped off his work boots in the entryway, then headed upstairs—as if he had not seen Chris at all. As if his middle son had become invisible.

The passive rejection left Chris staring at the bits of waterlogged tea leaves at the bottom of his empty cup. He wished his mother and brother had not witnessed the humiliation.

His mother patted his knee, then stood and shuffled toward the stairs. "I'll be back."

"Sorry," Jordan muttered.

"No worries." Chris walked his cup to the sink, then returned and grabbed his jacket. "I need to get back. Tell Mum, okay?"

"Wait!" His mother called, descending the stairs.

"I've gotta go," he explained. "I'll miss the train." He addressed Jordan, who still sat on the sofa, teacup in hand. "Sorry I didn't bring a present, mate. Happy birthday anyway, for what it's worth."

Again, his mother threw her arms around him. When she pulled back, she handed him a piece of paper. "Your birth certificate."

"It won't do you any bloody good," his father announced, marching downstairs. "You're still underage."

Chris avoided what he imagined was his father's disapproving glare. "We know a bloke in London."

"As in a forged passport?" George reproached him with disapproving eyes.

He looked down and away.

Lynda gasped, clutching her chest.

Jordan appeared beside him. He hugged him, then jogged upstairs. Chris watched him retreat into his room and close the door.

His father stood stone-faced beside his mother. "When do you need it?"

"Oh George, no," Lynda cried, wringing her hands. "He's only seventeen!"

George patted his wife's shoulder. "This is what he needs to do." He drew Chris in for a hug. "I'll meet you in London next week and help you arrange a real passport."

Chris closed his eyes. "Thanks, Dad."

Pulling away, he grabbed a handkerchief from his pocket to wipe his face.

"But George!" Lynda protested.

"It's okay, Mum," Chris said. "We're not going anywhere. Not yet, at least. It's to have, just in case." He slipped on his jacket.

Lynda held the door as Chris stepped onto the stoop. "You'll let me know before you go making any trips, then?"

George extended his hand. "Name the day, lad. We'll grab a bite."

Chris shook his father's hand, promised his mother to call once a week, then left for the train.

Nothing had gone down like he had anticipated. He had expected his mother to shame him. For Jordan to remain indifferent. And certainly, for his father to shun him. Their mercy had restored him, while evoking regret for every problem he had ever caused them. All the fires he had started in their Bledlow community. The money he had stolen. School problems. The years he had let them worry and wonder.

Ben's appearance at the Marquee made sense. Maybe their mother had asked him to go and make sure he was all right. Maybe they were still family after all.

He hoped to keep his word to his mum about calling. Something in her eyes had told him she doubted he would follow through. Given his nature, she was probably right. But he would try.

"Hi, Chris."

He turned, startled at the unexpected greeting. Recognizing the owner of the familiar voice, his jaw slacked. "Penelope?"

She smiled. A knowing smile. A smile that said she, too, had matured. "How are you? It's been a long time."

"It has." He stood still, unsure if he should approach her. "I'm good. How about you?"

Two years had passed since he had seen her. She was as stunning as ever. All the more since she had grown into her body. Fourteen looked a sight different than sixteen. Her jet-black hair still fell long and straight down her back. Fuller hips made attractive curves in her frame. Her soulful, almond-shaped emerald eyes gave the impression she possessed great wisdom. Or maybe it was just the confidence with which she held herself. He tried not to stare at her perfectly plump breasts.

She slid her hands into her back pocket. "Jordan said you started a band. That you're living in London."

"It's hard, but better than here."

"I guess." Her cheery expression dimmed to something Chris could not read.

When she looked down, her hair spilled forward about her face like a curtain closing after a performance. Regret riddled him. He had not told her goodbye before leaving Bledlow. He had left her in a delicate situation without a single word of acknowledgement.

His voice lowered. "I'm...I'm sorry, Penelope."

She toed the pavement with her chunky t-strap platform heels. "You didn't force me to do anything I didn't want to, right?"

"Still..."

"Your mum and dad barely speak to me in town."

"They know it was my fault."

She spared him a biting glance. "Doesn't change things, does it?"

"I suppose not. Was it bad with your parents?"

Penelope rattled her head. "You don't wanna know."

"I should've been there with you."

"Right." She snorted. "Like my dad would've let you anywhere near me."

Chris rubbed his jaw. "Guess you're right."

He wanted to stay and chat. To reconnect. Penelope drew him out like none of the girls he met in the clubs. Plentiful as they were, he wondered how keen they would be to do the things they did if he were just some nobody from Bledlow.

"I hate to go. I need to get to the train."

She looked at him, arms crossed, an expression he could not read covering her face.

He advanced for a hug, but she held up her hand between them.

"I really am sorry, Pen."

She rolled her shoulder. "Maybe we'll see each other again someday when I move to London."

He looked at her, unsure what to say. Unsure how to make it up.

She stepped forward and cupped his cheeks, drawing him in for a kiss. Quick, soft lips upon his. Her breath was sweet and warm. With that, she turned and walked away.

He thought about her the entire train ride back and all through Mirage's gig that night. When they went to eat after the show, he homed in on a similarly beautiful dark-haired bird amongst the crowd waiting for the band outside. She had a car. And a place of her own.

Hours later, thoughts of Penelope fueled his private performance.

CHAPTER 25

UNLIKE HER HUSBAND AND DAUGHTER, Beth O'Conner was not a music lover. She did not know all the Top 40 tunes or sing along with the radio that Kelley and Farin always kept on when they drove in the car. Music simply did not affect her as it did them.

Nonetheless, today she found herself humming as she baked. Five dozen oatmeal cookies. *"No raisins, Mom, ewww!"* Too many for an after-school snack for two ten-year-old girls. Well, a ten-year-old and a nine-year-old whose birthday they would celebrate the next day.

She switched off the oven and transferred the piping hot treats to a cookie rack, then dug through her Tupperware cupboard for a receptacle into which she could send half home with Joseph, for he and Carol to enjoy while they decorated their house. Pulling off a midweek birthday celebration, particularly a "milestone birthday" celebration, was no easy task. Even if they did grant the guest of honor special permission for a school night sleepover with her best friend. Honestly, with all Joseph and Carol did for Kelley and her, how could she not offer?

When she had packed up the to-go portion of her home-baked goods, she trotted upstairs to get the presents, which she would wrap and send home with Joseph for tomorrow's party.

Only after she had finished every self-assigned task would she make her call. The closer she got, the livelier her tuneless humming.

Ten years old. Farin's January birthday, followed by Marci's two months to the day later, had triggered a bit of depression. A decade. The girls had both passed the midway point before they would be grown and looking toward college. Though she had not discussed it with Kelley, she knew he must feel the same. Simply put, they were not prepared for Farin to grow up and leave home. Carol and Joseph were so much more casual when it came to these things. These realities of life. They loved Marci as much as Beth and Kelley loved Farin, but took the idea of her growing up and making her own way in stride.

Beth hoped her phone call would help ease, and delay, her years-too-early empty nest syndrome.

She ran the vacuum, prepped dinner, and put the wrapped cookies and

Marci's gifts by the door so she would remember to send them home with Joseph. Beth and Kelley had gotten her a gold necklace with a heart-shaped pendant set with a pink gemstone at the very bottom tip of the heart. Not the traditional aquamarine birthstone one might expect. Nothing but pink would do for this birthday girl. In Beth's opinion, it was infinitely more thoughtful than the Led Zeppelin *IV* album Farin had insisted on getting her friend.

"Marci isn't into music like us," Kelley had unsuccessfully argued the day they had gone shopping.

"Daddy!"

"Wouldn't you rather get her a nice doll, or some Barbie clothes?" Beth had suggested.

But Farin would not be moved. "She already has tons of dolls. Dolls are for babies. We're not babies anymore. Besides, 'Stairway to Heaven' is on Led Zeppelin *IV*! Marci loves that song! Even the bridge!"

Kelley had tried the practical approach. "Sweetie, Marci doesn't have a record player."

"She can play it at our house, though."

"Are you sure you wanna get her something she can only use at our house?" Beth asked.

"Momma!"

So, Led Zeppelin *IV* it was. As a concession, Farin had agreed to the pink wrapping paper her mother had picked out.

When Joseph and the girls arrived, Beth was just finishing a call. They bounded inside, giggling and chattering as they rushed to greet her. Beth held her index finger to her lips when they barreled into the kitchen. Joseph followed a few feet behind. She gestured to the plate of cookies and empty glasses.

"Oh, thank you," she said. "Next week's perfect. Thursday at one. Thank you again."

She hung up the phone and kicked back into gear, pouring milk for the girls, who had taken the entire plate of cookies to sit at the kitchen table. "Now don't go spoiling your dinner, little ladies."

They promised through full mouths, dangling their legs as they sat and munched their snack. Beth watched them a beat, noting with bittersweet nostalgia how close their toes were to the floor. Soon, the little girls' foot-swinging would give way to the young ladies' leg-cross.

When she asked Joseph if he wanted to stay for a cookie break, he declined. She caught his inquisitive glance and the wink as he nodded toward the phone. Beth ran her pinched index finger and thumb across her lips. She looked at the girls, then back to him, and mouthed, "Don't tell Kelley." He nodded and crossed his heart.

"I put Marci's things at the foot of the stairs," he said as she walked him to the front door. "Their homework's done. I took them by the office after I picked them up. They worked while I finished a couple of things."

"Did Kelley say if he'll be home for dinner?"

"Yes. He promised the girls. No work tonight."

She sidestepped to refold the afghan draped across the chair nearest the door. "I hope so. It's getting so Carol and I hardly see our husbands anymore."

Joseph paused at the screen door to fish his car keys from his pocket. "It'll get better. We've identified several strong candidates. We'll make a decision sometime late next month."

"Before Easter break," Beth insisted. "We want you men present for the trip."

"I've already started prepping the camping equipment. We'll make our decision by then."

She indicated the Tupperware container and the gifts. "Can you take these with you? I packed up some of the cookies. Oatmeal. It'll give you two some decorating energy."

He gathered the presents and the treat, then called goodbye to his daughter. "You be good for Aunt Beth. I'll see you tomorrow, kiddo."

Before he could leave, Farin and Marci came running out of the kitchen. Marci hugged his waist. "Bye, Daddy. See you tomorrow."

Farin's eyes bulged as she poked her mother's side. "Momma, he's taking my present!"

"It's Marci's present," Beth corrected.

"But she needs to open it here."

"Don't you want her to open it at the party?" She looked at Joseph, hands raised. "Whaddya think, Joe?"

"Doesn't matter to me." He looked down at his daughter. "How 'bout it, princess? Want an early present?"

"Sure!" Marci cheered. She turned to Farin. "Which one?"

Farin grabbed the thin, square present with the hot pink wrapping paper. "This one. You'll love it."

Beth gave Joseph a doubtful, surreptitious brow lift.

Joseph stayed long enough for Marci to tear open the paper. She surprised both adults with her open-mouthed glee.

"It's Led Zeppelin!" she cheered, hugging Farin's neck. "Thanks, Farin!"

"It's got 'Stairway to Heaven!'"

"It does?"

"Yeah! Wanna go upstairs and listen?"

They left the adults without a backward glance and bounded up to the attic.

Beth shook her head as Joseph headed out the door. "I guess Farin was right."

"Best friends are always right."

Beth waved as he drove off, then stepped back into the house and closed the door. She tenderly rubbed her abdomen as she considered his words. Best friends were, indeed, always right. Just yesterday, Carol had told her everything would be okay. That she would warm to the idea of having a second child. That everything would work out.

From all indications, Carol's assertions had manifested themselves to reality. She would find out next week, one way or another.

As she prepared dinner to the blaring echo of Led Zeppelin *IV*, she mused over several possible ways to share with Kelley the news he had waited to hear for the last year and a half.

***

Jameson had to hand it to Faith. Despite her initial brooding over their break-up, she was a good sport. Not to mention her enthusiastic, if unsuccessful, campaign to change his mind. At least it relieved the tension after their long flight across the pond. The periodic physical release she continued to educe from their occasional dalliance kept him laser-focused on his agenda. This last step in his plan was questionable. Half a million pounds questionable. The answer, risky.

He had contacted Leslie Payne before planning the trip. Years had passed since the man had left the Firm on less-than-amicable terms. The Krays had paid enforcer Jack "the Hat" McVitie to get rid of him, concerned Payne knew too much about the Firm's operations and might grass. But in the end, the failed hit had turned the tide of the twins' untouchable status in both legal and political circles. Reggie Kray stabbed McVitie to death at a party, in front of witnesses. Those Detective Nipper Read had not subsequently nicked, who were not current residents at one of Her Majesty's Prisons for McVitie's murder—or for Ronnie Kray's previous murder of George Cornell at the Blind Beggar, had scattered to the wind. The Krays received thirty-year sentences, each. Leslie Payne had gone off-radar in 1969.

The time spent laying low had paid off for Jameson. In the end, he had emerged a hero in the eyes of his former gangland bosses. He was one of few close associates who had not turned Queen's evidence. Loyalty mattered above all.

Payne no longer managed or had knowledge of the financial details, but he knew who did. "I always liked you," he had told Jameson. "The plan's brilliant. A bit bold. I wish you the best."

"I can always use your expertise if you want a change."

He had declined, but promised to set up the meeting. For a cut, of course.

Jameson and Faith had checked in to Claridge's in Brook Street, Mayfair, the night before. During their flight, he had passed time scribbling his vision for Lockhardt Sound in a spiral notebook. Faith slept mostly, using his shoulder as a pillow. When the plane prepared for landing that early evening, she had awoken to take in the aerial view of the city. London's illuminated cityscape had dazzled her.

At first, she claimed to have gotten her second wind. She had begged him to get a cab and show her around the city. However, by the time they had collected their luggage and gone through Customs, she had changed her mind, which was fine with Jameson. He knew London better than his own body, at least the London he had escaped in 1968. No part of him wanted to explore a city he would just as soon forget. After tonight's meeting, he hoped to never make this trip again.

To her credit, Faith had not flinched when he told her why he had come or why he had agreed to let her accompany him. Not that he told her everything. Just that he had a meeting, that it would make or break his dream of starting Lockhardt Sound, and that he needed a pretty escort on his arm to make the deal.

The next morning as she showered, the phone rang. Jameson picked up on the second ring. When he greeted the caller, he was met with a predictably hostile response.

"You're bloody mad, Ron. Even if this weren't the stupidest play I ever heard, it's mad."

Jameson ignored the rebuke. "Have you spoken to them?"

"I have."

"And?"

"Meet me at the Speak at ten. I'd stay put until then. It's never over with the Yard."

But Jameson knew. He had known all along.

Faith emerged from the steamy bathroom, wrapped in a plush hotel robe, combing out her damp red curls. "Who was that?"

"The man who's going to make both our dreams come true."

She plopped down on the sofa, sliding close to him. "It's done, then? Why'd we fly all this way if all it took was a phone call?"

"Because it's important to look people in the eye."

Faith nodded thoughtfully, the way she often did when Jameson gifted her with pearls of wisdom. "So, what now?"

"Now, I'm going to shower. Then, I'm taking you shopping at the sad remnant of what was once the beating heart of Swinging London. You'll choose the perfect outfit for an evening out at one of the city's most important nightclubs. Afterwards, we'll have a late lunch at one of the dirtiest pubs in London. Then, back here to get ready."

"Ready for what?" Her eyes sparkled with anticipation. She linked her arm in his, resting her head on his shoulder.

His robe dampened with her freshly shampooed mane. "Ready to start your new life."

She perked up to face him. "Can we see where you grew up? Your house? Your school? Maybe meet a few of your old friends?"

Jameson ambled to their bathroom as if the innocent request had not affected him in the slightest. "No," he said simply.

They followed their agenda to the letter. Faith marveled at the Union Jack-saturated shops along the deteriorated, T-shirt-rack-laden Carnaby Street with its tacky but colorful panels of pedestrian-trampled rubberized pavement. Things had changed over the last five years. Jameson felt like a stranger. He no longer belonged here. Maybe he never did.

He longed to return to New York, even if only long enough to arrange the move to Los Angeles. His transformation was nearly complete. No more a pathetic post-war orphan who had buried his sister with his bare hands. No more a car for hire or an East End villain. A glorious future lay before him.

Throughout their day, echoes of his promise to Polly filled his head. *I swear on my life. After the war ends, I'll get the house we dreamed of. Even if I have to build it with my bare hands.*

Everything hinged on this evening.

They took afternoon tea at the hotel, then napped in their room until eight. Faith showered again, then spent an hour fixing her hair, her makeup, and pouring herself into her new outfit. He did not personally find her mostly leather ensemble appealing. On the other hand, she looked her part.

Jameson had not seen Laurie O'Leary, the Speakeasy's manager and a lifelong friend of the Krays, since Sibylla's, another in a long line of former London clubs. The jolly-faced man recognized Jameson the moment he descended the steps of the club with Faith on his arm. Laurie nodded as if expecting them.

As Laurie escorted them to a table, Faith's eyes flickered wondrously about the small venue, starting with the coffin at the front entrance, which elicited an approving bark of laughter. Back at the hotel, she had chatted nonstop as she had primped for their evening. So many famous names had played the iconic club. Jimi Hendrix, King Crimson, Pink Floyd, the Who. The list was endless.

A part of him wished he were so easily impressed. He wished he loved music for music's sake, and not merely as a slick way to make his mark on the world and finally win back his wife. In truth, Jameson felt a greater connection to the enormous Al Capone poster on the Speak's wall than he did to any of the notable clientele sitting at their various tables, or others there, hoping to make deals or sign contracts—even if, tonight, he was one of them.

Laurie did not stay long after seating them, but he did give Jameson a knowing, if serious, nod of approval before leaving them to order their drinks.

Faith leaned into him, elbow perched upon their table. "Who's that man over by the bar? He's been staring at you since we walked in."

Jameson glanced casually around the room as if admiring the atmosphere. The man in question made little effort to pretend they had not noticed each other. When their eyes locked, neither turned away. Jameson sized him up. Suited. Side-parted sandy brown hair slicked down with too much hair grease. Unremarkable facial features. Sharp, close-set eyes.

"Well?" Faith pressed.

He averted his gaze to the stage, where a band prepared for their set.

"He's no one to worry about."

"Why's he staring? Do you know him?"

Jameson's voice grew stern. "While I appreciate your keen observations, Faith, I can't have you prattling on all night."

She flounced back, deflated. When their drinks came, she sucked back half her cocktail in a single slurp.

He peered down at her glass, nose wrinkled. "Pace yourself."

"You don't have to be an asshole. I can handle my alcohol."

"I can't coddle or focus on you tonight, Faith."

She set her jaw slightly off-center. "Wow. Thanks for that."

"You said you understood."

Her lips protruded into an irritated pout. When the music started, she pointed to the stage. "Can we at least dance?"

Jameson noted Tommy Crowley's arrival. A furtive glance at the bar told him the man at the bar did as well. Jameson lifted a finger when the small, redheaded man spotted him.

Tommy's steely eyes fixed upon him as he approached. "I'm not here to dance," he told Faith. I'm here for business. Do as we discussed. Keep quiet."

Her countenance turned cold. Jameson worried fleetingly he may have erred in bringing her. Worse, the man at the bar had pulled out from his breast pocket a small notebook and a pen.

When Tommy reached the table, Jameson rose to shake his hand.

Rumor had it Tommy Crowley had gone legit years ago. Pure tosh. Everyone knew he still laundered money. He had as much to lose by publicly meeting with Jameson as Jameson did by being seen with him.

"Let's get this over with," he spat, sitting down opposite Jameson. He did not so much as glance Faith's way.

"You might want to order a drink and relax," Jameson suggested. "Maybe put a smile on that face."

Crowley's eyes twitched about the crowded club. He was a small, rodent of a man. Pale eyes and skin. The freckles of a boy in his mid-fifties. Nervous countenance. When he caught sight of the man at the bar, he jerked his head back at Jameson, demanding, "Is this a setup?"

Eyes anchored to his acquaintance, Jameson inclined his head at Faith. "Time to dance."

She brightened and sat forward.

He nodded. "You go."

"Alone?" When he did not reply, she bolted from her chair, jaw set, and stared daggers at him.

His eyes narrowed at Tommy as he addressed her. "Don't make me tell you again."

Her lips parted, then clamped shut. Without a word, she stomped toward the dance floor.

When she left, the man at the bar stood and headed for their table.

"Where's my receipt?" Jameson asked coolly.

Crowley retrieved a folded piece of paper from his trousers pocket and slid it across the table. When Jameson reached for it, the man from the bar lunged forward, slamming his hand down on top of it. He stood between the two men, a look of self-satisfaction across his plain features. "Ronald Nock, we meet at last."

Jameson laced his fingers atop his lap, unmoved. Crowley stared wide-eyed at the man, corpselike, as the sparse amount of color in his skin drained.

The man slid the paper to the seat closest to him and lowered himself into the chair.

Nonplussed, Jameson said, "The name's Lockhardt."

"Is it, then?" he sneered, revealing perfectly straight, white teeth above thin, curled lips. He consulted his notes. "Never heard of any Lockhardt. You sure look like Ronald Nock."

Jameson regarded him, deadpan.

The man glanced left. "And Mr. Crowley. We meet again."

Tommy swallowed hard.

"I'm afraid I'm going to have to insist you state your business or leave us be," Jameson said. "I'm on an extremely tight schedule."

"Is that so?" The officer chuckled. "Right, then. Let's get on with it. I'm not sure where you've been hiding all this time, Nock, but don't think we've stopped looking into your lot once we cut off the twin heads of the snake. The others got theirs. I'm sure you understand why they'd want to let us know about you. Now's your turn."

Jameson glimpsed Faith on the dance floor. As instructed, she had cut loose. He had rather expected she would find someone to pair up with. Instead, she gyrated her hips and shimmied as if in solo performance. Midway through, she gravitated toward the stage. She had caught the attention of two of the band members. They watched her with lustful eyes as they played.

The spectacle disillusioned him. At that moment, he felt the full weight of their three-decade age difference. Even if intended to make him jealous, which it did not, he found her behavior undignified.

The officer reached into his pocket, pulling out a copy of Ronald Nock's private hire driver's license. He sucked his teeth. "Uncanny, the resemblance."

Jameson leaned in to scrutinize the paper. "Astonishing." He reached into his suit pocket, producing his passport. "But again, my name's Lockhardt. Mr. Crowley, here, is my accountant. Can't say as I'm familiar with any *Ronald Nock*, though the chap does look like he could be my twin."

"What's this, then?" The cop snatched up the paper Tommy had slid across the table. He unfolded and scanned it, whistling through his teeth. "That must be some business."

Jameson remained the embodiment of nonchalance. "Indeed."

"And what business might require your 'accountant' to wire you five hundred thousand pounds?"

He withdrew a business card and handed it over. "It's for my record label."

"Lockhardt Sound," the cop read. "Impressive. Says here you're based in New York?"

"I am."

"So why come all the way to London," he shook the receipt in his hand, "if it's a bank wire and all?"

Jameson glanced at Crowley, who had started to sweat. Disappointing, but expected. "You can go," he informed his old acquaintance. "I'll be in touch if there's a problem with the transfer."

When Tommy shot up, the cop stood as well. "Not so fast. We're not done here."

The band had ended their song. The crowd whistled and applauded. As they launched into their next tune, the lead singer knelt down to steal a moment of conversation with Faith. She inclined her ear to him but stared Jameson's way. The obvious flirtation irritated him.

From across the table, Tommy stared at him with pleading eyes.

Jameson remained seated, hands in his lap. "If you're after this Nock fellow, officer, your time would be better spent moving on. Mr. Crowley's done nothing wrong. He simply wired the money promised from some private investors. As for my trip to England, I'm starting a record label in

America. I took advantage of the opportunity to personally oversee the money transfer—an impressive sum as you've said yourself—while also scouting local talent."

The cop narrowed doubtful eyes upon him. "Yeah? Find any must-have acts, have you?"

"Tonight?" He raised an indignant brow.

The man shrugged. "All right, then. *Tonight.*"

"So far?" Jameson chin-pointed to the stage. "One."

The good news was, the bobby let Tommy go about his business without further question. The bad news was, he lingered to observe Lockhardt Sound's supposed acquisition. Something for which Jameson had not prepared.

He waited for the band's set to end, then stood and marched to join Faith at the front of the stage. "Time to go," he said.

"What? No! C'mon, Jameson. Let's stay. These guys are really good."

Jameson peered up at the platinum blond lead singer bobbing his head down at him. "Faith says you're starting a label."

"Did she?"

"In America."

He regarded the youth coolly.

The singer waved his bandmates over to join him. "We'd like to meet with you. Show you some of our stuff."

Jameson scrutinized their attire and setup. He wished he had paid closer attention to their sound. Especially with the Yard in attendance. Stealing a glance back to the bar, he saw the bartender deliver the man a fresh drink.

He weighed his options but could think of only one solution. He needed the officer to buy his story. "What's your name, son?"

"Todd Dalton." The boy extended his hand. "Our band's name is Mirage."

The name elicited a bark of laughter. "Mirage? You don't say."

The band members exchanged puzzled looks. "You don't like our name?" their drummer asked from behind the others.

"On the contrary," Jameson said, a thin smile breaching his stern exterior. "It's perfect. Welcome to Lockhardt Sound, gentlemen."

The four-boy band broke into excited cheers of astonishment. They exchanged back slaps and congratulatory hugs, talking over each other to thank the unknown stranger.

Faith stood on the sidelines, arms straight at her sides, seething at the announcement.

Jameson cupped her elbow amid the raucous, speaking as they backed away from the stage. "Meet us tomorrow at the Claridge for lunch. Say, two. And mind you, I'm a stickler for punctuality."

In that moment, Jameson realized Lockhardt Sound had officially launched. Without ceremony. Without the money that would still take a few days to clear his account. And without a valid business address.

As for the band, who knew? For now, they made an ideal alibi. He could always get rid of them later if he decided they held no promise.

Jameson escorted Faith out of the Speakeasy, nodding grandly at the officer as they passed.

Faith did not speak to him the entire way back to the hotel, through the lobby, or in the elevator ride up to the fifth floor. He did not protest. Their relationship had ended weeks ago, though a casual dalliance had continued. Tonight, she had played her part. And she had gotten a free trip to England for her inconvenience. He was not the least bit interested in indulging any petty complaint she might lodge.

The minute they stepped into their room, she disappeared into the loo. He took the opportunity to call Ross, grateful for the time difference. It would not bode well for either of them if he were to call too late and disturb Josephine.

"It's done," he told him. "The money was wired Wednesday. It should clear by the time we get back."

"No hiccups?"

"A couple. None of which matter. I did sign our first band." When the line fell silent, Jameson chuckled.

"You signed someone?" Ross asked.

"Well, it's in process. The cost of doing business. Or at least staying out of jail."

"So, you're heading back tomorrow?"

"Actually, I'm having lunch with Mirage."

"Mirage?"

"Lockhardt Sound's first official band. Start the paperwork. Also, you'll need to start arranging visas for this lot of budding young rock stars."

"And you're determined to go to Los Angeles?"

Jameson paused. "We'd agreed."

"I know."

"Is there a problem?"

"Actually...yes. A couple."

"Josephine?"

A sigh filled the line. "First things first. Did you leave your son my phone number?"

The hair on the back of Jameson's neck stood on end. "Why?"

"He called me. He's pretty shaken up."

"Is Sarah all right?"

"Bobby says she's lost her mind."

CHAPTER 26

"I'M SORRY *I LET YOU* down, Sarah. I love you."

"I love you too, Jameson. It's not that."

He heard her sniff, then sigh, as if gently weeping. His voice softened. "Please come home."

"What about your...job?"

Every conversation they had had since she walked out five years ago came down to this.

Jameson propped an elbow on the shabby nightstand next to his bed, upon which he sat. He pinched the bridge of his nose. "I can't discuss business, love."

"Business," she echoed. "Is that what you call it? If I were to return, could you leave that 'business' behind?"

"It's not that easy."

"Easy enough to get into, though, wasn't it?"

If she only knew.

The line fell silent. Either she did not believe him, or she did not care. Both possibilities crushed him. As the pain of her stubbornness overcame him, his cheeks warmed with anger. His lips parted to let loose a biting comment to justify his position, but he choked back the impulse. Truth told, he was not mad at her. He was mad at the choices he could never unmake. "Remember the night we met?"

She "mm-hmmed" into the line.

"I was then who I am now, my love. You knew. You didn't mind before."

"I never objected to your driving a cab. I never cared that you were poor."

"You mean, it never mattered until it did. Until you lived in a council flat smaller than your childhood bedroom."

Mournful sobs filled the line.

"Please don't cry. I'm sorry. I could've never been the man you deserved back then."

"And now? Do I deserve to worry that, every time you're away, you may be arrested? Or worse, leave me a widow? Your son an orphan?"

He heard the hitch in her breath, as if she regretted bringing up a potentially painful memory. She swiftly apologized. He accepted.

The recollection of those years on the streets of a war-damaged Canning Town held little power over him anymore, though he did suffer occasional nostalgia over the family of his youth. In some ways, it now seemed as if the Nocks resided in an alternate universe somewhere in the deep recesses of his memory. Jameson had turned forty-one mere weeks ago. As he had aged, he had overcome the painful details of his past—in no small way, thanks to his wife.

Sarah sniffed again, then cleared her throat. "I should go. I want to make cookies before Bobby gets home from school."

"How is he? How're his marks?"

"He's a bright boy. His marks aren't the issue."

"There's an issue?"

"Of course there's an issue. He's a ten-year-old boy who wonders where his father is, and why he never sees you. Twice a year, he receives some grand present from you. Maybe that often, a phone call. Just enough to keep him pining away."

"Then let me come out on holiday. I need to see him. I need to see you."

She snorted. "You? Come to America?"

Jameson scanned his bleak surroundings. Gray walls. Sparse, dingy furnishings. A small, ill-repaired table and a single chair where he could eat or drink away the ugliness of his day. And the rickety, rusting springs of his bed, upon which lay his lumpy, stained mattress.

Appearances to the contrary, he made good money. But every pound he made, he stashed away as a down payment for a future he had not so much as planned. All he knew was, he needed to make a change. Soon.

"I could maybe plan a trip for next summer. Be there for his birthday?"

"And your 'bosses' would approve?"

He ignored the barb. "I miss you. If you won't come back to me, let me come to you."

Her lack of response impaled him.

He stood and stretched, then consulted his clock. Nine PM. He needed to be at the club in an hour. "Is that a yes, then? Shall I start planning?"

"I don't know. We'll discuss it after the new year. June's months away."

He plopped back down upon his bed. "I'll do whatever it takes, my darling. Just tell me you miss me, too."

"Of course I miss you. But we must be sensible. How long can we keep saying how much we love and miss each other when there seems no hope for reconciliation? We've been apart for years now."

He stood and moved the few feet to his table for a half-full bottle of scotch. The phone cord stretched its limit. "Are you seeing anyone?" He poured a sloppy drink.

"You work for the most fearsome villains in England—you think I'd tell you anything about my private life?"

His forehead creased. "Private life? So, you're dating? Who is he?"

"I didn't say I was dating. I said I wouldn't discuss it."

He chewed the inside of his cheek. "Maybe I should get your dad to find out."

The comment elicited an indignant huff. Simultaneously, the call disconnected with an ear-ringing slam of the phone on the American end.

Jameson swore through flattened lips and responded in kind. Just what he needed. A bad call before what he anticipated would be a bad night.

Lately, there had been more bad nights than good for the Firm.

The invincibility his gangland bosses had achieved had preceded a trail of destruction felt by all its members and associates. Jameson did not know whether Reggie had laxed in giving twin Ronnie the much-needed Stemetil that curbed his psychosis, or if the drug no longer worked. Either way, much had transpired since their triumphant celebration at the West End's El Morocco club.

Their South End rivals, referred to by some as the "Torture Gang," formed by brothers Charlie and Eddie Richardson, had a reputation for torturing victims in unspeakable manners. For the most part, there had existed for some time an uneasy coexistence between the Firm and the Richardsons. At least until last Christmas, 1965, when a party at the Astor club in Mayfair had devolved into a brawl.

Reggie and Ronnie warned of the inevitability of a turf war. Everyone was on high alert. Three months later, the Richardsons arrived at a Rushey Green club, Mr. Smiths, and a brief gun battle had ensued. It was rumored that the Richardsons' intent had been to wipe out the Firm. But neither Ron nor Reg was present. In fact, none of the Firm members were there. Unfortunately, a good friend of the twins was. He was shot dead.

That next night, Ronnie had single-handedly changed the course of his, his brother's, and all of their associates' futures when he killed the Richardsons' loudmouthed, fearless enforcer, George Cornell, in full view of about a dozen witnesses at a club called the Blind Beggar.

Meanwhile, Reggie's infamous marriage to his "cockney princess" had crumbled within months of their wedding. Inarguably fragile, the young and stunning Mrs. Kray had moved out of Reggie's flat, leaving him in a consistently inconsistent state of agitation.

The twins had, most recently, orchestrated the escape of Frank Mitchell from his current detainment in Dartmoor prison. Frank was an armored tank of a man and a friend of Ronnie's from a previous stint in Wandsworth Prison back in the '50s. The brothers believed the escape would lead to a successful petition of the courts for a final release date for Mitchell, who had spent years inside without being given a promised date of release. Mitchell's escape made the national news. This type of publicity served no one well. Especially East End villains.

Ultimately, their plan collapsed. The Home Office refused to negotiate with an escaped inmate. Mitchell grew increasingly unruly. His unbridled strength and volatile temper made his minders uncomfortable. They could not return Mitchell to jail. Likewise, they could not risk letting him leave the Barking Road flat in which they kept him, for fear of prosecution should Mitchell talk.

Essentially, Frank Mitchell had traded one jail cell for another. He was not happy about it. No one could guess when Frank would turn on those who had set out to help him.

Tomorrow, Freddie would solve the problem. Permanently.

Jameson told no one, not even Sarah, how desperate he was to extricate himself from a life in which he no longer felt safe. It did not matter that the Firm had "disincentivized" witnesses to Cornell's murder from talking. It did not matter that Frank Mitchell's body would never be found. It did not matter that the removal of the Richardsons by Scotland Yard had enabled the Firm to expand their territory and further solidify their reputations as villains who one dared not challenge. All that mattered was that things were getting worse, not better.

One by one, Jameson saw his fellow Firm members participate in increasingly riskier crimes. Crimes carrying with them far longer sentences should they be nicked. Something told Jameson that, soon, he would be called upon to step up his own duties, which had thus far allowed him to stay out of the more serious capers by serving in various capacities in any one of their many clubs. How did he know his time would come? Because, as of tomorrow, they told him he would go back to driving his cab. Instinct told him no good would come from the change.

Maybe by the summer of '67, he would not only be able to visit his estranged wife and son, as he had told Sarah he would, but he could disappear from England—and the Krays—altogether.

***

Bobby came to amidst the pounding on his front passenger's window and accompanying shouts of his name. They sounded muted and far away. Filtered through wads of thick cotton. As his waking mind fused with the acute awareness of aching legs, dry mouth, and a stiff neck, he pried open one eye, then the other.

"Are you listening to me?!"

He bolted upright with a start and a hitch of his breath.

"Robert Jameson Lockhardt Jr., what on Earth are you doing?" his mother demanded, banging the window with her fists. "You'll come inside straightaway. I'm not joking!"

He smacked his dry lips, then turned to train his heavy, unfocused eyes her way, still not fully comprehending his circumstances. Why he sat in his car, he could not immediately recall. Especially through his mother's angry rant.

"I mean it, Bobby! Now!"

Anymore, he did not care. It did not matter whether he played the part of an obedient son or that of a rebel. Either way, things always ended the same.

Squinting at her through bleary eyes, he lifted his index finger. The impassive response sent his mother over the edge. She gathered the folds of her robe, turned on her slippered heel, and marched up their driveway toward the front door.

Random observations assaulted his consciousness. It impressed him that he had not, in his altered state, sideswiped his mother's Buick Electra when he had returned from wherever he had been. His mouth felt like sandpaper. He was hungry. His legs tingled and throbbed from having fallen asleep sitting up in the Porsche's frame-hugging leather seats. Either he had yet to wake up enough to register the agony of his hangover, or he was still drunk.

A far-off image danced in his memory. Last night, he had had a blast. He had needed it after the humiliation he had suffered. He also recollected making a call. He had spoken with his father's friend.

Ross Alexander was a kind man, and perhaps the nicest adult he had ever talked to.

If only his father were here.

Desperate for something to drink, he checked his immediate

surroundings for a remnant of a beer or a can of soda. On the passenger side floorboard, he found a small paper bag. He snatched it up but wrinkled his nose when he saw that it contained a half-full pint of tequila. He hated tequila. It must belong to one of the guys.

His mother screamed at him from the front doorway. "Are you coming?!"

He nodded, then once again held up his index finger. Sarah huffed inside and slammed the door.

Bobby opened the tequila bottle and took a hefty gulp, nearly gagging as he swallowed, then screwed the cap back on and tossed it back to the floorboard. Almost immediately, he felt it come back up on him. He barely got his car door open in time to spill the contents of his stomach onto the driveway instead of his lap.

At that moment, his curiously absent hangover arrived.

Head throbbing, he stumbled out of his car. He staggered up the driveway, but bypassed the front door to procure the garden hose.

Again, his mother opened the door. She glared at him expectantly.

"Gimme a sec, Mom. I need to hose down the driveway."

She glimpsed the vehicle-obstructed cement, then disappeared inside with another slam of the door.

Bobby winced at the noise but stayed the course. He sprayed the alcohol-infused bile off the driveway, over the sidewalk, and into the gutter. Once he stowed the hose and locked up his car, he went inside, prepared for the worst.

His mother sat on the living room sofa, arms and legs crossed. With a nod, she indicated the recliner opposite her. "Sit."

At least she had not attacked him. Yet.

When he sat down, he realized she had set a glass of water and some aspirin on the coffee table. At least he hoped it was aspirin. He scooped up the pills and downed them with the full glass of water, then excused himself to get a second glass. Hopefully, he would not throw up the pills before they kicked in.

"Where were you?" she asked once he settled in.

"I told you last night. Adam Utely invited me to a party."

"And I told you I didn't want you to go."

He looked down at the floor.

"I'm worried about you, Bobby. Your behavior's becoming erratic."

His eyes widened at the irony, but he said nothing.

"What's going on?"

Everything. Everything and nothing.

Sixteen years old and ending his junior year of high school. Total parties: one. Total dates with girls: zero. His most recent humiliation? Friday afternoon.

For years, Bobby had pined for Wendy Myers. Especially after the beautiful note she had written in his seventh-grade yearbook when she encouraged him not to be nervous around girls—to be himself. She had treated him kindly, at first, even after his mother had scared her off later that same summer when she tried to call. Since then, they had periodically exchanged brief hallway greetings as they rushed to get to their next class.

Friday, he had finally made his move.

"Wendy, wait up!" he had called when he saw her crossing the quad.

She had smiled when he approached her. "Hi, Bobby. How are you?"

He tried not to appear awkward as they chatted. Then, he heard himself from somewhere outside his body. "Wendy, would you like to go to a movie with me tomorrow? I know it's short notice, and you probably have plans and all, but—"

The disappearance of her beautiful smile, coupled with her downcast eyes, had stopped him mid-sentence.

"I'm sorry, Bobby," she had told him. "I'm seeing someone. Besides, you and I are just friends, right?"

She had never before that moment said she considered him a "friend." And as kind as she was, he knew a lie when he heard one.

Mercifully, she had not lingered to witness his abasement. She painted on a smile, pecked his cheek with her excruciatingly soft lips, then scampered off to catch up with a group of friends.

His heart had ached at the rejection, however unsurprising. He had trudged to his car in deep thought. Mostly, he felt sorry for himself. He was lonely.

A voice from behind him had shaken him from his thoughts. "What's up, Bobby?"

Isaac Fett had appeared from nowhere. Bobby glanced around the parking lot and spotted the boy's usual group of stoner friends waiting in the car. Adam Utely waved out the window. Bobby waved back.

"Adam wants to know if you wanna come to his party tomorrow," Isaac told him matter-of-factly.

Bobby frowned at the invitation. "Why?"

Isaac lifted his shoulders.

"He wants to give me that tape, doesn't he?"

Isaac bowed his head, toeing the pavement with his brand-new Puma Clydes. "Maybe."

"Why not ask me himself?"

"I dunno. You in or not?"

Bobby pressed his upper teeth with his tongue as he thought. The idea of escaping the pain of Wendy's rejection appealed to him. Besides, he had always complained about not having friends. Maybe stoner friends were better than none.

"I'm in," he said at last.

"Really? Cool!" Isaac peered over at his friends and gave Adam a thumbs up. Inside the car, the boys high-fived each other.

Bobby tore off a piece of scrap paper and had Isaac write down the address.

"The party's at nine," he said. "And maybe you'll let us take a spin in that cool car of yours, eh?"

Bobby gave a noncommittal snort.

"I know we haven't really talked much all these years, but I'm stoked you're coming." Isaac handed back the pen and paper with the address, then jogged off toward his friends. "See ya tomorrow!"

The invitation had lightened his spirits. At least until he got home. His mother became irate when he confessed the reason for his somber mood. "You're too young to start thinking about girls!"

Hoping to avoid further confrontation, he had delayed telling her about the party. When he finally did, she forbade him from going. So, he went anyway.

From what little he remembered, the party was worth the present inquisition.

"I thought you wanted a job," she scolded. "Isn't that a better use of your time?"

"I tried, Mom! But it's not easy keeping a job when you keep calling me home."

"Don't you dare blame your bad behavior on me!"

He set his jaw. For too long, he had enabled her abuse. Today, he was just sick and tired enough to give a little back.

Bobby stood and towered over her. "Let's talk about 'behavior,' Mom, okay? How about all the times I hear you talking to yourself in your room?"

Her eyes widened in undiluted shock.

His arms flailed in frustration. "Or about the ants, huh? There are no ants, Mom. There never has been. Our house has stunk of insecticide for seven years!"

The weight of his accusations riddled her. She covered her face with her hands and began to weep. The reaction did not faze him. He had seen it all before. In fact, it emboldened him.

He ticked off years of built-up complaints on his fingers. "You've scared away every friend I ever nearly had. You lose the car when you go out. Sometimes, you sit on the couch for hours without a word. It's strange, Mom. You're strange!"

Her crying morphed into pitiful, heaving sobs. At last, she shouted, "Apple favors! Scalpel thief!"

The tension in his shoulders deflated like a flattening tire. He shook his head. "Really, Mom? What does that even mean? Do you hear the things you say?"

Slowly, her hands slid away from her face. She reached for the tissue box on the end table, grabbed two sheets to blot her eyes, and then blew her nose. For a second, Bobby thought he recognized the mother who still possessed what little loyalty he still felt.

"I'm sorry," she squeaked. She uncrossed her legs and repositioned herself on the sofa, tucking her legs beneath her. "I know I have problems, son. I do. I just...can't."

The explanation made no more sense than anything else in his life. "I'm sorry, too, Mom. But you need to hear the truth."

She cocked her head, giving him a quizzical look.

Bobby grabbed his refilled glass of water and downed it in full. He replaced the glass on the coffee table, then stared at her with stolid indifference. "I called Dad yesterday."

The last thing he saw before everything went dark was her bolting up from the sofa with a rageful shriek.

***

Jameson had not expected much when he signed Mirage without even listening to their music. A means to an end, really. He had planned to cut them loose before boarding his return flight. And, given Faith's negative attitude, he considered leaving her with them.

In fairness, he had been distracted during their Sunday lunch. The call with Ross echoed in his mind. Something had happened in Santa Barbara.

The details were sketchy. Sarah? "...she's lost her mind..." Ross had relayed the message. Jameson could imagine no such thing. In the years he had known his wife, she had impressed him as a sober-minded, logical, sane woman.

"I'll call Bobby when I return to the states," he had told Ross. "It doesn't sound right. Maybe Bobby got into some trouble and wants attention."

"I don't know," Ross had said. "He seemed pretty upset."

As usual. Young Robert was often upset.

Jameson did not know his son well. Certainly not as he would have preferred. It had been difficult to get to know him, given the distance. Still, that distance had kept his son and wife safe during his former, less-respectable career. But soon, everything would change. The one thing he did know about Bobby was their common desire to reunite their family. Perhaps this outburst was his attempt to step up the calendar.

"Before I have the contracts drawn up, I'd like to hear you once more. I've arranged some studio time tomorrow afternoon at Olympic. Just an hour or so. When we're finished with lunch, I'd recommend you lot go home and prepare three of your best songs. No covers. I want to hear your sound. Are we clear?"

Nothing he threw at the band members dissuaded them. If anything, they grew more enthusiastic with each deterrent he introduced.

They would need to leave England for America almost immediately. "No problem."

They would need to have enough material for a full album—and all songs would be subject to his pre-approval. "Sounds great!"

They would need to work hard. No matter what they had read in the trades or the various rags, the music business was just that: business. They were all young chaps. Plenty of energy. No excuses. "Agreed!"

Faith remained uncharacteristically silent during their meal. Jameson ignored her. After her outburst before bed the night before, he had decided to sever all ties with her.

She had confronted him after his phone call with Ross. "You promised to sign me. You said I'd be the first artist on the Lockhardt Sound label. Where's my contract?"

"Tell me you'll do an album of classical music, and I'll sign you right now."

Her eyes had become angry slits. "We already talked about that."

"Fair enough. Give me the name of one successful solo rock pianist."

"Jerry Lee Lewis," she had countered.

Jameson had guffawed. "I guess I must have missed his recent chart-toppers."

"It still counts."

"So it does. Now, name a female solo rock pianist."

The challenge had infuriated her, but at least it shut her up so he could get some sleep.

Still doubtful, Jameson spent Monday morning verifying the wire transfer for which Tommy Crowley had given him the receipt. He had spent much of his personal savings on this trip. Without the promised five hundred thousand pounds—over one point two million American dollars at the current exchange rate—he had no company, no reason to sign Mirage, and no way back to the states, with or without Faith.

When everything went through, his mood lightened. Now, anything was possible. Including the success of his first signed act.

To say Mirage impressed him that afternoon at the studio was an understatement. In fact, it eventually discharged his final obligation.

Elliot Lawrence, Mirage's bassist, was a musical genius. He wrote most of their material. And each one was a potential hit. "Oil" impressed him the most. It took no time to earmark it as their first single.

Todd Dalton, their lead singer, had a three-octave set of golden pipes. Still, his youth, high-spiritedness, and what felt like an air of discontented anger gave Jameson pause. He suspected the lad had a taste for hard partying. Something he would make a point to take in hand. Initially, he considered finding a replacement. He made a mental note to keep an ear out for just that.

Drummer Lance Turner kept the energy high. More than proficient with his sticks, only his gregarious attitude impressed Jameson more. A keeper, for sure.

Then, there was the lead guitarist. Chris Grant was a shoe-in. Something about the lad reminded Jameson of himself. He possessed a darker, more serious disposition. Like Todd Dalton, there was a potent air of sexuality about him. A confident swagger that belied his youth. If his instinct proved accurate, Chris would quickly become his favorite of the lot. Plus, Jameson knew his brother, Ben, by reputation. Instinct told him Chris would become the solid foundation upon which Mirage would fully materialize.

"But right there," Elliot blurted out, stopping them in the middle of their third piece. "It's missing something."

Chris threw back his head. "Not again, El."

The bassist ignored the rebuke. He pointed to the control room where Jameson and Faith sat behind the console, listening. "You," he called.

Faith's eyes widened. She pointed to herself.

Elliot nodded.

Faith glanced at Jameson as if seeking his approval. He waved his hand. "Go ahead."

Eight minutes later, Jameson concluded their session. He instructed the group to meet him at their hotel tomorrow morning at ten sharp. "Pack everything you need, boys, and don't forget your birth certificates and passports. Tomorrow, we fly to LA. I've arranged a little surprise for you. You'll get it when we land. And by the way—you're officially a quintet, now. Congratulations on your new keyboardist."

"Yes!" Elliot brought his hands together with a single, victorious clap.

Todd Dalton slapped Chris Grant's chest with the back of his hand. "See?"

Jameson called Ross with the news and, in a rare moment of sincerity, thanked him when the man offered to help arrange the flight for everyone. Ross would meet them in LA. Josephine had reluctantly given her blessing for the trip. Not only did it make sense to facilitate the signing of the contracts, it would ensure he was on hand to assist Jameson if the situation in Santa Barbara declined.

That night after they finished packing their own luggage, Faith thanked Jameson one last time in her own special way.

CHAPTER 27

"OH GEORGE, DO HURRY," LYNDA pleaded. Handbag tucked close beside her, she fidgeted with her fingers. "I should've had breakfast ready earlier. It's all my fault."

"Don't you think on it," George admonished. His hands firmly gripped the wheel of their '65 Vauxhall Victor 101 Escape. Head lowered and eyes laser-focused on the road before them, he motored southeast down the A4010 through West Wycombe, then turned right on Chapel Lane, heading toward Handy Cross roundabout. "What time's their flight again?"

"He said nine," Ben answered from the back seat. He checked his watch. "It'll be close, but I think we can still make it."

Lynda released a mournful sigh.

"Please don't worry, Mum," Jordan piped up from his seat beside his oldest brother, directly behind their mother. He scooted forward and rested a hand on her shoulder.

She reached up and gave it a loving pat.

"Heathrow would've been closer. By half," George grumbled under his breath.

Lynda retrieved a handkerchief from her purse and dabbed her eyes.

It was more than simply giving his wife the opportunity to see her son off before he flew to America. Far more.

Who was this Jameson Lockhardt, anyway? How was it that he had just met his son three days ago and now had him and his bandmates flying halfway across the world? It made no sense. Chris should have swallowed his bloody pride and called earlier with the news. George certainly could have handled the negotiations—for all of Mirage. He could have checked the man out. Did it not concern this Mr. Lockhardt that their son was only seventeen? As a matter of fact, not one of the band members had reached the legal age of majority, to his knowledge.

"I've heard of him," Ben had told them Sunday when he had surprised his mother with a rare appearance for Sunday dinner. "He works for an American label—GPG. He's their A&R man. Hard-nosed. Quite a good reputation, actually. He's well-known for his superior instinct. You know, maybe this isn't such a bad thing after all. I say, good on Chris."

But that was Sunday, when Chris's call had merely mentioned the fact that, after their gig at the Speak Saturday evening, they had been approached by a gentleman who said he might want to sign Mirage to a recording contract. Surely they had time to meet up and discuss his intentions, George had thought at the time. Surely Chris would wait for his father to talk to this man and size him up.

Instead, they had received a second call late last night.

"We're leaving tomorrow morning," Chris had announced, breathless with excitement. "We'll be in Los Angeles, California, Mum! And when we're big stars, I'll fly you out and treat you like a queen!"

Chris had hung up before his father could snatch the phone away from his stunned wife.

George chastised himself for not immediately heading to London Monday morning. He could have gone to Chris and demanded to be taken to this Lockhardt's hotel. He could have done his job, as both a manager and a father.

The more he dwelled upon the situation, the angrier he grew. Defying the posted speed limit signs, he depressed the gas petal. The four-speed push rod engine hummed in response.

Lynda grabbed the door handle with her left hand, her right shooting out to clutch the dash. "George Grant, are you trying to get us all killed? Mind your speed!"

He reluctantly decelerated to the point where she leaned back and appeared to relax in her seat.

Battling the clock, he navigated the natural beauty of the English countryside, lined with all its lush green ash and elm. If not for the somber, sun-obscured sky, it could have been an ideal day for a drive. Instead, he took full advantage of the new-ish, though only partially completed, M40 motorway to just past Gerrards Cross.

"Construction everywhere," George spat bitterly. "Bloody progress."

"What if we don't make it?" Lynda whimpered beside him.

Jordan's hand still clasped his mother's shoulder. He gave her a tender squeeze.

George inclined his head back toward his oldest. "How're we on time?"

"It's tight, Dad."

Ben had arrived late last night at his father's request. No matter how their familial ties had loosened over the past few years, George had explained, they were still family. All of them. Family mattered. Even if that meant meandering along at a frustratingly inconsistent rate of speed through rural English roads to try to reach his rebel son before he disappeared from their lives for who knew how long, with who knew what type of man this Jameson Lockhardt might be. They needed to show up and lend their support. Even if they did not, in fact, support him.

George glimpsed Ben through the rearview mirror. Ben gave a doubtful shake of his head. George increased his speed in response, slowly at first, so as not to alarm his wife.

"Maybe we should've taken the train," Jordan suggested.

"It would've taken nearly double the time—and with all the morning commuters?"

Jordan released his grip on his mother's shoulder and scooted back into his seat. "It'll be okay, Mum. You know how mean Chris can be. He can take care of himself."

As they approached Heathrow to the east, George gritted his teeth behind pinch lips. He squeezed the steering wheel until his hands reddened around his white knuckles.

He glimpsed Lynda out of the corner of his eye. She looked oddly relaxed. Or perhaps she had resolved to expect the worst. Still clutching her dampened handkerchief, her hands rested atop her lap as she stared out the passenger's window at the gray morning. "The telly weatherman said it's rain before noon," she muttered, her voice little more than a whisper.

Ben glanced at Jordan, then cocked his head, squinting at their mother. "You okay, Mum?"

She did not look back. "We've lost him, Ben. I feel it in my bones."

"Rubbish," George argued. "We'll make it."

"You know, Mum, I'm going to America in a few months. I can leave early and fly to Los Angeles if I need to."

George flourished an upturned hand toward his wife. "See there? Now, no more talk of losing Chris. We know our son, love. He's got himself a wild streak, that one."

Lynda propped her elbow atop the door handle and rested her head upon her closed hand.

As their Vauxhall Victor sped past Smallfield, some two and a half miles from Gatwick Airport, Ben announced the nine o'clock hour.

George began decelerating. His facial muscles slackened, pulling down his cheeks and parting his lips. He said nothing as he prepared to turn around and head back to Bledlow. His eyes remained glued to the road before them.

Jordan hunched down and across Ben's lap to peer out the window closest to the airport. Ben lifted his arms, pressing back into his seat to accommodate. For some time, Jordan stared in the direction of the airport.

As George engaged his turn signal to exit the road, Jordan pointed at the sky. "Look!"

A Boeing 707 with a blue Pan Am logo on its tail rose above the Gatwick Airport terminal and hurtled upward toward the dark, cloudy sky.

George pulled to the side of the road and stopped. They watched, expressionless, as the aircraft battled gravity. The high-pitched whir of its mighty engine softened to a confident rumble as the vessel climbed ever upward and began veering west. Eventually, it disappeared into a blanket of angry nimbostratus clouds.

Lynda covered her face with her trembling hands and wept.

***

In their nineteen years of marriage, Ross had rarely traveled without his bride. Even while on his periodic business trips. He preferred having Josephine along with him, and she preferred accompanying him. Packing for one was a lonely prospect.

But he had not even suggested Josephine fly to Los Angeles. He did not need to. She had spent the last week hinting at her various obligations. Charity work. A prearranged lunch with Betty that she could not cancel. Volunteering at the hospital. Unavoidably busy, both of them. It all sounded so reasonable.

So, he packed alone for his two weeks in California. And as he packed, a pair of disapproving eyes scrutinized his every move. What slacks and sports coats he chose. His shirts. Ties. How many socks and pairs of boxer shorts he threw in his suitcase. His shaving kit. Shoes. Belts. A pair of swim trunks.

Josephine watched, arms folded, from the upholstered armchair in their bedroom. Legs crossed, she bounced her foot on the floor. The expression painted across her lovely features did not look as cold as they did disappointed. He hated disappointing her.

"Maybe you can help him find a replacement," she said, more a concession than anything else. "I'm not suggesting you just disappear. I realize you've committed to helping him find his legs."

Ross ran his thumb across a minor smudge on one of his fine leather

Oxfords, then slid the pair into their velvet shoe covers and stowed them atop his underwear.

"Have you told him yet?" The familiar, if rare, edge in her voice assured him she already knew the answer.

With a deep intake of breath, he stopped packing and faced her. "My love, there are some rather complicated matters involved at this time. I'll have the discussion while we're there. It's unfair to tell him over the phone."

"What complicated matters? How complicated can it be? He wants us to move. We're not going to. Case closed. LA's filled with lawyers. He can find a replacement."

"Yes." A grin played at the corner of his mouth as he continued filling and organizing his suitcase. "We're a dime a dozen, aren't we?"

"I didn't say that." Josephine stood and padded over to the bed where he had splayed his various items. She nudged him out of the way, removed everything in his suitcase and garment bag, then began refolding and reorganizing his things in a more efficient manner. "You know what I mean."

He kissed the base of her neck, then went to the bathroom for his toothbrush.

Josephine's refusal to move had come as no surprise. She had never lived outside of New York, save their months-long stay in London back in 1967. Even that had left her homesick. Her friends and family lived here in New York. She loved her church. The notion she would agree to pack up and go to California had been ridiculous. He had not thought it through very well.

Something about Jameson Lockhardt's plans for the future had skewed his judgment. He found himself swept up in the excitement of belonging to something instinct told him would find profound success. The justification for that belief lie in the few years Jameson had worked in the music industry and the reputation he had earned.

"Where are your undershirts?" Josephine called from the bedroom. "I don't see them here."

"I must have forgotten," he called back. "See? I need you with me. Pack your bags. I'll arrange your ticket."

She chuckled. Hearing her lighthearted side eased the tension in his shoulders.

Of course, that laughter would cease had she known the full extent of his association with the man he now prepared to visit. If she knew what that man had done. How her husband was not only an unwitting accessory after the fact, but that a case could be made that he had been directly involved.

Ross tried not to focus on such things. The case had closed before one even existed.

For his part, he had learned two things about his now-closest friend: he was smart, and he was dangerous. The part of himself Josephine did not know, despite nearly two decades of marriage, was the part drawn to both those aspects of Jameson's nature. Though not so naïve as to believe Jameson had told him everything the night they had laid their proverbial cards upon the table, he had learned enough. Somehow, the mutually assured destruction was thrilling.

"Remind me what time you have to leave?" Josephine called once again.

"The car should be here in an hour."

"Well, I'll need every bit of that time to make sure you're properly packed."

He grinned to himself as he packed his travel comb and razor into the zippered leather bag. "And I'll love you all the more for it."

"Which you'll prove by way of bringing me back something stunning from Rodeo Drive."

"Ah—spoiling the surprise already, are we?"

Her guilty giggle stirred him.

"Will you have time to call Lockhardt's son back before your flight? That poor boy. What a horrible situation."

He stared at, and through, his bathroom faucet. "I'm sure he's at school."

Bobby had called him again last night. The environment in Santa Barbara had passed the point of bizarre and crossed straight into unsafe.

"I'm scared," the young man had confided, his trembling voice assuring Ross that he had not embellished his story. "She locked me in my room yesterday and didn't even let me out to go to school today. Then tonight, she unlocked my door as if nothing happened. Should I go to school tomorrow? Or maybe call the police? Have you talked to Dad?"

Ross had made every attempt to calm the boy down. At first, he did not know what advice to give him. Any involvement with the authorities would create a scandal he preferred to avoid. Yet he could not ignore

Bobby's situation. "Your father arrives in LA late tomorrow night. I'll be there earlier, around three. We're booked into the Beverly Hills Hotel. Call me there if you need to. I'm sure your father will be in touch, but likely not until Wednesday morning. Between the signing and the appointments I've made for us, our schedule's fairly full. Is there someone you can stay with if you need to until we can get there?"

The pause that followed his simple question had saddened Ross. "Anyone, son?"

"Um...not really."

"I see. Well, you do what you need to do. It's only a little over twenty-four hours now. If you must call the police—"

"I don't really want to do that, Mr. Alexander. She's...she's still my mom."

"I agree. And Bobby? For what it's worth, I'm sorry you have to go through this. We'll get things sorted out. You have my word."

Josephine glided into the bathroom to hurry him along. She scanned his bag, nodded her approval, then zipped it closed. "You need to shower. I'll have your things waiting at the door."

He kissed her. "You're too good to me."

She gave his forearm a firm but gentle squeeze. "Promise you'll tell Jameson sooner rather than later. There's something I can't put my finger on. I can't help feeling there's nothing but trouble ahead if we make that move."

He reached into the shower to engage the water. "I understand. But we don't have a lot of options now that Conserves is folding."

"There are always options."

Another of her unsubtle hints. "Are you suggesting I quit entertainment law, Jo?"

She said nothing. She did not have to.

He stripped off his clothes and tested the water. "Maybe we should discuss this later."

As she left, he called after her. "Is this purely an issue of geography?"

She slowed her pace for a moment, then continued on. "I'm not sure."

Her answer told him everything he needed to know. He only wished he could convince Jameson to change his mind and build Lockhardt Sound here in New York. Given the brewing trouble in Santa Barbara, he could not imagine how he might pull that off.

***

Each time Jameson landed in LA, he made the same observation. The startling lack of trees was as astonishing to behold as the oily brown haze that seemed to permanently cover the vast, flat, sprawling metropolis like a toxic tarp. Night landings such as these were marginally more tolerable. The birds-eye view of grays and beige that made up the daytime landscape of the Greater Los Angeles area transformed each evening like a Seurat original, the pointillism of smog-filtered streetlights, office building lights, headlights, neon lights, and klieg lights painting the night. Past the jagged sandy coast to the west, the Pacific Ocean churned. Its frothy, white-edged blackness ebbed with the pull of the moon. An impressive transformation.

But, for all its crime and grit, Manhattan still appealed to him. It reminded him of a more garish, less historic London. Often miserable weather. Congested. But at least one did not require a car to move around.

Living in LA would take some getting used to.

He considered waking his travel mates as the pilot navigated the plane in preparation for landing but decided against it. The twelve-hour flight had taken its toll. That and the alcohol they had consumed. It never failed to astonish him how many substances those in the entertainment business could consume. Sure, he could hold his own and did enjoy his scotch. But he fell far short in an industry where grass, amphetamines, and gallons of booze were consumed with shocking regularity.

From the moment of Lockhardt Sound's conception, he had determined it would have standards. He was no prude, but he refused to let something he worked so hard for go the way of other mismanaged labels that pandered to the base personality of the increasingly worshipped "artists" who buttered their bread.

"And that's lesson one," he had informed Elliot and Chris, who had appeared to use their flight time as a crash course to learn about the forthcoming Lockhardt Sound's culture. "I can't speak to your 'process' when it comes to writing or performing. But when it affects my business, I have zero problem replacing people with those more serious about the music. If you want to destroy yourselves, go somewhere else. Or form your own label and take your chances."

For the first three hours of their trip, they had hung on his every word while Faith partied with Todd and Lance a few rows behind them. Lance shared his large cache of crisps and biscuits with them. Todd turned his nose up at the offering, preferring his liquid treats. They chatted and flirted with Faith nonstop, talking about music and asking endless questions about America.

"Thursday," Jameson had said, "Ross Alexander and I have appointments to view office space. I've my eye on a particularly nice spot on Sunset. Tomorrow night, I'll show you around the local clubs. But you're on your own during the day. However you spend it, I expect you back at the hotel and ready for dinner at seven. I've made reservations. And, of course, there's the signing on Friday, and then the party Saturday night."

"When will we get the contracts to review?" Elliot asked.

Jameson suppressed a grin. An astute young man, that Elliot.

"Ross is bringing them to the hotel. They'll be available immediately. You'll have time to review them, of course. Don't want to take too long, though. We need to get Mirage booked into the local clubs as soon as possible. We also need to find more permanent lodging."

Jameson observed their overwhelming joy, even if he did not share it. Always stars in the eyes with newcomers. He could not remember a time at their age when anything had so excited him.

They discussed the long-term plans of Lockhardt Sound to create an in-house recording studio with state-of-the-art equipment and to set up a publishing rights company. One by one, the band partied themselves to sleep. Elliot was the last of the group to fall out.

By the time they landed, arranged for the delivery of their bags to the hotel, and cleared Customs, it was midnight. Fully awake after their long, if uncomfortable, nap, they gawked at the fully stocked limousine Ross had ordered to ferry them to the Beverly Hills Hotel. While they absorbed their surroundings and checked out the various amenities of the car, Ross and Jameson discussed the forthcoming articles of incorporation they would file once Lockhardt Sound had an official address, as well as the contracts the lawyer had already drawn up for the band's signature.

Every so often, Jameson would catch Faith staring at him. She sat opposite him, her anger over the perceived betrayal of their relationship draped like a sandwich board over her shoulders. He knew it would pass eventually. On the upside, she appeared to get on well with her new band.

But as the limo pulled up to the iconic Pink Palace with its green and white striped porte-cochère and red-carpeted entrance, even she could not conceal her excitement.

Jameson ignored the wide-eyed, slack-jawed response of his young companions. He exited the vehicle as soon as the attendant opened the door, followed by Ross. One by one, they emerged, stunned as the reality of their situation settled upon them.

When Chris passed him, Jameson raised his hand to separate him from the others, who Ross ushered inside.

"A quick word, son," he said.

With a curt nod, Chris closed his mouth and followed him some feet from the front of the limo. "B-loody hell, Mr. Lockhardt, this is...I don't know what this is."

"I managed to speak to both Todd's and Elliot's families, but you never gave me your parents' number. Now, I've chosen to believe—what with your brother's career and that of your father's back in the day—that they know you're here."

An expression Jameson could not readily label covered Chris's face. "They know," he grumbled.

"So I shouldn't expect the police to raid my bungalow tonight after you call to let them know you've landed safely?"

The boy shook his head.

"Good. Then let's get checked in, shall we? I'm more than twice your age, with a busy few days ahead. I'm ready to turn in."

He marched toward the entrance full stride. Before he reached the steps, Ross exited the door with the others in tow. The man passed out their room keys. Todd and Lance would share a Junior Suite configured with two twin beds, as would Chris and Elliot. Faith had her own room with a patio. Jameson and Ross each had a bungalow.

Ross slid his hand inside his sports coat and retrieved five envelopes, which he passed out to each member of Mirage.

"I'm giving you each two hundred dollars," Jameson announced.

The boys exchanged looks of shock and elation while Faith eyed him suspiciously.

"Consider it an advance against future royalties and spend it wisely. As for the hotel, you may charge your meals and necessities, as well as reasonable calls to your families to let them know where you are and that you're safe. All such expenses shall likewise be recouped against your earnings, so be mindful. While Ross and I handle business over the next couple of days, this should tide you over."

While the others talked over each other and pocketed their small fortune, Elliot appeared less enthusiastic. His brows arched with concern above narrowed eyes as he folded the envelope and slid it into his back pocket.

"Problem?" Jameson asked.

The boy gave an awkward shrug. "It's very generous of you, sir. But it's not like we can go anywhere. A couple of us have driver's licenses, but we've never driven in America even if we could rent a car."

Ross shot Jameson a knowing grin.

"Hmm. That's true. Los Angeles certainly isn't London, is it? You'll need a car to get around." Lips pushed out, Jameson lifted his chin. He peered at the menagerie as if looking down his nose through a pair of spectacles. "Which of you have licenses?"

Everyone but Todd raised their hands.

"Well, then. Faith has her license. Perhaps she'll spend some time letting you practice driving on the right side of the road. What-say you, my dear?"

She looked away, aloof. "Fine with me. Gonna leave us the limo?"

They shared a lighthearted chuckle, then noticed Jameson trudging out into the parking lot. Ross motioned for them to follow. Murmuring with curiosity, they complied. Jameson strode to the far end of the lot to a largely unoccupied area where five highly polished vehicles sat. Every one a brand new, current-year model. Each without its permanent plates.

Jameson stopped, waited for the others to catch up, then swept his hand in a grand flourish toward the vehicles. "Gentlemen, and lady," he said, dipping his chin to the only female in their group, "I believe I mentioned something about having a surprise for you."

The vehicles had been backed into each space, the last near the corner end of the tree-lined barrier separating the hotel from Sunset Blvd. Closest to them sat a Ravenna green Porsche 914. To its left, a blue-green poly Corvette convertible.

Faith gaped at the vehicles, blinked, then looked back at her now ex-boyfriend. Fingers shaking, she pointed. "Are these for us?"

A rare smile stretched across Jameson's lips.

Lance eyeballed his bandmates as if they were competitors at a scavenger hunt.

Beside the Corvette, a BMW 3.0 CSi coupe in gulf yellow caught Elliot's attention.

After confirming Jameson's generous gift, Faith marched purposefully to the red Mercedes 450 SL parked between the BMW and the black Targa Porsche 911 Carrera at the end of the row. "You guys need to learn to take what you can get when it's offered. This one's mine." She looked askance at Jameson. "I've earned it."

Lance followed Faith's lead. He beelined to the Corvette. "Come to papa, you bloody beauty."

Todd and Chris sized one another up, then dashed to claim the Porches at either end of the row. Todd marveled at the stunning green of the 914. Chris opened the 911's passenger's door by habit, then jogged around to the left and eased himself into the driver's side leather seat.

Elliot watched the others stake their claims. One by one, Ross handed them each the keys to their vehicles.

Jameson stabbed at the air. "Not one inch before you get your license," he warned Todd. With a disappointed nod, the boy combed back his platinum locks with his fingers.

A chorus of engines revved as they turned ignitions and pressed gas pedals. They rolled down their windows, whooped, and thanked their benefactor machine-gun style.

Jameson realized the BMW remained unclaimed. When he turned to Elliot, he frowned at the sight of the lad's eyes brimming with tears. He went to him. "I trust the BMW's to your liking. If not, we can exchange it for something more your style."

"It's not that." Elliot fixed his gaze on the car. "I've never had much of anything, Mr. Lockhardt. Certainly nothing I haven't worked for. I'm not sure what to do."

"I believe Faith answered that question already, however inelegantly."

A bark of laughter escaped Elliot's otherwise flat features. "But I haven't earned this."

"You will. You're a talented songwriter. 'Oil' is going to be a big hit. If you can write that well, I see a bright future for you. It'll be hard work."

"Thank you, sir. For everything."

Jameson clapped his hand on Elliot's shoulder and squeezed, then sent him on his way. He accepted the keys from Ross as the man wandered back to have a private word.

"It's been a long day," Ross said, hands in his pockets. He rocked on his heels as they watched the joyous tumult in the parking lot.

"How was your flight?" Jameson asked.

"Uneventful. Especially compared to the night before."

Jameson cocked his head. "Everything all right?"

Ross gave a curt nod. "We should talk as soon as possible. I heard from your son again. I realize you've been on two continents today and intended to rest before we start office hunting, but you need to get up to Santa Barbara. Bobby's scared to death. And, from what he's told me, he has reason to be."

His eyes narrowed. "It's not just another attempt to—"

"It's serious. There may be some abuse."

Jameson battled the urge to protest aloud the absurdity of such a suggestion. When he met Ross's gaze, he realized their carefully planned trip had already taken a detour. The last thing he wanted to do tomorrow was take a road trip. What had Sarah done?

As Ross filled him in on the details, he eyed the fleet of Mirage vehicles, wondering which one he would borrow.

CHAPTER 28

*"Y*OU'LL NEED TO GET IN *and have a look around, first," they explained. "Get to know the place a bit. Find your exit. No mistakes. Understand?"*

The day Jameson dreaded had finally arrived. He had known his time would come. But never in his wildest imagination had he anticipated he would make his buttons doing a civilian. The Kray twins had lost control—of themselves and others. They believed they had no choice.

They were mad. Ronnie with his mental illness; Reggie with his booze-infused grief.

"He's away on business a lot. And when he's home, he's cocked up on pills and drink. It shouldn't be a problem getting in and out."

Years had passed since Glasgow crime lord, Arthur Thompson, had discouraged the twins from making a move into the music business in any meaningful way. Yes, there was money to be made managing bands. Especially the already-famous bands the Krays had set their sights upon. And yes, the American mafia had made successful inroads into the entertainment industry. But the downside far outweighed the inconvenience.

The first objection Arthur Thompson had raised? The average East End villain did not possess a disciplined work ethic, let alone the required energy to manage such aboveboard undertakings. Ronnie Kray's ill-fated dalliance in Enugu, Nigeria back in 1964, investing thousands of pounds in a major housing and factory development project, had made for a painful example. In the main, the twins wanted money, fame, and respect—not a grueling, if legitimate, day's work.

Thompson's second objection? Reputation. Should London's most infamous villains successfully wrestle away the world's most popular band from its high-profile manager, it could only damage the group's established brand and ultimately destroy their future success.

Another consideration? Loyalty. This objection the Kray twins fully understood. As with all of gangland, loyalty mattered. The metaphorical objects of the twins' affections were fiercely loyal to their troubled young manager. They would never submit to a group of thugs muscling their way in to take them over.

At the time of their discussion with Arthur Thompson, it seemed Ronnie and Reggie had accepted the reality that their plans would never materialize. Instead, they had capitalized on their strength: blackmail. But in a strange twist of fate, the murder of George Cornell had brought them full circle.

Jameson had arrived at E. Pellicci's on Bethnal Green Road early, as requested. Only a few of the Firm, their top guys, joined them. He had never before found himself included in such an exclusive meeting. Almost immediately, a cup of tea and a full English breakfast was slid in front of him.

He nodded his gratitude to proprietor Nevis Pellicci, though he had no appetite. Even so, he grabbed his fork and dug in.

When Ronnie Kray gave Jameson his marching orders, he nearly choked on his blood sausage.

Ever since Cornell's murder that night at the Blind Beggar, Jameson had heard rumors. Reggie had handled the witnesses in the same way they always managed such things: fear and intimidation. They had even tracked down the ones who had tried to hide. But who would have guessed that one of those witnesses might have an intimate connection to the very entertainment impresario the twins had, as a concession, been blackmailing all this time?

"And if you get caught, you're on your own," one of them warned, though in Jameson's shocked state he was unclear which twin had addressed him. "This doesn't touch us. Understand?"

Having no other choice, Jameson nodded. "Consider it done."

They discussed the details over the next half hour. Jameson participated fully, though he felt himself many miles away. Dozens of questions swam in his head. Most, he dared not ask.

"Do I ring Fred afterward to take care of the bod—"

"Leave it," they instructed.

He put his full attention on his meal, or at least he gave that appearance. Had they noticed he had begun to sweat? This was not villain-on-villain crime. Scotland Yard would be fully invested.

"When you're done, lay low. We'll be in touch. We'll find you."

Jameson wondered why they would consider terminating a steady source of dosh. To date, the blackmail scheme against Brian Epstein had worked. Maybe Epstein's secret stalker, the man who had caused the music manager such grief over the last few years—indeed, the source of the compromising photos the twins had come into possession of—had started causing problems. As fate would have it, the man had been at the Blind Beggar that night. What better way to send a message to a psychotic sometimes-boyfriend that he had best not grass? If the twins could make an example of Epstein, who could they not reach?

The twins might lose some monthly scratch, but if it ensured Ronnie Kray's continued freedom, perhaps they considered it a fair price.

Unfortunately, Jameson had been chosen to pay it.

The twins insisted he stay for more tea. He refused them nothing. And as they discussed other business matters, Jameson's mind coursed with fear. The one thing he had prided himself on all these years was that he had avoided the difficult jobs. Now, they had assigned him a more dangerous job than any one of them, including the twins themselves, had ever undertaken.

"How go the plans for America?" he asked when he found a natural opportunity in their conversation.

"Still just that," Ronnie said. "Plans."

"Maybe I can help you out, there," he told them.

"Yeah? How so?"

He gave a casual shrug. "I've been studying up. Hoping to make myself useful when the time comes."

The twins stared at one another, communicating in that way of theirs that outsiders could never understand. Serious at first, they eyeballed each other. For a moment, it seemed they might consider his offer. Then, they burst into a laughing fit. "Good on you, Ron! We'll let you know."

As they mocked his tireless efforts to learn as much about the music business as he could in anticipation of becoming their liaison in America, Jameson found his rage. He felt the urge to do what the rest of the Firm had only ever hinted at—ending both men—then and there. All his free time in the last six months, he had spent in the library. He had absorbed everything he could get his hands on about running a business. About the pitfalls and nuances of the entertainment industry. Books. Newspapers. And all for naught?

His last conversation with Sarah looped in his mind. He needed her back. To accomplish this, he needed to get to America. He had told Sarah he would do whatever it took to get there.

"Get to it, then," Reggie said once their bellies were full of Pellicci's fine fare, and they had concluded their business.

It was agreed that Jameson should distance himself from physical contact with the Firm until after he completed his assignment, and they could assure no blow back. The Yard had made no secret that they watched them closely these days. Ronnie had spotted a car outside when he arrived. Inside sat two men he suspected were from the Met. It was not the first time.

As they dispersed, Jameson used the back entrance to slip away undetected. Might as well start distancing himself right away. And as much as the idea of taking a man's life disturbed him, maybe it was the answer for which he had searched. He had tried to find a way to break free from the Firm once and for all.

If only no one had to die to purchase his freedom.

***

Farin frowned at her plate. "Mommy usually makes bacon and eggs. Or cereal."

"Mommy's sick. She gets to sleep in this morning," Kelley explained. He whistled a tune as he sat down with coffee and the morning paper. He sorted through the pages until he found the business section, opened the newspaper with a crisp crack, and began skimming articles.

"But I hate oatmeal, Daddy."

The top half of the paper bowed over. "You do?"

She pushed her lips into a pout.

"I see," he said, in feigned contemplation as he glanced at the ceiling, tapping his index finger against his lips. "That's a problem, isn't it? My girl needs a good breakfast before school, and I can't cook."

She hopped out of her seat and dashed around to her father's side, eyes sparkling, a coy grin tickling the sides of her mouth.

He wrapped an arm around her waist and pulled her close, kissing the top of her head. "Any suggestions?"

Her body wriggled excitedly. She gave him an innocent shrug.

"I'll make you a deal," he whispered in her ear. "You get rid of the oatmeal and then get your lunch box out of the fridge. I'll take out the garbage and grab my briefcase."

Eyes wide with the thrill of their innocent conspiracy, she nodded. "Can we get donuts?"

Kelley held her gaze, shushing her. He whispered, "You can't tell Mom."

He did not have to tell her twice. She scampered back to her side of the table, snatched up the bowl holding the unappetizing mush, then scraped its contents into the trash. As directed, she rinsed the remaining gunk from the bowl and left it in the sink. By the time she brushed her teeth and gathered her things for school, her father waited at the door.

They mince-stepped from the house, their bodies bobbing up and down like a couple of cartoon villains. Farin quietly turned the doorknob and pulled the door shut behind her, then dashed down the porch steps to the car while Kelley locked up.

As usual, the second he turned the ignition, Farin reached for the radio. Stevie Wonder's "You Are the Sunshine of My Life" blared into the silence of the spring morning. Kelley quickly dialed down the volume. As they pulled out of the driveway, he glanced up and saw Beth at their bedroom window. She wagged her finger down at them, then smiled and shook her head. He lifted his shoulders and hands, then looked askance at their daughter and backed out. Farin waved happily at her mother. Beth air-kissed her, then retreated from the window.

"Mommy doesn't look sick to me," she observed as they drove off.

"If you'd have heard her in the bathroom earlier, you wouldn't say that. We don't want to take any chances with our camping trip next week."

He took the long way to the donut shop. They had plenty of time before school. Besides, for the last few weeks, he and Joseph barely saw their families at night. Their practice had thrived to a point the workload was scarcely manageable. Not only did they need to bring in a new partner immediately, they might need two. And so, whenever he could, he stole moments like these to spend with his daughter.

When Helen Reddy's "Peaceful" came on the radio, he listened contentedly to Farin sing the entire song. Every so often, he would glance her way, concealing his pride as she shut her eyes and gently swayed her head to belt out the ballad with feeling.

"Got any plans this summer?" he asked when the tune finished.

Farin frowned his way. "Aren't we going to Hawaii?"

"We are. But that's only two weeks, and it's not until after the Fourth of July."

She thought about it as "Tie a Yellow Ribbon Round the Ole Oak Tree" began. "Marci and I have our tree house. And the beach."

"I don't know, hon." He exhaled an exaggerated breath. "That doesn't seem like much of an itinerary."

"How come?"

"Well," he said, as if speaking to a colleague, "I think it's time to start considering your future."

The suggestion sparked a laugh. "Daddy, I'm in fourth grade!"

"Exactly." He winked.

"You know I don't want to be a lawyer, right?"

"Oh, you've made that clear." He chuckled as he signaled to make a left on State Street.

"I'm gonna be a singer," she added.

"I know," he said. "That's why you should start practicing."

She turned to him, confused and curious. "I practice all the time. Don't you hear me?"

"Of course I do. But is that enough?"

"What else can I do? Singers sing, Daddy."

They tabled their conversation long enough to procure their sugary meal, some milk for Farin, and some black coffee for himself. From there, they drove back down State Street to park near the beach and enjoy their breakfast.

The clear sky and crisp ocean breeze made for a perfect spring morning. Seagulls and pelicans scavenged the sand and pier. A handful of people lounged on the sand or strolled along the boardwalk.

"So, I was thinking," Kelley said around a mouthful of apple fritter. He swallowed and sipped his coffee. "Are you sure you wanna be a singer?"

She jerked her head to gaze at him. Lips outlined in powdered sugar, she gulped her milk. "Of course I am."

"What would you think about taking some voice lessons?"

Farin's happy enthusiasm evaporated into the sea air.

He squinted at her. "What's wrong, angel?"

She peered out at the water.

"Tell me."

"I thought you said I'm a good singer."

"You are."

"Then why take lessons?"

He rubbed a crooked index finger along her cheek. "Do you think Daddy's a good lawyer?"

"I guess so. You're always at the office or in court."

The unintended slight stung. He knew things had to change. How many times lately had Beth made similar, less innocent, comments to the same effect? "Well, I had to go to school to learn how to be a lawyer. And even if you're the greatest singer in the world—which, of course, you are— you still need to train your voice."

She listened with interest. "Will it help me get on the radio?"

"It may, yes."

He watched as she twisted her mouth to one side and considered his advice. Her eyes flickered as she watched the rolling ocean waves. "Will you help me if I get a contract?"

"You mean *when* you get a contract?"

Her smile returned at last.

"You bet I will. But for now, you should think about getting those lessons. Your mom and I can find someone. It's important, Farin, to work hard for what we want. It doesn't matter how good we are at something. We work hard. We do the right thing. That's the best anyone can do in life. No one's going to come along and hand you what you want. That's not the way things are. You have to work to make your dreams come true. If you do, you'll find success."

Farin collected his pearls of wisdom as if intending to string them into a necklace. She hung on his every word, ignoring the half-consumed donut lying atop the napkin on her lap.

They chatted as they finished breakfast, then tossed their garbage in a nearby trash can and headed on to Franklin Elementary School.

"We'll start keeping an eye out for contests and talent shows as well," he said as he rounded the corner of her school. "Let me know if you hear anything from your teachers."

"Okay." She gathered up her lunch box. Before getting out of the car, she scooted across the station wagon's bench seat and kissed his cheek. "Are you gonna be late again tonight, Daddy?"

He peered out the windshield, blowing out a bubbly sigh. "I'll try not to be, hon, but we're making our decision about a new partner soon, and I have court tomorrow. It's a pretty big case. I need to be ready."

She snuggled into his hug, then hopped out of the car. "It's okay, Daddy. It's important to work hard, right?"

He gave her a wink and a smile. "Exactly. I love you, sweetie. Have a good day. Hopefully, Mom will be better tomorrow and we can have our eggs and bacon. This weekend, you can help me get things ready for Yosemite."

He waited until she skipped off toward her classroom, then turned up the radio. Gladys Knight and the Pips' "Neither One of Us (Wants to Be the First to Say Goodbye)" began as he drove away.

***

Jameson awoke to the perfect stillness of his darkened bungalow.

Wrapped in crisp, cool linen sheets, he lay silent and content. The first good night's sleep he could remember...ever, really. The embodiment of the ridiculously clichéd but optimistic saying about the first day of the rest of one's life. He felt it in his bones. That person was him. And this was his day.

He rolled his head left to peer at the bedside clock. Nine AM. Still a couple of hours to relax before Ross arrived for their champagne breakfast. He would make good use of every peaceful second of that time.

When his bladder protested his idle repose, he pulled back the sheets and sat up on the side of the bed. He yawned and stretched his arms wide, then scratched his head. His messy mop of blond hair alternately spiked and flattened from a full eight hours' rest. He would need a haircut before their appointments tomorrow.

Skinning on a luxurious white cotton bathrobe with the Beverly Hills Hotel logo on its breast pocket, he headed for the bathroom. On the way, he pulleyed open the room-darkening drapes. Bright, piercing sunlight flooded the space. He squinted against the blinding morning rays as he hastened to the bathroom to relieve himself.

A complimentary copy of the *LA Times* lay on the welcome mat outside his front door. He retrieved the paper and padded to the sofa. Yawning again, he propped his feet atop the glass and brass coffee table.

He had arranged for room service to deliver their breakfast at eleven thirty, but decided to order a tea service to tide him over. With a grunt, he stood and went to the desk to plug in the phone cord. His blissful night's sleep had demanded he temporarily thwart Faith's ability to call and beg him to let her come over.

The moment he restored the connection, the phone rang. He hesitated to pick up. He hated to begin his day before tea and the paper, but suspected his relaxing morning had already ended.

"I'm coming over," Ross announced. His voice sounded strained.

"You're not due for a couple of hours. Is there a problem?"

"Pick up your messages."

He wondered how many Faith had left.

"I just got off the phone with Bobby. He's going to school today, but asked if we'd be there this afternoon. I told him we would be."

Jameson promised to call the front desk. "There's nothing we can do before he gets home. Be here at eleven as planned."

When they hung up, he rang the front desk. Only three messages.

Predictably, the first was from Faith, asking him to come by her room. The second, an urgent request from Bobby to call him back. The third stole his attention.

"A Mr. Crowley, from London. He asked that you return his call right away."

He jotted down the number, barked a less than congenial "thank you," then severed their connection. Tommy Crowley had no reason to contact him. Not unless they had run into a problem with the money. He glanced at the clock, mentally calculated the time difference, then lifted his finger off the switch-hook and dialed the international number.

"They've been checking on you," Tommy told him.

"Checking on me, how?" Jameson demanded.

"That investigator from the Yard? He's been following up. I hear he's asking about you, your company, and that band you told him you signed."

"Why would he do that?" Stupid question.

"If they keep digging into the money…"

Jameson made a note to have Ross call the investigator's boss. "I'll handle it."

But Tommy would not be talked down. A nervous type for as long as Jameson had known him.

He assured the accountant that he would take care of it and promised to call him back as soon as he had more information. When they hung up, he shaved, showered, and dressed in a pressed gray suit, starched white shirt, a wide tie with black stripes, and a pair of black Oxfords.

The thought of Scotland Yard's unanticipated queries niggled his thoughts. He wanted to believe he had abandoned his days of worry at the Speakeasy last Saturday evening. For years, he had successfully avoided any close scrutiny.

Or had he?

He called Ross back, filled him in, and directed him to make inquiries. Unwilling to sit and stew for another hour about matters he could not control, he decided to check on the band before breakfast. In all likelihood, they were still asleep.

Nearing Todd and Lance's suite, he detected laughter and boisterous chatter competing with blaring music from the room's tinny radio. When he knocked on the door, there came several shushing noises, followed by guilty chuckles.

Chris Grant opened the door. Bleary-eyed, he teetered on wobbly legs as he greeted, "Mr. Lockhardt. Come in."

Jameson looked past him to the others gathered around the sofa in various states of intoxication. Liquor bottles littered the sitting area. The last thing he wanted to do was join them. The room reeked of stale alcohol, marijuana, and perspiration. "Have any of you slept?"

A chorus of uncontained guffaws blown out raspberry-style answered his question. Jameson beckoned Mirage's lead guitarist out into the hallway for a quick word.

"I'll need your car," he announced pointedly. "Around noon."

Chris frowned and squinted, as if processing the request. "My car?"

Jameson nodded.

"Where are we going?"

"*We* aren't going anywhere. *I* am." He lifted his palm. "Keys."

The young man fished through his jeans pockets, procured the keyring, then dutifully handed them over. "Where are we going again?"

Jameson turned on his heel and stomped back down the hall. "I'll see you for dinner. Get some sleep."

At breakfast, he declined the champagne he had ordered. His mood had soured with the obligations of his day. "You should probably stay here," he told Ross. "The band's wasted. I'd hate to think what they'll do if we both leave."

Ross nodded. "I'll stay on the grounds in case you need to have me paged. I've confirmed our appointment with the realtor tomorrow."

By one o'clock, Jameson strode purposefully across the parking lot toward the Carrera. The drive to Santa Barbara would take a couple of hours. It occurred to him he did not know what time his son returned home from school. With any luck, he would arrive in time for a private chat with his wife.

"Jameson, wait!"

He stopped and turned to find Faith jogging up behind him.

"Take me with you," she called. "Please."

His nose wrinkled at the suggestion.

She moved in close, resting her hands on his chest. "*Please.*"

With slow but exaggerated movements, he placed her hands at her sides. "I'm going to see my wife, Faith. We've discussed this. Our relationship's over."

Lips quivering, her bloodshot eyes welled. She shook her head, pleading.

"Don't be that girl, my dear. The girl who chases the unattainable man. I'm not Mr. Beam."

The arrow found its mark. She stared up at him, hurt and betrayal contorting her sallow, inebriated features. "Why would you say that?"

He ignored the question. "You're a grown woman, now. With a promising career. Mirage will be a remarkable success. That's a promise, and I don't make promises lightly. When we met, you said that was all you wanted."

Mascara-infused tears spilled down her cheeks. "But I want *you*."

"Enough," he spat cruelly. "I'm a married man. Now, go back inside. Rest. Get yourself together. We have a long night ahead of us."

He left her sobbing in the parking lot without a backward glance. When he unlocked the Porsche's driver's side door to lower himself into the snug bucket seat, he noticed with a start that Chris sat in the passenger's seat, shirt wrinkled and only half-tucked into his jeans, head propped against the window, mouth open, and passed out cold.

"Get up!" he ordered, nudging his shoulder.

The boy snored beside him, undisturbed.

He considered his options. Should he stop Faith and get her keys? Drag Chris out of the car and leave him sleeping in the parking lot?

Jameson swore under his breath as he buckled himself into his seat. He had allotted no time in his schedule to sort out drunken stowaways. Chris would simply have to make the trip with him. At least Jameson could ensure the lad was sober by the time they returned for dinner.

"You'd better be bloody worth all this," he growled.

He revved the engine in a final attempt to wake his unconscious companion. Nothing. A moment later, he shifted into gear and sped through the parking lot toward the exit to the street. No morning paper. No haircut. No celebratory champagne breakfast. No lasting assurances that he had finally left his days in gangland behind him.

Could his day get any worse?

CHAPTER 29

ETH SAT AT THE DINING room table, alone. An untouched table setting lay before her. A second setting lay at the opposite end, likewise pristine. Thankfully, she had not plated the food. She had wisely decided to wait until she saw the whites of her husband's eyes.

The homemade Beef Wellington recipe Carol had recommended had taken the majority of the afternoon to prepare. She had taken painstaking care to ensure she got the pastry right. To be honest, she did not care for the required duck liver the recipe demanded. Nonetheless, she had soldiered on, producing a visually impressive meal. At least it had looked impressive before she had to leave it warming in the oven at 170°.

"'I'll be home at a reasonable time. I promise,'" she mocked aloud, arms crossed as she stole a bitter glance at the wall clock. Reasonable could not, by any rational person's estimation, mean after 10 PM.

Hours earlier, Farin had enjoyed a simpler meal of hot dogs and chips. Not the most nutritious fare for a ten-year-old girl, but it was mercifully quick. An episode of the *Sonny and Cher Comedy Hour*, followed by her nightly bath, and she had gone off to bed more than satisfied.

Beth stared sullenly at the two wrapped packages sitting atop the middle of the table. The smaller of the two, an old jewelry gift box she had saved from the earrings Kelley gave her last Christmas, was wrapped in navy and teal geometric-patterned paper with a navy bow. Inside, she had placed a pair of earplugs. The label affixed to the gift read "Bad News." Inside the slightly larger second gift box was a baby bib with the words "World's Greatest Dad - Again" stitched on its front. She had wrapped it in red paisley paper with a purple ribbon. Its label read "Good News."

As minutes-late bled into hours, her enthusiasm to proceed with their romantic evening waned. Tonight was supposed to be special.

"So much for promises," she spat when she gave in at last and called Kelley at the office.

He groaned apologetically into the receiver. "I'm sorry, honey. I completely lost track of time."

"What's kept you?" She hated the nagging tone in her voice. Though an arguably soft interrogation, it was not her style. She attributed it to hormones. "I have news."

"Are you crying? Is everything okay?"

She sniffed, then cleared her throat. "I made a special dinner. It's probably ruined now."

"I'm sure it'll be fine."

"It's not supposed to be *fine*. It's supposed to be *special*. And now, well, it's just not special anymore."

"Don't say that, sweetheart."

Her anger fizzled to that of mere disappointment. "How soon can you be here?"

"I just have to pack up my files, and I'll hurry home. I really am sorry. It's just that, with this big case going to court tomorrow and our vacation next week, I wanted to handle as much as I could. It'll be better once Joseph and I make our decision on the partnership. I prom—"

"You promise. I know."

The partnership. For over a year now, she and Carol had heard nothing but promises to bring in a new partner. In the meantime, their workload had become unbearable. Anymore, the kids rarely saw their fathers beyond periodic weekends and morning breakfasts. Marci missed Joseph so much, she had recently announced to Carol her intention to go to law school so that she might one day hire on to O'Conner, Williams & Associates.

"Can you give me a hint about this news of yours?" he asked, as if trying to coax her into a lighter mood. "Is it good news or bad news?"

Her eyes flitted toward the gifts. "Yes. Yes, it is."

He chuckled. "A mystery. I'm intrigued."

"You're not intrigued," she accused playfully. "You're changing the subject."

"I'm eight minutes away. Think dinner'll last that long?"

"Probably not. I'm sure the pastry's either dried out or soggy by now."

"Pastry? Yum!"

"I tried the Wellington recipe Carol gave me."

"Well hell, Beth. If you'd told me that, I'd have been home on time."

"If I'd have told you why you really needed to be home on time, you would have been."

"Hmm," he pondered aloud. "The mystery deepens. Any additional hints?"

"Not until you get here, Counselor."

He paused. "Can I guess?"

"I'd prefer you didn't."

"Aw, c'mon. You're no fun."

She propped her free hand to her hip. "Kelley Rowyn O'Conner, you're stalling."

"You're pregnant," he blurted out offhandedly.

The unexpected statement took her aback. Her lips parted as she hitched her breath.

Kelley paused again. His voice deepened. "You're pregnant?"

Beth's eyes misted. "You weren't supposed to guess."

"That's it, isn't it?"

She heard the shuffling of papers and imagined him stuffing his briefcase as his pace quickened. "The surprise is ruined, now. Just like dinner. Oh Kelley, how could you? I even made up the little 'Good News Bad News' gifts, like you did for me back in Seattle when you told me we were moving."

"Beth?"

"What?" she asked with a deflated pout.

"I love you."

"I love you, too. But I hate your powers of deduction."

He snickered. "I'll be home as soon as humanly possible."

"Will you tell me the Wellington's perfect? Even if it's not?"

"Especially if it's not. And I promise to act surprised when I open my gifts. Does Farin know yet?"

"I thought we'd tell her together. Maybe go out Friday for dinner? Just the three of us?"

"You mean the four of us?"

She smiled at last, echoing, "The four of us."

"I'm leaving this second, so start dishing me up some of that Wellington, little mama."

She hooked the receiver onto the wall phone, then busied herself in the kitchen. Moving about with a pronounced bounce in her step, she donned her oven mitts and retrieved their meal. It looked fine. When she tapped the top of the pastry to get an idea for its consistency, it felt a bit soggy but certainly passable. It smelled scrumptious.

The salad she had prepped and stored in the fridge was still crisp. At least her husband's tardiness had not ruined that part of their dinner. She set the bowl of fresh greens, tomatoes, and cucumbers on the counter, then shuffled into the dining room to light the tapered candles.

Within five minutes, she had everything in place. It might not be what she planned, but it would be special after all.

The four of us, she thought. Tomorrow, while Kelley was in court, she would make their Friday dinner reservations.

She rubbed her belly as she grabbed the novel she had been trying to finish, turned on the stereo for some background music, and sat down to wait. The savory aroma of their almost-gourmet dish wafted in the air. Food had challenged her over the last few days, but she realized she was starving.

Glancing up from her book and out the living room window for signs of Kelley's headlights, she hummed a lullaby. Tonight might not have gone according to schedule, but she could not complain.

Her life was perfect.

***

Bobby spent the entire school day anxious about his father's impending arrival. His mother knew nothing. At least nothing more than what he had told her before she knocked him out last Sunday afternoon and then locked him in his room for twenty-four hours.

"I'm so sorry, son," she had wept pitifully when she had finally released him after school on Monday. "Please remember your promise. Tell no one. I can't live if I lose you."

She had embraced him, sobbing and shuddering into his shoulder. Bobby had endured the physical contact, but it had brought him no comfort. In fact, it had made his skin crawl.

Upon his arrival at San Marcos High Tuesday morning, Isaac and Adam had riddled him with questions and teased him about not being able to hold his drugs and alcohol. Bobby never confirmed it, but his would-be friends assumed he had stayed home to nurse a hangover. They called him a lightweight.

Today, he had successfully slipped out of the house without encountering his mom. One of the school office's student teacher aides told him at lunch that Sarah had called to make sure he had gotten to class. After school, he asked Isaac if he could hang out for a bit.

Isaac winced at the suggestion, rubbing the back of his neck. "Gee, I don't know, Bobby. My mom doesn't know we've been hanging out."

"Come to my house," Adam offered. "My mom doesn't care."

"My dad's coming to see me," Bobby explained. "I wanted to be closer to the house."

"Is everything okay with your mom?" Isaac asked, sizing him up, perhaps looking for marks or bruises. Surely, the Fett family heard Sarah's periodic shrieks and screams.

When Bobby did not answer right away, Isaac and Adam had glanced at each other.

"Your dad's coming?" Adam's expression turned hopeful. "You gotta come over, then. I need to give you my tape."

In the end, they made a deal. Bobby would go to Adam's and stay there until Isaac called and told him Bobby's dad had arrived. Adam would give Bobby the tape before he left, and Bobby would give the tape to his dad.

But as soon as Bobby arrived at the Utely residence, the phone rang.

"Your dad's already here," Isaac told him. "He was here when I got home. And there's some guy with him. He's our age, I think. He's asleep in the car. You never said you and your dad had matching wheels. That's far out, man!"

Little about the call made sense, but Bobby knew he needed to get home right away. "I'm sorry, Adam. I gotta go."

He spied the similar, if newer model, Porsche as he pulled into the driveway around 4 PM. The property was still and quiet, save the snoring emanating from the open passenger's window of his father's vehicle. Before he went in, he stalked to the curb to take a closer look at his dad's friend.

As he approached, the snoring stopped with an abrupt snort. The passenger awoke with a start, then looked around in confusion.

"Hey," Bobby casually greeted.

The kid looked untidy and disoriented as he stretched his arms, arched his back, and let out a protracted moan. Stringy dark hair, wrinkled T-shirt, in need of a shave—and some mouthwash. "Where am I?"

Bobby half-leaned, half-sat to the front of the door. "You must be with the new band my dad's signing."

He nodded through slit eyes, then glanced up at the house. "Is Lockhardt inside?"

"I think so. I just got here. I'm Bobby. Lockhardt."

"Chris," the boy responded in kind. "Grant."

"Wanna come inside?" Bobby asked awkwardly. "I wouldn't recommend it, but you're welcome."

Chris Grant squinted up at him, one eye shut. "Why wouldn't you recommend it? Is the place haunted or something?"

"If only," Bobby countered with a sardonic cough of laughter.

"Well, I need to whiz, so...guess I'll chance it." He climbed out of the Porsche on unsteady legs, then followed Bobby up the driveway, tucking his shirt as he walked. "Where are we?"

"Santa Barbara."

"Is that near LA?"

"A couple hours north."

Chris nodded, obviously unclear on the geography.

By the time they reached the door, they heard the shouting. Bobby's cheeks flushed with humiliation.

To his credit, Chris pretended not to notice. "You know what, mate? If it's all the same, I'll just slip over to the side of the house behind that tree."

"Want anything? Water or something? We're out of juice and soda."

He waved him off as he stumbled off to handle his business. "Tell your dad I'll be in the car."

As soon as Bobby walked through the front door, he regretted involving his father in his personal problems.

"You'll never take my son!" Sarah shrieked from somewhere in the kitchen.

"You're not well!" Jameson roared back from the center of the living room, where he stood, pristine in his suit, as if the idea of relaxing on their old sofa physically nauseated him. "Someone needs to take care of the boy!"

"I've taken care of him for seventeen years! With no help from you!"

"Need I remind you who left who?"

Bobby froze in the entryway, afraid or unwilling to go to his father. He did not know what to say, or what Sarah might do.

At last, Jameson noticed him. Bobby hoped the man would raise his arms and greet him with a hug—or even a handshake. Instead, he nodded an acknowledgment and continued in battle, though he lowered his tone. "I'm taking you somewhere for an evaluation. Your behavior's unacceptable. You need help. And I'm here, now. You'll not lose your son, Sarah. Not forever. Now, be reasonable." He addressed Bobby with a stern nod. "Go pack a bag, son. I'm taking you back to LA with me."

Before Bobby reached the hallway, he saw a flash of movement. His mother rushed into the living room toward his father, a large kitchen knife gripped firmly in her raised hand. Bobby caught her by the waist as she passed, then held her from behind.

"No!" She dropped the knife but wriggled against his grasp. "You promised you wouldn't say a word! Not people numbers! You promised!"

Jameson tucked his chin, frowning at the outburst. He lifted his hands as he went to his son. "Does she have anything that calms her? A prescription?"

Bobby struggled to contain his mother. He wove his head right and left as she flailed in his arms. "She doesn't have anything. She won't go see a doctor."

His father nodded as he thought. Eventually, he moved between Bobby and Sarah, looped his arms around her waist, and nodded toward the hallway. "I've got her. Now, listen to me," he said, leveling his eyes on his son.

Sarah shrieked in agony as she struggled to break free. She hopped up and down, twisting her body while alternating between pummeling Jameson's arms and trying to pry them apart.

"Pack a bag," Jameson repeated.

Bobby nodded.

"When you're done, I want you to leave. There's a young man waiting outside. About your age. I need you to take him somewhere. Perhaps for a meal. Anywhere. Just go. I'm taking your mother to hospital. I'll need a few hours to get her settled. I'll meet you back here."

Sarah screamed in protest.

Bobby trembled as he dumped out the contents of his backpack, then stuffed a handful of briefs, two pairs of jeans, and several T-shirts inside. When the pack bulged and could not hold anything else, he found an old Macy's bag at the back of his closet and used it to pack some shoes and socks. He stared straight ahead as he carried the bag and the backpack toward the front door, trying to ignore his mother's pleading screams.

"No! He's my son, Jameson! Mine! Bobby!"

He swallowed hard, set his jaw, then marched down the driveway toward his father's car. Chris sat again in the passenger's seat, his head propped atop his closed hand.

"Hey," Bobby said. "You need to come with me."

Chris looked askance, glancing at Bobby's things. "What are you on about?"

Bobby rounded the vehicle, reached inside the opened driver's side window, and pulled the trunk release handle. "You must be hungry," he told Chris Grant matter-of-factly. "Dad asked me to take you out."

Chris grabbed the keys from the ignition, exited his vehicle, and hiked up his jeans as Bobby shoved his things into the front trunk, then shut the hood. "Be careful with my car, mate. I just got it. Don't want any scratches, do I?"

Bobby froze, gaping at him. "This is *your* car?"

Chris nodded. "Got it from your dad yesterday." He gestured toward Bobby's similar model in the driveway. "We must have the same taste."

"How long have you known my dad?"

He lifted a shoulder. "A few days. We met Saturday night."

"And he gave you a *car*?"

"He gave us all cars. The whole band. Generous bloke, your old man."

Bobby flattened his lips. He fished his keys out of his front pocket and motioned toward his older, suddenly less special, car. "C'mon. What're you hungry for?"

"I wouldn't mind a hair of the dog," Chris told him as he slid into the passenger's seat.

He folded his arm on the roof and peered at the kid through his opened driver's side window. "I don't know what it's like in England, but you gotta be twenty-one to buy liquor here."

"Really? Bloody hell. It's eighteen where I'm from."

Bobby glanced away, weighing his options. He bit the inside of his cheek. "Wait here."

He slipped through the side gate, into the heavily overgrown backyard that neither he nor his mother bothered to tend. Since hanging out with Isaac and Adam, he had established an easy way to get in and out of the house without notice.

His parents' angry shouting sounded to have subsided as he snuck inside his mother's bedroom and into her alcohol stash. It sounded as if his father was on the phone. "I need you here as soon as possible," Bobby heard him say.

Peering at the recently restocked inventory, he spied two bottles of Jack Daniels. He scooped them both up, then grabbed a bottle of Crown Royal as well.

As he returned with the booty, Chris whistled with approval. "Look at you."

Bobby handed him each bottle, which Chris stowed as much out of sight as he could, then slid into his seat and engaged the engine. "Hungry?"

"I could eat. Let's get some takeaway and find a park or something."

They grabbed some burgers at the Habit off Hollister, then doubled back past the high school and over to La Cumbre Country Club. Since Bobby had gotten his own wheels, he regularly hid out to drink in a secluded area off the golf course. He had never shared his secret spot. Not even with Isaac or Adam.

As they ate and shared their first bottle of Jack, they made idle conversation. For the most part, Bobby listened. Something about Chris rubbed him the wrong way. Probably the fact that his father seemed to have spent more quality time with Chris since meeting him five days ago than he had with him in seventeen years.

The sun set around six, but they did not leave the club grounds. Instead, they opened the second bottle of whiskey. Bobby wondered where his father had taken his mother, and if they had returned yet. He did not want to babysit a snobby English musician all night. Then again, anything beat getting home too early and risking another confrontation.

Sometime after nine, Bobby decided they should get back.

"You okay to drive?" Chris asked as they gathered their trash and snuck back to the car.

Bobby belched. "Not really. You wanna drive?"

"Un-bloody-likely," he snickered, dumping the trash into a receptacle near the parking lot. "I had my first go last night in the hotel parking lot. Haven't quite figured out driving on the left side of the car on the right side of the road. You Yanks are a backward lot."

They piled into the car and drove back to Hope Ranch. When they arrived, Chris's car still sat parked on the curb. The Renault was gone.

"You know, your dad was supposed to take us back to LA hours ago. He'd said he'd take us to dinner and out to the clubs."

The statement wounded Bobby. All evening, Chris Grant had talked about Bobby's father as if he had known him for years. It irritated him. Plus, he had assumed his father would stay at least one night in town.

"Do you have a dad?" Bobby snapped.

Chris blinked. "Of course."

"Good."

"Why?"

Bobby shook his head. "No reason. Just wanted to remind you that my dad isn't your dad."

"Pfft. Sensitive chap, are we?"

"Better than being an asshole."

"Arsehole?"

"You heard me."

Chris raised his eyebrows, the corners of his mouth arching downward. A moment later, he exited Bobby's car and staggered toward his own. "Think I'll wait for 'your' dad in *my* new car."

Bobby reached down to his floorboard for the bottle of Crown Royal, noting the bagged bottle of tequila he had not yet disposed of from last weekend. He checked his watch. Nine thirty. He wished his father would return, but found consolation that the delay had ruined Chris Grant's night. "Damn right, he's my dad," he muttered to himself, cracking the seal on the Crown.

Minutes later, Chris returned to lean down on Bobby's passenger window. "Where are they?"

"Out," Bobby spat. He sipped his bottle.

"I need to get back to LA."

"You've got a car. Go."

Chris snatched the bottle out of Bobby's hand and took a greedy gulp. "And what if I did?"

"You'd be dead before you reached the city limits."

"Is that so?"

"That's what you said." Bobby adopted a pompous, British affectation. "'Bloody Yanks don't know how to drive,'" he mocked. "'Mummy, what side of the road shall I use, Mummy?'"

"At least my mum doesn't scream like a barmy old cow at my dad."

Bobby barreled out of the car and stalked after Chris, who staggered down the driveway. "What did you say about my mother?"

Chris spun around, stopping Bobby in his tracks and nearly falling down in the process. "What are you on about, mate? You sound absolutely mad."

"Maybe so, but at least I know how to drive."

"I know how to drive, you tosser. Probably better than you."

"You think so?"

He shoved the bottle into Bobby's chest. "Have another drink, Johnny swerve-about."

Bobby took a final gulp of Crown before heaving it at the Carrera. The bottle shattered against the passenger's door.

Chris's lips parted. He jerked his head to stare at the shards of glass on the cement. They shimmered like jewels in the refracted light from the surrounding streetlamps. "Good thing your dad's rich," he seethed. "If I find so much as a scratch—"

"What does it matter if there's a scratch if all you ever do is ride in the passenger's seat?"

Chris dug in his pocket for his keys. He dangled the keyring in Bobby's face. "You're just cheesed off because mine's newer."

When their relentless one-upmanship escalated to near-blows, Bobby made the challenge. "Let's see what that newer model can do. I know a place we can race."

"You're off your bloody nut," Chris snarled.

"All talk? Figures."

Chris thought about it. "You know your car. You've been driving her almost a year. I'd call that an unfair advantage."

"You're scared," Bobby sneered, inching closer.

"I'm not scared. I'm just not stupid."

"Fine," Bobby growled. He tossed his keys to Chris. "Gimme yours. We'll switch."

"Switch?"

"Yeah. If you're such a great driver, why not?"

"Because you're bloody wasted, and I don't want you to do any more damage."

Bobby scoffed in disgust. "I knew it."

Chris tossed his keys to Bobby and marched to the other vehicle. "Fine. Lead the way."

Seventeen years of neglect fueled Bobby's dogged determination as he wove through back roads and out of Hope Ranch, cursing under his breath at the vehicle's new car smell. His parents had still not returned before they took off. He worried about his mother. About his father's chummy relationship with what Bobby could only assume was the son his father would have preferred. Every cell in Bobby's whiskey-soaked body wanted to put this interloping, golden-fingered snob in his place.

It brought him great satisfaction to watch Chris through the rearview mirror. The kid periodically wove in and out of the correct lane, as if not only blinding drunk but struggling to remember he needed to drive in the right-hand lane. Had it not been his car, Bobby would have wished Chris would veer off into a tree. He hoped the Crown Royal had done at least a little damage.

"This is mad," Chris yelled out the driver's window when they came to their starting place at the corner of Castillo and West Cabrillo. "Let's switch back. It's stupid to switch cars."

Bobby glinted his way. He shot him a challenging smile and revved the engine.

Chris wiggled his body into place and clutched the wheel. "You'd better not wreck my car, Lockhardt!"

"*GO!*" Bobby shouted.

They took off with a sustained screech of tires, leaving behind them several feet of black tire tracks as they sped east on Cabrillo. Plenty of evening traffic still dotted the boulevard hugging the Pacific coastline, but the teens wove through and navigated the slower-moving cars with ease despite their intoxicated state.

Chris lagged behind at first, still trying to master his ability to shift with his right hand. Bobby glanced at his rearview mirror. He cackled gleefully as he raced toward the cemetery, where he would pull over and wait for his lesser to arrive.

The two Porsches careened toward State Street. Bobby glanced up again. When he did not spy Chris behind him, he frowned. Seconds later, he heard a self-satisfied guffaw as the kid raced past him on his right. Momentarily stunned, Chris blew past him, then moved into his lane.

Bobby stomped on the accelerator. He watched Chris, who once again began veering to the left. He laughed as he reduced the distance between them.

But when Chris failed to immediately correct his position, Bobby's smile vanished. His eyes darted ahead to the intersection at State.

He instinctively waved his hand from left to right. "You're on the wrong side of the road, asshole!" he shouted, knowing Chris could not hear him.

Too late, Bobby watched his 16th birthday present ram its left front end into the passenger's door of an oncoming vehicle. The contact caused the Porsche to spin around until it skidded backward and came to a rolling stop.

Unfortunately, the other vehicle did not fare as well. The station wagon absorbed the full impact of the hit, sending it careening headfirst into a thick palm tree west of the intersection.

Bobby stomped on the brakes. The tires locked up, leaving another trail of skid marks as he screeched to a stop in the middle of eastbound traffic.

He heard screaming as other cars stopped their vehicles and got out to help. Passengers who had witnessed the crash rushed to one or the other cars to check on their occupants. Eventually, he saw Chris exit his car on wobbly legs.

When he peered over at the station wagon, he swallowed hard. The front end looked like it had smashed all the way up to the steering wheel. Smoked hissed and rose from the engine. The windshield had shattered.

He heard the urgent plea of a woman standing outside the front passenger's door. "Someone call an ambulance! He's not moving!"

Startled, drunk, and unsure what to do, he glanced again at his damaged Porsche. Outside, Chris wandered uneasily across the street and toward the beach. He did not seem to register what had just happened.

Minutes later, Bobby heard sirens.

***

"Dad?" Bobby's voice trembled over the line.

Jameson stood alone in the empty kitchen. His stance grew rigid. "Where are you, son?"

"There was an accident."

"Is Chris with you? Is anyone hurt?"

Bobby wept into the receiver, spitting and slurring his words as he spoke. "Why don't you ask if *I'm* hurt? Why *him*?"

Jameson's forehead creased in confusion. "Where are you?"

"By Stearns Wharf. The police just got here."

Eyes fused and stomach falling, Jameson exhaled through his nose. He had finished the paperwork a mere hour earlier. Sarah had been placed under mandatory psychiatric observation for the next seventy-two hours, under what California law called a "5150." He had hoped to make it back to LA this evening, as planned. Lockhardt Sound did not, officially, exist yet. He could not have a scandal on his hands. Especially with the Yard poking about his business.

"Are you all right, Robert?" he demanded.

"It wasn't me."

"What do you mean? Is Chris—"

"Please get down here, Dad," Bobby sobbed. "I think someone's dead."

CHAPTER 30

*J*AMESON BROUGHT HIS CAB TO *a rolling stop outside the five-story home in Chapel Street. He eyed their surroundings, scouting for a parking space. Unfortunately, the press had already taken all the convenient spots. "Go ahead. I'll park down the street. It's a bit crowded."*

"Nonsense! I invited you here today as a friend, not as a hired car. Go ahead and drive up a little. We can both walk back."

The friendship Ross Alexander referenced had come as a providential surprise. He and his wife had come to London for business—music business—a few months back. As fate would have it, they had booked Jameson's cab. He and Jameson had immediately connected and, since that time, Ross had booked him exclusively to take him to and from his temporary residence at the Park Lane Hotel to his frequent stops at Olympic Studios, the Conserves Records offices, and even when he and his wife, or "bride" as he called her, went out on evenings or weekends.

It was a lucrative arrangement. Never more so than today.

"It's a press launch," Ross had explained when he extended the invitation. "Just a small dinner party. We probably won't stay for dinner, but I have to go. Professional courtesy and all. Josephine's not feeling well, and I'd rather not go alone."

Far be it from Jameson to let his friend attend the launch party alone. Especially one at this particularly well-known Belgravia residence. But while most people gifted with such an opportunity would be excited for the chance to meet the world's most famous band, Jameson's gratitude lay in the knowledge that he would not have to break into the Georgian townhouse to get his bearings after all.

"Go straight in. They're up there somewhere," directed the gentleman who answered the door. Ross nodded an acknowledgment as they passed through the open doors.

The minute Jameson peered into the elegantly appointed, smoky room and laid eyes on his target standing beside a shelf on the right talking and smiling with a small group of men, his heart rate quickened. He felt like a lion stalking unsuspecting prey. Given his current occupation, perhaps he should feel the thrill of the hunt. However, he did not. Instead, his wife's name echoed in the chambers of his mind.

Sarah, I told you I'd do anything.

He laser-focused on his surroundings rather than the notable photographers, journalists, and DJs who had come to get a sneak peek at Sgt. Pepper's Lonely Hearts Club Band, *the Fab Four's eagerly anticipated new album. He made note of the home's layout and the placement of its furnishings. No dog, which was nice. What mattered to Jameson was an easy entrance, getting a handle on who regularly occupied its space, and identifying any physical obstacles that might slow him down in the unlikely event he needed to make a quick exit.*

The drawing room into which they were directed was sparsely appointed. A couple of chairs. A settee. Not overflowing with bric-a-brac. Jameson imagined how the arrangement might differ when not overrun by the press. In the center of the room sat a table set up with eggs, various salads, hams, cheeses, and other sumptuous fare. His stomach protested its empty state.

Ross moved through the crowd of people like a seasoned pro, mingling with those who had not turned up to merely take photos or conduct interviews. He shook hands with DJs Alan Freeman and Jimmy Savile, exchanged pleasantries, and introduced Jameson as a friend instead of a hired driver.

"Can I get you anything?" asked the pretty brunette fluttering about the space as another man approached them with flutes of champagne.

Ross accepted the carbonated libation and greeted the woman with a jovial smile and a cheek kiss. "We're fine, thanks, Joanne. Have you met my friend, Jameson Lockhardt?"

When Ross introduced the woman as his mark's secretary, Jameson smiled and extended his hand.

"And the bearer of the bubbly, here, is Peter."

Jameson took the offered drink, shook the man's hand, and gave him a curt nod. "Grand to meet you." Congenial but unremarkable. It was bad enough Ross was giving everyone his name.

Press secretary Tony Barrow ushered the group of photographers down the stairs and out the front doors. "Just one more shot on the doorstep, boys."

As the horde filed past those mingling on the main floor, he spotted the flamboyantly dressed lads everyone had come to see. They struck him as slightly shorter than he had imagined the few times he had glimpsed them on interviews or variety shows—shows he had taken an interest in over the last six months. They also looked to be cocked up on something. Particularly the bespectacled, frilly-shirted front man who could not string two coherent words together, yet bloviated about how the new project had enabled him to "...understand my own feelings."

Amidst the gaiety and enthusiasm of the press, Jameson seized the opportunity. He asked Joanne for directions to the loo. She pointed to the stairs and sent him on his way.

He crept through the house quickly and quietly, noting bedrooms, bathrooms, and an office. Window placements, rooftop access, physical placement of furniture, should he arrive at night. The one wrinkle in formulating his plan came when he overheard that the housekeeper and her husband resided on the premises, taking up the entire ground floor.

The more he poked about, the more real the situation became. He wondered if he had the stomach to follow through—if he had a choice at all. Epstein seemed nice enough, in a soft sort of way. Different than someone brought up on the East End, but that was no crime. Still, no one said no to Ronnie and Reggie Kray. If Jameson wanted to live without looking over his shoulder for the rest of his life, he knew what he needed to do.

After getting a lay of the land, he doubled back down to the restroom he had sought and flushed the toilet. Inside the otherwise all-white bathroom, covering one full wall, was the painting of a bullfighter. Jameson shook his head at the odd choice of bathroom decor.

Downstairs, the tone of the event audibly shifted from business to social. The formality of the group posing together in front of the fireplace mantel or out on the doorstep had given way to a casual mingling of the guests with individual members of the band. If he did not return soon, Ross might wonder where he had run off to. Slipping back into the crowd in the sitting room, he noted his friend had become immersed in conversation.

Jameson wanted to leave. He had accomplished what he had come for, and had done so without detection. No sense in hanging around, pretending to fawn over the guests of honor. He slipped over to Ross and stood unobtrusively behind him, eyes narrowed in concentration as they darted around the space for ideas or precautions.

"Find what you're looking for?"

When he turned around, he saw the champagne-offering Peter behind him. The man looked like a thirty-something Ernest Hemingway.

"Sorry," Jameson said, cocking his head. "Looking for...?"

The man inclined his chin to the stairs. "The loo?"

"Ah, yes. All sorted. Cheers."

He turned away, at once the embodiment of ease and comfort, until he caught a glimpse of their previously smiling, convivial host at the far end of the room, staring at him with what looked like suspicious eyes. The hair on Jameson's neck prickled. He tried to convince himself he was being paranoid. When Peter joined the man, leaning in to listen as Epstein whispered in his ear, Jameson admonished himself for indulging his doubts.

The media passed around a copy of the garish cover for the album that would be released the first of the following month. On its front, the moustache-sporting band, donning ornate and colorful uniforms, congregated around a large bass drum, which depicted the album's title. Dozens of images of famous and infamous people appeared behind them, as if cardboard cutouts. At the band's feet, an arrangement of funeral flowers spelled out the word "Beatles" on top of a mound of fresh soil, as if the band had been recently buried.

On the main, Jameson disliked the chaotic images and flashy display. But as he stared at it, he realized he appreciated the message. The Beatles had buried themselves, only to emerge as a new creation: Sgt. Pepper's Lonely Hearts Club Band.

Jameson took it as a sign, even though he did not believe in such rubbish. Soon, he would reinvent himself, as well. Again.

The key to his future incarnation still stared at him from across the room. For a moment, they locked eyes. Had Jameson believed in telepathy or mind-reading or other such tosh, he might have suspected Epstein saw him for who, and what, he was. Slowly, the sides of Jameson's lips curled into a knowing, almost warning, grin.

By the time Ross finished his casual conversations and decided they had best head out, Jameson had tabled his anxiety. He resigned himself to his fate. Now, all that mattered was to complete the deed. And although Ross did not yet know it, he would assist.

***

Carol held Beth's hand as she sped toward the hospital. Such an unconscionable turn of events. For two days, the O'Conners had stayed with the Williamses, grieving Kelley's shocking death. The girls alternated between tears and shock. Farin and Beth were inconsolable. They had lost their family patriarch. And now, this?

Beth sobbed and groaned with each contraction, squeezing Carol's hand.

"We're close," Carol promised. "Hang in there."

"I can't lose this baby, too," Beth insisted through her tears.

"It'll be okay, hon. It's just the stress."

"It's more. I know it. I don't think I can bear it."

Carol and Joseph had received the news of Kelley's fatal car accident just past 1:30 AM Thursday morning. The police had called from the O'Conner home, reporting that Beth and Farin were in shock and needed someone to come be with them. Carol had not hesitated.

When she had arrived, she found Beth sitting on the living room sofa, staring at nothing. Farin was upstairs, sobbing atop her parents' disheveled bed. Her hands were bloody. According to the police officer who had tried to comfort her, she had clawed the covers and then the mattress until she had ripped a couple of nails off her fingers.

From that moment on, time had blurred. Joseph acted as the family representative, calling the coroner and the funeral director. He made inquiries to the police, helped Beth write an obituary, visited the scene of the crash, and pressed for information on the occupant of the other vehicle. More than once, he had voiced his frustrations to Carol. Historically, he had found the police quite helpful. Something felt wrong.

But all those concerns faded to background noise as Carol parked at the emergency room entrance of Cottage Hospital. Beth O'Conner could not lose this baby on top of everything else.

"Will you stay with me?" Beth begged, still gripping Carol's hand as a nurse got her into a wheelchair and rolled her inside.

Carol rushed alongside the wheelchair. She glanced at the nurse for confirmation. When the woman nodded, Carol gave Beth's hand a tender squeeze. "Of course I will."

"How far along is she?" The nurse asked Carol.

"Don't act like I'm not here!" Beth snapped. She gritted her teeth and winced as she doubled over, her eyes fusing in pain. "Fourteen weeks."

The bleeding had started the morning after the accident. At first, they had believed it was spotting. Then, the pain started. Today, it increased to the point that Beth agreed to let Carol take her in to see a doctor.

Carol helped Beth into a gown, then onto an exam table, all the while holding her hand. Hospital staff flitted in and out, taking her vital signs and some blood as they waited for a physician.

When the doctor arrived, he confirmed Beth's fears. He explained that spontaneous miscarriages were not uncommon at this stage of pregnancy.

However, it could take some time for the process to complete. With little more than the obligatory, "I'm sorry for your loss," he wrote a prescription to help facilitate the process, then left. Carol's eyes pooled with tears as the nurse gave them final instructions and prepared Beth's discharge.

At last, Beth released Carol's hand. "That's it, then. It's over."

Carol shook her head. She shut her eyes against the pain. "Oh, Beth."

"I—what am I going to do?"

She gave her shoulder a gentle squeeze. "That's not a question for today. Not today. And not here."

Carol collected the paperwork and the prescription as Beth dressed. Anything to minimize the pain of her friend's circumstances. Privately, she wondered whether losing the baby, while unbearable, might not be a blessing in disguise. How could Beth take care of two children with no husband?

As they drove home, the women fell silent. Periodically, Beth would wince in pain. Carol hoped the medication the doctor had prescribed would hasten the end of this tragic nightmare.

"Should we have them move in?" Joseph asked later that night, after he tucked the girls in and Carol settled Beth into the spare room with her prescription and a two-finger pour of whiskey to help her sleep.

"I don't know what to do," Carol confessed. She collapsed, exhausted, onto the couch and snuggled into his embrace. "It doesn't seem real, Joe. Not Kelley."

When she began to weep, he drew her closer. She whispered against his chest, "All I know is, whatever they need, we'll be there."

"Kelley had the forethought to get a hefty life insurance policy. Financially, I think they'll be fine."

"Beth's not fine. She's in shock. How was Farin today?"

Joseph grimly shook his head.

They held one another in the darkness of their living room. Sometime later, they heard the screams. It did not take long until Marci hastened downstairs, rubbing her sleepy eyes.

"What's wrong with Farin, Momma?" She cuddled into her mother's arms.

Carol stroked her dark hair. "She's having another nightmare."

"It scares me."

"I know, sweetheart. But you're her friend, right?"

She nodded, lips trembling as she fought back tears.

"Then see her through it. That's what friends do."

"How long's it gonna last?"

"We can't know that," Joseph told her in his gentlest voice. "We'll just take each day as it comes. And someday, they'll be gone."

Marci sat forward and glanced at her father. "Does Aunt Beth have nightmares, too?"

"I don't think so."

"Well, I'll take care of Farin. Even if it takes forever."

"You're a good friend, sweetie. She's lucky to have you. I'm sure it won't take that long."

"I hope not."

The funeral was set for Saturday. Carol hoped both Beth and Farin would begin to heal once their living nightmare ended, but her gut told her it had just begun.

***

"I thought you were basing the company in LA," Faith spat over the phone.

"There's been a change of plans," Jameson told her.

"What sort of change?" she demanded.

"The sort that requires me to call and tell you I need you to get the boys back to New York. I won't be more than a few days behind."

She questioned and protested each request. Probably because he refused to give her details. But in the end, she agreed. "What about the cars?"

"I'll handle it. For now, just take the boys to my place. You can stay there until Ross and I return. From there, we'll arrange permanent accommodations."

"Lockhardt Sound isn't happening, is it?" she asked.

"Of course it is! Now, we can stay on the phone and chat, or you can let me finish my business. The sooner I'm done here, the sooner I fly back."

"Is your wife coming back to New York with you?"

"Goodbye, Faith. I'll see you next week."

Jameson had gone into damage control mode the moment he received the phone call from his son. His already-endless day had extended into an even longer night. By morning, Ross had sorted the police, they had returned a still-inebriated Chris Grant to his suite at the Beverly Hills Hotel, and Bobby would wake up in his bed as if the previous night was no more than a bad dream. Their agonizing hangovers would work to Jameson's advantage.

No way would he risk losing his recording empire. Especially before it had launched.

"If Chris is named as the driver of the vehicle, all's lost," Jameson said as he and Ross sat together in Sarah's kitchen, sipping tea, mildly distracted by the pungent chemical odor permeating the house. "He's an underage foreigner. Legally, I'm not even his guardian."

Ross drank his tea in silence, offering little to the conversation beyond supportive grunts of agreement.

"I've lost my wife," Jameson admitted aloud. "I won't lose Lockhardt Sound as well."

"I'm afraid I have more bad news," Ross told him. "Josephine's refused to relocate."

The announcement changed everything.

Jameson arranged to have Faith accompany Mirage back to New York. With Sarah's unexpected illness, he had no reason to plant his flag in sunny Southern California. New York was more manageable, geographically. Besides, Ross was not expendable.

"Go to the funeral," Ross advised. "Maybe offer the widow some monetary compensation for her loss. She'll probably need it. It could help."

Jameson agreed. "We'll need to keep an eye on her. If she needs anything, make sure she gets it. Whatever it takes to keep her quiet."

"And the girl?"

He gave Ross a quizzical look. "Girl?"

"The man has a ten-year-old daughter."

Jameson closed his eyes and slowly shook his head. "Orphan," he whispered under his breath.

Ross tilted his head. "Say again?"

"Nothing." Jameson stood and walked his cup to the sink. "I want that child taken care of. Are we clear?"

Ross's lips flattened into a straight line. "I'm sure I don't need to tell you this is becoming a very costly complication."

"Money's no longer a problem."

"Since when?"

"Since my wife's incapacitated, and I'm in control of the finances."

Jameson eased back into the kitchen chair. Once he elaborated on the details of the sizable Wellingham estate, Ross expressed no further doubts.

They discussed their few remaining loose ends while they waited for Bobby to wake up. Though Ross did not feel entirely comfortable with the concept of rewriting the events of last night to fit their purpose, Jameson drew upon all his life experience to make fantasy reality.

"After all, it was Bobby's car."

"They couldn't have been that drunk," Ross argued, astonished by his friend's proposal.

"Chris has been drunk since the flight from London. I can imagine how he'd just...forget."

"And Bobby? Why would he agree?"

"My son's confused. He's had a rough go of it. And with the trauma of his mother..."

"Still."

Jameson lifted his brows. "It was his car. And he has the least to lose."

Ross stared at him, open-mouthed.

"He'll come back to New York with us. It'll be fine. We can put this all behind us."

In his bones, he felt he was right. No one could bring back the man in the station wagon. What justice would be served by ruining the lives of so many others? How would such collateral damage console a widow and her child? In Jameson's experience, money was a tool. It could do what time and justice never could.

Money would seed Lockhardt Sound.

Money would allow him to finally fulfill his decades-old promise to Polly.

Money would wash clean the memory of every soul-altering compromise he had ever made in the name of love or survival.

And maybe eventually, money would recover everything the war, the streets, and forty-seven years of desperation had stolen from him.

Ross swallowed the last of his tea, then replaced the cup to its saucer with an unsteady hand. "It appears you have everything figured out."

"I couldn't have done it without you, my friend."

"It isn't finished yet," Ross warned. "We'll need to stick around a while. Make sure we've put out a few potential fires. I have some ideas."

Jameson decided the time had come to rouse his sleeping son. Time to start the wheels in motion. He rose from the table and gave his colleague a curt nod. "I'll leave you to it, then."

"If we're ever caught—"

Jameson did not share his friend's apprehension. He had avoided a lifetime of detection. As he disappeared down the hall, he vowed, to himself and to Ross, "No one will ever know."

THE END

About the Author

Heather O'Brien lives in Nevada with her husband. She enjoys music, travel, cooking, documentaries, and research.

To learn more, or to read excerpts from the Music is Murder saga, visit: www.booksbyheather.com.

Iconic Moments in Music History

The 1800s:

February 19, 1877 — Thomas Edison invents first recorded sound

November 8, 1887 — Emile Berliner invents Gramophone

1887 — Columbia Records founded
It remains the oldest surviving brand name in recorded sound.

The 1940s:

July 1940 —1st Pop Music Concert

September 10, 1940 — South Hallsville School bombing

October 1, 1943 — Birth of Vinyl Records

October 12, 1944 — The Columbus Day Riot

The 1950s:

1951 — Alan Freed popularizes term "Rock'n'Roll."

March 21, 1952 —1st Rock'n'Roll Concert

October 7, 1952 — American Bandstand airs

July 9, 1955 — "Rock Around the Clock" hits Billboard Charts

November 21, 1955 — Sam Phillips sells Elvis to RCA

February 3, 1959 — The Day the Music Died

May 4, 1959 — 1st Annual Grammy Awards

The 1960s:

April 4, 1960 — Motown Records is founded

Iconic Moments in Music History (cont.)

The 1960s (cont.):

April 25, 1960 — Payola Investigations

November 1961 — Phil Spector's "Wall of Sound"

October 24, 1962 — James Brown at the Apollo Theater

August 30, 1963 — Introduction of the Cassette Tape

January 1, 1964 — Top of the Pops first airs

February 9, 1964 — The Beatles on Ed Sullivan

July 20, 1965 — Dylan Goes electric

September 15, 1965 — 8-Tracks introduced

June 16, 1967 — Monterey Pop Festival

August 27, 1967 — Beatles manager, Brian Epstein, found dead

August 15-17, 1969 — Woodstock

December 6, 1969 — Altamont

The 1970s:

October 4, 1970 — Janis Joplin joins the "27 Club"

November 8, 1971 — Stairway to Heaven is released

April 7, 1973 — Mirage plays the Speakeasy Club

December 10, 1973 — Hilly Kristal opens CBGB

December 19, 1975 — Stax Records closes

October 20, 1977 — Lynyrd Skynyrd plane crash

April 22, 1978 — Bob Marley's One Love Peace Concert

July 12, 1979 — The Day Disco Died

Iconic Moments in Music History (cont.)

The 1980s:

August 1, 1981 — Video Killed the Radio Star

1982 — Hair bands

October 1, 1982 — first CD is released

March 25, 1983. — Michael Jackson moonwalks on VH1 Music Awards

March 5, 1984 — Jordan Grant signs with Lockhardt Sound, Inc.

January 28, 1985 — We Are the World is recorded

July 13, 1985 — Live Aid concert

1987 — record labels consolidate to the "Big Six"

June 9, 1988 — Jordan Grant meets Farin O'Conner at Le Dome

August 6, 1988 — *Yo!* MTV Raps first airs

March 3, 1989. — "Like a Payer" video is released

July 21, 1989 — Milli Vanilli

August 29, 1989. — "Down Deep in Love" hits #1

The 1990s:

March 20, 1990 — Gloria Estefan bus crash

May 6, 1991 — Pro Tools released

November 24, 1991 — Freddie Mercury dies

November 30, 1991 — Mirage's farewell concert

January 26, 1994 — Chris Grant signs with Minor 6th Records

April 5, 1994 — Kurt Cobain dies

Iconic Moments in Music History (cont.)

The 1990s (cont.):

circa July 1995 — Suzanne Vega's "Tom's Diner"
used to test MP3 technology

November 14, 1995 — Jameson Lockhardt's retirement roast

March 9, 1997 — Hip-Hop rivalries

1998 — Graveyard Summer's debut album

December 10, 1998 — Big 6 record labels consolidate to Big 5

January 25, 1999 — Eminem's "My name is…"

June 1, 1999 — Napster

The 2000s:

June 11, 2002 — American Idol airs

April 28, 2003 — iTunes

January 6, 2004. — GarageBand released

August 5, 2004 — Big 5 record labels consolidate to Big 4

July 23-24, 2005 — the return of Lollapalooza

February 8, 2009 — Death Cab for Cutie's Grammy protest of Auto-Tune

The 2010s:

August 2, 2010 — "Jaded" released on Minor 6th Records

July 23, 2011 — Amy Winehouse dies

September 21, 2012 — Big 4 record labels consolidate to Big 3

www.ingramcontent.com/pod-product-compliance
Lightning Source LLC
Chambersburg PA
CBHW031203310726
48969CB00001B/191